Looking @t Languages

A Workbook in Elementary Linguistics

Third Edition

Paul R. Frommer

University of Southern California

Edward Finegan

University of Southern California

THOMSON

WADSWORTH

Australia Canada Mexico Singapore Spain United Kingdom United States

Looking at Languages: A Workbook in Elementary Linguistics
Third Edition
Paul R. Frommer / Edward Finegan

Publisher: *Michael Rosenberg*
Acquisitions Editor: *Stephen Dalphin*
Development Editor: *Leslie Taggart*
Production Editor: *Samantha Ross*
Executive Marketing Manager: *Carrie Brandon*
Senior Print Buyer: *Mary Beth Hennebury*
Compositor: *Datapage Technologies, Inc.*
Project Manager: *Christine Wilson*
Cover Designer: *Gina Petti, Roundhouse Design*
Printer: *Globus Printing*

Printed in the United States of America.

2 3 4 5 6 7 8 9 10 07 06 05 04

For more information contact Wadsworth, 25 Thomson Place, Boston, MA 02210 USA, or you can visit our Internet site at http://www. wadsworth.com.

For permission to use material from this text or product contact us:
Tel   1-800-730-2214
Fax   1-800-730-2215
Web   www.thomsonrights.com

ISBN: 0-8384-0795-1

Preface

A word to students . . .

Like the ability to play the piano, ride a bicycle, or solve a calculus problem, the ability to analyze linguistic data can be acquired and refined only through practice. To fully appreciate the principles of linguistic analysis and the structure, organization, and use of languages, you need to "get your hands dirty" in the data of a wide range of languages, both familiar and unfamiliar. This book provides just that opportunity.

Looking at Languages examines data from thirty natural languages, including Akan, Wichita, and a few others that might be considered "exotic" by the majority of readers. For most beginning students, however, the phenomena of better-known languages like Arabic, Greek, Chinese, Japanese, Indonesian, Persian, and Turkish are exotic enough, and the accessibility of native speakers—sometimes sitting right next to you in class—who can pronounce the examples, offer observations about them, and provide you more data can infuse an exercise with immediacy and added life. Besides these natural languages, this book also lets you tackle such fictitious ones as Spiiktumi and Klingon.

The major innovation in this edition of *Looking at Languages* is the opportunity for you to *hear* most of the data as well as see it. When you see the sound icon ⌂ in an exercise, point your browser to *http://english.wadsworth.com/finegan-frommer/*, find the data reproduced there, and click on each example to hear it pronounced authentically by a native speaker. Although the problems can be solved without recourse to the sound files, hearing speakers pronounce their own languages will bring the printed page to life, making the exercises more interesting and exciting for you. Particularly in the case of the phonology problems, it will also add clarity and understanding. Books play a crucial role in university education, but human languages are, in the first instance, produced by the vocal apparatus and captured by the ear.

. . . and to instructors . . .

Designed to accompany *Language: Its Structure and Use* by Edward Finegan, *Looking at Languages* is nevertheless largely self-contained and can be used with other introductory textbooks.

Innovations in this third edition include not only the introduction of the sound files referred to above but also a modification to the phonetic transcription. Paralleling changes in *Language: Its Structure and Use* and a growing international trend, this edition employs symbols of the International Phonetic Alphabet more fully. Where we have used other symbols, we have indicated the IPA equivalents at the start of the problem.

As in the previous edition, the problems reflect an English/Other-Languages division. All the exercises from the second edition have been retained, some in revised form, and several new problems have been added. At the suggestion of instructors, we have included a sample exercise and solution in morphology (Exercise 1.00) and in phonology (3.00). For answers to other exercises, instructors can obtain a key from the publisher or publisher's representative.

*   *   *

As always, we welcome comments on *Looking at Languages* from both students and instructors.

Paul R. Frommer
(frommer@marshall.usc.edu)

Edward Finegan
(finegan@usc.edu)

Acknowledgments

Our thanks to the following linguists, language experts, and friends who read portions of the manuscript, offered suggestions, supplied data and intuitions, or tried out the problems with their students: John E. Brinkley, Paul Bruthiaux, Edward Chisholm, Larry Da Silva, Eric Du, Christine Cox Eriksson, Charles S. Fineman, the late Sylvia Frommer, Patricia Hunt, Larry Hyman, Min-Kyong Ju, Dino Koutsolioutsos, Martin Lo, Terry Loop, Andrew Meisel, Fred Nager, George Schlein, Julian Smalley, Donald Stilo, Terry Szink, and especially Ger-Bei Lee. Our book is a better one because of their help.

Special thanks also to the following students at the University of Southern California who generously offered their time and native-speaker expertise to record the sound files that augment this edition of *Looking at Languages:* Fahad Al-Deweesh (Arabic), Aang Angkasa (Indonesian), Sona Azatyan (Russian), Omar Beas (Spanish), Monica Cabrera (Spanish), Martina Campos (Portuguese), Leila Chachil (French), Ju-An Du (Mandarin Chinese), Michael Friedlander (Hebrew), Teruhiko Fukaya (Japanese), Shadi Ganjavi (Persian), Fetiye Tunc Karabay (Turkish), Miae Lee (Korean), Roberto Mayoral Hernandez (Spanish), Ashish Mestry (Hindi), Simona Montanari (Italian), Ana Sánchez Muñoz (Spanish), Jens Stephan (German), Despoina Theodorou (Greek), and Chen-Kang Yang (Mandarin Chinese).

Contents

Note: When you see the sound icon 🎧 , go to *http://english.wadsworth.com/finegan-frommer/* to hear all or part of the data pronounced by a native speaker.

CHAPTER 3 Phonology   77

KEY TERMS AND SYMBOLS   77

CHAPTER **4** Syntax 145

CHAPTER **5** Semantics 191

CHAPTER 6   Pragmatics   215

CHAPTER 7   Register   237

CHAPTER 8   Dialect   261

Appendixes 368

Bibliography 373

1

Morphology

KEY TERMS AND SYMBOLS

See the glossary at the end of the workbook.

Adjective	Determiner	Number
Adverb	Free morpheme	Personal pronoun
Affix	Gender	Prefix
Blend	Indefinite article	Preposition
Borrowing	Infinitive	Productive process
Bound morpheme	Inflectional morpheme	Pronoun
Compound	Invention	Root
Conjunction	Lemma	Semantic shift
Constituent	Lexical category	Shortening
Conversion	Metaphor	Stem
Coordinating conjunction	Monomorphemic word	Stress
Definite article	Monosyllabic word	Subordinating conjunction
Derivation	Morpheme	Suffix
Derivational morpheme	Noun	Verb

Name _____   **Section** _____   **Date** _____

1.00 SOLVED PROBLEM

MORPHEMES: Hungarian Morpheme Identification

Below you will find a number of simple sentences in Hungarian. The sentences have been translated, but individual words and morphemes have not been identified. Examine the data carefully, comparing the different sentences and their translations. Without looking at the discussion and solution that have been provided, answer the questions for yourself. Then check your answers. (Data adapted from Hudoba n.d.)

The data are given in standard Hungarian spelling. In Hungarian:

gy represents a sound similar to the *dy* combination in *did you*

s is pronounced like the *sh* in *show*

a is pronounced somewhat like the *o* in *above*

1.	Mi magasak vagyunk.	'We are tall.'
2.	Én beteg vagyok.	'I am sick.'
3.	Ti betegek vagytok.	'You (pl.) are sick.'
4.	Lankadtak vagyunk.	'We are weary.'
5.	Te magas vagy.	'You (sg.) are tall.'
6.	Mi betegek vagyunk.	'We are sick.'
7.	Én lankadt vagyok.	'I am weary.'
8.	Ti nagyon kedvesek vagytok.	'You (pl.) are very nice.'
9.	Beteg vagy.	'You (sg.) are sick.'
10.	Beteg vagyok.	'I am sick.'
11.	Ti nagyon magas vagytok.	'You (pl.) are very tall.'
12.	Magasak vagyunk.	'We are tall.'
13.	Te kedves vagy.	'You (sg.) are nice.'
14.	Nagyon betegek vagytok.	'You (pl.) are very sick.'

A. Isolate and identify all the morphemes in the data, grouping them into categories (adjectives, pronouns, etc.) and stating the meaning or function of each one. Note that one morpheme in the data has two different forms.

B. Which morpheme has two forms? Based on this limited data, what would be your hypothesis as to when each form is used?

C. Based on this data, are subject pronouns optional or obligatory in Hungarian? Explain.

Discussion and Solution:

A. A useful approach in problems like this is to isolate pairs in the glosses or translations that differ by only one element. By comparing the differences in such glosses with the corresponding differences in the non-English data, you will be able to match morphemes with their meanings.

For example, by comparing 2 and 6, you can conclude fairly safely that *én* means 'I' and *mi* means 'we.' In the same way, you can compare 5 and 11 to conclude that the second word in each sentence corresponds to the adjective in the translation.

Solution:

Adjectives		Personal Pronouns		Verb Agreement Suffixes	
beteg	'sick'	én	'I'	ok	1st person singular
kedves	'nice'	te	'you (sg.)'	unk	1st person plural
lankadt	'weary'	mi	'we'	tok	2nd person plural
magas	'tall'	ti	'you (pl.)'		

Others

vagy	stem of 'to be'
ak/ek	plural agreement suffix for adjectives
nagyon	'very'

B. The plural agreement suffix for adjectives has two different forms, *ak* and *ek*. The data show that *ak* attaches to *lankadt* and *magas*, while *ek* attaches to *beteg* and *kedves*. You might suspect, though, that *ak* and *ek* have more general distribution than these particular words; if so, you might note that *ak* attaches to an adjective containing *a* vowels, while *ek* attaches to an adjective containing *e* vowels. (Additional data would show this to be part of an even more general process in Hungarian, whereby vowel sounds within a root or stem govern the form of an affix.)

Solution:

The morpheme with two forms is *ak/ek*, the plural agreement suffix for adjectives. Based on this limited data, you can form the following hypothesis:

    ak is used with adjectives containing *a* vowels.

    ek is used with adjectives containing *e* vowels.

C. The data allow you to form the following hypothesis about subject pronouns in Hungarian:

Solution:

Subject pronouns for 1st person and 2nd person are optional. The omission of the subject pronoun doesn't cause confusion because the verb suffix—or lack of suffix in the case of the 2nd person singular—indicates the person and number of the subject unambiguously.

Name _____   Section _____   Date _____

EXERCISES BASED ON ENGLISH

1.01   LEXICAL CATEGORIES: Lexical Categories in English

Above each highlighted word in the following paragraphs, write its lexical category. The three versions proceed from a relatively easy to a relatively difficult selection of categories. (The passage is adapted from *Newsweek,* July 7, 1997.) Use these abbreviations:

N = noun	Pro = pronoun	Det = determiner
V = verb	Prep = preposition	Conj = conjunction
A = adjective	Adv = adverb	TO = infinitive marker

1. Will Smith has **a dark, fatal** flaw. It's **an** obsession of sorts, the kind **of** thing that can drive loved ones crazy and might even, if allowed to run amok, derail and debilitate an otherwise **promising** career. *He hates **bad** grammar.* Pronunciation errors, mistakes of any **linguistic** sort—**they** make him **nuts.** His girlfriend, the actress Jada Pinkett, knows **it.** His friends, family, and **close** associates know it. Occasionally, **in** their **gentlest,** most **caring** way, **they** try to caution **him about** the seriousness **of** his affliction. Sitting down **over** breakfast one morning **in** their Spanish-style villa outside L.A., Pinkett casts a **tentative** glance **in** his direction. "**What** were **you** telling **me the** other day?" **she** says. "That people say **the** word 'often' like 'of-fen,' when **it**'s really pronounced 'of-*t*en'?" Smith, looking sporty and **proper in** a **white** Ralph Lauren polo shirt, **white** sweatpants and Nike Air Up-tempos, sets down a platter **of** banana pancakes **with** a **disapproving** thud. "No, *no,*" **he** says. "The **right** way is 'offen.' People **who** pronounce **the** *t* are trying to sound sophisticated, but **they** just sound wrong." Pinkett giggles, then affects a Superman tone of voice. "It's **a** noun . . . It's **a** verb . . . No, it's *Captain Correction!*"

2. Will Smith **has** a dark, fatal **flaw.** It's an **obsession** of sorts, the kind of **thing** that can **drive** loved ones crazy and might even, if allowed to run amok, **derail** and **debilitate** an otherwise promising **career.** *He hates bad grammar.* **Pronunciation** errors, **mistakes** of any

linguistic **sort**—they **make** him nuts. His girlfriend, the **actress** Jada Pinkett, **knows** it. His friends, family, and close **associates** know it. Occasionally, in their gentlest, most caring way, they try to **caution** him about the **seriousness** of his **affliction.** Sitting down over **breakfast** one **morning** in their Spanish-style **villa** outside L.A., Pinkett casts a tentative **glance** in his **direction.** "What were you telling me the other **day?**" she **says.** "That people say the **word** 'often' like 'of-fen,' when it's really pronounced 'of-*t*en'?" Smith, looking sporty and proper in a white Ralph Lauren **polo shirt,** white **sweatpants** and Nike Air Uptempos, sets down a **platter** of banana **pancakes** with a disapproving **thud.** "No, *no,*" he **says.** "The right **way is** 'offen.' **People** who **pronounce** the *t* **are trying** to sound sophisticated, but they just **sound** wrong." Pinkett **giggles,** then **affects** a Superman tone of voice. "It's a **noun** . . . It's a verb . . . No, it's *Captain* **Correction!"**

3. Will Smith has a dark, fatal flaw. It's an obsession of **sorts,** the kind of thing **that** can drive **loved** ones **crazy** and might **even,** if allowed **to** run **amok,** derail and debilitate an **otherwise** promising career. *He hates bad* **grammar.** Pronunciation **errors,** mistakes of **any** linguistic **sort**—they make him nuts. **His** girlfriend, the actress Jada Pinkett, knows it. **His** friends, family, and close associates know it. **Occasionally, in their** gentlest, **most** caring way, they **try to** caution him about the seriousness of **his** affliction. Sitting **down** over breakfast one morning in **their Spanish-style** villa **outside** L.A., Pinkett **casts** a tentative glance in his direction. "What were you telling me the other day?" she says. "**That people** say the word 'often' **like** 'of-fen,' **when** it's **really** pronounced 'of-*t*en'?" Smith, looking sporty **and** proper in a white Ralph Lauren polo shirt, white sweatpants and Nike Air **Uptempos, sets down** a platter of **banana** pancakes with a disapproving thud. "No, *no,*" he says. "The right way **is** 'offen.' People who pronounce the *t* are trying **to sound** **sophisticated, but** they **just** sound **wrong.**" Pinkett giggles, **then affects** a **Superman tone** of voice. "It's a noun . . . It's a **verb** . . . No, it's *Captain Correction!"*

Name _____   **Section** _____   **Date** _____

1.02   LEXICAL CATEGORIES: Stress and Lexical Categories in English

In English, it often happens that two words are spelled the same but pronounced differently. Sometimes the difference in pronunciation is mostly or entirely a matter of stress.

A. Read each of the following sentences out loud, and note the pronunciation of the underlined words. Then, for each underlined word, indicate whether the stress falls on the first or the second syllable and give its lexical category.

EXAMPLE

		Syllable	Category
a)	Who is the <u>object</u> of your affection?	1st [✓] 2nd [ ]	**noun**
b)	They didn't <u>object</u> to the decision.	1st [ ] 2nd [✓]	**verb**
1. a)	I don't think a jury will <u>convict</u> her.	1st [ ] 2nd [ ]	_____
b)	A former <u>convict</u> often has a hard time finding a job.	1st [ ] 2nd [ ]	_____
2. a)	What an <u>insult</u>!	1st [ ] 2nd [ ]	_____
b)	Why would you want to <u>insult</u> me like that?	1st [ ] 2nd [ ]	_____
3. a)	Their unruly classroom <u>conduct</u> made teaching difficult.	1st [ ] 2nd [ ]	_____
b)	At work, <u>conduct</u> yourself in a professional manner.	1st [ ] 2nd [ ]	_____
4. a)	We don't <u>permit</u> that sort of thing around here.	1st [ ] 2nd [ ]	_____
b)	Do I need a <u>permit</u> to carry a concealed weapon?	1st [ ] 2nd [ ]	_____
5. a)	My karate instructor said I'm making excellent <u>progress</u>.	1st [ ] 2nd [ ]	_____
b)	You won't <u>progress</u> unless you practice a lot more.	1st [ ] 2nd [ ]	_____
6. a)	My dentist wants to <u>extract</u> all four of my wisdom teeth!	1st [ ] 2nd [ ]	_____
b)	Don't use anything but pure vanilla <u>extract</u> in this recipe.	1st [ ] 2nd [ ]	_____
7. a)	Try to <u>project</u> your voice to the very last row.	1st [ ] 2nd [ ]	_____
b)	What are you doing as a final <u>project</u> in your statistics class?	1st [ ] 2nd [ ]	_____
8. a)	<u>Refuse</u> collection is suspended on national holidays.	1st [ ] 2nd [ ]	_____
b)	I made them an offer they couldn't <u>refuse</u>.	1st [ ] 2nd [ ]	_____

		Syllable	Category

9. a) She can <u>converse</u> in Mandarin, Cantonese, and Taiwanese!   1st [ ] 2nd [ ] _____

   b) Be careful—the <u>converse</u> of this theorem is false.   1st [ ] 2nd [ ] _____

10. a) "Round up the usual <u>suspects</u>," said Captain Renault.   1st [ ] 2nd [ ] _____

   b) I think he <u>suspects</u> you work for the CIA.   1st [ ] 2nd [ ] _____

11. a) An advertising <u>insert</u> fell out of the magazine.   1st [ ] 2nd [ ] _____

   b) <u>Insert</u> plug A into socket B and push button C.   1st [ ] 2nd [ ] _____

12. a) Do you think this <u>conflict</u> will ever be resolved?   1st [ ] 2nd [ ] _____

   b) Eating pork would <u>conflict</u> with our religious beliefs.   1st [ ] 2nd [ ] _____

13. a) I'd like to <u>invite</u> you to my party.   1st [ ] 2nd [ ] _____

   b) Hey! We just got an <u>invite</u> to a party Saturday night!   1st [ ] 2nd [ ] _____

14. a) The <u>proceeds</u> from the dinner will go to fight AIDS.   1st [ ] 2nd [ ] _____

   b) She pauses, takes a drink, and then <u>proceeds</u> with her talk.   1st [ ] 2nd [ ] _____

15. a) Sometimes a country will try to <u>annex</u> its weaker neighbor.   1st [ ] 2nd [ ] _____

   b) We'll meet in the <u>annex</u>, not in the main building.   1st [ ] 2nd [ ] _____

B. Examine the results of your analysis. Judging from these data, what generalization can you make?

_____

_____

_____

Name _____   **Section** _____   **Date** _____

1.03 MORPHEMES: Types of English Morphemes

A. For each italicized word in the passage below, identify its lexical category and specify whether it is a member of an open or a closed class. Then list the morphemes that make up the word, and, in the columns to the right, indicate for each constituent morpheme whether it is a stem (Stem), prefix (Pre), or suffix (Suf); a bound (Bound) or free (Free) form; and, for prefixes and suffixes, whether they are inflectional (Inflec) or derivational (Deriv) morphemes.

Even the *skeptical* historian develops a humble respect for religion, since he sees it functioning, and *seemingly indispensable,* in every land and age. To the *unhappy,* the suffering, the bereaved, the old, it has brought supernatural comforts valued by millions of souls as more precious than any *natural* aid. It has helped parents and teachers to discipline the young. It has conferred meaning and dignity upon the *lowliest existence,* and through its sacraments has made for *stability* by transforming human covenants into solemn *relationships* with God. It has kept the poor (said Napoleon) from murdering the rich. For since the natural inequality of men dooms many of us to poverty or defeat, some supernatural hope may be the sole alternative to despair. (From Will and Ariel Durant, *The Lessons of History* [New York: Simon and Schuster, 1968])

EXAMPLE: NATURAL

Lexical category _____ Adjective _____   Open/Closed _____ Open _____

Morphemes	Stem/Pre/Suf	Bound/Free	Inflec/Deriv
nature	Stem	Free	—
-al	Suf	Bound	Deriv

1. SKEPTICAL

Lexical category _____   Open/Closed _____

Morphemes	Stem/Pre/Suf	Bound/Free	Inflec/Deriv
_____	_____	_____	_____
_____	_____	_____	_____
_____	_____	_____	_____

2. SEEMINGLY

Lexical category _____   Open/Closed _____

Morphemes	Stem/Pre/Suf	Bound/Free	Inflec/Deriv
_____	_____	_____	_____
_____	_____	_____	_____
_____	_____	_____	_____

3. INDISPENSABLE

Lexical category _____   Open/Closed _____

Morphemes	Stem/Pre/Suf	Bound/Free	Inflec/Deriv
_____	_____	_____	_____
_____	_____	_____	_____
_____	_____	_____	_____

4. UNHAPPY

Lexical category _____   Open/Closed _____

Morphemes	Stem/Pre/Suf	Bound/Free	Inflec/Deriv
_____	_____	_____	_____
_____	_____	_____	_____
_____	_____	_____	_____

Name _____   **Section** _____   **Date** _____

5. LOWLIEST

Lexical category _____   Open/Closed _____

Morphemes	Stem/Pre/Suf	Bound/Free	Inflec/Deriv
_____	_____	_____	_____
_____	_____	_____	_____
_____	_____	_____	_____

6. EXISTENCE

Lexical category _____   Open/Closed _____

Morphemes	Stem/Pre/Suf	Bound/Free	Inflec/Deriv
_____	_____	_____	_____
_____	_____	_____	_____
_____	_____	_____	_____

7. STABILITY

Lexical category _____   Open/Closed _____

Morphemes	Stem/Pre/Suf	Bound/Free	Inflec/Deriv
_____	_____	_____	_____
_____	_____	_____	_____
_____	_____	_____	_____

8. RELATIONSHIPS

Lexical category _____   Open/Closed _____

Morphemes	Stem/Pre/Suf	Bound/Free	Inflec/Deriv
_____	_____	_____	_____
_____	_____	_____	_____
_____	_____	_____	_____
_____	_____	_____	_____

B. Identify and list eleven monomorphemic words in the passage, including four monosyllabic ones, four disyllabic ones, and three consisting of more than two syllables. An example of each is given:

Monosyllabic	Disyllabic	Multisyllabic
EXAMPLE: young	humble	poverty
_____	_____	_____
_____	_____	_____
_____	_____	_____
_____	_____	_____

C. List all monosyllabic words in the passage with more than one morpheme:

_____	_____	_____
_____	_____	_____
_____	_____	_____
_____	_____	_____

Name _____   **Section** _____   **Date** _____

1.04   MORPHEMES: Derivational Prefixes and Suffixes

I. Derivational Prefixes

A. Each derivational rule below attaches a prefix to a word of a specific lexical category to create a different word. An example has been given in each case. Give three more examples for each and then answer the questions that follow.

1. **MIS- + Verb   →   Verb**
    direct   misdirect

    _____   _____

    _____   _____

    _____   _____

2. **UN- + Adjective   →   Adjective**
    cool   uncool

    _____   _____

    _____   _____

    _____   _____

3. **IN- + Adjective   →   Adjective**
    sincere   insincere

    _____   _____

    _____   _____

    _____   _____

4. **UN- + Verb   →   Verb**
    clog   unclog

    _____   _____

    _____   _____

    _____   _____

5. **IM- + Adjective   →   Adjective**
    proper   improper

    _____   _____

    _____   _____

    _____   _____

6. **UNDER- + Verb   →   Verb**
    bid   underbid

    _____   _____

    _____   _____

    _____   _____

7. **RE- + Verb   →   Verb**
    phrase   rephrase

    _____   _____

    _____   _____

    _____   _____

8. **EX- + Noun   →   Noun**
    cop   ex-cop

    _____   _____

    _____   _____

    _____   _____

B. With respect to IN- + Adjective and IM- + Adjective, can you make any generalization about the initial sounds of the adjectives that follow IN- versus those that follow IM-?

_____

C. What other prefix has the same meaning as IN- and IM- but precedes certain other adjectives?

_____

II. Derivational Suffixes

Each of the following derivational rules attaches a suffix to a word of a specific lexical category to create a word of a different lexical category. An example has been given in each case. Supply three more examples for each.

1. **Noun + -FUL** → **Adjective**
   doubt   doubtful

2. **Adjective + -LY** → **Adverb**
   beautiful   beautifully

3. **Verb + -ER** → **Noun**
   surf   surfer

4. **Adjective + -EN** → **Verb**
   light   lighten

Name _____   **Section** _____   **Date** _____

1.05   ORGANIZATION OF MORPHEMES:
Constituency and Word-Formation Rules in English

For each word that follows, identify its root; then give the sequence of additions for each word in the left column, the morphological rule for marking the addition in the middle column, and the bracketing for the word in the right column.

EXAMPLE: UNENLIGHTENED

Stem	Rule	Bracketing
light	root	[light]
light + en	adj + en → verb	[[light] en]
en + lighten	en + verb → verb	[en [[light] en]]
enlighten + ed	verb + ed → adj	[[en [[light] en]] ed]
un + enlightened	un + adj → adj	[un [[en [[light] en]] ed]]

1. REAPPEARANCE

Stem	Rule	Bracketing

2. UNTOUCHABLE

Stem	Rule	Bracketing

3. OWNERSHIP

Stem	Rule	Bracketing
_____	_____	_____
_____	_____	_____
_____	_____	_____
_____	_____	_____
_____	_____	_____

4. UNSHOCKABILITY

Stem	Rule	Bracketing
_____	_____	_____
_____	_____	_____
_____	_____	_____
_____	_____	_____
_____	_____	_____

5. RECOLONIZATIONS

Stem	Rule	Bracketing
_____	_____	_____
_____	_____	_____
_____	_____	_____
_____	_____	_____
_____	_____	_____

Name _____   **Section** _____   **Date** _____

1.06   INCREASING VOCABULARY: Morphological Processes in English

The following expressions are adapted from two *Newsweek* articles. Next to each word (or underlined word, where a whole phrase is given) name the morphological process or processes that allow for the word's particular use here. Choose from among the processes listed below. (*Note:* Some listed processes may not be illustrated.)

COMPOUNDING	SHORTENING	BORROWING
METAPHOR	CONVERSION	BLENDING
SEMANTIC SHIFT	DERIVATION	INVENTION

EXAMPLES   a <u>tariff-free</u> zone   COMPOUNDING
defenders   DERIVATION

A. From an article discussing electronic commerce (*Newsweek,* July 7, 1997):

1. Netheads   _____

2. encryption technologies   _____

3. <u>techno-hostile</u> initiatives   _____

4. a <u>hard-disk</u> crash   _____

5. pretty <u>cheeky</u>   _____

6. his own White House <u>run</u>   _____

7. a <u>history-making</u> blueprint   _____

8. administration <u>train wrecks</u>   _____

9. cyberwonks   _____

10. Netizens   _____

11. media-ites   _____

12. anti-censorship   _____

B. From George F. Will, "Sex, Fat and Responsibility" (*Newsweek,* July 7, 1997):

1. cyberspace   _____

2. worsening   _____

3. victimhood   _____

4. predisposition   _____

5. slothful   _____

6. gauche   _____

7. CDA ('Communications Decency Act')   _____

8. the Court ('the Supreme Court')   _____

9. modem   _____

10. an <u>underage</u> recipient   _____

11. log cabin   _____

12. <u>marketplace</u> of ideas   _____

13. <u>gateway</u> technologies   _____

14. electronic world   _____

15. criminalized   _____

16. Lincoln's log cabin was not <u>wired</u>   _____

17. The Court <u>swatted</u> aside that argument _____

Name _____   **Section** _____   **Date** _____

1.07   INCREASING VOCABULARY:
English Past-Tense Productivity Experiment

A. Consider the following pairs of English verbs:

A	B
live	give
fake	take
like	strike
leak	speak
side	ride
link	think
sin	spin

1. How do the A-verbs form their past tense?

   _____

2. How do the B-verbs form their past tense?

   _____

B. Here are some brand-new, just-coined English verbs, with definitions and examples:

bive   'gulp down'
(rhymes with *give*)   Why do you always bive your food?

vake   'have someone vacation'
                              I think I'm going to vake my mother in Tahoe this year.

slike   'attend only the last half of a class, lecture, concert, etc.'
                              You shouldn't slike math so often.

deak   'have a strong feeling of distaste or revulsion'
                              I deak whenever I hear him sing.

mide   'pour honey over'

                                He usually mides his pancakes.

strink   'drive a vehicle within the speed limit'

                                You'd better start strinking—here comes the Highway Patrol!

lin   'stare with narrowed, accusing eyes'

                                Don't you lin at me like that!

You are going to conduct some linguistic research, and you will need to find an informant to help you. Your informant may be anyone at all—a family member, friend, person you meet on the street—just so long as she or he is

- At least six years of age
- A native speaker of English
- A "civilian"—i.e., not a linguistics student, language major, etc.

Your job is to elicit the past tense forms of the "new" verbs from your informant.

The way *not* to do this is to say something like "Here's a new verb—*bive*. It means 'gulp down.' What's the past tense?" Rather, you want to elicit the desired forms as *naturally* as possible. Besides, you can't expect your informant necessarily to know the meaning of 'verb' or 'past tense.' So you will want to proceed along the following lines:

1. Teach your informant to play a language game with you. You will ask a question, and he or she will respond with a "long" answer.

    EXAMPLE You say, "Did you eat lunch at noon?"
                 Informant replies, "Yes, I ate lunch at noon."

    Try your informant out on a few random verbs, such as *eat, take, walk, go, hit, beg.* Make sure this is proceeding smoothly before going on to the next step. (You will probably want to work with a prepared "script" rather than trying to ask questions extemporaneously.)

2. Now teach your informant each "new" verb in turn. Give the meaning plus an example of its use. When you are satisfied he or she has grasped the idea, try the question/answer game as in part 1.

    EXAMPLE You say, "Did you bive your dinner last night?"
                 Informant replies, "Yes, I _____ my dinner last night."

Remember—we are interested in *speech.* The entire experiment is to be conducted orally. Do not let your informant see anything written, and do *not* spell the words—just pronounce them. You may ask your informant to repeat the answer or say it slowly, but you may not ask him or her to spell anything.

Name _____   **Section** _____   **Date** _____

Record here all the past tense forms you get.

Verb	Past Tense Form Elicited
bive	_____
vake	_____
slike	_____
deak	_____
mide	_____
strink	_____
lin	_____

3. (a) Summarize the results of your experiment.

_____

_____

_____

_____

_____

_____

_____

_____

_____

_____

_____

(b) A *productive* process in a language is one that is "alive," in the sense it can be applied to new forms entering the language. Considering the results of your experiment, comment on the productivity of the two kinds of past tense formation in English, "A-type" and "B-type."

_____

_____

_____

_____

_____

_____

(c) It has been proposed that the strong ("B-type") verbs in English form a closed set—English has a fixed number of such verbs and will never have any more. Is this prediction borne out by your experiment? Explain.

_____

_____

_____

_____

_____

_____

Name _____   **Section** _____   **Date** _____

EXERCISES BASED ON OTHER LANGUAGES

🎧 1.08   MORPHEMES: Spanish versus Hebrew Gender and Number

A. Examine the following Spanish data, given in phonetic transcription. Then identify all the morphemes, and state the meaning or function of each. (*Note:* In these examples, the symbol č represents a sound similar to the *ch* in *chance*.)

1.	amigo	'male friend'	5. amigos	'male friends'
2.	amiga	'female friend'	6. amigas	'female friends'
3.	mučačo	'boy'	7. mučačos	'boys'
4.	mučača	'girl'	8. mučačas	'girls'

_____

_____

_____

_____

B. Do the same for the following Modern Hebrew data. (*Note:* In these examples, the *x* does not represent a *ks* sound as it does in English but rather a sound similar to the *ch* in the German pronunciation of the name *Bach*. The symbol ɔ represents a sound similar to the *o* in *or*.)

1.	xavɛr	'male friend'	5. xavɛrim	'male friends'
2.	xavɛra	'female friend'	6. xavɛrɔt	'female friends'
3.	talmid	'male student'	7. talmidim	'male students'
4.	talmida	'female student'	8. talmidɔt	'female students'

_____

_____

_____

_____

Note: Whenever you see the sound icon 🎧 , go to http://english.wadsworth.com/finegan-frommer/ to hear all or part of the data pronounced by a native speaker.

C. Based on what you have discovered, explain how Spanish and Hebrew differ in the way they mark gender and number.

_____

_____

_____

_____

_____

Name _____   **Section** _____   **Date** _____

🎧 1.09   MORPHEMES: Malay/Indonesian Morpheme Identification

Malay (known in Malaysia as Bahasa Malaysia, 'the Malaysian language') and Indonesian (known in Indonesia as Bahasa Indonesia) are essentially the same language, differing only slightly more than do British and American English. Malay/Indonesian (MI) is among the top ten languages in the world in terms of number of speakers.

Examine the following MI sentences. One possible translation has been given for each.

1. Ini kuda.   'This is a horse.'
2. Ini Ali.   'This is Ali.'
3. Ali bagus.   'Ali is good.'
4. Ali menjual kuda itu. 'Ali sells that horse.'
5. Kuda Ali bagus.   'Ali's horse is good.'
6. Jualan ini bagus.   'This merchandise is good.'
7. Kuda ini dijual oleh Ali. 'This horse is sold by Ali.'
8. Ali penjual kain.   'Ali is a cloth seller.'

A. List all the *morphemes* in the data, giving their meanings or explaining their uses in each case.

_____

_____

_____

_____

_____

B. Identify one *inflectional* and two *derivational* morphemes in the data.

_____

_____

C. Based on the prior data, are these statements true or false?

1. Every MI sentence must have a verb.   [ ] T   [ ] F
2. MI has no possessive morpheme.   [ ] T   [ ] F
3. MI has no indefinite article.   [ ] T   [ ] F

D. Translate into English:

Kuda bagus ini kuda ali.

_____

E. Translate into MI:

1. 'Ali's merchandise is cloth.'

   _____

2. 'This is a good horse.'

   _____

3. 'This horse is good.'

   _____

F. If *mendidik* means 'educate,' what is the probable meaning of the following?

1. pendidik

   _____

2. didikan

   _____

Name _____   **Section** _____   **Date** _____

🎧 1.10   MORPHEMES: Persian Morpheme Identification 1

Here are some data in Modern Colloquial Persian, given in phonetic transcription.

Note: In these examples,

    š represents a sound similar to the *sh* in *show*

    x represents a sound similar to the *ch* in the German pronunciation of the name *Bach*

    æ represents a sound similar to the *a* in *cat*

1.	mæn mixunæm	'I am reading.'
2.	šoma ketab mixunin	'You are reading a book.'
3.	šoma ketabro næxundin	'You didn't read the book.'
4.	mæn ketab nemixunæm	'I am not reading a book.'
5.	mæn næxundæmeš	'I didn't read it.'
6.	šoma xundineš	'Did you read it?'
7.	šoma xundineš	'You read it.' (past tense)

A. Isolate and identify *all* the morphemes in the data, and state the meaning of each one. (Note that the negative morpheme has two pronunciations.)

_____

_____

_____

_____

_____

_____

_____

B. Translate into Persian:

'You aren't reading it.'

_____

C. How do you suppose yes/no questions are formed in Colloquial Persian? (A yes/no question has an answer of either yes or no.)

_____

_____

_____

D. Consider the following additional data: (* indicates that something is ungrammatical.)

8.   *mæn šoma mibinæm   'I see you.'

9.   mæn šomaro mibinæm   'I see you.'

How will you have to revise your original analysis, if at all, to account for these new data? Explain.

_____

_____

_____

E. To express a past progressive verb ('was reading,' 'were eating,' etc.), the two morphemes you isolated in part A that relate to tense or aspect are used _together_.

Translate into Persian:

'I wasn't reading the book.'

_____

Name _____   Section _____   Date _____

 1.11   MORPHEMES: Persian Morpheme Identification 2

Below you will find a number of sentences in Modern Formal Persian. The sentences have been translated, but individual words and morphemes have not been identified. Examine the data carefully, comparing the different sentences and their translations, and then answer the questions that follow.

Note: In these examples,

   ǰ   represents a sound similar to the *j* in *joke*

   š   represents a sound similar to the *sh* in *show*

   x   represents a sound similar to the *ch* in the German pronunciation of the name *Bach*

   æ   represents a sound similar to the *a* in *cat*

1.	šoma koǰa budid	'Where were you?'
2.	mæn bæd næbudæm	'I wasn't bad.'
3.	mæn emruz ketab mixanæm	'I am reading a book today.'
4.	an zæn bæd bud	'That woman was bad.'
5.	mæn ketabra mixanæm	'I am reading the book.'
6.	an mærd ketabra xand	'The man read the book.'
7.	ketab xub bud	'The book was good.'
8.	aya šoma ketab mixanid	'Are you reading a book?'
9.	in mærd xub bud	'This man was good.'
10.	zæne mæn ketabra anǰa nemixanæd	'My wife doesn't read the book there.'
11.	mæn diruz ketab næxandæm	'I didn't read a book yesterday.'
12.	šoma ketabra inǰa xandid	'You read (PAST) the book there.'
13.	aya šoma ketabe an mærdra mibinid	'Do you see the man's book?'
14.	aya in zæn šomara mibinæd	'Does this woman see you?'
15.	mæn ura nædidæm	'I didn't see him.'
16.	u zænra did	'She saw the woman.'
17.	nanra nædaræm	'I don't have the bread.'
18.	zænra did	'He saw the woman.'

Note: One possible translation has been given for each sentence. Other translations may be possible as well.

A. Isolate and identify all the morphemes in the data, *stating the meaning or function* of each one. When giving your answers, group the morphemes into categories (nouns, verb roots, verb suffixes, etc.). Note that the negative morpheme has two pronunciations.

_____

_____

_____

_____

_____

_____

_____

B. What are the two forms of the negative morpheme?

_____

C. What is unusual about the way Persian expresses the verb 'see'?

_____

_____

D. The verb 'have' is somewhat irregular in many languages. How about Persian? Explain.

_____

_____

E. Translate into English:

mæn ketabe zæne šomara nædidæm

_____

F. Translate into Persian:

'Do you have her bread?'

_____

Name _____   **Section** _____   **Date** _____

1.12   INFLECTIONAL MORPHOLOGY: Latin Declensions

Latin, the ancestor of the modern Romance languages, has nouns that change their form according to their grammatical role in the sentence. In this problem you will examine some different forms, or *cases*, of certain Latin nouns.

Examine the Latin sentences given below in standard orthography, and answer the questions that follow.

Note: Since Latin has distinctive vowel length, long vowels are sometimes represented with a macron (¯), even though the Romans themselves did not do this. You need not try to account for any changes in vowel length in your solution to this problem.

1. Senātor gladiātor erat.   'The senator was a gladiator.'
2. Crātēr senātōris est.   'It is the senator's bowl.'
3. Structor senātōrem aspexit.   'The carpenter looked at the senator.'
4. Senātōrem aspexit structor.   'The carpenter looked at the senator.'
5. Senātor aspexit structōrem.   'The senator looked at the carpenter.'
6. Structōrem senātor aspexit.   'The senator looked at the carpenter.'
7. Senātor sorōrem gladiātōris aspexit.   'The senator looked at the gladiator's sister.'
8. Structor crātērem senātōrī dedit.   'The carpenter gave the bowl to the senator.'
9. Gladiātōrī crātērem dedit senātor.   'The senator gave the bowl to the gladiator.'

A. List the nouns in the data, and divide them into their component morphemes. Then state the meaning or function of each of these morphemes.

_____

_____

_____

_____

_____

_____

_____

_____

B. Examine carefully sentences 3 through 6. Compared to English, is word order in Latin more or less important in determining the meaning of a sentence? Justify your answer.

_____

_____

_____

_____

C. Translate into English:

Gladiātōrī structōrem senātor commendāvit. (commendāvit = 'recommended')

_____

D. Translate into Latin:

'The gladiator gave the carpenter's bowl to the senator's sister.'

_____

Name _____   **Section** _____   **Date** _____

1.13   INFLECTIONAL MORPHOLOGY: Lakota Verbs

Lakota belongs to the Siouan family of Native American languages. Today it is the most widely spoken language in the Siouan group, with six thousand native speakers. You can hear the language spoken in the film *Dances with Wolves*.

Examine the following inflected forms for several Lakota verbs. By comparing the given forms, you can identify the morphemes and state their meanings or functions.

Note: Some of the Lakota sounds are represented by symbols that may be unfamiliar to you. Although you don't need this to solve the problem, here is some information about the pronunciation of these symbols.

č	represents a sound similar to the *ch* in *chance*
š	represents a sound similar to the *sh* in *show*
ĩ, ũ	represent nasalized vowels
ʔ	represents a glottal stop
k'	represents a glottalized consonant, produced when air is set in motion by raising the larynx with the glottis closed. A distinct break is heard between such a consonant and the following vowel.

A. Identify the morphemes in the data given below. You should be able to isolate the verb stems as well as several agreement markers. Indicate which such markers are prefixed to the stems in these data and which are suffixed. In one case, you also should indicate the semantic effect of using two of the markers in combination.

Note that two abbreviations have been used in the glosses:

we$_1$ = you (sg.) and I

we$_2$ = she/he and I, or several of us (more than two)

1.	wahi	'I arrive'
2.	cĩ	'she/he wants'
3.	ũk'upi	'we$_2$ give to him/her'
4.	ʔũpi	'they are'
5.	gili	'she/he arrives here'
6.	yačĩpi	'you (pl.) want'
7.	wak'u	'I give to him/her'
8.	ũpsičapi	'we$_2$ jump'
9.	škatapi	'they play'
10.	ũhi	'we$_1$ arrive'
11.	yaʔũ	'you (sg.) are'
12.	yapsičapi	'you (pl.) jump'
13.	ũškata	'we$_1$ play'
14.	yagili	'you (sg.) arrive here'

Verb Stems	Agreement Markers

B. Now, using the morphemes you have identified, give the complete paradigm of the verb t^hi 'to live or dwell':

_____ 'I dwell'

_____ 'you (sg.) dwell'

_____ 'he/she dwells'

_____ 'you (sg.) and I dwell'

_____ 'she/he and I/several of us dwell'

_____ 'you (pl.) dwell'

_____ 'they dwell'

2

Phonetics

KEY TERMS AND SYMBOLS

See the glossary.

Affricate
Alveo-palatal consonant
Approximant
Aspiration
Back vowel
Bilabial consonant
Central vowel
Consonant
Final position
Fricative
Front vowel
Glottal stop
High vowel

Initial position
Interdental consonant
Intervocalic position
Labial
Labialized consonant
Labiodental consonant
Lax vowel
Liquid
Low vowel
Nasal
Orthography
Palatal consonant
Pharyngeal consonant

Phonetic symbol
Phonetic transcription
Round vowel
Stop
Stress
Tense vowel
Uvular consonant
Velar consonant
Voicing
Vowel
Vowel length

Name _____   **Section** _____   **Date** _____

EXERCISES BASED ON ENGLISH

2.01   SOUNDS AND SPELLINGS: English Consonants

1. For each of the following words, fill in the phonetic symbol that represents the pronunciation of the final consonant sound.

   EXAMPLE   wished [t]

bananas	[ ]	tarts	[ ]	potatoes	[ ]
apples	[ ]	pies	[ ]	beans	[ ]
oranges	[ ]	cookies	[ ]	turnips	[ ]
peaches	[ ]	biscuits	[ ]	rutabagas	[ ]
melons	[ ]	cakes	[ ]	carrots	[ ]
avocados	[ ]	puddings	[ ]	cucumbers	[ ]
grapes	[ ]	sorbets	[ ]	parsnips	[ ]
lemons	[ ]	custards	[ ]	onions	[ ]
kicked	[ ]	watched	[ ]	agreed	[ ]
swooned	[ ]	eliminated	[ ]	strained	[ ]
pushed	[ ]	studied	[ ]	stretched	[ ]
looked	[ ]	typed	[ ]	measured	[ ]
surrounded	[ ]	quashed	[ ]	erased	[ ]
kicks	[ ]	watches	[ ]	agrees	[ ]
swoons	[ ]	eliminates	[ ]	strains	[ ]
pushes	[ ]	studies	[ ]	stretches	[ ]
looks	[ ]	types	[ ]	measures	[ ]
surrounds	[ ]	quashes	[ ]	erases	[ ]

2. For each of the following words, give the phonetic symbol for the sound represented by the underlined letters:

brea<u>th</u>	[ ]	lei<u>s</u>ure	[ ]	bu<u>dg</u>et	[ ]
brea<u>the</u>	[ ]	in<u>j</u>ure	[ ]	<u>sh</u>ovel	[ ]
<u>th</u>istle	[ ]	in<u>s</u>ure	[ ]	bo<u>ss</u>y	[ ]
<u>th</u>wart	[ ]	bu<u>s</u>y	[ ]	di<u>s</u>ease	[ ]
<u>th</u>ough	[ ]	in<u>ch</u>ed	[ ]	di<u>s</u>use	[ ]
<u>th</u>rough	[ ]	in<u>s</u>ulate	[ ]	disabu<u>se</u>	[ ]
mea<u>s</u>ure	[ ]	tou<u>ch</u>ed	[ ]	resi<u>s</u>ted	[ ]
a<u>ss</u>ure	[ ]	wi<u>sh</u>ed	[ ]	re<u>s</u>entment	[ ]

Name _____   **Section** _____   **Date** _____

2.02   PHONETIC TRANSCRIPTION: Reading Practice 1

Using standard English orthography, identify the English words represented by the following phonetic transcriptions. (*Note:* Aspiration and stress have not been indicated.)

1. ɪnstənsəz   _____

2. ənawnsmənts   _____

3. gɪglɪŋ   _____

4. nɑrəd   _____

5. tiðɪŋ   _____

6. notwərðinɪs   _____

7. ɪspɛʃəli   _____

8. tʃuzəz   _____

9. ʌnhæpinɪs   _____

10. mɛnʃənɪŋ   _____

11. lokweʃəs   _____

12. dɪsplɛʒər   _____

13. blʌdʒənd   _____

14. ʌnθrɪfti   _____

15. kənspɪrətɔriəl _____

16. mɪsfɔrtʃən   _____

17. fɑrməsurəkəl   _____

18. sajkoənæləsɪs _____

19. æŋkʃəs   _____

20. nɑlɪdʒəbəl   _____

21. səksɛʃən   _____

22. juθəneʒə   _____

23. fɪziks   _____

24. sɪnəsɪzəm   _____

25. fɛðərwet   _____

26. ɑnərɛri   _____

27. kənsivd   _____

28. kjukʌmbər   _____

29. risɛst   _____

30. əkɑmədeʃənz   _____

31. rilɪŋkwɪʃt   _____

32. tərbjələns   _____

33. ɪgzæktɪŋ   _____

34. homonər   _____

35. kəredʒəs   _____

36. pətɛnʃəli   _____

37. æmətʃər   _____

38. lidʒəner   _____

39. ɔθɛntəket   _____

40. ʃuʃajn   _____

Name _____   **Section** _____   **Date** _____

2.03 PHONETIC TRANSCRIPTION:
Reading Practice 2—English Homophones

Each of the following phonetic transcriptions represents two or more different English words with different spellings. In each case, give the possible spellings the transcriptions represent. The numbers following the transcriptions indicate the number of possibilities that have occurred to the authors. Try to find as many of these as you can. For a few of the more esoteric vocabulary items, a dictionary may be helpful. (Note: In pʰ, tʰ, and kʰ, the small raised h indicates aspiration.)

EXAMPLES   tʰu 3   <u>to, too, two</u>
                 si 3   <u>see, sea, c</u>

1. so 3	_____	17. kʰju 3	_____
2. ber 2	_____	18. mit 3	_____
3. brɛd 2	_____	19. aj 3	_____
4. dʒinz 2	_____	20. sajt 3	_____
5. rid 2	_____	21. fɔr 3	_____
6. sɛnt 3	_____	22. gron 2	_____
7. ruts 2	_____	23. ren 3	_____
8. dajd 2	_____	24. lut 2	_____
9. siz 4	_____	25. hərts 2	_____
10. mud 2	_____	26. sajz 3	_____
11. rez 3	_____	27. rɛst 2	_____
12. hid 2	_____	28. noz 3	_____
13. pʰækt 2	_____	29. ædz 2	_____
14. ju 4	_____	30. fɪltər 2	_____
15. rajts 3	_____	31. hil 3	_____
16. tʰod 3	_____	32. er 3	_____

33. ajl 3 _____

34. pʰɑks 2 _____

35. rʌf 2 _____

36. sɔrd 2 _____

37. swit 2 _____

38. ven 3 _____

39. lɑgər 2 _____

40. kʰi 2 _____

41. nid 3 _____

42. flu 3 _____

43. hɑstəl 2 _____

44. pʰɔz 2 _____

45. awr 2 _____

46. majt 2 _____

47. pʰʊrɪŋ 2 _____

48. dɪskrit 2 _____

49. kʰɑmpləmɛntri 2 _____

_____

50. kʰɔrs 2 _____

51. steʃənɛri 2 _____

_____

52. pʰroz 2 _____

53. pʰrɪnsəpəl 2 _____

_____

54. lirər 2 _____

55. dez 2 _____

56. frajər 2 _____

57. kʰærət 4 _____

_____

58. ərn 2 _____

59. fajl 2 _____

60. ɔrəl 2 _____

English has many more such examples. See if you can come up with three of your own:

61. _____   _____

62. _____   _____

63. _____   _____

Name _____   Section _____   Date _____

2.04   PHONETIC TRANSCRIPTION:
Reading Practice 3—Film and Play Names

Using standard English orthography, identify the following film and play titles transcribed phonetically:

1. rɑki hɔrər pʰɪktʃər ʃo _____

2. sajko _____

3. tʰajtʰænɪk _____

4. hæri pʰɑɾər ən ðə fələsəfərz ston _____

5. æn əmɛrəkən wɛrwʊlf ɪn pʰærɪs _____

6. tʰərmənəɾər θri ðə rajz əv ðə məʃinz _____

7. ðə kʰɪŋ ən aj _____

8. gosbʌstərz _____

9. ðə mæn ɪn ði ajərn mæsk _____

10. ɛle kʰanfədɛnʃəl _____

11. bɔjz ɪn ðə hʊd _____

12. ə hʌndrəd ən wʌn dælmeʃənz _____

13. θɛlmə ən luwiz _____

14. ðə lɔrd əv ðə rɪŋz ðə fɛloʃɪp əv ðə rɪŋ _____

15. pʰærɪs ɪz bərnɪŋ _____

16. rɑbən hʊd pʰrɪns əv θivz _____

17. bɪl ən tʰɛdz ɛksələnt ədvɛntʃər _____

18. sevɪŋ pʰrajvɪt rajən _____

19. mɪdnajt ɪn ðə gardn̩ əv gʊd n̩ ivəl _____

20. huz əfred əv vərdʒɪnjə wʊlf _____

21. maj bɪg fæt grik wɛrɪŋ_____

22. rozənkræns ən gɪldənstərn ər dɛd_____

23. ðə sajləns əv ðə læmz _____

24. mɛʒər fər mɛʒər _____

25. maj bjurəfəl lɔndrɛt _____

26. ðə fæntəm əv ði ɑprə_____

27. sno wajt ən ðə sɛvən dwɔrfs_____

28. ðə pʰərfɪkt stɔrm _____

29. læst ɛgzɪt tʰə brʊklɪn _____

30. bæk tʰə ðə fjutʃər pʰart θri _____

31. tʰinedʒ mjutn̩t nɪndʒə tʰərtl̩z_____

32. nekɪd gʌn tʰu ən ə hæf ðə smɛl əv fir _____

33. ə stritkʰar nemd dəzajr _____

34. bolɪŋ fər kʰaləmbajn _____

35. kʰɔl θiɾər fər ʌðər pʰrogræmz _____

Name _____   **Section** _____   **Date** _____

2.05   PHONETIC TRANSCRIPTION: Reading Practice 4

I. Convert the broad phonetic transcription below into standard English orthography; / is used to indicate original sentence breaks. [From *The Buddha of Suburbia* by Hanif Kureishi (New York: Penguin, 1990)]

aj ræn ən fɛtʃt dædz prəfərd jogə bʊk jogə fər wɪmən wɪθ pɪktʃərz əv hɛlθi wɪmən ɪn blæk liətɑrdz frəm əmʌŋ hɪz ʌðər bʊks ɑn bʊɾɪzəm sufɪzəm kənfjuʃənɪzəm ən zɛn wɪtʃ hi hæd bɔt æt ði ɔriɛntəl bʊkʃɑp ɪn sisəl kɔrt* ɔf tʃærɪŋ krɔs rod / aj skwɑrəd bəsajd hɪm wɪð ðə bʊk / hi brɪðd ɪn hɛld ðə brɛθ brɪðd awt ən wʌns mɔr hɛld ðə brɛθ / aj wɑzənt ə bæd rɪɾər ænd aj əmædʒənd majsɛlf tə bi ɑn ðə stɛdʒ əv ði old vɪk æz aj diklemd grændli səlambə sərsɑsənə** rivajvz ən mentɛnz ə spɪrət əv juθfəlnəs ən æsɛt bijɑnd prajs / ɪt ɪz wʌndərfəl tə no ðæt ju ɑr rɛri tə fes ʌp tə lajf ænd ɪkstrækt frəm ɪt ɔl ðə ril dʒɔj ɪt hæz tu ɔfər

* Cecil Court (a place name)   ** Salamba Sirsasana (a person's name)

_____

_____

_____

_____

_____

_____

_____

_____

_____

_____

_____

_____

II. Below you will find transcriptions of the casual, colloquial English of a particular American speaker.

Write the English versions of each sentence in two ways: the first time using standard English spelling, the second time with the kind of colloquial spellings you are used to seeing in comic strips or in the dialog sections of a script. (*Note:* Stress has been indicated by an acute accent mark over the vowel [´].)

EXAMPLE   ɑmnátgənəgó

       1.   I'm not going to go.
       2.   I'm not gonna go.

A. wénərjəgənəgímiðəglǽsəwórərajǽstfɔr

    1. _____

    2. _____

B. soiséztəmi júənájkənmekbjúrəfəlmjúzəktəgéðər

    1. _____

    2. _____

C. ɪfjəwúdn̩májn knájsipʰárrəjərnúzpʰepər

    1. _____

    2. _____

D. tʰéləmajdʒʌ́skʰǽntʰékɪrenimɔr ajmáwrəhir

    1. _____

    2. _____

E. djəwánəgóruətʃájnízərənətʰǽljənréstrɑnfərdínər

    1. _____

    2. _____

Name _____   **Section** _____   **Date** _____

2.06   PHONETIC TRANSCRIPTION: Writing Practice 1

I. Transcribe the following one-syllable words and names phonetically.

1. who _____
2. soot _____
3. soothe _____
4. these _____
5. knead _____
6. few _____
7. wrong _____
8. barks _____
9. heart _____
10. used _____
11. cause _____
12. chance _____
13. housed _____
14. shopped _____
15. Ives _____
16. wished _____
17. height _____
18. heir _____
19. Fritz _____
20. pure _____

21. phone _____
22. suit _____
23. myth _____
24. theme _____
25. pro _____
26. quake _____
27. rouge _____
28. brains _____
29. heard _____
30. leased _____
31. strengths _____
32. choir _____
33. laughed _____
34. oiled _____
35. eaves _____
36. schemed _____
37. eighth _____
38. Leigh _____
39. struck _____
40. psalm _____

41. ledge _____
42. suite _____
43. phlegm _____
44. hymn _____
45. guides _____
46. tried _____
47. catch _____
48. George _____
49. aisle _____
50. teased _____
51. vague _____
52. chef _____
53. screeched _____
54. clicked _____
55. fixed _____
56. Schwinn _____
57. sleigh _____
58. isle _____
59. warmth _____
60. drunk _____

II. Pronounce these words aloud, and transcribe your pronunciation phonetically.

1. mosquitoes   _____

2. suitcases   _____

3. jubilantly   _____

4. bicycled   _____

5. fanatical   _____

6. possession   _____

7. opinionated   _____

8. accented   _____

9. characteristics   _____

10. potpourri   _____

11. psychological   _____

12. pneumonia   _____

13. machinations   _____

14. calming   _____

15. introductions   _____

16. thistle   _____

17. requirements   _____

18. persuasive   _____

19. immeasurable   _____

20. breathed   _____

Name _____   **Section** _____   **Date** _____

2.07   PHONETIC TRANSCRIPTION: Writing Practice 2

I. American English contains a number of written forms that can be pronounced in more than one way. Sometimes the different pronunciations reflect different regional or social dialects (*aunt:* [ænt], [ɑnt]; *root:* [rut], [rʊt]). Less often, the different pronunciations are simply in free variation (*either:* [iðər], [ajðər]; *economics:* [ɛkənɑmɪks], [ikənɑmɪks]). This exercise is concerned with a third category: written forms whose different pronunciations reflect differences in meaning and/or function.

   For each of the following English spellings, give two different phonetic transcriptions representing two possible pronunciations. For each transcription, give an example of a sentence using the word pronounced in that way. For words of more than one syllable, indicate stress. In some cases, the two pronunciations will represent completely unrelated words; most often, however, you will find that the different pronunciations reflect grammatical differences among related items (noun/verb differences, for example). In two cases, you will have to capitalize the word to find the other pronunciation!

   EXAMPLE   protests
   1. [prótɛsts]   The station received a number of protests from irate viewers after airing a condom commercial.
   2. [prətésts]   I'd say she protests just a little too much.

A. read

   1. _____   _____

   2. _____   _____

B. record

   1. _____   _____

   2. _____   _____

C. present

   1. _____   _____

   2. _____   _____

D. live

   1. _____   _____

   2. _____   _____

E. dove

    1. _____

    2. _____

F. conduct

    1. _____

    2. _____

G. bow

    1. _____

    2. _____

H. address

    1. _____

    2. _____

I. house

    1. _____

    2. _____

J. perfect

    1. _____

    2. _____

K. minute

    1. _____

    2. _____

Name _____ **Section** _____ **Date** _____

L. polish

    1. _____ _____

    2. _____ _____

M. refuse

    1. _____ _____

    2. _____ _____

N. progress

    1. _____ _____

    2. _____ _____

O. resume

    1. _____ _____

    2. _____ _____

P. affect

    1. _____ _____

    2. _____ _____

Q. rebel

    1. _____ _____

    2. _____ _____

R. content

    1. _____ _____

    2. _____ _____

S. estimate

   1. _____   _____

   2. _____   _____

T. job

   1. _____   _____

   2. _____   _____

II. Write the sentences below in phonetic transcription.

   1. She said you laid the plaid tie on the couch.

   _____

   _____

   2. I'm not in a good mood, for it's no great treat to sweat blood.

   _____

   _____

   3. If the bough breaks, the cradle will fall through the roof . . .

   _____

   _____

   4. . . . but the tough little kid with asthma, although coughing, will be OK.

   _____

   _____

Name _____   **Section** _____   **Date** _____

2.08   CONSONANTS AND VOWELS: Identifying C/V, Describing C

A. Using only C for consonants and V for vowels, represent the ordinary pronunciation of each of the following words.

EXAMPLE   devastate   CVCVCCVC

1. redeem   _____

2. temptation   _____

3. resistance   _____

4. booklet   _____

5. crutches   _____

6. botched   _____

7. original   _____

8. quickly   _____

9. linguistics   _____

10. readily   _____

11. psychological   _____

12. phony   _____

13. intimate   _____

14. autumn   _____

15. accommodation   _____

B. Give a brief phonetic description in terms of voicing, place of articulation, and manner of articulation for each of the consonant sounds listed. Then give examples, in both standard orthography and phonetic transcription, of English words that contain the sound in *initial, inter-vocalic* (i.e., between vowels), and *final* position. If no examples of the sound in a certain position exist, indicate this with a dash.

		Initial	Intervocalic	Final
EXAMPLE				
ʃ	voiceless alveo-palatal fricative	chevron [ʃɛvrən]	nation [neʃən]	rush [rʌʃ]
1. b	_____ _____	_____	_____	_____
2. s	_____ _____	_____	_____	_____

	Initial	Intervocalic	Final
3. h	_____	_____	_____	_____
	_____			
4. r	_____	_____	_____	_____
	_____			
5. z	_____	_____	_____	_____
	_____			
6. θ	_____	_____	_____	_____
	_____			
7. n	_____	_____	_____	_____
	_____			
8. v	_____	_____	_____	_____
	_____			
9. ŋ	_____	_____	_____	_____
	_____			
10. ð	_____	_____	_____	_____
	_____			
11. j	_____	_____	_____	_____
	_____			
12. k^h	_____	_____	_____	_____
	_____			

Name _____   **Section** _____   **Date** _____

EXERCISES IN GENERAL PHONETICS

2.09   DESCRIBING SOUNDS: Communicating about Pronunciation

Part of the value of phonetic transcription and related linguistic terminology lies in the fact these tools help make communication about pronunciation precise, concise, and unambiguous.

One place where pronunciation is almost always discussed is at the beginning of language textbooks, phrasebooks, and dictionaries. The authors of such works are faced with a dilemma: They need to explain certain matters of pronunciation, but direct demonstration is not a possibility. This is a place where linguistic terminology could make a big difference. In most cases, however, the target audience can't be expected to have a background in linguistics, and terms such as "voiced velar fricative" will be mysterious to most readers. Given this predicament, writers have come up with various alternative methods for describing sounds, some more successful than others. In this exercise, you'll see and comment on some of the problems inherent in these alternative descriptions.

A. Sometimes authors compare the sounds they are describing with sounds in particular varieties of English or in other foreign languages. For each of the following examples, comment on how useful you find the comparison.

1. From a Portuguese phrasebook:

   "*o* is pronounced as in f*oo*d when unstressed, otherwise either as in r*o*ck or as in Scottish l*o*w, usually depending upon the next sound"

   _____

   _____

   _____

2. From a Dutch phrasebook:

   "*g* is pronounced gutturally something like *h* in *hue* (with a little exaggeration)"

   _____

   _____

   _____

3. From a Maori textbook:

   "*Wh.*—Say the English word *what,* then say it without the *t* at the end, and you will have as near as possible the correct sound of *wh,* e.g.:—

   Wha-ka-ta-ne   Wha-ka-ki"

   _____

   _____

   _____

4. From an Icelandic phrasebook:

   "*a*—like the same letter in the north of England."

   _____

   _____

   _____

5. From a Latin/English dictionary:

   "*y* is a Greek sound and is pronounced (both short and long) as *u* in French."

   _____

   _____

   _____

6. From a Spanish textbook:

   "[Spanish *r:*] Slightly trilled by vibrating the tongue slightly against the hard palate. Like *r* in the English *very.*"

   (*Note:* Chances are that the *r* in your pronunciation of *very* is not at all what the author has in mind!)

   _____

   _____

   _____

Name _____   **Section** _____   **Date** _____

B. For this last group of examples, comment on how effectively the description offers the reader a clear understanding of the sound described.

1. From a Yiddish textbook:

   "[The letter *samekh*] has the sound of S."

   _____

   _____

   _____

2. From an Indonesian phrasebook:

   "*ng* may occur at the beginning, as well as the middle and end of a word. *ng* is always pronounced like the *ng* in *sing,* never as in fi*ng*er. The sound which comes in the middle of fi*ng*er is spelled and transcribed *ngg*."

   _____

   _____

   _____

3. From an Indonesian textbook:

   "*k* at the beginning of a syllable sounds like English *k* in 'king,' but is pronounced without an 'explosion.'"

   _____

   _____

   _____

4. From a Swahili textbook:

   "E is like the *a* in *say,* without the final sound we give it in English by slightly closing the mouth."

   _____

   _____

   _____

5. From a Spanish textbook:

    "[Spanish *g* is pronounced] as *g* in English before *a*, *o*, and *u* or a consonant, at the beginning of a word, and before *n* and *l*. In all other positions similar to *g* in *big,* but prolonged."

    _____

    _____

    _____

6. From a German textbook:

    "*ch* = no English sound. It is nearest to English *k*, which, however, cannot be made into a continuous sound, but comes to an abrupt stop. German *ch*, on the other hand, is produced by contracting the air passages just enough to cause audible friction, but not enough to cause a stop as in *k*. German *ch* can be continued indefinitely as a sound."

    _____

    _____

    _____

Name _____   **Section** _____   **Date** _____

2.10   CONSONANTS AND VOWELS: Classification and Experimentation

I. Classification Practice 1

A. In each case, circle the sound that doesn't fit the description.

	EXAMPLE Consonants	ʒ	h	(æ)	ŋ
1.	Voiced stops	g	b	z	d
2.	Affricates	z	tʃ	dʒ	
3.	Back vowels	u	e	o	
4.	Tense front vowels	i	e	ɪ	
5.	Voiceless sounds	m	s	θ	h
6.	Fricatives	s	ʒ	ð	dʒ
7.	Nasals	m	l	ŋ	ɲ
8.	High vowels	o	i	u	ü
9.	Round vowels	o	i	u	ü
10.	Liquids	r	l	y	
11.	Velars	x	ŋ	d	g
12.	Voiced labials	m	b	f	

B. Circle the sound that doesn't belong, and name the category.

EXAMPLE	Voiceless stops	t	p	(s)	k
1.	_____	i	æ	s	u
2.	_____	pʰ	n	m	w
3.	_____	dʒ	ʃ	s	ʒ
4.	_____	a	ɔ	u	æ
5.	_____	b	g	k	d

6. _____   f   s   z   ʃ

7. _____   tʰ   pʰ   t   d

8. _____   i   æ   ü   u

9. _____   β   ð   ɸ   ɣ

10. _____   e   ɔ   ɛ   ɪ

II. Ease-of-Articulation Experiment

1. Below you will find five sets of nonsense words. Pronounce each set several times at normal conversational speed, noting how each word "feels" in your mouth.

   You may find that one word in each set, compared to the other two, seems easier for the vocal apparatus to articulate. Circle whichever words seem "easier" to you in this sense.

	A	B	C
Set 1	[wambi]	[wanbi]	[waŋbi]
Set 2	[plimd]	[plind]	[pliŋd]
Set 3	[ɛmko]	[ɛŋko]	[ɛnko]
Set 4	[aŋgosi]	[angosi]	[amgosi]
Set 5	[sunpi]	[suŋpi]	[sumpi]

2. Many people find that the "easier" words are 1A, 2B, 3B, 4A, and 5C. What is it about the relationship between the nasal and its following stop in these words that makes them easier to articulate than the others?

_____

_____

_____

_____

_____

Name _____   **Section** _____   **Date** _____

2.11   CONSONANTS AND VOWELS: Classification Practice 2

A. The same consonant chart is reproduced several times here, each time with a different group of segments highlighted. In each case, give the term that identifies and defines the group of segments in the gray area.

EXAMPLE

pʰ			tʰ			kʰ	
p			t			k	
b			d			g	
				tʃ			
				dʒ			
ɸ	f	θ	s	ʃ	ç	x	h
β	v	ð	z	ʒ		ɣ	
m			n		ɲ	ŋ	
w					j		
			l				
			r				

_____ Voiced stops _____

1.

pʰ			tʰ			kʰ	
p			t			k	
b			d			g	
				tʃ			
				dʒ			
ɸ	f	θ	s	ʃ	ç	x	h
β	v	ð	z	ʒ		ɣ	
m			n		ɲ	ŋ	
w					j		
			l				
			r				

_____

2.

Bilabial	Labiodental	Dental	Alveolar	Postalveolar	Palatal	Velar	Glottal
pʰ			tʰ			kʰ	
p			**t**			**k**	
b			d			g	
				tʃ			
				dʒ			
ɸ	f	θ	s	ʃ	ç	x	h
β	v	ð	z	ʒ		ɣ	
m			n		ɲ	ŋ	
w					j		
			l				
			r				

(The row p, t, k is highlighted.)

3.

Bilabial	Labiodental	Dental	Alveolar	Postalveolar	Palatal	Velar	Glottal
pʰ			tʰ			kʰ	
p			t			k	
b			d			g	
				tʃ			
				dʒ			
ɸ	**f**	**θ**	**s**	**ʃ**	**ç**	**x**	**h**
β	**v**	**ð**	**z**	**ʒ**		**ɣ**	
m			n		ɲ	ŋ	
w					j		
			l				
			r				

(The fricative rows ɸ … h and β … ɣ are highlighted.)

4.

Bilabial	Labiodental	Dental	Alveolar	Postalveolar	Palatal	Velar	Glottal
pʰ			tʰ			kʰ	
p			t			k	
b			d			g	
				tʃ			
				dʒ			
ɸ	f	θ	s	ʃ	ç	x	h
β	v	ð	z	ʒ		ɣ	
m			**n**		**ɲ**	**ŋ**	
w					j		
			l				
			r				

(The nasal row m, n, ɲ, ŋ is highlighted.)

Name _____   **Section** _____   **Date** _____

5.

Bilabial	Labiodental	Dental	Alveolar	Postalveolar	Palatal	Velar	Glottal
pʰ			tʰ			kʰ	
p			t			k	
b			d			g	
				tʃ			
				dʒ			
ɸ	f	θ	s	ʃ	ç	x	h
β	v	ð	z	ʒ		ɣ	
m			n		ɲ	ŋ	
w					j		
			l				
			r				

6.

Bilabial	Labiodental	Dental	Alveolar	Postalveolar	Palatal	Velar	Glottal
pʰ			tʰ			kʰ	
p			t			k	
b			d			g	
				tʃ			
				dʒ			
ɸ	f	θ	s	ʃ	ç	x	h
β	v	ð	z	ʒ		ɣ	
m			n		ɲ	ŋ	
w					j		
			l				
			r				

7.

Bilabial	Labiodental	Dental	Alveolar	Postalveolar	Palatal	Velar	Glottal
pʰ			tʰ			kʰ	
p			t			k	
b			d			g	
				tʃ			
				dʒ			
ɸ	f	θ	s	ʃ	ç	x	h
β	v	ð	z	ʒ		ɣ	
m			n		ɲ	ŋ	
w					j		
			l				
			r				

8.

	Bilabial	Labiodental	Dental	Alveolar	Postalveolar	Palatal	Velar	Glottal
	pʰ			tʰ			kʰ	
	p			t			k	
	b			d			g	
					tʃ			
					dʒ			
	ɸ	f	θ	s	ʃ	ç	x	h
	β	v	ð	z	ʒ		ɣ	
	m			n		ɲ	ŋ	
	w					j		
				l				
				r				

9.

	Bilabial	Labiodental	Dental	Alveolar	Postalveolar	Palatal	Velar	Glottal
	pʰ			tʰ			kʰ	
	p			t			k	
	b			d			g	
					tʃ			
					dʒ			
	ɸ	f	θ	s	ʃ	ç	x	h
	β	**v**	**ð**	**z**	**ʒ**		**ɣ**	
	m			n		ɲ	ŋ	
	w					j		
				l				
				r				

10.

	Bilabial	Labiodental	Dental	Alveolar	Postalveolar	Palatal	Velar	Glottal
	pʰ			tʰ			kʰ	
	p			t			k	
	b			d			g	
					tʃ			
					dʒ			
	ɸ	f	θ	s	ʃ	ç	x	h
	β	v	ð	z	ʒ		ɣ	
	m			n		ɲ	ŋ	
	w					**j**		
				l				
				r				

Name _____   **Section** _____   **Date** _____

B. Now do the same for the following vowel classes:

1.

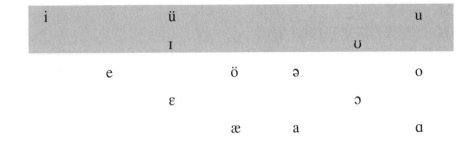

```
        i                ü                              u
                 ɪ                            ʊ
            e              ö        ə              o
                 ɛ                        ɔ
                 æ        a                ɑ
```

_____

2.

```
        i                ü                              u
                 ɪ                            ʊ
            e              ö        ə              o
                 ɛ                        ɔ
                 æ        a                ɑ
```

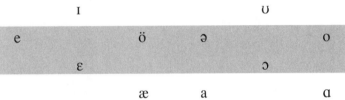

_____

3.

```
        i                ü                              u
                 ɪ                            ʊ
            e              ö        ə              o
                 ɛ                        ɔ
                 æ        a                ɑ
```

_____

4.

```
        i                ü                              u
                 ɪ                            ʊ
            e              ö        ə              o
                 ɛ                        ɔ
                 æ        a                ɑ
```

_____

5.
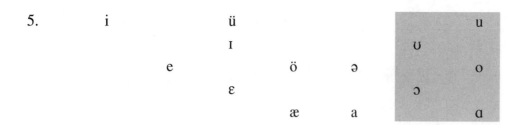

_____

6.
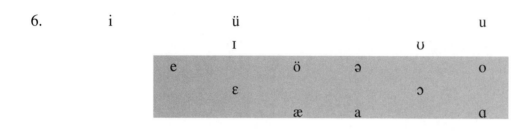

_____

7.

_____

8.
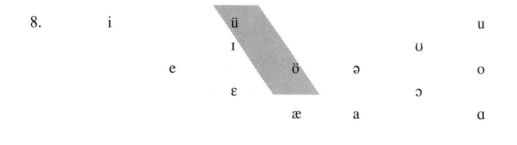

_____

9.

_____

Name _____   **Section** _____   **Date** _____

EXERCISES BASED ON OTHER LANGUAGES

2.12   CONSONANTS AND VOWELS: Hawaiian C/V Inventory

The Hawaiian language has an unusually small inventory of distinct sounds. You can discover all but one of these by analyzing the Hawaiian words you know. (For most people, these will be largely place names.)

For this exercise, you may regard the usual spelling of Hawaiian words as equivalent to a phonetic transcription.

Note: The sound referred to above that is usually not indicated in the spelling is the glottal stop, [?]. This is sometimes notated with a single open quotation mark in the orthography. (You may have noticed such spellings as *Hawai'i* and *Pepe'ekeo*.)

A. Referring to a map or atlas if necessary, list all the sounds of Hawaiian, with an example to justify each one.

_____

_____

_____

_____

_____

_____

_____

_____

B. Now answer these questions:

1. How many consonants does Hawaiian have?

_____

2. How many vowels?

_____

3. List the Hawaiian nasals.

_____

_____

4. List the voiceless stops in Hawaiian.

_____

_____

5. Stops, affricates, and fricatives together are known as *obstruents*. How many voiced obstruents does Hawaiian have?

_____

6. How many fricatives?

_____

7. What are the front vowels in Hawaiian?

_____

8. In contrast, how many consonants and vowels does English have?

_____

_____

Name _____   **Section** _____   **Date** _____

2.13   CONSONANTS AND VOWELS: Wichita C/V Inventory

Wichita is a Native American language in the Caddoan family, originally spoken in parts of Texas, Oklahoma, and Kansas. Among the world's languages, its inventory of distinctive sounds is quite unusual. (Data adapted from Rood 1975.)

A. The twelve Wichita words below contain all the consonants and vowels found in the language. Enter these consonants and vowels in the appropriate places on the standard charts that follow—this will give you a graphic picture of the Wichita inventory of distinctive sounds. (*Note:* [t͡s] represents an affricate similar to the *ts* sequence in the English word *cats*. [kʷ] is a labialized voiceless velar stop. [a] is a low central vowel. [ː] indicates a long, and [ːː] an extralong, vowel. An accent over a vowel indicates one of two distinctive pitches, the other being unmarked.)

1. khat͡s	'white'	7. t͡sheːt͡sʔa	'dawn'
2. ksaːrʔa	'bed'	8. rhiʔirt͡skhaːrʔa	'trousers'
3. haːt͡sarijarit͡s	'saw'	9. kskhaːrʔa	'hip joint'
4. kʔítaːks	'coyote'	10. t͡skhaːrʔa	'night'
5. thárah	'close'	11. waːkhat͡sijeːs	'calf'
6. kʷhaːt͡s	'red'	12. isseːːwa	'you better go'

Consonants

	Labials	Alveolars	Palatals	Velars	Glottals
Stops					
Affricates					
Fricatives					
Nasals					
Approximants					

Vowels (Just fill in the basic vowels—disregard length and pitch distinctions.)

	Front	Central	Back
High			
Mid			
Low			

B. Examine the consonant chart you've constructed, and then explain what is so unusual about Wichita's consonant inventory. Your answer should refer to *classes* of sounds, not just to individual segments.

_____

_____

_____

_____

C. Repeat question B for the Wichita vowels: Explain what makes this set of vowels highly unusual. As before, you should refer to classes of sounds.

_____

_____

_____

_____

D. As you have seen, Wichita vowels each come in three different degrees of length—short, long, and extralong—and two different pitch values. Taking length and pitch distinctions into account, how many different CV syllables (syllables consisting of consonant + vowel) can this language have? Explain.

_____

_____

_____

_____

_____

Name _____   Section _____   Date _____

🎧 2.14 CONSONANTS AND VOWELS:
Biblical Hebrew Consonant Inventory

The following is a phonetic transcription of an Old Testament passage in its original language, Biblical Hebrew (BH). This is the familiar section of *Ecclesiastes* (3:1–5) that begins, "To every thing there is a season . . ." The first five verses are given below.

Your task is to determine the consonant sounds that occur in BH. Although the passage is brief, all but two of the BH consonants can be found in it.

You already should be acquainted with most of the notation used in this phonetic transcription. For the symbols that may be new to you, see Appendix B.

Ecclesiastes 3:1–5

1   lakkol zᵊmaːn   wᵊʕeθ lᵊxɔl ħeɸɛṣ taħaθ haʃʃaːmaːjim

2   ʕeθ laːlɛðɛθ   wᵊʕeθ laːmuːθ
     ʕeθ laːṭaʕaθ   wᵊʕeθ laʕᵃqoːr naːṭuːaʕ

3   ʕeθ lahᵃroːɣ   wᵊʕeθ lirpoː
     ʕeθ liɸroːṣ   wᵊʕeθ liβnoːθ

4   ʕeθ liβkoːθ   wᵊʕeθ liśhoːq
     ʕeθ sᵊɸoːð   wᵊʕeθ rᵊqoːð

5   ʕeθ lᵊhaʃliːx ʔᵃβaːniːm   wᵊʕeθ kᵊnoːs ʔᵃβaːniːm
     ʕeθ laħᵃβoq   wᵊʕeθ lirħoq meħabbeq

A. Enter the BH consonants in their appropriate places on the following consonant chart. The two consonants not found in the data have been entered for you.

	Bilabial	Labio-dental	Inter-dental	Alveolar	Alveo-palatal	Palatal	Velar	Uvular	Pharyngeal	Glottal
Stops										
voiceless										
voiced				d			g			
Nasals										
Fricatives										
voiceless										
voiced										
Affricates										
voiceless										
voiced										
Approximants										
voiced central										
voiced lateral										

B. 1. How many phonetic consonants does BH have?

_____

2. Which BH consonants are not found in English?

_____

_____

3. Which English consonants are not found in BH?

_____

_____

4. *(Optional)* Notice that in this corpus, the "common" stops [p], [t], [k], [b], [d], and [g] seem to occur relatively rarely. Four of them occur only once each (counting [bb] as one occurrence) and two do not occur at all. Assuming the corpus is representative of the language as a whole, speculate on why this might be so.

_____

_____

_____

_____

C. Over the millennia, the Hebrew sound system has changed considerably. The following is a transcription of the same passage in modern Israeli Hebrew (IH) pronunciation. Compare this with BH, and on a separate sheet of paper make a list of the consonant changes you find. (Example: BH [q] → IH [k].) Try to form generalizations whenever possible.

Note: [t͡s] is a voiceless affricate similar in sound to [ts] in *cats*.

[ʁ] is a uvular approximant similar to "Parisian r."

1	lakɔl zᵊman	vᵊʔɛt lᵊxɔl xɛfɛt͡s taxat haʃamajim
2	ʔɛt lalɛdɛt	vᵊʔɛt lamut
	ʔɛt lataʔat	vᵊʔɛt laʔakɔʁ natua
3	ʔɛt lahaʁɔg	vᵊʔɛt liʁpɔ
	ʔɛt lifʁɔt͡s	vᵊʔɛt livnɔt
4	ʔɛt livkɔt	vᵊʔɛt lisxɔk
	ʔɛt sᵊfɔd	vᵊʔɛt ʁᵊkɔd
5	ʔɛt lᵊhaʃlix ʔavanim	vᵊʔɛt kᵊnɔs ʔavanim
	ʔɛt laxavɔk	vᵊʔɛt liʁxɔk mɛxabɛk

Name _____   **Section** _____   **Date** _____

2.15   CONSONANTS AND VOWELS: Sound Symbolism in Lakota

In this exercise you will investigate a very interesting phenomenon in the Lakota language called *sound symbolism.* (For some general information on Lakota, see exercise 1.13.)

In certain sets of related vocabulary items, the meaning differences represent different points on an increasing scale of intensity, such as the English terms *big* and *huge* or *damp*, *wet*, and *soaked.* Unlike English, however, Lakota mirrors these semantic differences in the sounds of the terms themselves through a definite and consistent progression of sound changes.

The data below are given in phonetic transcription. A small raised vowel represents a very short unstressed vowel that breaks up a consonant cluster by "pre-echoing" the vowel in its following syllable. The mark ˜ above a vowel indicates nasalization. An apostrophe denotes a *glottalized* consonant, produced when air is set in motion by raising the larynx with the glottis closed; a distinct break is heard between such a consonant and the following vowel. Certain required prefixes in the data have been omitted. (Data adapted from Boas and Deloria 1941.)

A. Examine the following sets of Lakota words and glosses. *Based entirely on the meanings of the words within each set,* rewrite the words in their order of "intensity," going from the least to the most intense. (The exact nature of "intensity" will vary from set to set.) In certain cases the words are already in the required order; in other cases you will have to rearrange them.

1. *a)* paʒa   'it has a thick-skinned blister'

    b) paza   'it has a thin-skinned blister'

    Order of intensity _____, _____

2. *a)* ptuɣa   'small pieces are cracked off so they fall off'

    b) ptuza   'it is bent forward'

    c) ptuʒa   'small pieces are cracked but not broken off'

    Order of intensity _____, _____, _____

3. *a)* pʰãʒa   'it is porous and soft'

    b) pʰãɣa   'it is porous and hard'

    Order of intensity _____, _____

4. *a)* mⁱniɣa   'it is shrunk permanently'

    b) mⁱniʒa   'it is curled, contracted, or wrinkled but can be smoothed again'

    Order of intensity _____, _____

5. *a)* mᵘnuza   'it gives a crunching sound (said of something easily broken)'

   b) mᵘnuɣa   'it gives a crunching sound (said of something hard)'

   c) mᵘnuʒa   'it gives a crunching sound (said of something of moderate resistance)'

   Order of intensity _____, _____, _____

6. *a)* ʃuʒa   'it is badly bruised'

   b) suza   'it has a slight bruise'

   c) xuɣa   'it is fractured'

   Order of intensity _____, _____, _____

7. *a)* pʰexniɣa   'it is red hot, quivering with heat'

   b) pʰeʃniʒa   'sparks'

   Order of intensity _____, _____

8. *a)* ʒata   'it forks into two parts'

   b) ɣata   'it is branching with many angles'

   Order of intensity _____, _____

9. *a)* izuza   'a smooth whetstone'

   b) iɣuɣa   'rough sandstone'

   Order of intensity _____, _____

10. *a)* nuɣa   'it is hard and immovable (e.g., gnarl on a tree)'

    b) nuʒa   'it is semihard and movable (e.g., cartilage)'

    c) nuza   'it is soft and movable (e.g., an enlarged gland under the skin)'

    Order of intensity _____, _____, _____

11. *a)* gᵉlɛɣa   'striped with wide, strongly contrasting colors'

    b) gᵉlɛza   'striped with narrow, indistinct lines'

    Order of intensity _____, _____

12. *a)* kĩza   'a single high-pitched tone sounds'

    b) kĩʒa   'several high-pitched tones sound and blend together'

    Order of intensity _____, _____

Name _____   **Section** _____   **Date** _____

13. *a)* k'ɛɣa   'it is in a scraped condition'

    b) k'ɛza   'it is in a scratched condition'

    Order of intensity _____, _____

14. *a)* ʃli   'semiliquid matter is being squeezed out'

    b) xli   'it is muddy material'

    c) sli   'a thin liquid (e.g., water) is being squeezed out'

    Order of intensity _____, _____, _____

15. *a)* zi   'it is yellow'

    b) ʒi   'it is tawny'

    c) ɣi   'it is brown'

    Order of intensity _____, _____, _____

B. Now compare the words in each intensity-ordered list you have determined. You should discover that the sounds that change from word to word are always in a definite and consistent order, correlating with the changes from lower to higher intensity in the meanings.

1. The data have two such series of sounds. List both series in order, giving a brief but clear phonetic description of each sound you list.

		Lower	**I N T E N S I T Y**	**Higher**
Series I	*Sound*	_____	_____	_____
	Description	_____	_____	_____
		_____	_____	_____
		_____	_____	_____
Series II	*Sound*	_____	_____	_____
	Description	_____	_____	_____
		_____	_____	_____
		_____	_____	_____

2. What is the relationship between Series I and Series II?

_____

_____

3. Explain how increases in the intensity scale are mirrored in the articulation of these sounds. In other words, how are changes in the meanings of the given words correlated with what's going on in your mouth as you say them?

_____

_____

_____

_____

_____

_____

_____

3

Phonology

KEY TERMS AND SYMBOLS

See the glossary.

Allomorph	Minimal pair	Romanization
Allophone	Morpheme	Surface form
Complementary distribution	Phoneme	Transcription
Contrast	Phonological rule	Transliteration
Distinctive	Predictable difference	Underlying form

3.00 SOLVED PROBLEM

Phonemes and Allophones: [ç] and [x] in Irish and German

Both Irish and German contain the voiceless palatal fricative [ç] and the voiceless velar fricative [x]. The data below consist of words in each language, given in the standard spelling and in phonetic transcription, that contain these sounds. Examine the data carefully. Without looking at the discussion and solution that have been provided, answer the questions for yourself. Then check your answers.

A. Irish.

(Note: Although this is not relevant to the problem at hand, Irish words can change their initial sounds depending on the immediately preceding word. Some of the data below are listed in these "mutated" forms.)

	Spelling	Transcription	Meaning
1.	choiche	xiːçə	'ever, forever'
2.	chun	xun	'towards'
3.	loch	lox	'lake'
4.	chi	çiː	'see'
5.	siochánta	ʃiːxaːntə	'peaceful'
6.	chúb	xuːb	'coop'
7.	brachai	braxiː	'bleary'
8.	cheol	çoːl	'music'
9.	chiúb	çuːb	'cube'
10.	oichi	iːçə	'nocturnal'
11.	iochtarach	iːxtərəx	'lower'
12.	chan	xan	'not'
13.	seicheamh	ʃeçəv	'sequence'
14.	cheal	çal	[used in certain interrogatives]

Determine whether the voiceless fricatives [ç] and [x] are different phonemes in Irish or allophones of a single phoneme. If the former, justify your answer. If the latter, state the rule that describes the distribution of each allophone.

Discussion:

Examining the data carefully shows that in Irish, [ç] and [x] can occupy the same kind of position in a word. For example, they can both appear initially before [iː] (1 and 4), before [a] (12 and 14), and before [uː] (6 and 9). In fact, 6 and 9 are a *minimal pair*: two words that differ by only a single sound in the same position.

So we can conclude the following:

Solution:

Since a minimal pair for [ç] and [x] exists in Irish, the two sounds represent different phonemes in that language.

B. German.

Spelling	Transcription	Meaning
1. dich	dɪç	'you (sg. obj.)'
2. machen	maxən	'to make'
3. auch	aux	'also'
4. Bücher	büçər	'books'
5. Bach	bax	'brook'
6. durch	dʊrç	'through'
7. Chirurg	çɪrʊrk	'surgeon'
8. doch	dɔx	'yet, but'
9. hoch	hox	'high'
10. Richard	riçart	'Richard'
11. Buch	bux	'book'
12. Bächlein	bɛçlajn	'little stream'
13. chinese	çinezə	'Chinese'

Name _____   **Section** _____   **Date** _____

14.	sprechen	sprɛçən	'to speak'
15.	Achim	axim	'Achim' (a man's name)
16.	recht	rɛçt	'right'
17.	Milch	mɪlç	'milk'
18.	Bruch	brʊx	'breach'

Analyze these data just as you analyzed the Irish data—that is, determine whether the voiceless fricatives [ç] and [x] are different phonemes in German, or whether they are allophones of a single phoneme. If the former, justify your answer. If the latter, state the rule that describes the distribution of each allophone.

Discussion:

Upon examining the data, you'll see that [ç] and [x] are in *complementary distribution*—that is, they do not occupy the same positions with respect to surrounding sounds:

    [x] occurs only after the vowels [u] (3, 11), [ʊ] (18), [o] (9), [ɔ] (8), and [a] (2, 5, 15).
    [ç] occurs in all other places.

When two sounds in a language are in complementary distribution and are phonetically similar, as are [ç] and [x], we say they are *allophones of the same phoneme*.

So at this point you could form the following rule to describe the distribution of the two allophones:

    [x] occurs after [u], [ʊ], [o], [ɔ], and [a].
    [ç] occurs elsewhere.

If you stopped there, you would have a workable rule that accounts for the data. But you would not have gotten to the heart of the matter, since you would have missed an important generalization. Are the five vowels mentioned in the rule an arbitrary set, or do they share some features?

You can see that these five vowels are *back* ([u], [ʊ], [o], [ɔ]) or *central* ([a]) vowels. The feature they share is that they are *non-front*. Not only that, but these are the only non-front vowels in the data. So you can revise your original rule, stating it more simply and more generally:

Solution:

[ç] and [x] are allophones of the same phoneme in German.
    [x] is found after non-front vowels.
    [ç] is found elsewhere.

Name _____   **Section** _____   **Date** _____

EXERCISES BASED ON ENGLISH

3.01   PHONEMES AND ALLOPHONES: Modern English [k] and [kʰ]

A. For the words below, determine whether the sound represented by <k>, <c>, <ck>, or <q> is aspirated or not. Then answer the questions that follow.

A	B	C	D
kinder	skillet	slicker	sequester
cooler	skimmed	wicket	secrete
kangaroo	skewed	docket	include
correct	scope	hacker	incorporate
kosher	squadron	pickle	incurable
kudos	scandal	recondite	recall

1. In column A, do initial <k> and <c> represent [k] or [kʰ]?

   _____

2. In column B, do <k>, <c>, and <q> represent [k] or [kʰ]?

   _____

3. In column C, do <c> and <ck> represent [k] or [kʰ]?

   _____

4. In column D, do <c> and <q> represent [k] or [kʰ]?

   _____

5. Give the distribution of these allophones of /k/ in English.

   [k] is found   _____

   _____

   [kʰ] is found   _____

   _____

B. You are teaching English in a foreign country. Your students are having some pronunciation problems. They can't distinguish between [i] and [ɪ] or between [kʰ] and [k]. Since your time is limited, you want to give your priority to the more serious problem.

You have decided on this philosophy with respect to teaching pronunciation: It is not so important to try to make students sound exactly like native speakers, but it *is* important for their speech to be clear and completely comprehensible so that they will not be misunderstood.

Which of the two problems mentioned above would you expect to be the more serious? Why? Make sure you include examples to support your statements and justify your choice. You may want to mention the terms *contrast* and *complementary distribution* in your discussion.

Name _____   **Section** _____   **Date** _____

3.02   PHONOLOGICAL RULES: A Phonological Rule of Old English

A. Examine the words below, given in both Old English (OE) spelling and phonetic transcription. For the words in column A, <f> represents the sound [f]; for those in column B, it represents [v].

A			B		
fæst	[fæst]	'fast'	wifung	[wiːvʊŋg]	'wedlock'
fisc	[fɪʃ]	'fish'	hlaford	[hlaːvɔrd]	'lord'
fæder	[fædɛr]	'father'	æfre	[ævrɛ]	'ever'
wif	[wiːf]	'woman'	wifel	[wɪvɛl]	'weevil'
ceaf	[tʃæəf]	'chaff'	cealfian	[tʃæəlvɪan]	'to calve'
cealf	[tʃæəlf]	'calf'	ofer	[ɔvɛr]	'over'
æfter	[æftɛr]	'after'	hræfn	[hrævn]	'raven'

1. Identify any minimal pairs among the words above.

   _____

   _____

   _____

2. Determine whether [f] and [v] occur in complementary distribution, and specify the distribution if they do.

   _____

   _____

   _____

3. What can you conclude about the phonemic status of [f] and [v] in OE?

   _____

   _____

   _____

4. On the basis of your analysis, give underlying forms for *fisc, ofer,* and *wif,* and state a phonological rule that will generate the correct surface forms.

_____

_____

_____

_____

B. Now examine the OE words below. For the words in column A, <s> represents the sound [s]; for those in column B, it represents [z].

	A			B	
fæst	[fæst]	'fast'	wisa	[wiːza]	'leader'
sæd	[sæd]	'sad'	wesan	[wɛzan]	'to be'
sticca	[stɪkka]	'stick'	risan	[riːzan]	'to rise'
sendan	[sɛndan]	'send'	ælsyndrig	[ælzündrij]	'separately'
wis	[wiːs]	'wise'	glesan	[gleːzan]	'to gloss'
mos	[mɔs]	'moss'	ceosan	[tʃeːəzan]	'to choose'
spell	[spɛl]	'story'	glisian	[glɪzɪan]	'to glitter'

1. Identify any minimal pairs among the words above.

_____

_____

_____

2. Determine whether [s] and [z] occur in complementary distribution, and specify the distribution if they do.

_____

_____

_____

3. What can you conclude about the phonemic status of [s] and [z] in OE?

_____

_____

_____

Name _____ **Section** _____ **Date** _____

4. On the basis of your analysis, give underlying forms for *fæst, sæd,* and *wisa,* and state a phonological rule that will generate the correct surface forms.

_____

_____

_____

_____

C. Examine the words below. For the words in column A, both <þ> and <ð> represent the sound [θ]; for those in column B, they represent [ð].

A			B		
ðing	[θɪŋg]	'thing'	oðer	[ɔːðɛr]	'other'
bæð	[bæθ]	'bath'	cweðan	[kwɛðan]	'to speak'
wiþ	[wɪθ]	'with'	baþian	[baðian]	'to bathe'
þurh	[θʊrx]	'through'	weorðe	[wɛɔrðɛ]	'worthy'
þridda	[θrɪdda]	'third'	wiþoban	[wɪðɔban]	'collarbone'
ðunor	[θʊnɔr]	'thunder'	mæðel	[mæðɛl]	'council'
þrotu	[θrɔtʊ]	'throat'	hæþen	[hæːðen]	'heathen'
hæþ	[hæːθ]	'heath'	hæðung	[hæːðʊŋg]	'heating'

1. Identify any minimal pairs among the words above.

_____

_____

_____

2. Determine whether [θ] and [ð] occur in complementary distribution, and specify the distribution if they do.

_____

_____

_____

3. What can you conclude about the phonemic status of [θ] and [ð] in OE?

_____

_____

_____

4. On the basis of your analysis, give underlying forms for *bæð, þrotu, weorðe,* and *baþian,* and state a phonological rule that will generate the correct surface forms.

_____

_____

_____

_____

D. Examine sections A, B, and C, and determine what your three phonological rules have in common. Write a single rule that captures the content of the three separate rules. (Think of the natural classes of sounds represented in the rules you devised.)

_____

_____

_____

_____

_____

Name _____   **Section** _____   **Date** _____

3.03   SYLLABLE STRUCTURE:
Constraints on Consonant Clusters in English

A. Initial Consonant Clusters

Syllables in English can begin with up to three consonants. Your task is to discover the rules that specify which initial sequences of consonants are possible. In other words, what are the rules that allow *play* but not *pnay, stray* but not *stpay*, etc.?

The rules you create should be as general as possible. For example, it is quite true that English syllables can begin with p + r, but a list of specific cases of this sort is not what you're after as a final result. The p + r case is part of a more general pattern, which is what you are to discover.

You may find it helpful to discuss the 1-consonant, 2-consonant, and 3-consonant cases separately. (In the 1-consonant case, determine which English consonant cannot begin a syllable.)

Finally, consider some foreign terms that have become part of the English vocabulary of some speakers: *shtick, shnook, knish,* and *shlemiel*. Do these recent imports obey the rules or constraints you have proposed? Explain.

_____

_____

_____

_____

_____

_____

_____

_____

_____

_____

_____

_____

B. Final Consonant Clusters

Now consider consonant clusters at the end of a syllable. Do the constraints you discovered for initial consonant clusters hold for final ones as well? Give examples to support your answer.

_____

_____

_____

_____

_____

_____

_____

Name _____   **Section** _____   **Date** _____

3.04   MORPHOLOGY/PHONOLOGY INTERACTION: Articles in English

In this exercise you will examine certain variants of the English articles and determine when they are used.

A. The indefinite article.

The indefinite article appears in two forms in English, *a* and *an,* which differ in both spelling and pronunciation.

    For each of the following words (given in standard English spelling), write the correct form of the article before the word, and *transcribe* the *initial sound* of the word after it.

       EXAMPLE   __an__ ape   [e]

1. _____ door [ ]	8. _____ monster [ ]	15. _____ use [ ]
2. _____ window [ ]	9. _____ hour [ ]	16. _____ Oscar [ ]
3. _____ tree [ ]	10. _____ ounce [ ]	17. _____ island [ ]
4. _____ apple [ ]	11. _____ pound [ ]	18. _____ eye [ ]
5. _____ child [ ]	12. _____ house [ ]	19. _____ ewe [ ]
6. _____ onion [ ]	13. _____ ear [ ]	20. _____ cheese [ ]
7. _____ union [ ]	14. _____ humidor [ ]	21. _____ vineyard [ ]

What rule determines which form of the indefinite article is used?

_____

B. The definite article.

In some varieties of English, including SAE (Standard American English), the definite article *the* appears in two forms—[ðə] and [ði]—which differ in pronunciation but not in spelling.

    In each of the following spaces write the transcription of the correct form of the definite article. The data are the same as in part A.

1. _____ door   [ ]   8. _____ monster [ ]   15. _____ use   [ ]

2. _____ window [ ]   9. _____ hour   [ ]   16. _____ Oscar   [ ]

3. _____ tree   [ ]   10. _____ ounce   [ ]   17. _____ island   [ ]

4. _____ apple   [ ]   11. _____ pound   [ ]   18. _____ eye   [ ]

5. _____ child   [ ]   12. _____ house   [ ]   19. _____ ewe   [ ]

6. _____ onion   [ ]   13. _____ ear   [ ]   20. _____ cheese   [ ]

7. _____ union   [ ]   14. _____ humidor [ ]   21. _____ vineyard [ ]

What rule determines which pronunciation of the definite article is used?

_____

Name _____   **Section** _____   **Date** _____

3.05   MORPHOLOGY/PHONOLOGY INTERACTION:
A Negative Prefix in English

1. Consider the following English words, each of which includes a prefix spelled *in-* or *im-:*

insurmountable	indefinable	inexhaustible
inanimate	impartial	involuntary
indignity	inexplicable	inoperable
insufferable	indecisive	impossible
inordinate	inappropriate	independent
imbalance	inexpressible	infamous
ineligible	impractical	inutile
inarticulate	invalid	inalienable

   What determines for each of the adjectives or noun roots whether the negative prefix is *im-* or *in-?*

   _____

   _____

   _____

2. Now consider the following words:

incomplete	inconclusive	incorrigible
incoherent	incommodious	inconsiderate
incomprehensible	ingratitude	inconvenient
incompetence	inconsistency	incurable

   What two different pronunciations of the negative prefix occur in these words? What accounts for the variant pronunciations?

   _____

   _____

   _____

3. Next to each of the following words, write its negative form:

   legible _____   legitimate _____

   literate _____   logical _____

   legal _____

4. Another set of words, like those in number 3 above, requires a special form of the negative prefix. Give some members of this set along with their negative forms.

_____

_____

_____

_____

5. Now summarize your findings: What generalizations can be made about the distribution of the allomorphs of this negative prefix?

_____

_____

_____

Name _____ **Section** _____ **Date** _____

EXERCISES BASED ON OTHER LANGUAGES

3.06   PHONEMES AND ALLOPHONES: Spanish [ɾ] and [r̃]

Spanish has two different r-sounds. The first, transcribed as [ɾ], is a single alveolar flap. The second, transcribed as [r̃], is a strong trill. Your job is to discover whether these sounds contrast in Spanish and to determine their phonemic status in the language.

Examine the following data carefully, and then answer the questions. Note that the data are given in transcription, which is not necessarily identical to standard Spanish spelling.

1.	peɾo	'but'	10.	per̃o	'dog'
2.	kar̃o	'cart, car'	11.	bar̃a	'bar, rod'
3.	r̃estaɾ	'to remain'	12.	r̃eiɾ	'to laugh'
4.	r̃aton	'mouse'	13.	r̃emoxaɾ	'to soak'
5.	r̃umba	'rumba'	14.	kaɾo	'dear'
6.	daɾ	'to give'	15.	r̃io	'river'
7.	iɾ	'to go'	16.	aɾaɾe	'I will plow'
8.	r̃oxa	'red'	17.	er̃oɾ	'error'
9.	baɾa	'runs aground'	18.	r̃opa	'clothing'

A. Fill in the following chart, which will give you a clear picture of the distribution of [ɾ] and [r̃] in three positions in a word: *initial position* (at the beginning of a word), *medial position* (between vowels), and *final position* (at the end of a word). Use a checkmark to indicate the sound occurs in the position and a zero to indicate it does not.

	Initial Position	Medial Position	Final Position
[ɾ]	_____	_____	_____
[r̃]	_____	_____	_____

B.   Do [ɾ] and [r̃] contrast in *initial position*? Justify your answer.

_____

_____

C. Do [ɾ] and [r̃] contrast in *medial position*? Justify your answer.

_____

_____

D. Do [ɾ] and [r̃] contrast in *final position*? Justify your answer.

_____

_____

E. What can you say about the phonemic status of [ɾ] and [r̃] in Spanish? Again, justify your answer.

_____

_____

Name _____   **Section** _____   **Date** _____

🎧 3.07   PHONEMES AND ALLOPHONES: Spanish [s] and [z]

In Spanish, /s/ is pronounced [z] in certain positions in a word. Your job is to discover which environment the rule operates in.

Examine the following data carefully, and then answer the questions. Note that the data are given in transcription, which is not necessarily identical to standard Spanish spelling. (For the meaning of the symbols ɾ and r̃, refer to exercise 3.06.) In certain cases, word boundaries have not been indicated.

1.	mizmo	'same'	16.	lazletɾas	'the letters'
2.	dezðe	'from'	17.	ezβeɾde	'it's green'
3.	este	'this'	18.	ezmoɾeno	'it's brown'
4.	izla	'island'	19.	esamaɾijo	'it's yellow'
5.	aspiɾas	'you seek'	20.	ezneɣɾo	'it's black'
6.	fosko	'irritable'	21.	eskoloɾðeɾ̃osa	'it's pink'
7.	r̃iezɣo	'risk'	22.	espuɾo	'it's clean'
8.	lasuɲas	'the fingernails'	23.	dospeɾ̃os	'two dogs'
9.	lozlaβios	'the lips'	24.	dozðeðos	'two fingers'
10.	lazmanos	'the hands'	25.	dozɣatos	'two cats'
11.	laspelotas	'the balls'	26.	dosoɾuɣas	'two caterpillars'
12.	losaɾkos	'the arches'	27.	dostapetes	'two rugs'
13.	loskaɾ̃os	'the cars'	28.	dozlutʃas	'two fights'
14.	lostamales	'the tamales'	29.	dosizlas	'two islands'
15.	loseɾmanos	'the brothers'	30.	doskesos	'two cheeses'

A. Before what vowels does [s] occur?

_____

B. Before what vowels does [z] occur?

_____

C. Before what consonants does [s] occur?

_____

D. Before what consonants does [z] occur?

_____

E. What features do the consonants you listed in question C have in common?

_____

F. What features do the consonants you listed in question D have in common?

_____

G. Formulate a concise statement that explains the distribution of [s] and [z]. Your statement should be of the following form:

[s *or* z] occurs _____; [s *or* z] occurs in all other places.

_____

_____

Name _____   **Section** _____   **Date** _____

3.08   PHONEMES AND ALLOPHONES: Hindi and Japanese

I. Hindi, along with some other languages of the Indian subcontinent, contains a number of *voiced aspirated* sounds, which are much rarer among the world's languages than their unaspirated counterparts. This exercise focuses on Hindi's two voiced bilabial stops, [b] and [bʰ]. The data below will allow you to determine whether these two sounds represent different phonemes in Hindi or are allophones of the same phoneme.

Examine the data, and then answer the questions that follow. The transcription is phonetic; the tilde mark (˜) over a vowel represents nasalization.

1.	bʰut	'ghost'	11.	bʰi	'also'
2.	bitʃ	'middle'	12.	dʒibʰ	'tongue'
3.	gəmbʰir	'serious'	13.	ʊbalna	'to boil'
4.	bar	'occasion'	14.	abʰari	'grateful'
5.	bʰãdʒi	'sister's brother'	15.	bʊzʊrg	'elderly'
6.	dʒəvab	'answer'	16.	dobara	'again'
7.	səbʰi	'all'	17.	bʰar	'burden'
8.	bʰabʰi	'brother's wife'	18.	tʃabi	'key'
9.	dʒeb	'pocket'	19.	bãka	'crooked'
10.	ləgbʰəg	'approximately'	20.	bɪkna	'to be sold'

A. Do the sounds [b] and [bʰ] contrast in Hindi, are they in free variation, or are they in complementary distribution? If in either contrast or free variation, justify your answer from the data. If in complementary distribution, state the distribution of the two sounds.

_____

_____

_____

_____

B. Do the two sounds in question represent different phonemes in Hindi, or are they allophones of the same phoneme?

_____

_____

_____

II. The following three sounds exist phonetically in Japanese: [h], [ɸ], and [ç]. ([ɸ] is a voiceless bilabial fricative; it is usually romanized in transliteration as <f>. [ç] is a voiceless palatal fricative. Note also that [ɯ] is a high, back, and unrounded vowel. [ː] indicates a long vowel.) Examine the data below, given in phonetic transcription, and then determine which of these three possibilities is the case for Japanese:

A. The three sounds are allophones of a single phoneme.

B. Two of the three sounds are allophones of one phoneme, while the third belongs to another phoneme.

C. The three sounds represent three different phonemes.

Justify your answer. If you find that some or all of these sounds belong to the same phoneme, give the rule or rules determining the distribution of allophones. If you find that some or all of these sounds contrast, prove it.

1.	çito	'person'
2.	haha	'mother'
3.	çiɸɯ	'skin'
4.	asaçi	'morning sun'
5.	heta	'awkward, unskillful'
6.	ɸɯne	'ship'
7.	hon	'book'
8.	haʃi	'chopsticks'
9.	hohei	'infantryman'
10.	ɸɯhenɸɯtoː	'neutrality'

_____

_____

_____

_____

_____

_____

_____

Name _____   **Section** _____   **Date** _____

🎧 3.09 PHONEMES AND ALLOPHONES:
[t], [ṭ], and [θ] in Biblical Hebrew and Standard Arabic

Biblical Hebrew (BH) and Standard Arabic (SA) both contain the sounds [t], [ṭ], and [θ]. (For information on the velarized or "emphatic" stop [ṭ] and other sounds you may be unfamiliar with, see Appendix B.)

A. Examine the following BH words:

1.	ṭɛrɛm	'not yet'	9.	tᵊxelɛθ	'violet-blue'
2.	tuːr	'seek out'	10.	ʃɛlɛṭ	'shield'
3.	haʃʃabbaːθ	'the Sabbath'	11.	laːθuːr	'to seek out'
4.	maːṭaːr	'rain'	12.	wajjeʃt	'and he drank'
5.	liʃħoṭ	'to slay'	13.	maːθaj	'when'
6.	paːθaħtiː	'I opened'	14.	ṭuːr	'row'
7.	ruːθ	'Ruth'	15.	uːθᵊxelɛθ	'and violet-blue'
8.	ṭabbaʕaθ	'ring'	16.	liɸtoᵃħ	'to open'

On the basis of these data, determine whether BH [t], [ṭ], and [θ] are different phonemes, or whether two or three of them are allophones of a single phoneme. If the former, justify your answer. If the latter, state the rule that describes the distribution of each allophone.

_____

_____

_____

_____

_____

_____

_____

_____

_____

B. Now consider the following SA words:

1.	ṭuːb	'bricks'		9.	baħθ	'discussion'
2.	θawb	'garment'		10.	θalaba	'he slandered'
3.	ʔassabt	'the Sabbath'		11.	baħt	'pure'
4.	maṭar	'rain'		12.	qaħṭ	'drought'
5.	ṭalaba	'he searched'		13.	mataː	'when'
6.	tuːb	'repent'		14.	maṭlab	'quest'
7.	ʔaθar	'effect'		15.	ʃabaθ	'spider'
8.	taθbiːt	'strengthening'		16.	mutaṭallabaːt	'requirements'

Analyze these data just as you analyzed the BH data—that is, determine whether SA [t], [ṭ], and [θ] are different phonemes, or whether two or three of them are allophones of a single phoneme. If the former, justify your answer. If the latter, state the rule that describes the distribution of each allophone.

_____

_____

_____

_____

_____

_____

_____

C. As you've seen, on the phonetic level BH and SA both contain the sounds [t], [ṭ], and [θ]. Are these languages also the same on the *phonological* level with respect to these three sounds? That is, do the sounds have the same phonological status in the sound patterns of BH and SA? Explain.

_____

_____

_____

_____

_____

Name _____   **Section** _____   **Date** _____

🎧 3.10   PHONOLOGICAL RULES: Tokyo Japanese

Examine the following Japanese words, transcribed phonetically as they are pronounced by some speakers in Tokyo:

1. gakkoo   'school'
2. giri   'obligation'
3. ginza   'Ginza' (well-known street)
4. geta   'wooden clogs'
5. naŋai   'long'
6. amaŋɯ   'raincoat'
7. daiŋakɯ   'university'
8. miŋi   'the right side'

A. State the distribution of the sounds [g] and [ŋ]. Does this constitute complementary distribution?

_____

_____

_____

B. What can you say about the phonemic status of [g] and [ŋ] in the Tokyo dialect?

_____

_____

_____

C. Choose an underlying form for each word given above, and provide a rule that will generate all the correct surface forms. If you find more than one way of doing this, give the alternative analyses as well.

_____

_____

_____

_____

_____

_____

_____

_____

_____

_____

_____

_____

D. *(Optional)* Here are the same words as they are pronounced by some other Japanese speakers. Compare the two different pronunciations. How does this additional information help you decide which of the alternative analyses you found in part C is preferable?

1. gakkoo   'school'
2. giri   'obligation'
3. ginza   'Ginza' (well-known street)
4. geta   'wooden clogs'
5. nagai   'long'
6. amagɯ   'raincoat'
7. daigakɯ   'university'
8. migi   'the right side'

_____

_____

_____

_____

_____

_____

Name _____   **Section** _____   **Date** _____

 3.11   PHONOLOGICAL RULES: Italian [s] and [z]

This exercise concerns the sounds [s] and [z] in three regional varieties of Italian. Each of the three dialects has both of these alveolar fricatives in its sound system. However, the distributional patterns of these sounds differ from one dialect to another.

In the data below (given in phonetic transcription, *not* necessarily standard Italian spelling!) you will see how certain Italian words are pronounced in the north and south of Italy, as well as in a third area that includes the city of Florence. Examine each dialect in turn to determine whether in that dialect [s] and [z] are allophones of a single phoneme or members of two different phonemes. If the former, describe the distribution of allophones; then give the underlying form and state the phonological rule that yields the correct surface forms. If the latter, justify your answer.

	NORTHERN	FLORENTINE	SOUTHERN	
1.	sugo	sugo	sugo	'juice'
2.	kaze	kase	kase	'houses'
3.	znɛllo	znɛllo	znɛllo	'slender'
4.	fuzo	fuzo	fuso	'melted'
5.	pasta	pasta	pasta	'pasta'
6.	zdentato	zdentato	zdentato	'toothless'
7.	korsa	korsa	korsa	'race'
8.	skuzi	skuzi	skusi	'excuse me'
9.	rizo	riso	riso	'rice'
10.	meze	mese	mese	'month'
11.	zbruffone	zbruffone	zbruffone	'braggart'
12.	fuzo	fuso	fuso	'spindle'
13.	pensare	pensare	pensare	'to think'
14.	zvenire	zvenire	zvenire	'to faint'
15.	zradʒonare	zradʒonare	zradʒonare	'to talk nonsense'
16.	dispari	dispari	dispari	'uneven'
17.	sadizmo	sadizmo	sadizmo	'sadism'
18.	autopsia	autopsia	autopsia	'autopsy'
19.	dizdire	dizdire	dizdire	'to cancel'
20.	sfortuna	sfortuna	sfortuna	'bad luck'
21.	falso	falso	falso	'false'
22.	illuzione	illuzione	illusione	'illusion'

A. Northern dialect:

_____

_____

_____

_____

_____

_____

B. Florentine dialect:

_____

_____

_____

_____

_____

_____

C. Southern dialect:

_____

_____

_____

_____

_____

_____

Name _____   **Section** _____   **Date** _____

 ## 3.12   PHONOLOGICAL RULES: A Phonological Rule of Russian

In the data below you will find several examples of a certain class of Russian noun. Each example is given in two different forms, the nominative singular and the genitive plural. Your task is to isolate all the morphemes in the data in their *unique underlying forms* and to propose a general phonological rule that will account for all the surface forms.

Examine these data, given in broad phonetic transcription. Then answer the questions that follow.

Note: Certain aspects of the surface phonetics—e.g., palatalization before front vowels, stress, and vowel reduction—have not been indicated. [ɯ] is a high, back, and unrounded vowel.

	Nominative Singular			Genitive Plural	
1a.	reka	'river'	1b.	rek	'of the rivers'
2a.	kniga	'book'	2b.	knik	'of the books'
3a.	rɯba	'fish'	3b.	rɯp	'of the fish'
4a.	rana	'wound'	4b.	ran	'of the wounds'
5a.	rabota	'work'	5b.	rabot	'of the works'
6a.	moda	'fashion'	6b.	mot	'of the fashions'
7a.	opira	'opera'	7b.	opir	'of the operas'
8a.	rosa	'dew'	8b.	ros	'of the dews'
9a.	repa	'turnip'	9b.	rep	'of the turnips'
10a.	duʃa	'spirit'	10b.	duʃ	'of the spirits'
11a.	platforma	'platform'	11b.	platform	'of the platforms'
12a.	loʒa	'boxseat'	12b.	loʃ	'of the boxseats'

A. Give a single, unique underlying form for each morpheme in the data.

_____

_____

_____

_____

_____

B. Propose a phonological rule that will account for all the surface forms. Your rule should be as general as possible.

_____

_____

_____

_____

C. Show the derivation of 'book' and 'of the books':

'book'

Underlying form: / _____ /

Application of P-rule: _____

Surface form: [_____]

'of the books'

Underlying form: / _____ /

Application of P-rule: _____

Surface form: [_____]

Name _____   **Section** _____   **Date** _____

 3.13   PHONOLOGICAL RULES: Cuban Spanish and "R-Less" English

In this exercise you will take a look at two different phonological processes, one in Cuban Spanish and the other in certain types of English, which share an interesting similarity.

A. Cuban Spanish.

The data below, given in phonetic transcription, provide pairs of Spanish words in two alternate pronunciations. Column 1 gives a standard pronunciation in many parts of the Spanish-speaking world; column 2 gives the corresponding pronunciation in one variety of Cuban Spanish.

Assuming that the forms in column 1 represent the underlying forms for those in column 2, state a phonological rule that accounts for the Cuban pronunciations. Carefully and explicitly state the environment in which the rule operates.

	1		2	
1a.	eso	1b.	eso	'that'
2a.	esta	2b.	ehta	'this'
3a.	sabɾoso	3b.	sabɾoso	'delicious'
4a.	dos latinos	4b.	doh latinoh	'two Latins'
5a.	buskaɾ	5b.	buhkaɾ	'to look for'
6a.	ospital	6b.	ohpital	'hospital'
7a.	asistentes	7b.	asihtenteh	'assistants'
8a.	mostasa	8b.	mohtasa	'mustard'
9a.	eski	9b.	ehki	'ski'
10a.	kuɾso	10b.	kuɾso	'course'

Rule:

_____

_____

_____

B. "R-less" English.

Standard British, Australian, and New Zealand English, along with several varieties of regional American English, are referred to as "r-less" dialects, since in these types of English *r* is dropped in certain linguistic environments.

In the following list of words, the underlined *r*'s are the ones that may drop in the "r-less" dialects. First transcribe the words in phonetic notation; then state the rule that determines which *r*'s are lost.

1. Robe<u>r</u>t   _____   10. ba<u>r</u>e   _____

2. sta<u>r</u>   _____   11. ca<u>r</u>e   _____

3. pa<u>r</u>k   _____   12. ca<u>r</u>ed   _____

4. horro<u>r</u>   _____   13. caring   _____

5. strike<u>r</u>   _____   14. ca<u>r</u>etaker   _____

6. starry   _____   15. tea<u>r</u>   _____

7. ha<u>r</u>de<u>r</u>   _____   16. to<u>r</u>e   _____

8. clea<u>r</u>   _____   17. pou<u>r</u>   _____

9. cleare<u>r</u>   _____   18. pou<u>r</u>ed   _____

Rule:

_____

_____

_____

C. What do the rules you discovered for Cuban Spanish and "r-less" English have in common?

_____

_____

_____

_____

Name _____   Section _____   Date _____

🎧 **3.14   PHONOLOGICAL RULES: Mandarin Tone Change of _pù_ and _ī_**

Mandarin Chinese has four distinctive tones:

1st Tone: high level	**EXAMPLE**	fāŋ	'square'
2nd Tone: rising		fáŋ	'house'
3rd Tone: low falling/rising		fǎŋ	'copy'
4th Tone: falling		fàŋ	'release'

Although tone is an intrinsic part of a Mandarin syllable, some tones change depending on their environment.

A. Consider the following data involving the words for 'one' and 'no, not.' In isolation, these are respectively [ī] and [pù].

1a.	xǎo	'good'		1b.	pù xǎo	'not good'
2a.	gāo	'tall'		2b.	pù gāo	'not tall'
3a.	nién	'year'		3b.	ì nién	'one year'
4a.	twèi	'correct'		4b.	pú twèi	'not correct'
5a.	tǎ	'hit'		5b.	pù tǎ	'not hit'
6a.	mièn	'side'		6b.	í mièn	'one side'
7a.	tʰài	'too'		7b.	pú tʰài	'not too'
8a.	tà	'big'		8b.	pú tà	'not big'
9a.	tʰiēn	'day'		9b.	ì tʰiēn	'one day'
10a.	lái	'come'		10b.	pù lái	'not come'
11a.	pʰà	'fear'		11b.	pú pʰà	'not fear'
12a.	tiěn	'dot, bit'		12b.	ì tiěn	'one bit'

State the rules that determine the tones of 'not' and 'one' in Mandarin.

_____

_____

_____

_____

_____

B. The word for 'type, kind' is [jàŋ]. The expression for 'not the same' is literally 'not one kind.' How do you say 'not the same' in Mandarin? Explain how you determined the tones.

_____

_____

_____

_____

_____

Name _____   **Section** _____   **Date** _____

 3.15   PHONOLOGICAL RULES: Voiceless Vowels in Japanese

One phonological rule in Japanese *devoices* certain vowels, with an effect something like a whispered vowel. Whether or not this devoicing occurs depends on several factors, including the rate and style of speech: The faster and more casual the speech, the more the devoicing.

The data below, given in phonetic transcription, illustrate this phenomenon. Some of the symbols used deserve special comment. [ɯ] represents a high, back, and unrounded vowel; [ɸ] is a voiceless bilabial fricative; [ç] is a voiceless palatal fricative, similar to the first sound of the English word *hue*. If a vowel has a small circle beneath it, it is "eligible" for devoicing, in the sense that it will be devoiced in at least some styles of speech; vowels without this symbol are never devoiced. The apostrophe indicates the position of the Japanese pitch accent[*].

Analyze these data to discover the rule or rules that determine which vowels are eligible for devoicing. Your goal is to write a brief paragraph that will describe in general terms—as far as can be determined from the data—the exact conditions for devoicing. The following questions should guide your analysis:

- Do all Japanese vowels participate in the process or only certain ones? If the latter, what if anything sets these vowels apart from the others?
- Does the process depend on the neighboring sounds? If so, how?
- Does it depend on the vowel's position in the word (initial, medial, final)?
- Is the accent involved? If so, what effect does it have on whether or not devoicing can occur?

Make sure your analysis correctly accounts for all the data presented. (Data adapted from Jorden 1963.)

1.	hatake	'dry field'	12.	kitto	'certainly'
2.	soʃite	'and then'	13.	sɯki'	'pleasing'
3.	watarɯ	'go across'	14.	sɯʃi'	'sushi'
4.	t͡sɯki'	'moon'	15.	çikima'ʃita	'pulled'
5.	saʃimi'	'raw fish dish'	16.	itʃi'	'one'
6.	çito'ri	'one person'	17.	kɯt͡sɯ'ʃita	'socks'
7.	sɯko'ʃi	'a small quantity'	18.	kabɯki	'kabuki' (theater)
8.	ɸɯkɯ'	'clothing'	19.	çikatet͡sɯ	'subway'
9.	ha'ʃi	'chopsticks'	20.	kakika'ta	'style of writing'
10.	haʃi'	'bridge'	21.	sɯkijaki	'sliced beef dish'
11.	sɯgi'rɯ	'exceed'	22.	mɯra'saki	'purple'

[*]The nature of the pitch accent, while not relevant to this problem, is quite interesting. The accent indicates the location of a high-to-low pitch transition: The syllable or part of a syllable preceding the accent is at a high pitch and is immediately followed by a fall in pitch. When the accent occurs after the last syllable, the pitch fall is "potential" and is only manifested when certain particles are attached to the word. Note that it is perfectly possible for a multisyllabic word not to have a pitch accent. (See Shibatani 1990: 177 ff.)

23. watasɯ̥   'hand over'

24. t͡sɯ'kɯ   'arrive'

25. mo'ʃimoʃi̥   'hello (on telephone)'

26. çi̥to't͡sɯ   'one unit'

27. bo'kɯ̥tatʃi̥   'we'

28. kimotʃi̥   'mood'

29. gakɯ̥sei   'student'

30. ɸɯ'kɯ   'blow'

31. ʃinbɯɯn   'newspaper'

32. kɯ̥ʃi'   'a comb'

33. watakɯ̥ʃi̥   'I'

34. sɯmi'   'ink stick'

35. tʃi'tʃi̥   'father'

36. ɯsagi   'rabbit'

37. çi̥ka'ʃi̥t͡sɯ   'basement'

38. ne'kɯ̥tai   'necktie'

39. sɯ̥pɯ'ɯn   'spoon'

40. ito'ko   'cousin'

Name _____   **Section** _____   **Date** _____

3.16   PHONOLOGICAL RULES: Tones in Akan

Akan, also known as Twi, belongs to the Kwa branch of the Niger-Congo family of languages. It is spoken by about 5 million to 8 million people, mainly in Ghana. Like almost all the languages south of the Sahara, Akan is a tone language. Recall that a tone language uses pitch along with consonants and vowels to distinguish syllables and hence words.

Unlike the Chinese languages, in which the tones can involve a *change* of pitch on a single syllable, the tones of Akan are all level, differing among themselves only in relative pitch. Three such tones exist, indicated in the data below by diacritics written over the segment that bears the tone:

á   high tone   a̍   mid tone   à   low tone

The following data, given in phonetic transcription, provide a number of two-syllable words exhibiting different tonal patterns. The list is exhaustive with respect to these patterns, in the sense that all the permissible combinations of tones in two-syllable words are illustrated. Examine the data carefully, and then answer the questions that follow.

1.	kírà	'to leave'	11.	pépà	'paper'
2.	pàpà	'a palm-leaf fan'	12.	séέ̍	'as, like'
3.	bʊ̀à	'to help'	13.	bípɔ́	'mountain, hilltop'
4.	kírà̍	'soul'	14.	fùæ̀	'to hold, seize'
5.	kása̍	'a language'	15.	fîtá	'to fan a fire'
6.	pápá	'good'	16.	káà	'automobile'
7.	fùǽ	'single, one'	17.	sísí	'a bear'
8.	kàsà	'to speak'	18.	kɔ́tà	'quart'
9.	sὲὲ	'to use up'	19.	kàá	'ring, bracelet'
10.	pàpá	'father'	20.	bʊ̀á	'to tell a lie'

A. Determine which of the following statements is true with respect to *high tone* and *low tone* in Akan. Circle the number of the correct statement, and then give the evidence for your conclusion: If 1, prove it; if 2, state the complementary distribution; if 3 or 4, explain.

1. These two tones contrast.

2. These two tones are in complementary distribution.

3. No conclusion can be drawn from the data.

4. Other (state): _____

Evidence or explanation: _____

_____

_____

B. Repeat part A for *low tone* and *midtone*.

1. These two tones contrast.
2. These two tones are in complementary distribution.
3. No conclusion can be drawn from the data.
4. Other (state): _____

Evidence or explanation: _____

_____

_____

C. Repeat part A for *high tone* and *midtone*.

1. These two tones contrast.
2. These two tones are in complementary distribution.
3. No conclusion can be drawn from the data.
4. Other (state): _____

Evidence or explanation: _____

_____

_____

D. In general, given three distinct tones—call them H, M, and L for short—how many logical or mathematical possibilities exist for different sequences of two tones (e.g., HH, HM, etc.)? _____

List all these logical possibilities: _____

E. Now go back to the Akan data and determine which of the logical possibilities you listed in part D actually exist in the language. (It may help to write the tone sequence of each Akan word next to it, using H, M, and L. For example, pápá HH.) Circle the actually occurring tonal sequences on your list.

F. State a rule or generalization that characterizes all the "good" sequences. Your rule must correctly predict precisely which logically possible sequences of tones can and cannot exist in two-syllable words in Akan.

_____

_____

Name _____   **Section** _____   **Date** _____

🎧 3.17   SYLLABLE STRUCTURE: Japanese versus English

Syllable structure is generally thought of in terms of the sequences of consonants and vowels a language allows. Thus, CVC represents a syllable of the pattern consonant-vowel-consonant; this is a very common pattern for English (*hat, shack, thought,* etc.), but other languages—Hawaiian is an example—may totally disallow this kind of syllable.

This problem contrasts Japanese and English syllable structure. You choose the English data on your own. For the Japanese examples, use the phonetically transcribed words in the following representative list, which have been divided into syllables for you. (Note: [ɯ] is a high, back, unrounded vowel.)

1.	a na ta	'you'	10.	ke i san ki	'calculator'
2.	to mo da tʃi	'friend'	11.	an ra kɯ	'comfort'
3.	o too to	'younger brother'	12.	gjɯt to	'tight'
4.	ɯn tʃin	'fare'	13.	kjoo kɯn	'instruction'
5.	da i ga kɯ	'university'	14.	mja kɯ	'pulse'
6.	hak ki ri	'clearly'	15.	rjok ka	'tree planting'
7.	oo kii	'big'	16.	i dʒip pa ri	'obstinacy'
8.	ha dʒi me ma ʃi te	'How do you do?'	17.	kjo ʃin	'open mind'
9.	den wa	'telephone'			

A. Fill in the following spaces with two Japanese and two English examples for each of the syllable types given. For your Japanese examples, write the Japanese word and underline the syllable; for your English examples, write the word in ordinary spelling and in phonetic transcription, and underline the syllable in the transcription.

EXAMPLE

	Japanese	English
CV	a<u>na</u>ta	to [tʰu]

1. **CV**   _____ _____   _____ _____

2. **V**   _____ _____   _____ _____

3. **VC**   _____ _____   _____ _____

4. **CVC** _____ _____   _____ _____

5. **CVV** _____ _____   _____ _____

	Japanese		English	
6. **CCV**	_____	_____	_____	_____
7. **CCVC**	_____	_____	_____	_____
8. **VCC**	_____	_____	_____	_____
9. **CVCC**	_____	_____	_____	_____
10. **CCVCC**	_____	_____	_____	_____
11. **CCCVC**	_____	_____	_____	_____
12. **CVCCC**	_____	_____	_____	_____
13. **CCVCCC**	_____	_____	_____	_____
14. **CCCVCCCC**	_____		_____	

(One example is enough!)

B. Now answer these questions:

1. Which language has the wider variety of possible syllable types? _____

2. Assuming the given data are representative, which syllable type predominates in Japanese?

    _____

3. What can you say about the kinds of *consonant clusters* (sequences of two or more consonants) that may begin a syllable in Japanese? Does this hold true for English as well?

    _____

    _____

4. What can you say about the kinds of consonant clusters that may end a syllable in Japanese? Is this also true for English?

    _____

    _____

Name _____   **Section** _____   **Date** _____

 3.18   SYLLABLE STRUCTURE: Mandarin Chinese

Syllable structure in Mandarin Chinese is traditionally analyzed in terms of *initials* (onsets) and *finals* (rhymes). The 22 initials* exhaust the possibilities for the start of a syllable, while the 37 finals give all the possible continuations.

   If all the initials and finals could combine with each other freely, then $22 \times 37 = 814$ syllables would be possible, ignoring tonal differences. In fact, however, only a little more than 400 of these exist. This is because constraints limit the free combination of initials and finals.

A. Here are the fricative initials or onsets of Mandarin:

   [f], [s], [ʂ], [ç], [x]

   Recall that [ç] is a voiceless palatal, as in German *ich*. [x] is a voiceless velar, which often tends toward [h]. [ʂ] is similar to [ʃ] but is retroflexed, i.e., articulated with the tip of the tongue curled back toward the hard palate.

   Consider the following eight finals or rhymes:

   [u], [in], [ou], [aŋ], [ü], [iaŋ], [ei], [üe]

   If these rhymes could combine freely with the fricative onsets, how many syllables (ignoring tone) could be constructed from them?

_____

B. The following words will show you which combinations of these onsets and rhymes actually exist. (Tones are indicated, but are not relevant for this problem.) The list is exhaustive, in that if a particular combination of the given onsets and rhymes isn't present, it doesn't exist in Mandarin. (Mandarin has an abundance of homonyms; the glosses indicate only one of a sometimes very large number of possible meanings for each word.)

1.	ʂàŋ	'up'	11.	xēi	'black'
2.	fú	'clothes'	12.	çǘe	'study'
3.	ʂéi	'who?'	13.	fǒu	'deny'
4.	çiǎŋ	'think'	14.	sù	'tell'
5.	sāŋ	'funeral'	15.	xáŋ	'line'
6.	çǖ	'empty'	16.	xǔ	'tiger'
7.	xòu	'rear'	17.	fēi	'fly'
8.	fáŋ	'house'	18.	sōu	'search'
9.	çīn	'new'	19.	ʂǒu	'hand'
10.	ʂū	'book'			

*Twenty-one single consonants plus the "zero" initial (absence of a consonant).

The following grid will help you see the patterns in the data. The boxes of the grid represent all the logically possible combinations of onsets and rhymes. Referring to the data, check the boxes that represent actually occurring syllables in Mandarin.

	in	iaŋ	ü	üe	u	ei	ou	aŋ
f								
s								
ş								
ç								
x								

Now state the generalization that captures which of the given onsets combine with which rhymes.

_____

_____

_____

_____

C. One potential syllable exists whose absence will not be accounted for by the general rule you formulated in part B. Which syllable is this? What are some possible reasons for its nonexistence?

_____

_____

_____

Name _____   **Section** _____   **Date** _____

🎧 3.19   STRESS: Icelandic, Swahili, Modern Greek, and Standard Arabic

In some languages, stress is *phonemic* or *distinctive*—i.e., the placement of stress in a word is not generally predictable and can therefore be used to distinguish words that would otherwise be identical. In other languages, stress is *predictable*—i.e., the placement of stress in a word is determined by phonological rules and is therefore not capable of distinguishing words. (In still other languages, stress is extremely weak or nonexistent; French is an example of such a language.)

Examine the Icelandic, Swahili, Modern Greek, and Standard Arabic words given below. The main stress in each word has been indicated by ´. For each language, determine whether stress is distinctive or predictable. If the former, justify your answer. If the latter, state the rule or rules that determine the placement of stress in a word.

A. Icelandic.

The data are given in standard Icelandic orthography: <þ> = [θ], <j> = [j], <ð> = [ð], and <æ> = [æ]. Although some of the words below have secondary stress, only the main stress has been indicated and is relevant to the problem.

1.	éftir	'after'	8.	skípbrotsmaður	'shipwrecked man'
2.	dískur	'plate'	9.	kénnari	'teacher'
3.	svéfnherbergi	'bedroom'	10.	éftirlæti	'favorite'
4.	drótning	'queen'	11.	þéssvegna	'therefore'
5.	vérzlunarviðskifti	'commerce'	12.	jókulbunga	'rounded summit
6.	élska	'(I) love'			of a glacier'
7.	kærleikur	'love' (n.)	13.	élskuðum	'(we) loved'

In this language, stress is   [   ] distinctive

[   ] predictable

Explanation:

_____

_____

_____

_____

_____

B. Swahili.

The data are given in standard Swahili orthography, which has been influenced by English spelling. Thus, <sh> = [ʃ], <ch> = [tʃ], and <j> = [dʒ]. In most other respects, the orthography is phonetic. Note that <ng> = [ng], not [ŋ]. (The latter is written <ng'>.)

As in the Icelandic data, only the main stress has been indicated. Note that in these examples, word-initial <m> before a consonant represents a syllable by itself. Thus, *mbu* has two syllables.

1.	watóto	'children'
2.	símba	'lion'
3.	ḿto	'river'
4.	Kiswahíli	'Swahili language'
5.	Kiingeréza	'English language'
6.	ḿbu	'mosquito'
7.	walijitazáma	'they looked at themselves'
8.	nimesikía	'I hear'
9.	kilichotutósha	'which was enough for us'
10.	mchúngwa	'orange tree'
11.	amekwénda	'he has gone'
12.	amekwendápi	'where has he gone?'
13.	zitakazowaharibía	'which will ruin for them'

In this language, stress is   [   ] distinctive

[   ] predictable

Explanation:

_____

_____

_____

_____

_____

Name _____   **Section** _____   **Date** _____

C. Modern Greek.

The data are given in phonetic transcription.

1. ánθropos   'man'
2. staθmós   'station'
3. xóros   'spare room'
4. kinimatoɣráfos   'movie theater'
5. ðrómos   'road'
6. viós   'property'
7. eŋgonós   'grandson'
8. éðafos   'soil, earth'
9. víos   'life'
10. aðɛrfós   'brother'
11. naós   'temple'
12. karkínos   'cancer'
13. xorós   'dance, ball'

In this language, stress is   [   ] distinctive

[   ] predictable

Explanation:

_____

_____

_____

_____

_____

D. Standard Arabic.

The data are given in transcription. For a description of some of the phonetic symbols used, see Appendix B.

1. kálimatun   'a word'
2. muqáːtilun   'a fighter'
3. wáladun   'a boy'
4. ʔawláːdun   'boys'
5. dʒadáːwilu   'streams'
6. karíːmun   'generous'
7. ʕáːlimun   'learned, erudite'
8. ʃádʒaratun   'a tree'
9. ʔáswadu   'black'
10. ʔaswadáːni   'two black men'
11. ʃaríbtum   'you (m. pl.) drank'
12. dʒadíːdun   'new'
13. ʔadʒáddu   'newer'
14. ḍarabtúnna   'you (f. pl.) struck'
15. katábnaː   'we wrote'
16. katábtumaː   'you two wrote'
17. taláːmiðatun   'a student'
18. maʃɣúːlun   'busy (m. sg.)'
19. maʃɣuːláːtun   'busy (f. pl.)'
20. tardʒamtumúːhaː   'you (m. pl.) translated them'

In this language, stress is   [   ] distinctive
                                [   ] predictable

Explanation:

_____

_____

_____

_____

_____

Name _____   **Section** _____   **Date** _____

3.20 MORPHOLOGY/PHONOLOGY INTERACTION: Articles in French and Arabic

I. French

Many final consonants that appear in the spelling of French words are never pronounced. In certain circumstances, however, final consonants that are usually "silent" may in fact be pronounced.

This exercise focuses on the plural article in French, which appears as *les* in standard French spelling. You are to determine the different pronunciations of this article and then to discover the circumstances for using each pronunciation.

Examine the following data carefully, given in transcription. Word boundaries have been indicated.

1.	le ʃa	'the cats'	10.	le vag	'the waves'
2.	le garsõ	'the boys'	11.	lez urs	'the bears'
3.	lez ami	'the friends'	12.	le tapi	'the carpets'
4.	le kaʒ	'the cages'	13.	le muʃ	'the flies'
5.	le pwa	'the peas'	14.	lez jø	'the eyes'
6.	lez eta	'the states'	15.	le nüaʒ	'the clouds'
7.	le buʒi	'the candles'	16.	lez ɔm	'the men'
8.	lez üzin	'the factories'	17.	le fam	'the women'
9.	lez wazo	'the birds'	18.	lez ãfã	'the children'

A. What are the different pronunciations of *les*? _____

B. Formulate a rule that predicts when each of the variant pronunciations is used.

_____

_____

II. Arabic

A. Examine the following list of nouns in Standard Arabic. The nouns are given first without, and then with, the definite article. Then find an underlying form for the definite article in Arabic. (*Note:* [q] is a voiceless uvular stop. The vowel transcribed as [a] has some phonetic variation that has not been indicated.)

1. ?ab	?al?ab	'father'	9. waːdʒib	?alwaːdʒib	'duty'
2. baːb	?albaːb	'door'	10. ?ax	?al?ax	'brother'
3. xariːf	?alxariːf	'autumn'	11. bint	?albint	'girl'
4. faːris	?alfaːris	'knight'	12. funduq	?alfunduq	'hotel'
5. qabr	?alqabr	'tomb'	13. qism	?alqism	'part'
6. kalb	?alkalb	'dog'	14. kitaːb	?alkitaːb	'book'
7. madrasa	?almadrasa	'school'	15. madʒd	?almadʒd	'glory'
8. hilaːl	?alhilaːl	'crescent'	16. walad	?alwalad	'boy'

Underlying form of definite article _____

B. Now examine the following additional data. Notice that in these cases, the definite article is pronounced differently.

Formulate a rule that determines how the article is actually pronounced. Your goal is not to generate a large number of different rules for specific cases but, rather, to find one *general* rule that will work in every case.

17. tarbija	?attarbija	'education'	24. taʔriːx	?attaʔriːx	'history'
18. daːr	?addaːr	'house'	25. dars	?addars	'lesson'
19. raːkib	?arraːkib	'rider'	26. radʒul	?arradʒul	'man'
20. zajt	?azzajt	'oil'	27. zawaːdʒ	?azzawaːdʒ	'marriage'
21. salaːm	?assalaːm	'peace'	28. sinn	?assinn	'tooth'
22. ʃadʒara	?aʃʃadʒara	'tree'	29. ʃamaːl	?aʃʃamaːl	'north'
23. natiːdʒa	?annatiːdʒa	'result'	30. nabi	?annabi	'prophet'

Rule:

_____

_____

_____

_____

Name _____   Section _____   Date _____

🎧 3.21   MORPHOLOGY/PHONOLOGY INTERACTION: Malay/Indonesian Morphophonemics

A. Examine the following Malay/Indonesian words, given in transcription. The first column gives a number of verbs in their root forms, and the second gives the forms with a prefix attached. This prefix has a number of different allomorphs. (The forms in the second column have been glossed in only one of several possible ways.)

1a.	bawa	'bring'	1b.	məmbawa	'bringing'
2a.	dapat	'get'	2b.	məndapat	'getting'
3a.	gaŋgu	'bother'	3b.	məŋgaŋgu	'bothering'
4a.	doroŋ	'push'	4b.	məndoroŋ	'pushing'
5a.	ambil	'take'	5b.	məŋambil	'taking'
6a.	bwat	'do'	6b.	məmbwat	'doing'
7a.	hilaŋ	'disappear'	7b.	məɲhilaŋ	'disappearing'
8a.	utʃap	'say'	8b.	məɲutʃap	'saying'

List the different allomorphs of the prefix found among these data. Then propose a single, unique underlying form for the prefix, and state the rule or rules that will account for the appearance of the various allomorphs. Your rule(s) should be as general as possible.

Allomorphs: _____

Underlying form: _____

Rule(s):

_____

_____

B. Now consider the following additional data:

9a.	tari	'dance'	9b.	mənari	'dancing'
10a.	pandaŋ	'gaze'	10b.	məmandaŋ	'gazing'
11a.	tulis	'write'	11b.	mənulis	'writing'
12a.	kanduŋ	'contain'	12b.	məŋanduŋ	'containing'
13a.	pəgaŋ	'hold'	13b.	məməgaŋ	'holding'
14a.	kata	'say'	14b.	məŋata	'saying'
15a.	pakaj	'wear'	15b.	məmakaj	'wearing'
16a.	tərima	'receive'	16b.	mənərima	'receiving'

Propose an additional rule that will correctly account for the forms in the second column.

_____

_____

_____

C. The rules you proposed in parts A and B must be applied in a certain order. What is this order?

_____

_____

Show how the words for 'taking,' 'pushing,' and 'gazing' are derived.

	'taking'	'pushing'	'gazing'
Underlying Forms	/ _____ /	/ _____ /	/ _____ /
Rules	_____	_____	_____
	_____	_____	_____
Surface Forms	[_____]	[_____]	[_____]

Name _____   **Section** _____   **Date** _____

 ## 3.22   MORPHOLOGY/PHONOLOGY INTERACTION: A Derived Verb Stem in Arabic

As in other Semitic languages, most verb forms in Arabic and their corresponding noun forms are derived from a sequence of three root consonants or "radicals" to which are added various affixes. The three consonants embody a basic semantic notion, which the affixes modify, refine, and extend.

For example, the consonants ħ, k, and m relate to the idea of judging or ruling. These consonants, of course, are unpronounceable by themselves. However, with the insertion of vowels in various patterns; the addition of certain prefixes, infixes, and suffixes; and the lengthening of certain consonants and vowels, a wide range of Arabic words is produced with meanings related in various ways to judging or ruling. Here is a partial list of words derivable from the root *ħ-k-m* in this way:

Verbs

ħakama	'pass judgment, govern, rule, dominate'
ħukima	'be judged, receive judgment'
ħakkama	'appoint as judge or ruler'
ħaːkama	'prosecute, bring to trial'
ʔaħkama	'do expertly, be proficient in, master'
taħakkama	'pass arbitrary judgment, be in control'
taħaːkama	'appeal for a legal decision, be heard' (in court)
ʔiħtakama	'have one's own way, proceed at will, reign, hold sway'
ʔistaħkama	'be strong, firm, deep-seated, ingrained'

Nouns and Adjectives

ħukm	'judgment, legal decision' (pl.: ʔaħkam)
ħukmiː	'legal'
ħakam	'arbitrator, umpire, referee'
ħikma	'wisdom'
ħakiːm	'wise man, sage, physician'
ħukuːma	'government'
ħukuːmiː	'governmental, official'
ʔaħkam	'wiser'
maħkama	'court'
taħkiːm	'arbitration'
muħaːkama	'trial'
ʔiħkaːm	'perfection in performance'
taħakkum	'despotism, domination'
ħaːkim	'judge, ruler'

Arabic has ten common patterns or stems for verbs. Stem I is the basic, simplest pattern. This problem concerns Stem II, the second of these verbal patterns.

Each pair of words below consists of the Stem I form of the verb along with the Stem II form. Compare the forms and meanings carefully, paying particular attention to the meaning relationship between Stems I and II. Then answer the questions that follow.

Note: Arabic verbs are listed in dictionaries under their simplest forms, namely the third person singular masculine (Semitic verbs have gender!) of the perfect, Stem I. These are the "citation" forms—the forms people give when they wish to talk about the item in question. In English, we speak of the verb 'to write,' the citation form being the infinitive; Arabic speakers talk about the verb *kataba,* which means 'he wrote.' The words here are accordingly given in their third-person citation forms but glossed as English infinitives. Many of these verbs have a wide range of meanings, often including metaphorical ones; the glosses most clearly point to the systematic relationship between the two stems.

If you are unfamiliar with any of the phonetic symbols used in the transcription, see Appendix B.

1. I: nazala   'to descend, go or come down'
   II: nazzala   'to lower, let down'

2. I: baraza   'to come out, appear'
   II: barraza   'to bring out, expose, show'

3. I: baṭala   'to become null, void, invalid'
   II: baṭṭala   'to nullify, neutralize, invalidate'

4. I: nafaḍa   'to shake, shake off, shake out'
   II: naffaḍa   'to shake violently'

5. I: xasira   'to go astray'
   II: xassara   'to corrupt'

6. I: ʃarada   'to run away, flee, escape'
   II: ʃarrada   'to frighten or chase away'

7. I: θabata   'to stand firm, be fixed or stationary'
   II: θabbata   'to fasten, make fast, stabilize'

8. I: ḥasuna   'to be handsome, beautiful, proper'
   II: ḥassana   'to beautify, embellish, improve'

9. I: qatala   'to kill, slay'
   II: qattala   'to massacre, cause carnage'

Name _____   **Section** _____   **Date** _____

10. I: xalada   'to be immortal, eternal, everlasting'
    II: xallada   'to perpetuate, immortalize'

11. I: wasixa   'to be or become dirty'
    II: wassaxa   'to dirty, sully, soil'

12. I: raɣiba   'to desire, wish, crave'
    II: raɣɣaba   'to awaken a desire, excite interest'

13. I: kasara   'to break, shatter, break open'
    II: kassara   'to break into pieces, fragmentize, smash'

14. I: sakana   'to be tranquil; to calm down, abate, subside'
    II: sakkana   'to calm, placate, soothe'

15. I: ṭaraħa   'to throw away, discard'
    II: ṭarraħa   'to throw far away'

16. I: ʕalima   'to know, be informed'
    II: ʕallama   'to teach, instruct'

17. I: hataka   'to tear or rip apart'
    II: hattaka   'to tear to shreds, rip to pieces'

18. I: qaruba   'to be near, to approach'
    II: qarraba   'to bring into proximity'

19. I: labisa   'to put on, wear'
    II: labbasa   'to clothe, garb, attire'

20. I: matuna   'to be firm, strong, solid'
    II: mattana   'to strengthen, fortify'

A. If we call the three root consonants in each example above C_1, C_2, and C_3, what is the pattern or patterns for the Stem I verbs?

_____

_____

B. What is the pattern or patterns for the Stem II verbs?

_____

_____

C. You will have noticed that the meanings of the Stem II forms are related in systematic ways to those of the corresponding Stem I forms. Two basic semantic relationships exist between the two stems apparent in these data. One holds for the majority of examples, but a second, different relationship is evident as well.

Explain what these two relationships are; in the case of the "minority" relationship, include the numbers of the examples in the data that give evidence for it.

_____

_____

_____

_____

_____

_____

_____

_____

_____

D. Consider the following two verbs:

I: radʒaʕa   'to return'

II: radʒdʒaʕa   'to return'

Notice that they have been glossed identically. Are these words exceptions to the generalizations you found in C, or do they fit into the pattern? Explain.

_____

_____

_____

Name _____   **Section** _____   **Date** _____

 **3.23   MORPHOLOGY/PHONOLOGY INTERACTION:
Articles and Pronouns in Modern Greek
(or "The Girl or the Sailor?")**

Modern Greek has considerable inflectional morphology. The following data concern a subset of the Modern Greek articles and pronouns, both of which categories are inflected for gender, number, and case.

Nouns, pronouns, and adjectives in Modern Greek fall into one of three genders, traditionally referred to as masculine, feminine, and neuter. The data presented here are restricted to masculine and neuter genders. Note that the word for 'man' is, appropriately enough, masculine.

A. Examine the following sentences in Modern Greek. (The data are given in transcription; stress is indicated.)

1. *a)* o ándras íne ɛðó   'The man is here.'
    b) vlépo ton ándra   'I see the man.'
    c) ton vlépo   'I see him.'

2. *a)* to krasí inɛ ɛðó   'The wine is here.'
    b) pínumɛ to krasí   'We drink the wine.'
    c) to pínumɛ   'We drink it.'

3. *a)* o kafés íne ɛðó   'The coffee is here.'
    b) píno toŋ gafɛ́   'I drink the coffee.'
    c) tom bíno   'I drink it.'

4. *a)* o tíxos íne ɛðó   'The wall is here.'
    b) vlépumɛ ton díxo   'We see the wall.'
    c) ton vlépumɛ   'We see it.'

5. *a)* to pɛðí íne ɛðó   'The child is here.'
    b) ksɛ́ro to pɛðí   'I know the child.'
    c) to ksɛ́ro   'I know him/her.'

6. *a)* o kírios íne ɛðó   'The gentleman is here.'
    b) ksɛ́rumɛ toŋ gírio   'We know the gentleman.'
    c) toŋ gzɛ́rumɛ   'We know him.'

7. *a)* to pɛrioðikó íne ɛðó   'The magazine is here.'
    b) ɛ́xumɛ to pɛrioðikó   'We have the magazine.'
    c) to ɛ́xumɛ   'We have it.'

8. *a)* o páɣos íne eðó   'The ice is here.'

   b) éxo tom báɣo   'I have the ice.'

   c) ton éxo   'I have it.'

(1) Isolate all the morphemes in the data, giving each one in its underlying form. For the articles and pronouns, you may want to present your solutions in a chart like the following:

	Masculine	Neuter
Subj.	_____	_____
Obj.	_____	_____

_____

_____

_____

_____

_____

_____

_____

_____

_____

_____

_____

_____

_____

_____

_____

_____

Name _____   **Section** _____   **Date** _____

(2) State the rule or rules that will derive the surface forms from the underlying forms. For 'I have the ice,' give the underlying form, and show how your rule or rules apply to yield the surface form.

Rule(s):

_____

_____

_____

_____

'I have the ice.'

_____

Underlying Form   / _____ /

Rule(s)   _____

_____

_____

Surface Form   [_____]

B. Some of the *b)* and *c)* sentences in the data have alternate forms in spoken Greek. These are given below.

3. *b)* píno to gafé
    c) to bíno

4. *b)* vlépumɛ to díxo

6. *b)* ksérumɛ to gírio
    c) to gzérumɛ

8. *b)* éxo to báɣo

What additional rule is needed to account for these spoken variants? How must this rule be ordered with respect to the rule(s) you formulated in part A? Justify your answers.

_____

_____

_____

_____

_____

C. You overhear a conversation in an Athenian taverna concerning a sailor and a girl. The noise level is such that you can't follow the conversation completely. However, you clearly hear someone saying he knows the individual under discussion. What you hear is:

to gzéro

Is the speaker saying he is acquainted with the sailor (o náftis) or the girl (to korítsi)? How do you know?

_____

_____

_____

Name _____   **Section** _____   **Date** _____

3.24   MORPHOLOGY/PHONOLOGY INTERACTION:
The Definite Article in Welsh

A. Examine the data below, given in both standard Welsh orthography and phonetic transcription. Then answer the questions that follow.

1a.	y tŷ	[ə ti]	'the house'
2a.	y gwaith	[ə gwaiθ]	'the workplace'
3a.	yr ysgol	[ər əskol]	'the school'
4a.	y car	[ə kar]	'the car'
5a.	yr adeilad	[ər adeilad]	'the building'
6a.	yr eglwys	[ər egluis]	'the church'

1b.	yn y tŷ	[ən ə ti]	'in the house'
2b.	yn y gwaith	[ən ə gwaiθ]	'in the workplace'
3b.	yn yr ysgol	[ən ər əskol]	'in the school'
4b.	yn y car	[ən ə kar]	'in the car'
5b.	yn yr adeilad	[ən ər adeilad]	'in the building'
6b.	yn yr eglwys	[ən ər egluis]	'in the church'

1c.	i'r tŷ	[ir ti]	'to the house'
2c.	i'r gwaith	[ir gwaiθ]	'to the workplace'
3c.	i'r ysgol	[ir əskol]	'to the school'
4c.	i'r car	[ir kar]	'to the car'
5c.	i'r adeilad	[ir adeilad]	'to the building'
6c.	i'r eglwys	[ir egluis]	'to the church'

1d.	o'r tŷ	[or ti]	'from the house'
2d.	o'r gwaith	[or gwaiθ]	'from the workplace'
3d.	o'r ysgol	[or əskol]	'from the school'
4d.	o'r car	[or kar]	'from the car'
5d.	o'r adeilad	[or adeilad]	'from the building'
6d.	o'r eglwys	[or egluis]	'from the church'

1. What are the allomorphs of the definite article in Welsh?

_____

_____

2. What is the distribution of these allomorphs—i.e., what determines when each one is used?

_____

_____

_____

B.

1. Find a unique underlying form for the definite article from which all the allomorphs can be derived.

_____

2. Propose one or more phonological rules that will allow the surface forms to be derived. If more than one rule exists, do they have to be ordered with respect to each other? Explain.

_____

_____

_____

3. Show the derivation of 'in the house,' 'in the school,' 'from the house,' and 'from the school' by filling in the following chart. (Use phonetic transcription.)

	'in the house'	'in the school'
Underlying Forms	/_____/	/_____/
Phonological Rules	_____	_____
	_____	_____
Surface Forms	[_____]	[_____]

	'from the house'	'from the school'
Underlying Forms	/_____/	/_____/
Phonological Rules	_____	_____
	_____	_____
Surface Forms	[_____]	[_____]

Name _____   **Section** _____   **Date** _____

 **3.25   MORPHOLOGY/PHONOLOGY INTERACTION:
Vowel Harmony in Turkish**

Turkish vowels enter into a process known as *vowel harmony,* a type of assimilation whereby vowels within a word tend to share some of the same characteristics. It has been described as "basically a stringing together of vowels of similar quality, so that there is a sound harmony extending over the whole word" (Rona 1989). In this exercise you will become familiar with the Turkish vowel system and will explore some aspects of the vowel harmony that operates within Turkish words.

The data are given in standard Turkish orthography, which is quite close to a phonetic transcription. Here are some differences you should be aware of:

$$<c> = [d\!\!3]$$
$$<ç> = [t\!\!\int]$$
$$<ş> = [\int]$$
$$<y> = [j]$$

Most importantly for this problem, the undotted *i,* <ı>, represents a vowel similar to [u] except that it is *nonround*; such a vowel is also found in Russian and Japanese. Two different phonetic symbols for this vowel are [ɨ] and [ɯ].

A. Turkish has a particularly symmetric vowel system. You will be able to identify the Turkish vowels by examining the brief passage below, which contains them all. (Data and translation, Rona 1989, from a passage on visiting mosques in Turkey.)

Kadınların başlarını örtmeleri lazımdır. Yanınızda bir eşarp ya da başınızı örtecek bir şey olmayabilir. O takdirde oradaki bir görevliden bir başörtüsü isteyebilirsiniz, ve camiden çıkarken bunu geri verirsiniz.

'Women must cover their heads. It is possible you may not have with you a scarf or something else to cover your head. In that case, you'll be able to ask for a headscarf from one of the officials there, and when you go out of the mosque you'll give it back.'

1. List the eight vowels of Turkish:

_____

2. The symmetry of this vowel system becomes apparent when the vowels are analyzed according to the following criteria:

Height: High or nonhigh

Backness: Back or nonback (i.e., front)

Roundness: Round or nonround

Describe each of the Turkish vowels in terms of these criteria. (One vowel has been done for you as an example.)

a)   i   high, nonback, nonround

b) _____ _____

c) _____ _____

d) _____ _____

e) _____ _____

f) _____ _____

g) _____ _____

h) _____ _____

3. Now present the same information in a different form. Using the following chart (an example of a *distinctive feature matrix*), write the vowels in the left-hand column, and then enter a plus or minus in each blank according to whether the value of the feature is positive or negative for the vowel in question.

Vowel	High	Back	Round
_____	_____	_____	_____
_____	_____	_____	_____
_____	_____	_____	_____
_____	_____	_____	_____
_____	_____	_____	_____
_____	_____	_____	_____
_____	_____	_____	_____
_____	_____	_____	_____
_____	_____	_____	_____

Name _____   **Section** _____   **Date** _____

4. As an aid to visualizing the symmetry of the Turkish vowel system, assign each vowel to the appropriate vertex of this cube:

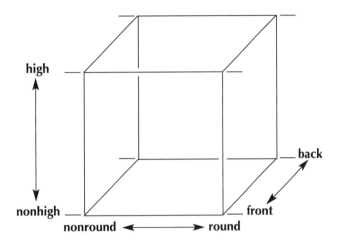

5. List all the Turkish vowels that are each of these:

   a) nonround: _____

   b) front and round: _____

   c) high and back: _____

   d) back: _____

   e) nonhigh, back, and nonround: _____

B. Having identified the vowels and their features, you are now ready to analyze some examples of vowel harmony.

   The following data show certain Turkish nouns with and without the suffix meaning 'in,' an example of what we may call a Class I suffix. Examine the data, and then answer the questions that follow. (*Note:* Turkish has no definite article; although the word 'the' appears in the glosses, it is not reflected anywhere in the Turkish.)

1a.	ev	'house'		1b.	evde	'in the house'
2a.	kutu	'box'		2b.	kutuda	'in the box'
3a.	köy	'village'		3b.	köyde	'in the village'
4a.	oda	'room'		4b.	odada	'in the room'
5a.	deniz	'sea'		5b.	denizde	'in the sea'
6a.	halı	'carpet'		6b.	halıda	'in the carpet'
7a.	gül	'rose'		7b.	gülde	'in the rose'
8a.	kol	'arm'		8b.	kolda	'in the arm'

1. What are the possible forms of the suffix for 'in'?

   _____

2. Referring to the vowel analysis you did in part A, fill in the following blanks to characterize precisely the two different vowels that can appear in this suffix:

   These are exactly the vowels that are both _____ and _____.

3. How do these vowels *differ*?

   _____

4. The next step is to determine when each variant of the suffix is used. The key is to look at the vowel in the syllable immediately preceding it.
       For each variant of the suffix, determine all the vowels possible in the preceding syllable. Then, looking at each set of vowels you've listed, characterize them precisely, again referring to your previous analysis:

   The variant _____ can follow the vowels_____; these are

   exactly the vowels that are _____.

   The variant _____ can follow the vowels_____; these are

   exactly the vowels that are _____.

5. What is the connection between each suffix variant and the vowels it can follow?

   _____

   _____

6. Now state the generalization for Class I suffixes by filling in the following blanks: _____

   vowels can appear in a Class I suffix, namely _____; these

   vowels are characterized by the fact that they are _____ and

   _____. The vowel in the suffix is chosen so as to agree in

   _____ with the vowel of the immediately preceding syllable.

Name _____   **Section** _____   **Date** _____

C. In the following data you will find all the variants of the Turkish suffix meaning 'with'—an example of what we may call a Class II suffix—along with a representative sampling of their distribution.

Examine the data carefully, and then analyze the distribution of the variants as you did for the Class I suffix in the previous section. You should proceed with the same six-step process above, ending with a generalization for Class II suffixes comparable to the one you formulated for Class I.

1a.	balık	'fish'	1b.	balıklı	'with fish'
2a.	biber	'pepper'	2b.	biberli	'with pepper'
3a.	süt	'milk'	3b.	sütlü	'with milk'
4a.	limon	'lemon'	4b.	limonlu	'with lemon'
5a.	tuz	'salt'	5b.	tuzlu	'with salt'
6a.	peynir	'cheese'	6b.	peynirli	'with cheese'
7a.	ordövr	'hors d'oeuvres'	7b.	ordövrlü	'with hors d'oeuvres'
8a.	çikolata	'chocolate'	8b.	çikolatalı	'with chocolate'

_____

_____

_____

_____

_____

_____

_____

_____

_____

_____

_____

_____

_____

_____

_____

_____

_____

_____

_____

_____

_____

D. The first column below lists eight Turkish verbs. Fill in the blanks in the other two columns by adding on the appropriate forms of the infinitive suffix *-mek* (Class I) in column 2, and the past tense suffix *-di* (Class II) in column 3.

1. gel	'come'	gelmek	'to come'	geldi	'came'
2. çevir	'dial'	_____	'to dial'	_____	'dialed'
3. gör	'see'	_____	'to see'	_____	'saw'
4. yüz	'swim'	_____	'to swim'	_____	'swam'
5. kal	'stay'	_____	'to stay'	_____	'stayed'
6. ısır	'bite'	_____	'to bite'	_____	'bit'
7. koy	'put'	_____	'to put'	_____	'put'
8. oku	'read'	_____	'to read'	_____	'read'

4

Syntax

KEY TERMS AND SYMBOLS

See the glossary.

Auxiliary	Indirect object	Relative clause
Clause	Interrogative sentence	Relative pronoun
Deep structure	Matrix clause	Subject
Direct object	Modal verb	Subordinate clause
Embedded clause	Noun phrase	Subordinate conjunction
Grammatical relation	Oblique	Surface structure
Head noun	Passive	Tree diagram

Name _____   Section _____   Date _____

EXERCISES BASED ON ENGLISH

4.01   SENTENCE TYPES: English Clauses

A. In the spaces provided, write S for sentences that contain only one clause and E for sentences that contain embedded clauses. Underline <u>subordinators</u>, bearing in mind that not all embedded clauses are marked by conjunctions. (Sentences taken or adapted from an article in the *New York Times*, February 13, 1998.)

EXAMPLE   <u>E</u>   <u>After</u> Mark left, Sally felt much more comfortable.

_____   1. As people get older, the male brain shrinks faster than the female brain.

_____   2. The study appears in the February issue of *The Archives of Neurology*.

_____   3. Many of those studies have looked to levels of education, exercise or nutrition to explain the differences, but the latest findings suggest that it might now be possible to see if structural changes lead to subtle differences in cognition.

_____   4. The study looked at the brains of 330 healthy people 65 to 95 years of age through the use of magnetic resonance imaging, a technique that reveals brain anatomy in exquisite detail.

_____   5. Men's brains are bigger than women's because men are larger.

_____   6. After allowing for such factors, it is possible to compare the size of various brain regions and to look for differences.

_____   7. One measure is the cerebral spinal fluid, a clear, watery substance that bathes the brain's outermost layer, called the cortex, and circulates between various cavities in the brain's deeper regions.

_____   8. Everyone loses brain mass as he or she ages, Coffey said.

_____   9. The people in the study were not demented.

_____   10. Such age-related changes in brain size could be normal and have little or no effect on memory and thinking, or they could indicate that brain cells are dying and that a person's cognitive functions are declining.

B. Underline the subject and verb of every clause contained in each of the following sentences. (Use a single underline for the subject and a double underline for the verb.) Then give the clause count for the sentence. (Sentences taken or adapted from an article in the *New York Times,* February 13, 1998.)

EXAMPLE   _4_   Joyce insisted that her brother Marvin worked out seven days a week but it seemed to me that he wasn't getting any bigger.

Clause Count

_____ 1. Jerry Seinfeld is moving away from Tom's Restaurant in more ways than one.

_____ 2. First he signed a $4.35 million contract for an apartment a couple of blocks south of his old one.

_____ 3. The Tenth Street Lounge between First and Second Avenues was jammed with twenty-something types whose off-the-rack suits suggested that they still inhabited the lower rungs of the corporate ladder.

_____ 4. The party was for *Swing* magazine, and a lot of networking was going on.

_____ 5. More than one woman who said she couldn't juggle a job and a relationship complained about so-and-so's marriage.

_____ 6. Some buyers insisted the cards were for nieces or nephews who have a thing for Rosie O'Donnell.

_____ 7. "It's like a writers' workshop," Mr. Coppola said as he celebrated the magazine's first anniversary at the TriBeCa Grill.

_____ 8. The deal for the apartment hinges on approval from the co-op board at the Beresford.

_____ 9. It was so noisy that Ms. Johnson could hardly hear the bids.

_____ 10. "No one's particularly worried—the building already has a celebrity quotient," said one person familiar with the deal.

Name _____   **Section** _____   **Date** _____

4.02   CONSTITUENCY AND TREE DIAGRAMS:
English Constituent Structure

Here is the first sentence of Lincoln's Gettysburg Address.* Several of its word sequences follow. Determine whether each of these is or is not a constituent of the sentence; if it is, indicate what kind.

Fourscore and seven years ago our forefathers brought forth on this continent, a new nation, conceived in Liberty, and dedicated to the proposition that all men are created equal.

	EXAMPLES	and seven	Not a constituent
		a new nation	Constituent: NP

1. our forefathers

   [   ] Not a constituent   [   ] Constituent: _____

2. forth on this

   [   ] Not a constituent   [   ] Constituent: _____

3. on this continent

   [   ] Not a constituent   [   ] Constituent: _____

4. on this continent, a new nation

   [   ] Not a constituent   [   ] Constituent: _____

5. all men

   [   ] Not a constituent   [   ] Constituent: _____

6. men are created

   [   ] Not a constituent   [   ] Constituent: _____

7. are created equal

   [   ] Not a constituent   [   ] Constituent: _____

8. all men are created equal

   [   ] Not a constituent   [   ] Constituent: _____

9. proposition

   [   ] Not a constituent   [   ] Constituent: _____

*Delivered in 1863, Lincoln's great speech long preceded current sensitivities to sexist language.

10. the proposition that all men are created equal

    [   ] Not a constituent   [   ] Constituent: _____

11. to the proposition that all men are created equal

    [   ] Not a constituent   [   ] Constituent: _____

12. a new nation, conceived in Liberty, and dedicated to the proposition that all men are created equal

    [   ] Not a constituent   [   ] Constituent: _____

13. brought forth on this continent, a new nation, conceived in Liberty, and dedicated to the proposition that all men are created equal

    [   ] Not a constituent   [   ] Constituent: _____

14. years ago our forefathers brought forth

    [   ] Not a constituent   [   ] Constituent: _____

15. Fourscore and seven years ago our forefathers brought forth on this continent, a new nation, conceived in Liberty, and dedicated to the proposition that all men are created equal.

    [   ] Not a constituent   [   ] Constituent: _____

16. a new nation, conceived in Liberty

    [   ] Not a constituent   [   ] Constituent: _____

17. dedicated to the proposition

    [   ] Not a constituent   [   ] Constituent: _____

Name _____   **Section** _____   **Date** _____

4.03   CONSTITUENCY AND TREE DIAGRAMS: English Sentence Trees

The following tree diagrams range from simple to fairly complex. These are basically "empty" trees that will each fit a large number of different sentences.

For each example, provide a sentence that fits the structure. Write the lexical items where they belong in the tree, and write the whole sentence below the tree in the space provided.

Note: Triangles have been used when the details of a particular structure are not required. Although in some theories of syntax the AUX node is always present, for simplicity AUX has not been consistently indicated in the diagrams. The same is true for the COMP node related to the matrix clause.

EXAMPLE

Diagram given

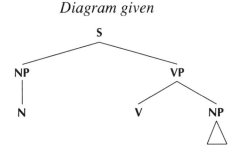

One possible answer

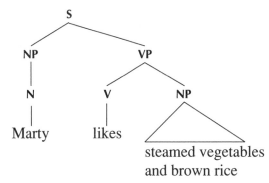

Marty likes steamed vegetables and brown rice.

1.

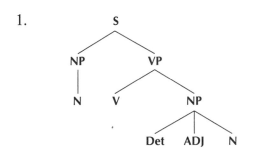

_____

_____

2.

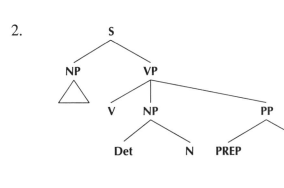

_____

_____

3.

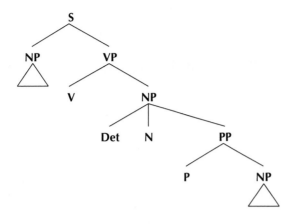

_____

_____

4.

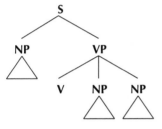

_____

_____

5.

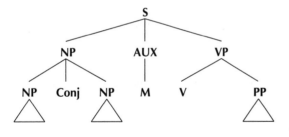

_____

_____

6.

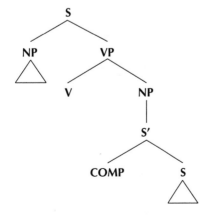

_____

_____

Name _____   **Section** _____   **Date** _____

7.

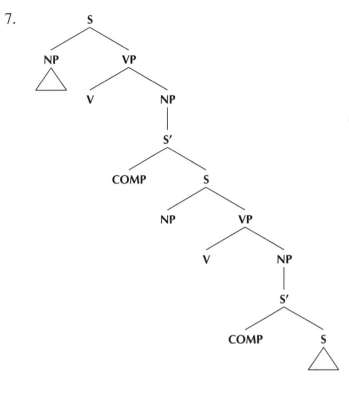

_____

_____

8.

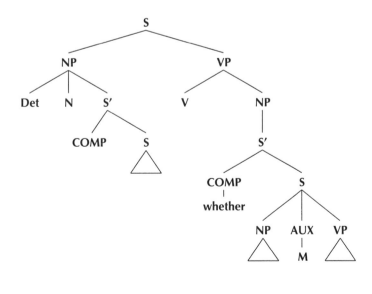

_____

_____

9.

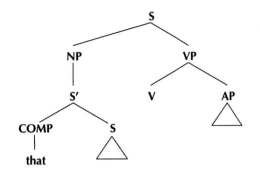

_____

_____

10.

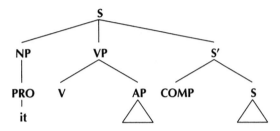

_____

_____

11.

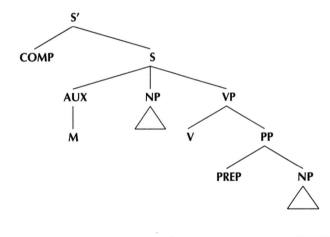

_____

_____

12.

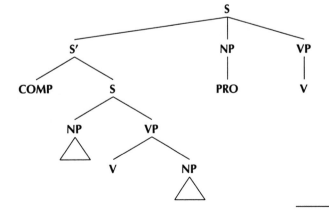

_____

_____

Name _____   **Section** _____   **Date** _____

4.04   CONSTITUENCY AND TREE DIAGRAMS:
Structural Ambiguity in English

Sentences can be ambiguous for many different reasons. The type of sentence ambiguity we are concerned with here is known as *structural ambiguity*. Sentences that are structurally ambiguous have two or more different interpretations, not because of any ambiguous words or morphemes they contain but rather because their words or morphemes can be organized in *different constituent structures,* resulting in different meanings.

A. The following sentence is structurally ambiguous:

I hate *raw fish and onions*.

1. Give an unambiguous paraphrase of the sentence if the italicized part has the following structure:

raw   fish   and   onions

Paraphrase: ___fish   and   onions   that   are   raw_____

2. Now give a second paraphrase if the italicized part has this structure:

raw   fish   and   onions

Paraphrase: ___fish   that   is   raw   and   onions_____

B. Consider this structurally ambiguous sentence found on a restaurant menu:

The price includes *soup or salad and french fries*.

You should have no trouble finding two different interpretations of this sentence. For each interpretation, draw a tree diagram as in part A of the italicized constituent (you needn't label the nodes), and give an unambiguous paraphrase.

Interpretation 1

Paraphrase: _____

Interpretation 2

Paraphrase: _____

Name _____   **Section** _____   **Date** _____

4.05   GRAMMATICAL RELATIONS: English

A. For each underlined noun phrase in the following sentences, identify the grammatical relation it has in its clause and write the abbreviation above it. Use SUB for subject, DO for direct object, IO for indirect object, OBL for object of preposition, and POSS for possessor. If an underlined noun phrase does not have one of these grammatical relations in its clause, write NOTA for "None of the above." (Sentences taken or adapted from *Rolling Stone,* June 12, 1997.)

                                        SUB   OBL

EXAMPLE   Jakob and the band are bone tired in the midst of a merciless string of one-
                              nighters.

1. She wrote a story about the freedoms and tyrannies of knowing.

2. Now I actually have a job.

3. Hadn't he shown all five children the rigors of the road?

4. Now, like some howling curse, he has descended upon the son.

5. He laughs, then reminds me that there have always been signs.

6. All spring, father and son crisscrossed the country separately.

7. Jake loves playing music; he likes writing songs.

8. Based on the information that he's given me so far, it doesn't add up.

9. Consumers loved the convenience of the new format and the promise of perfect sound.

10. Until this year, music recordings could not be sent across the Internet with speed and

    reliability.

B. In each sentence that follows, first underline all the noun phrases. Then identify the grammatical relation of each noun phrase and write the abbreviation above it. Use SUB for subject, DO for direct object, IO for indirect object, OBL for object of preposition, POSS for possessor, and NOTA for "None of the above." (Sentences taken or adapted from *Rolling Stone,* June 12, 1997.)

1. Jakob says he didn't have enough friends to sell tickets to.

2. Jakob is bleeding on the tablecloth of the meeting room.

3. Cigarette smoke contains carbon monoxide.

4. He won't tell me unless I conceal his identity.

5. You could make your own disc with a CD recorder.

6. But that still requires a sizable investment of time and money.

7. Me, I like the music—I just don't like hunting down the discs.

8. The title *Across America* refers to Garfunkel's walk across the country.

9. James Taylor duets with Garfunkel on a reading of Gerry Goffin and Carole King's "Crying

   in the Rain."

10. Revising history is a tricky business: it's hard to amend or adjust a classic album without

    marring its essence.

Name _____   **Section** _____   **Date** _____

4.06   SYNTACTIC OPERATIONS: English Passives

Underline each passive-voice verb and bracket the underlying (deep) subject of the passive-voice clause; if the underlying subject does not appear in the surface structure of the passive sentence, write NA for "No Agent" after the sentence. (Data taken from the *Los Angeles Times*.)

      EXAMPLE   The museum <u>is directed</u> by [Fernando Trevino Lozano].

      EXAMPLE   I <u>was told</u> that my mental circuitry was all twisted.   NA

1. He was once prescribed lithium to combat manic-depressive tendencies.

2. Slash was so unruly that he was kicked out of three high schools.

3. Rose was raised in such a strict family environment that for years he couldn't even listen to rock 'n' roll on the radio.

4. The CD is being played at a volume that would bring complaints if Guns N' Roses had not taken over the whole floor.

5. The song was widely attacked by critics and others who objected to the use of certain slur words to refer to blacks and homosexuals.

6. Across the Channel, the Jeu de Paume has been refurbished as a showcase for contemporary art.

7. Almost everything about the Museo de Arte Contemporaneo and its inaugural exhibition has been done on a grand and sumptuous scale.

8. Half the structure is devoted to 14 galleries, which yield more exhibition space than will be found in the Anderson Building.

9. MARCO is clearly designed to impress—and it does.

10. Salinas' rise to political power has been tied to his vigorous championship of privatization in the Mexican economy.

11. MARCO was organized and has been funded by an unusual partnership of private and government leaders.

12. Galan's highly decorated paintings are often populated by porcelain-skinned, doll-like heads.

13. He was paid $100 every two weeks to attend dance and theater classes at the Inner City Cultural Center.

14. He recalls being questioned about why people of color were not at the forefront of the National Endowment for the Arts protests.

15. But there's this other viewpoint, my idea, which is that before you can be censored, you have to be heard.

16. It is the subject matter, not the person, that is being censored.

Name _____   **Section** _____   **Date** _____

4.07   SYNTACTIC OPERATIONS: English Relative Clauses

For each of the following sentences:

- Bracket the relative clause.
- Insert a caret ($_\wedge$) in the gap where the relative pronoun originated.
- Underscore the head noun of the noun phrase that the relative clause is attached to.
- Above each relative pronoun indicate its grammatical relation in its clause: SUB = subject; DO = direct object; IO = indirect object; OBL = oblique (e.g., object of preposition); and POSS = possessor. Insert any omitted relative pronouns.

(Data taken from the *Los Angeles Times*.)

EXAMPLE   This is the <u>teacher</u> [that I told you about $_\wedge$]. (OBL)

EXAMPLE   Those <u>fans</u> [who braved the weather] paid a price. (SUB)

1. The new law has been cheered by developers and officials who have inundated prospective immigrants with investment options.

2. Armed Croatians and Serbians confront each other in Serbian enclaves of the Krajina, which has resisted Croatia's secession.

3. Activist Mike Hernandez is taking an "up-close and personal" approach that he hopes will help him win the council seat.

4. Pugnacious people on both sides use tax-deductible donations to carry on a fight that is really about values.

5. The environmental experts who conducted the study found that about one-third of the dangerous wastes are properly disposed of.

6. Without the benefits that free trade can provide, Mexico will never have enough money to clean up its environment.

7. Salinas must show good faith by using the limited resources that he has at hand to crack down now on polluters in Mexico.

8. Otherwise, environmental issues will continue to undermine the free-trade pact he so badly wants.

9. Axl Rose made news by decrying the forces that he believes can rob young people of their individuality and aspirations.

10. Rose—who is the hottest lightning rod for controversy in rock since Sinead O'Connor—suggested that many young people are like prisoners.

11. There's a Latino community, and then there's a Latino gay community, which is really invisible.

12. If they didn't have my older brother, who's a sports jock, it would have been more of a problem.

13. The postgame dramatics were as good as the game, which gave the Dodgers their second victory in three days.

14. The Angels, who collected only five hits against a rookie pitcher who was winless in his previous 10 starts, are in a slump.

15. Baker-Finch, whose 64 wiped out the Royal Birkdale course record, is a co-leader with O'Meara of the 120th British Open.

16. Born prematurely on a train and named after the doctor who was able to help, Rodney Cline Carew visited the Hall of Fame in May.

17. As the season went along and I saw the guys they were bringing off the bench, I asked myself what went wrong.

18. Tehran police have vowed to shut down any foreign company whose female staff members flout Iran's strict Islamic dress code.

19. This is my first trip to this land to which all our hearts are bound forever.

20. Every indication I see is that he is pulling out.

Name _____   **Section** _____   **Date** _____

4.08   SYNTACTIC OPERATIONS: English Question Formation with Modals

English has several types of auxiliary verbs, one of which is the set of *modals (will, would, shall, should, can, could, may, might,* and *must)*. Each of the sentences below contains a modal verb:

1. Harriet will slice the Brie.
2. Their uncle can tell them the answer.
3. Kittens should be fed seventeen times a day.
4. All employees in the accounting department must submit their timesheets to Carol in triplicate.
5. You could at least help me with the dishes once in a while.

A. For each of the above sentences, form the associated Yes/No question.

1. _____

2. _____

3. _____

4. _____

    _____

5. _____

    _____

B. Consider the following formulation of the rule of Yes/No question formation with modal verbs, a subpart of a more inclusive rule:

> R1: To form a Yes/No question for a sentence that contains a modal verb, move the modal to the front of the sentence.

Will R1 accurately generate the Yes/No questions you wrote in part A? (If the rule fails in any way with respect to these sentences, explain how.)

_____

_____

_____

C. Now apply R1 to the following sentences, and write down exactly what the results are in each case. If, by any chance, a result of applying the rule is ungrammatical, write the correct Yes/No question as well. If you find any cases where it is difficult to know how to apply the rule, explain what the problem is.

1. Anyone who can count to ten will know the answer.

_____

_____

2. The guy you should talk to is out sick today.

_____

_____

3. We shall give the $50,000 to a charitable organization that will use it to help the homeless.

_____

_____

4. Norbert seems to think that people will be living on the moon in thirty years.

_____

_____

5. The question of how state governments can simultaneously address the concerns of developers and environmentalists will be taken up at the next session.

_____

_____

_____

D. If you found that R1 is inadequate in any way, explain and illustrate exactly how it can be modified to avoid incorrect answers in the five cases.

_____

_____

_____

Name _____   **Section** _____   **Date** _____

4.09   SYNTACTIC OPERATIONS:
Constraints on Information Questions in English

The formation of WH questions can be thought of as a way of "questioning" various constituents of a sentence. For example, consider:

<u>John</u> devoured <u>several durians</u> in Kota Bharu.
   A   **B**

Each of the underlined constituents can be questioned by

- Substituting the appropriate WH expression (who, what, where, etc.)
- Moving that WH expression to the front of the sentence
- Making the necessary word order and verb adjustments

Thus, to question constituent A, we get

   Who devoured several durians in Kota Bharu?

and no further adjustments are necessary. To question constituent B, we get the following sequence of stages:

   John devoured what in Kota Bharu? (an *echo question*)

* What John devoured in Kota Bharu?

   What did John devour in Kota Bharu?

A large variety of constituents can be questioned in this way. Sometimes, however, the process unexpectedly yields an ungrammatical sentence. This is because constraints exist on which constituents can be moved by the WH process.

For the following sentences, form WH questions by "questioning" each of the indicated constituents as above. You needn't show the intermediate stages in your derivations—just give the final results. "Star" any sentences you derive that are ungrammatical.

1. Jerome emptied the liquid into a beaker.
     A   — **B** —   — **C**—

    A: _____

    B: _____

    C: _____

2. This problem was first solved by Einstein.
　　　— D ———   E

D: _____

E: _____

3. John and Mary like onions and garlic.
　　F —— H —— G ——   —— I —— K —— J ——

F: _____

G: _____

H: _____

I: _____

J: _____

K: _____

4. He$_i$ said Hermione kissed him$_i$. (The subscripts indicate coreference.)
　　L   M   N

L: _____

M: _____

N: _____

5. Jacqui has no idea how this computer works.
　　O   —— P ——

O: _____

P: _____

6. Mary felt Barbara wanted Herman to ask Carol to fire Timothy.
　　Q   R   S   T   U

Q: _____

R: _____

S: _____

T: _____

U: _____

Name _____   **Section** _____   **Date** _____

EXERCISES BASED ON OTHER LANGUAGES

4.10   CONSTITUENCY AND TREE DIAGRAMS:
Spanish, Japanese, and English

I. Analysis of a Japanese Simple Sentence

A. Consider the following representative Japanese sentence:

Biru ga Michiko ni kamera o yatta.

Bill   Michiko   camera   gave.

'Bill gave Michiko a camera.'

Note: In the sentence above,

ch = IPA [tʃ]

y   = IPA [j]

1. Judging from this sentence, what is the normal word order for subject, object, and verb in Japanese? (Circle the correct answer.)

OSV   OVS   SOV   SVO   VOS   VSO

2. Japanese has particles that indicate subject, direct object, and indirect object. What is their position relative to their associated NP?

_____

_____

B. Draw a tree diagram for this sentence, and alongside it list the phrase structure rules implied by your diagram.
   Note: Assume a noun plus a particle forms an NP.

II. Branching Structures in Spanish, Japanese, and English

In this section, you will diagram some embedded NPs in two languages, Spanish and Japanese, which consistently use different syntactic constructions for such phrases. Then you will examine a corresponding phrase in English, which makes use of both types of syntactic devices.

A. Spanish.

Glossary: el amigo   'the (male) friend'
                 el coche   'the car'
                 el maestro   'the (male) teacher'
                 la puerta   'the door'
                 de   'of'
Note: de + el is converted into *del* by a phonological rule.

For a phrase like 'Naomi's friend,' Spanish uses a word order corresponding to 'the friend of Naomi':

   el amigo de Naomi

This phrase has the following structure, where the node labels correspond to the English categories you are already familiar with:

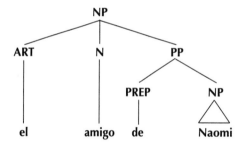

(The triangle symbol is used here in the usual way: to represent a node whose internal structure is irrelevant and therefore not indicated.)

1. Translate into Spanish:
    'Naomi's friend's teacher' _____

    Now draw a labeled tree diagram for this phrase.

Name _____   **Section** _____   **Date** _____

2. Now translate and diagram this:
    'Naomi's friend's teacher's car'

    _____

3. Finally, do the same for this:
    'the door of Naomi's friend's teacher's car'

    _____

    Choose one: A structure such as this is referred to as what?
    [   ] left-branching   [   ] right-branching

B. Japanese.

Glossary: doa   'door'
               kuruma   'car'
               sensei   'teacher'
               tomodachi   'friend'
               Note: Japanese has no definite article.

For a phrase like 'Naomi's friend,' Japanese uses a word order similar to English:

  Naomi no tomodachi

Here, the postposition *no* corresponds to the *'s* in English. This phrase has the following structure, where the node labels correspond to the English categories you are already familiar with, except that PP here means Postpositional Phrase, and POST means Postposition:

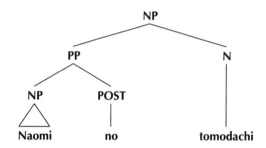

1. Translate into Japanese:
    'Naomi's friend's teacher' _____

    Now draw a labeled tree diagram for this phrase.

Name _____   **Section** _____   **Date** _____

2. Now translate and diagram this:
    'Naomi's friend's teacher's car'

_____

3. Finally, do the same for this:
    'the door of Naomi's friend's teacher's car'

_____

Choose one: A structure such as this is referred to as what?

[   ] left-branching   [   ] right-branching

C. English. English, as already noted, makes use of both the Spanish- and Japanese-style constructions you have previously analyzed.

Assume phrases like *John's house* and *the cover of the book* have the following structures:

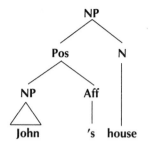
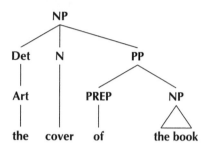

Here, Aff stands for Affix, and Pos for Possessive.

Draw a labeled tree diagram for the following English phrase:

the outside of the door of Lisa's mother's house

Name _____   **Section** _____   **Date** _____

4.11   PHRASE STRUCTURE RULES:
Articles, Demonstratives, and Possessives in English, Italian, and Greek

Every language contains the syntactic category NP with N as its head, but the distribution of the other elements found in noun phrases varies among languages. In this exercise you will examine some simple NPs containing articles, demonstratives, and possessives in three languages, and you will determine how the phrase structure rules that rewrite NP in these languages differ.

A. English. Consider the following simple phrase structure (PS) grammar that generates certain definite NPs in English.

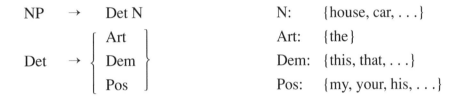

(Here, Det, Art, Dem, and Pos stand respectively for Determiner, Article, Demonstrative, and Possessive.)

1. Using the PS grammar above, draw labeled tree diagrams for the following English NPs:

    the house   my house   this house

2. Consider the following ungrammatical phrases in English: *the my house, *the this house, *this my house.

    Will the given PS grammar generate any of these phrases? Justify your answer.

    _____

    _____

B. Italian. Here are some grammatical and ungrammatical definite NPs in Italian:

la casa	'the house'
la mia casa (*mia casa)	'my house'
questa casa (*la questa casa)	'this house'

1. Using the same categories found in the English PS grammar in part A, write a comparable phrase structure grammar that will generate all of the grammatical phrases above and none of the ungrammatical ones. (*Hint:* You will have to make a distinction between obligatory and optional elements in one of your rules. Note that the parenthetical notation for optional elements—A → B (C)—collapses the two rules A → B and A → B C.)

    _____

    _____

    _____

2. Now draw a labeled tree diagram for *la mia casa* that uses your phrase structure rules.

C. Modern Greek. Examine these grammatical and ungrammatical definite NPs in Modern Greek, and answer the questions that follow:

to spiti	'the house'	afto to spiti	'this house'	*afto spiti
to spiti mu	'my house'	afto to spiti mu	'my house'	*spiti mu

1. Do the same for these Modern Greek data as you did for the Italian data, i.e., write a phrase structure grammar that will generate all and only the grammatical phrases. (*Hint:* Not all the categories used in the English and Italian sections may be appropriate here!)

    _____

    _____

    _____

2. Draw a labeled tree diagram for *afto to spiti mu* that uses your phrase structure rules.

Name _____   **Section** _____   **Date** _____

 4.12   SYNTACTIC OPERATIONS: French Interrogatives

A. French has several ways of forming interrogative sentences. Examine the data below, given in standard French orthography, and then answer the questions that follow.

1. *a)* Vous êtes Monsieur Renoir.

   You are

   'You are Monsieur Renoir.'

   b) Etes-vous Monsieur Renoir?

   are you

   'Are you Monsieur Renoir?'

   c) Est-ce que vous êtes Monsieur Renoir?

   is it that you are

   'Are you Monsieur Renoir?'

2. *a)* Vous aimez ces   croissants.

   you like   these croissants

   'You like these croissants.'

   b) Aimez-vous ces   croissants?

   like   you these croissants

   'Do you like these croissants?'

   c) Est-ce que vous aimez ces   croissants?

   is it that you like   these croissants

   'Do you like these croissants?'

   d) Pourquoi aimez-vous ces   croissants?

   why   like   you these croissants

   'Why do you like these croissants?'

   e) Pourquoi est-ce que vous aimez ces   croissants?

   why   is it that you like   these croissants

   'Why do you like these croissants?'

3. *a)* Ils   mangent du   gâteau tous les jours.

   they eat   some cake   all   the days

   'They eat cake every day.'

   b) Mangent-ils   du   gâteau tous les jours?

   eat   they some cake   all   the days

   'Do they eat cake every day?'

c) Est-ce qu'ils   mangent du   gâteau tous les jours?
    is it that-they eat   some cake   all the days
    'Do they eat cake every day?'

d) Quand mangent-ils   du   gâteau?
    when eat   they some cake
    'When do they eat cake?'

e) Quand est-ce qu'ils   mangent du   gâteau?
    when is it that-they eat   some cake
    'When do they eat cake?'

4. a) Vous voyez un pigeon sur le toit.
        you see   a   pigeon on the roof
        'You see a pigeon on the roof.'

    b) Voyez-vous un pigeon sur le toit?
        see   you a   pigeon on the roof
        'Do you see a pigeon on the roof?'

    c) Est-ce que vous voyez un pigeon sur le toit?
        is it that you see   a   pigeon on the roof
        'Do you see a pigeon on the roof?'

    d) Que voyez-vous sur le toit?
        what see   you on the roof
        'What do you see on the roof?'

    e) Qu'est-ce que vous voyez sur le toit?
        what-is it that you see   on the roof
        'What do you see on the roof?'

    f) Où   voyez-vous un pigeon?
        where see   you a   pigeon
        'Where do you see a pigeon?'

    g) Où   est-ce que vous voyez un pigeon?
        where is it that you see   a   pigeon
        'Where do you see a pigeon?'

1. Judging from the data, what are two ways of constructing Yes/No questions in French when the subject is a pronoun? Be as precise as you can.

_____

_____

_____

_____

Name _____   **Section** _____   **Date** _____

2. Repeat question 1 for the type of WH questions found in the data.

_____

_____

_____

B. Questions in colloquial French sometimes take a different form. Examine these very informal equivalents of the more formal French interrogatives already given, and then answer the questions that follow.

1. *d)* Vous êtes Monsieur Renoir?
       You are
       'Are you Monsieur Renoir?'

2. *f)* Vous aimez ces   croissants?
       you   like   these croissants
       'Do you like these croissants?'

    g) Pourquoi vous aimez ces   croissants?
       why   you   like   these croissants
       'Why do you like these croissants?'

3. *f)* Ils   mangent du   gâteau tous les jours?
       they eat   some cake   all   the days
       'Do they eat cake every day?'

    g) Quand ils   mangent du   gâteau?
       when   they eat   some cake
       'When do they eat cake?'

4. *h)* Vous voyez un pigeon sur le   toit?
       you   see   a pigeon on the roof
       'Do you see a pigeon on the roof?'

    i) Vous voyez quoi sur le   toit?
       you   see   what on the roof
       'What do you see on the roof?'

    j) Où   vous voyez un pigeon?
       where you   see   a pigeon
       'Where do you see a pigeon?'

1. Explain exactly what the differences are between the more formal and the more colloquial rules of question formation.

    _____

    _____

    _____

    _____

    _____

    _____

    _____

    _____

2. Change to informal colloquial French:

    Est-ce que vous voulez aller avec moi?

    is   it that you want   to-go with me

    'Do you want to go with me?'

    _____

3. Change to formal French:

    Ils   boivent quoi?

    they drink   what

    'What are they drinking?'

    _____

Name _____   **Section** _____   **Date** _____

🎧 4.13 SYNTACTIC OPERATIONS:
Chinese Noun Modifiers and Relative Clauses

In the first part of this problem, you will examine some simple noun modifiers in Mandarin Chinese. Then you will look at noun modifiers that are themselves clauses. The data are transcribed in the Pinyin system (see Appendix A).

A. Examine the following data and then answer the questions that follow.

1. wǒ de shū
   I   book
   'my book'

2. tāmen de péngyou
   they   friend
   'their friend'

3. shūfu   de yǐzi
   comfortable   chair
   'comfortable chair'

4. piàoliang de nǚpéngyou
   pretty   female friend
   'pretty girlfriend'

5. là   de cài
   spicy   food
   'spicy food'

6. lǎoshī   de qìchē
   teacher   car
   'teacher's car'

7. piányi de jiājù
   cheap   furniture
   'cheap furniture'

8. lǎoshī de piányi de qìchē
   teacher   cheap   car
   'the teacher's cheap car'

1. Which is the order of elements in Chinese?
   [   ] modifier + noun   [   ] noun + modifier

2. Explain the function of *de* as it appears in these data.

_____

_____

_____

B. Now examine these sentences and phrases, and answer the questions that follow.

1. *a)* Lǎoshī chī píngguǒ.

   teacher eat apple

   'The teacher eats apples.'

   b) chī píngguǒ de lǎoshī

   'the teacher who eats apples'

   c) lǎoshī chī de píngguǒ

   'the apples that the teacher eats'

2. *a)* Jīnglǐ   mài zìxíngchē.

   manager sell bicycle

   'The manager sells bicycles.'

   b) mài zìxíngchē de jīnglǐ

   'the manager who sells bicycles'

   c) jīnglǐ mài de zìxíngchē

   'the bicycles that the manager sells'

3. *a)* Háizi hē   jiǔ.

   child drink wine

   'The child drinks wine.'

   b) hē jiǔ de háizi

   'the child who drinks wine'

   c) háizi hē de jiǔ

   'the wine that the child drinks'

1. Do Chinese relative clauses precede or follow their heads? Taking a relative clause to be a modifier of its head noun, is this pattern consistent or inconsistent with the result you determined in part A for simple noun modifiers?

_____

_____

Name _____   **Section** _____   **Date** _____

2. The derivation of Chinese relative clauses such as the ones illustrated here becomes transparent if *the underlying form of the relative clause is taken to be a full sentence.* (In a comparable analysis for English, for example, the underlying form of *books that children read* is taken to be

    books$_i$ [children read books$_i$]

in which the two occurrences of *books* are coreferential, as indicated by the identical subscripts.)

    a) Under such an analysis, give the underlying form of 'the child who drinks wine.' What is the grammatical relation of the coreferential NP within the relative clause?

        _____

        _____

    b) What is the underlying form of 'the wine that the child drinks'? What is the grammatical relation of the coreferential NP within the relative clause?

        _____

        _____

    c) Show how the underlying forms you posited in questions *a)* and *b)* yield the correct surface forms. You will have to discover one or more transformations that apply consecutively to the underlying forms to give the surface forms. If you do this correctly, you will find that *exactly the same transformations can be used to arrive at the correct surface forms in both cases.*

*d) *(Optional)* Compare and contrast the Chinese relative clause strategy you have just analyzed with the corresponding strategy in English. What are the similarities and differences between the two strategies? (You can take as your English data the glosses of the Chinese relative clauses. Be sure to address the differences between *who* and *that*.)

_____

_____

_____

_____

_____

_____

_____

_____

_____

_____

_____

_____

Name _____   Section _____   Date _____

4.14 SYNTACTIC OPERATIONS: Case Marking and Relative Clauses in German

A. Examine the following sentences, given in standard German orthography. Then identify the *subject* and *object* forms (often referred to as *nominative* and *accusative cases*) of 'the man,' 'the woman,' 'the child,' and 'the dog.' What is the normal order of subject, object, and verb in main sentences such as these?

1. Der Mann liebt den Hund.	'The man loves the dog.'
2. Der Hund liebt den Mann.	'The dog loves the man.'
3. Der Mann liebt die Frau.	'The man loves the woman.'
4. Das Kind liebt den Mann.	'The child loves the man.'
5. Der Hund liebt das Kind.	'The dog loves the child.'
6. Die Frau liebt den Hund.	'The woman loves the dog.'

	'the man'	'the woman'	'the child'	'the dog'
Subject Form	_____	_____	_____	_____
Object Form	_____	_____	_____	_____

Word Order: _____

B. Now examine the following sentences, and determine the normal order of subject, object, and verb in subordinate (embedded) clauses.

7. *Ich weiss, dass der Mann liebt den Hund.   'I know that the man loves the dog.'

8. Ich weiss, dass der Mann den Hund liebt.   'I know that the man loves the dog.'

9. *Ich weiss nicht, ob der Hund liebt das Kind.   'I don't know whether the dog loves the child.'

10. Ich weiss nicht, ob der Hund das Kind liebt.   'I don't know whether the dog loves the child.'

Word Order: _____

C. A *relative clause* is an embedded sentence that modifies a noun. The modified noun is called the *head;* if the noun phrase that contains it is NP_i, then the embedded sentence also must contain this same NP_i; the two noun phrases are *coreferential.*

A large number of German relative clauses can be derived by the following rules:

• The relative clause comes after the head.

• Since they are embedded sentences, relative clauses follow subordinate-clause word order.

- Two operations apply in the following order to yield the correct surface structure:

  Attraction: The coreferential NP inside the relative clause is moved to the front of the clause, adjacent to the head.

  Noun Drop: The coreferential *noun* within the relative clause is dropped; the article retained functions as a relative pronoun.

> **EXAMPLE** To derive the German for 'the man who(m) the dog loves':
> We start with the NP 'the man' followed by the modifying sentence containing the coreferential NP:
>
> > the man [the dog loves the man]
>
> Remembering to use subordinate clause word order, the German for this is:
>
> > der Mann [der Hund den Mann liebt]
>
> Now we apply the two operations:
> *Attraction* gives: der Mann [den Mann der Hund liebt]
> *Noun Drop* gives: der Mann [den der Hund liebt]
> We now have the correct surface form:
>
> > der Mann den der Hund liebt

Translate each of the following phrases into German by going through a derivation like the one in the example. You can assume the head in each case is a subject.

1. 'the man who loves the dog'

    Start with: _____

    Attraction: _____

    Noun Drop: _____

    Surface form: _____

2. 'the dog that loves the man'

    Start with: _____

    Attraction: _____

    Noun Drop: _____

    Surface form: _____

3. 'the dog that the man loves'

    Start with: _____

    Attraction: _____

    Noun Drop: _____

    Surface form: _____

Name _____   **Section** _____   **Date** _____

4. 'the man who loves the woman'

   Start with: _____

   Attraction: _____

   Noun Drop: _____

   Surface form: _____

5. 'the man who(m) the woman loves'

   Start with: _____

   Attraction: _____

   Noun Drop: _____

   Surface form: _____

6. 'the woman who loves the man'

   Start with: _____

   Attraction: _____

   Noun Drop: _____

   Surface form: _____

7. 'the woman who(m) the man loves'

   Start with: _____

   Attraction: _____

   Noun Drop: _____

   Surface form: _____

8. 'the woman who loves the child'

   Start with: _____

   Attraction: _____

   Noun Drop: _____

   Surface form: _____

9. 'the woman who(m) the child loves'

Start with: _____

Attraction: _____

Noun Drop: _____

Surface form: _____

D. If you did the derivations in part C correctly, you will have noticed that German can run into a problem with relative clauses.

1. Identify the problem. Specifically, which pair of English phrases in part C does German have trouble with? What exactly is the problem? Why does German run into this difficulty?

_____

_____

_____

_____

_____

2. German speakers have not been observed to have any more trouble understanding each other than English speakers do. Speculate on how German speakers resolve the problem you identified in question 1.

_____

_____

_____

_____

_____

_____

Name _____   **Section** _____   **Date** _____

🎧 4.15 WORD ORDER: Yiddish and Turkish

A. Yiddish, like its sister language Modern German, is descended from Middle High German, spoken during the Middle Ages.

The data below, given in phonetic transcription, consist of a Yiddish sentence in twelve different versions, distinguished only by the word order. These all have basically the same meaning, although the pragmatics (how they are used in context) may vary. Ungrammatical variants are starred. The last four items are questions related to the original sentence.

Although quite a bit of word order flexibility is exhibited in these data, you should discover one overriding principle of Yiddish word order that will account for all the grammaticality judgments below. What is this principle? (Data adapted from Uriel Weinreich, *College Yiddish*.)

1. jɪdn rɛdn jɪdɪʃ   hajnt ɪn   a sax lɛndɛr.
   Jews speak Yiddish today in   many countries
   'Jews speak Yiddish today in many countries.'

2. hajnt rɛdn jɪdn jɪdɪʃ ɪn a sax lɛndɛr.

3. *ɪn a sax lɛndɛr hajnt rɛdn jɪdn jɪdɪʃ.

4. jɪdɪʃ rɛdn jɪdn hajnt ɪn a sax lɛndɛr.

5. *ɪn a sax lɛndɛr hajnt jɪdn rɛdn jɪdɪʃ.

6. ɪn a sax lɛndɛr rɛdn jɪdn jɪdɪʃ hajnt.

7. *ɪn a sax lɛndɛr jɪdn rɛdn hajnt jɪdɪʃ.

8. jɪdn rɛdn hajnt jɪdɪʃ ɪn a sax lɛndɛr.

9. *rɛdn jɪdn jɪdɪʃ hajnt ɪn a sax lɛndɛr.

10. jɪdɪʃ rɛdn hajnt ɪn a sax lɛndɛr jɪdn.

11. jɪdɪʃ rɛdn hajnt jɪdn ɪn a sax lɛndɛr.

12. *hajnt jɪdn rɛdn jɪdɪʃ ɪn a sax lɛndɛr.

13. t͡si rɛdn jɪdn jɪdɪʃ hajnt ɪn a sax lɛndɛr?
    'Do Jews speak Yiddish in many countries today?'

14. *t͡si jɪdn rɛdn jɪdɪʃ hajnt ɪn a sax lɛndɛr?
    'Do Jews speak Yiddish in many countries today?'

15. vu rɛdn jɪdn jɪdɪʃ hajnt?
    'Where do Jews speak Yiddish today?'

16. vɔs rɛdn jɪdn hajnt ɪn a sax lɛndɛr?
    'What do Jews speak today in many countries?'

_____

_____

_____

B. Examine the Turkish sentences below, given in standard Turkish orthography. (*Note: i* and *ı* are different vowels: *i* is the common high, front, unrounded vowel, while *ı* is the less common high, *back,* unrounded vowel. y = IPA [j].) As usual, an asterisk indicates ungrammaticality.

1.	Et aldım.	'I bought meat.'	6.	Eti aldı.	'He bought the meat.'
2.	Et aldı.	'He bought meat.'	7.	Et pahalı.	'Meat is expensive.'
3.	Mektup yazdım.	'I wrote a letter.'	8.	Et pahalı.	'The meat is expensive.'
4.	Mektup yazdı.	'He wrote a letter.'	9.	*Eti pahalı.	'The meat is expensive.'
5.	Mektubu yazdım.	'I wrote the letter.'	10.	Mektup güzel.	'The letter is beautiful.'

1. On the basis of the above data, do objects in Turkish come before or after the verb?

    _____

2. What is the difference in grammatical relation between *et/eti* and between *mektup/mektubu*?

    _____

3. What, besides grammatical relation, determines the choice between these word pairs?

    _____

    _____

Now consider the following additional data:

Kasaptan et aldım.	'I bought meat from the butcher.'
*Et kasaptan aldım.	'I bought meat from the butcher.'
Kıza mektup yazdım.	'I wrote a letter to the girl.'
*Mektup kıza yazdım.	'I wrote a letter to the girl.'
Kasaptan eti aldım.	'I bought the meat from the butcher.'
Eti kasaptan aldım.	'I bought the meat from the butcher.'
Kıza mektubu yazdım.	'I wrote the letter to the girl.'
Mektubu kıza yazdım.	'I wrote the letter to the girl.'

4. What is the rule in Turkish regarding the proximity of direct objects to their verbs?
    (*Note:* Turkish uses suffixes and postpositions, not prepositions: *kıza* 'to the girl,' *kızdan* 'from the girl.')

    _____

    _____

Name _____   **Section** _____   **Date** _____

4.16   WORD ORDER: Aspects of Klingon

Examine the sentences below in the Klingon language, devised for the *Star Trek*® feature films and the *Star Trek: The Next Generation*® television series by linguist Marc Okrand. Then answer the questions that follow.

Note: The data are adapted from Okrand's *Klingon Dictionary,* which contains the only grammatical sketch of the language so far available to non-Klingons, and are given in the transcription used in that work. Pronunciation is not relevant to this problem. Those who would like to pronounce these sentences as Klingons do, however, should note the following:

gh	=	[ɣ]
S	=	a voiceless fricative halfway between [s] and [ʃ]
H	=	[x]
j	=	[dʒ]
I	=	[ɪ]
tlh	=	apparently a *t* with an aspirated lateral release, equal to Aztec *tl*.
y	=	[j]
'	=	[ʔ]

1. puq legh yaS — 'The officer sees the child.'
2. yaS legh puq — 'The child sees the officer.'
3. puq vIlegh jIH — 'I see the child.'
4. jIH mulegh puq — 'The child sees me.'
5. puq vIlegh — 'I see the child.'
6. mulegh puq — 'The child sees me.'
7. puq lulegh yaSpu' — 'The officers see the child.'
8. Salegh — 'I see you (pl.).'
9. tlhIH Salegh — 'I see you (pl.).'
10. Salegh jIH — 'I see you (pl.).'
11. relegh — 'We see you (pl.).'
12. relegh maH — 'We see you (pl.).'
13. yaSpu' legh puq — 'The child sees the officers.'
14. jIH tulegh tlhIH — 'You (pl.) see me.'
15. nulegh yaSpu' — 'The officers see us.'
16. maH nulegh — 'They see us.'

A. Isolate all the morphemes in the data, giving the meaning or function of each.

_____

_____

_____

_____

_____

_____

B. What is the basic sequencing of subject, object, and verb in Klingon? Name any Earth languages you are familiar with that employ this particular sequencing as a basic word order.

_____

_____

_____

C. Judging from the data, what elements of a Klingon sentence are optional? Are these same elements optional in English? If not, what is it about Klingon grammar that allows the omission of these elements? Explain.

_____

_____

_____

_____

_____

D. Translate into English:

tlhIH relegh

_____

E. Translate into Klingon:

'The children see the officer.'

_____

5

Semantics

KEY TERMS AND SYMBOLS

See the glossary.

Affective meaning

Antonymy

Converseness

Definite NP

Deixis

Homonomy

Hyponomy

Indefinite NP

Lexical field

Lexicon

Metaphorical extension

Nonreferential NP

Polysemy

Referential meaning

Referential NP

Social meaning

Specific NP

Synonymy

Name _____   **Section** _____   **Date** _____

EXERCISES BASED ON ENGLISH

5.01   TYPES OF MEANING: Referential, Social, and Affective Meaning

After each utterance pair that follows, provide a *Yes* or *No* decision three times to indicate whether the utterances have the same (1) referential, (2) social, and (3) affective meaning. (See the glossary for definitions of these terms.) Then explain the differences you have indicated by any *No* decisions. Some utterance pairs may differ on more than one dimension of meaning.

EXAMPLE   *a)*   She's not my friend now.
              b)   She ain't my friend now.
              Y, N, Y.   *a)* and *b)* differ in social meaning in that *ain't* is frequently used by speakers of nonstandard English and by many other speakers in informal situations or to indicate emphasis.

1.   *a)*   She don't want no more.
     b)   She doesn't want any more.

     _____
     _____
     _____

2.   *a)*   She said she will select whichever one she wishes.
     b)   She said she'll pick the one she wants.

     _____
     _____
     _____

3.   *a)*   If the governor doesn't sign the bill . . .
     b)   If that sonofabitch doesn't put his John Hancock on that bill . . .

     _____
     _____
     _____

4.   *a)*   Me and him was friends in the army.
     b)   He and I were friends in the army.

     _____
     _____
     _____

5. *a)* Is there a Miss Smith in this office?
   b) Is it a Miss Smith in this office?

   _____

   _____

   _____

6. *a)* May I use your washroom?
   b) Where's the john?

   _____

   _____

   _____

7. *a)* My uncle often goes to the races.
   b) My aunt never squanders her money gambling.

   _____

   _____

   _____

8. *a)* The first American president chopped down a cherry tree.
   b) George Washington did not chop down a cherry tree.

   _____

   _____

   _____

9. *a)* Take the elevator to the first floor and find the exit.
   b) Take the lift to the ground floor and find the way out.

   _____

   _____

   _____

10. *a)* Let's go to the flicks together, but it'll be Dutch treat.
    b) Let's go to the movies together, but let's pay our own way.

   _____

   _____

   _____

Name _____   **Section** _____   **Date** _____

5.02   LEXICAL SEMANTICS: English Lexical Semantics

A. Lexical items can be compared along several dimensions. Two such dimensions are *sound* and *meaning,* which form the basis for concepts such as homonymy and synonymy. To these we can add *look,* referring to the way the word appears orthographically—its spelling, capitalization, abbreviations, etc.

The following chart gives all the mathematical possibilities for comparing pairs of words along the three dimensions of sound, look, and meaning. Provide one example for each of the eight categories in the chart. An example consists of a pair of English words that fits the description of the category. (S = Same, D = Different)

EXAMPLE   Category 7 asks for a pair of words that sound the same and look the same but have different meanings—that is, words that are spelled and pronounced identically but mean different things. A standard example is *bank* 'financial institution' and *bank* 'land along the edge of a river.'

Category	Sound	Look	Meaning	Examples		
1	D	D	D	_____	and	_____
2	D	D	S	_____	and	_____
3	D	S	D	_____	and	_____
4	D	S	S	_____	and	_____
5	S	D	D	_____	and	_____
6	S	D	S	_____	and	_____
7	S	S	D	_____	and	_____
8	S	S	S	_____	and	_____

B. Now answer the following questions:

1. Which category or categories represent(s) *synonymy?* _____

2. Which category or categories represent(s) *homonymy?* _____

3. Which category or categories represent(s) *alternate pronunciations of the same word?* _____

4. Which category or categories represent(s) *alternate spellings of the same word?* _____

C. Before each set of words write the abbreviation for the lexical relationship represented. For each set you mark as HYP, circle the higher term (the hyponym). (*Note:* Not every group of words captures a systematic relationship; those that do not should be marked N/A.) Use the following abbreviations:

Synonymy (SYN)   Hyponymy (HYP)   Converseness (CON)

Part/Whole (P/W)   Antonymy (ANT)   Homonymy (HOM)

Metaphorical extension (MET)

_____ 1. canary, parakeet, robin, cockatoo, pigeon, bird

_____ 2. tall/short; fat/skinny; bright/dull; hard/soft

_____ 3. carp, compute, bank, save, cardinal, element

_____ 4. teacher/student; buyer/seller

_____ 5. wry/rye; quay/key; there/their; freeze/frieze

_____ 6. drunk, intoxicated, inebriated, plastered

_____ 7. to dawn on one/ring a bell/devour a book/pie-eyed

_____ 8. wall/window; foot/toe; face/nose; shoe/sole

_____ 9. steal, frown, sad, with, cousin, friend

_____ 10. chinchilla, rat, mouse, rodent, squirrel, beaver

_____ 11. silver, iron, copper, magnesium, element, gold, sodium

_____ 12. ankle, foot, toe, heel, sole, arch

_____ 13. so/sew; too/two; carrot/caret; rest/wrest; bore/boar

_____ 14. freeze/thaw; light/heavy; clean/dirty; loud/quiet

_____ 15. head of the class, foot of a table, mouth of a river

_____ 16. lip, chin, jaw, nose, eye, face, forehead

_____ 17. borrow/lend; tenant/landlord; debtor/creditor

_____ 18. lose/find; add/subtract; go/come; occupy/vacate

_____ 19. tool, instrument, implement, organ, utensil

_____ 20. cold/hot; pleasure/pain; happy/sad; smile/frown

_____ 21. rotelli, spaghetti, pasta, vermicelli, linguini, rigatoni

_____ 22. couch potato, Achilles' heel, cold fish, tall tale, pie in the sky

_____ 23. regular, disturbed, sorry, smooth, red, gingerly

_____ 24. rye, wheat, corn, grain, sorghum, rice, barley

_____ 25. giant sequoia, beech, birch, tree, maple

Name _____   **Section** _____   **Date** _____

5.03   LEXICAL SEMANTICS: True Synonymy and the Rarity Thereof

We can say two words are strictly synonymous if in *every* utterance in which one of them occurs, the other can be substituted with no change in referential, social, or affective meaning. True synonyms, so defined, are rare.

The following pairs of words are often thought of as synonymous. In some contexts, however, only one of them is appropriate. For each pair of words, give *a)* both versions of a sentence where the words may be used interchangeably, and *b)* both versions of a sentence where substituting one for the other results in strangeness or a change of meaning. Explain the difference.

EXAMPLE   large, big

   a)   (1)   This plate is much too large to use for dessert.
          (2)   This plate is much too big to use for dessert.

   b)   (1)   This is Henry, my big brother.
          (2)   This is Henry, my large brother.

   In (1) "big brother" means elder brother. In (2) "large brother" cannot mean elder brother; it may be a way of saying Henry is obese.

1. small, little

   a)   (1) _____

          (2) _____

   b)   (1) _____

          (2) _____

   Explanation: _____

   _____

   _____

2. annoy, irritate

   a)   (1) _____

          (2) _____

   b)   (1) _____

          (2) _____

   Explanation: _____

   _____

   _____

3. inexpensive, cheap

    a) (1) _____

        (2) _____

    b) (1) _____

        (2) _____

    Explanation: _____

    _____

    _____

4. interfere, meddle

    a) (1) _____

        (2) _____

    b) (1) _____

        (2) _____

    Explanation: _____

    _____

    _____

5. correct, right

    a) (1) _____

        (2) _____

    b) (1) _____

        (2) _____

    Explanation: _____

    _____

    _____

Name _____   **Section** _____   **Date** _____

5.04   LEXICAL SEMANTICS: English Metaphors 1

Many common expressions have arisen from a metaphorical use of other expressions, as with *dove* and *hawk* to refer to opponents and supporters of the Vietnam War. Identify and underscore at least one metaphorical expression in each sentence; then indicate the term's literal meaning and the appropriateness of its extension to capture a phenomenon in the context used. The sentences are taken, slightly adapted, from *Time* magazine (July 22, 1991), in an article about France written by James Walsh.

1. It is a culture abrim with connoisseurs.

    _____

    _____

2. De Gaulle, father of the Fifth Republic, used to cite France's prodigious number of cheeses.

    _____

    _____

3. Why all the buzz about discontent, social gloom and political drift, a crisis of faith and a fading sense of identity?

    _____

    _____

4. It sounds as unlikely as Cyrano de Bergerac fumbling his sword or groping for the *mot juste*.

    _____

    _____

5. Not since Baron Haussmann thrust his boulevards through rancid slums has Paris experienced such a fever of renewal.

    _____

    _____

6. Judging by the diagnoses in the press, a country that long prided itself on being the *lumière du monde* is awash in dark soul-searching.

_____

_____

7. There is the hangover from the gulf war, an episode that deflated the vaunted image of French power and influence.

_____

_____

8. What the country preserved over the centuries it now risks losing in the homogenizing vat of that mysterious entity called Europe.

_____

_____

9. The French seem to be losing their bearings, their ideals and dreams.

_____

_____

10. It is a bitter vintage, all the more so considering how high expectations were running.

_____

_____

11. Just last year France looked well placed to become more than the center of gravity of a newly ascendant Europe.

_____

_____

12. Paris was confidently pulling the strings of Europe.

_____

_____

Name _____   **Section** _____   **Date** _____

5.05   LEXICAL SEMANTICS: English Metaphors 2

The phrases and clauses below are taken (sometimes slightly adapted) from *The New Yorker* magazine's "In Brief" movie reviews. Each contains at least one familiar metaphorical use of a word. Identify a metaphorical use in each, and briefly explain the difference between the literal and the metaphorical use of the word.

1. the kind of power that Kurosawa aims for

    _____

    _____

2. the second half of "Dreams" is weak

    _____

    _____

3. the fifth episode is a thin conceit

    _____

    _____

4. she's too decent and too timid to explode

    _____

    _____

5. Eugene O'Neill's play about a black man's disintegration

    _____

    _____

6. was conceived in a semi-Expressionist style

    _____

    _____

7. Yet there isn't a breath of life in it

    _____

    _____

8. a cold, clever period gangster movie

_____

_____

9. the action unfolds in and around a city

_____

_____

10. hushed and hypnotic, it makes you so conscious of its artistry

_____

_____

11. this tale of a sorrowful, wisecracking starlet

_____

_____

12. whose brassy, boozing former-star mother started her on sleeping pills

_____

_____

13. his tone keeps slipping around

_____

_____

14. She remains distant, emotionally atonal.

_____

_____

15. Marlon Brando, in his magnetic, soft-eyed youth

_____

_____

16. Atkinson's lethal genius at playing an articulate swine

_____

_____

Name _____   **Section** _____   **Date** _____

5.06   FUNCTION WORDS AND CATEGORIES OF MEANING:
Deictic Expressions

Briefly explain what makes each of the underlined words and phrases in the following utterances (reported in the *Los Angeles Times*) a deictic expression. (See the glossary for an explanation of *deixis*.)

EXAMPLE   I will be here tomorrow.
        The referent of I depends on who is speaking.
        The referent of here depends on the place of utterance.
        The referent of tomorrow depends on the time of utterance.

1. I think the people of this city have won.

_____

_____

2. We are in a position now where serious division can be healed.

_____

_____

3. We thought it was appropriate at this moment to just have it among us.

_____

_____

_____

4. He has promised to retire by the end of this year.

_____

_____

5. If he was concerned about how Friday's events would fly with his constituents, he wasn't showing it.

_____

_____

_____

6. "I really feel good about <u>this place</u>," he said.

_____

_____

7. <u>Last night</u> he gave his approval for an orderly process of change.

_____

_____

8. Within the <u>next few months</u>, the voters will express their views.

_____

_____

9. The result came <u>yesterday</u> when the chief of police indicated that he would retire at the end of <u>this year</u>.

_____

_____

_____

10. We can <u>immediately</u> begin to work changes in the city charter.

_____

_____

Name _____   **Section** _____   **Date** _____

5.07   FUNCTION WORDS AND CATEGORIES OF MEANING: Definiteness, Referentiality, and Specificity

Determine whether each of the following underlined phrases is *definite* or *indefinite, referential* or *nonreferential,* and *generic* or *specific.* (See the glossary for explanations of these terms.)

1. <u>A rather large possum</u> was outside the door, eating the cat food. The cat saw it and
          A

    stayed a few yards away, but <u>the possum</u> seemed oblivious to her presence.
                           B

    A: [ ] Definite   [ ] Referential   [ ] Generic
        [ ] Indefinite   [ ] Nonreferential   [ ] Specific

    B: [ ] Definite   [ ] Referential   [ ] Generic
        [ ] Indefinite   [ ] Nonreferential   [ ] Specific

2. <u>The unicorn</u> is <u>a mythical beast</u>.
      A   B

    A: [ ] Definite   [ ] Referential   [ ] Generic
        [ ] Indefinite   [ ] Nonreferential   [ ] Specific

    B: [ ] Definite   [ ] Referential   [ ] Generic
        [ ] Indefinite   [ ] Nonreferential   [ ] Specific

3. Have you seen <u>a little white kitten with gray and orange spots</u>? <u>She</u> must have gotten out
                                      A   B

    about fifteen minutes ago.

    A: [ ] Definite   [ ] Referential   [ ] Generic
        [ ] Indefinite   [ ] Nonreferential   [ ] Specific

    B: [ ] Definite   [ ] Referential   [ ] Generic
        [ ] Indefinite   [ ] Nonreferential   [ ] Specific

4. Hello, Crown Books? I'm looking for <u>a book on referentiality in Lithuanian</u>. Do you have
                                              A

    anything like that? [*pause*] Young man, I just bought <u>a book on definiteness in Hungarian</u>
                                                                        B

    from you last week, so you could at least take a look!

    A: [ ] Definite   [ ] Referential   [ ] Generic
        [ ] Indefinite   [ ] Nonreferential   [ ] Specific

    B: [ ] Definite   [ ] Referential   [ ] Generic
        [ ] Indefinite   [ ] Nonreferential   [ ] Specific

5. I've traveled far and wide in my quest for <u>the perfect cheeseburger</u>.
                                              A

    A: [ ] Definite   [ ] Referential   [ ] Generic
       [ ] Indefinite   [ ] Nonreferential   [ ] Specific

6. X. I'm <u>a highly experienced automotive engineer</u>.
                        A

    Y. Unfortunately we have no job here for <u>a highly experienced automotive engineer</u>.
                                                               B

    A: [ ] Definite   [ ] Referential   [ ] Generic
       [ ] Indefinite   [ ] Nonreferential   [ ] Specific

    B: [ ] Definite   [ ] Referential   [ ] Generic
       [ ] Indefinite   [ ] Nonreferential   [ ] Specific

7. X. All my life I've been searching for <u>someone who would worship me, support me, and</u>
                                           A

    <u>give me the space I need to be myself and do my own thing</u>. Are you <u>that person</u>?
                                                                                    B

    Y. Search no longer. I am <u>the one you've been dreaming of</u>. (Yeah, right.)
                                C

    A: [ ] Definite   [ ] Referential   [ ] Generic
       [ ] Indefinite   [ ] Nonreferential   [ ] Specific

    B: [ ] Definite   [ ] Referential   [ ] Generic
       [ ] Indefinite   [ ] Nonreferential   [ ] Specific

    C: [ ] Definite   [ ] Referential   [ ] Generic
       [ ] Indefinite   [ ] Nonreferential   [ ] Specific

8. <u>They</u>'re having <u>a Stallone retrospective</u> at <u>the Vista</u> this week. Do <u>you</u> want to go?
    A   B   C   D

    A: [ ] Definite   [ ] Referential   [ ] Generic
       [ ] Indefinite   [ ] Nonreferential   [ ] Specific

    B: [ ] Definite   [ ] Referential   [ ] Generic
       [ ] Indefinite   [ ] Nonreferential   [ ] Specific

    C: [ ] Definite   [ ] Referential   [ ] Generic
       [ ] Indefinite   [ ] Nonreferential   [ ] Specific

    D: [ ] Definite   [ ] Referential   [ ] Generic
       [ ] Indefinite   [ ] Nonreferential   [ ] Specific

Name _____   Section _____   Date _____

5.08   SEMANTIC ROLES AND SENTENCE SEMANTICS:
Semantic Roles in Headlines

Headlines tend to be telescoped clauses, with some function words unexpressed. Examine the following headlines, in which certain noun phrases have been underlined. (These headlines, sometimes adapted, have been taken from the *Los Angeles Times*.)

Above each underscored NP, identify its semantic role in its clause by writing the abbreviation for the role above it:

A	=	Agent	P	=	Patient	B	=	Benefactive
E	=	Experiencer	I	=	Instrument	C	=	Cause
R	=	Recipient	TM	=	Temporal	L	=	Location

For any NP you judge to play a role other than those listed above, propose a suggestive name for that role and explain it.

Then, for each underscored NP, add a *second* underscore if its grammatical relation is subject of the clause and a *second and third* underscore if its grammatical relation is object of the verb.

                           E   L
>   **EXAMPLE**   Actor Has Lived in the 'Hood

1. Network Fends Off Critics for Busting Embargo

2. Small U.S. Studios Delight Audience at Moscow Fair

3. Gay Men's Chorus Opens Doors in Europe

4. Boyhood Favorites Still Leave Critic Reeling

5. FBI Loses Lennon Papers Battle

6. Disney Seeks U.S. Highway Funds by August

7. James Hawkins, Who Defended Family From Gangs, Dies at 80

8. Shootings Mar 'BOYZ' Showings

9. Beleaguered <u>Governor</u> Needs a Winner on <u>Election Day</u>

10. <u>Smith</u> Tells <u>Officials</u> <u>He</u>'ll Quit

11. <u>Senator,</u> <u>Actors</u> Focus on <u>Bill</u> to Curb Paparazzi

12. <u>Hollywood</u> Backs Bill to Curb <u>Paparazzi</u>

13. <u>Welsh Settlers</u> in <u>Patagonia</u> Keep <u>Old Ways</u>

14. <u>Opening Ceremony</u> Plays on Past in Hopes of Igniting <u>Present</u>

15. <u>INS</u> Issues <u>New Rules</u> for <u>Foreign Performers</u>

16. 91,000 <u>Fans</u> Roar as <u>Mexico</u> Wins, 1–0

17. <u>Governor</u> Has Assets, But <u>Opponents</u> Have <u>Deep Pockets</u>

18. <u>Bill</u> Aims to Treat <u>Young Sex Offenders</u>

19. <u>Cahuilla Tribe</u> to Reopen <u>Long-Closed Canyon</u>

20. Tribe Plans <u>Fences</u> Before Reopening <u>Area</u> to <u>Public</u>

21. <u>Staffers</u> Brace for <u>Next Bump</u>

22. <u>Winds</u> Disable <u>4 Vessels</u> in <u>Gulf of Mexico</u>

23. <u>Search</u> Continues for <u>Bombing Suspect</u>

24. <u>Singapore</u> Sees <u>Efficiency</u> as Key to <u>Success</u>

Name _____   **Section** _____   **Date** _____

EXERCISES BASED ON OTHER LANGUAGES

🎧 5.09   LEXICAL SEMANTICS: Classifiers in Malay/Indonesian

In English, we can generally place numbers directly before nouns: 'five books,' 'twenty-three rabbits,' 'one computer.' Sometimes, however, a different structure is necessary. We don't normally say 'two chalks' or 'three breads' but 'two sticks (or pieces) of chalk' and 'three slices (or pieces or loaves) of bread.'

Although in English it is relatively rare that nouns like *stick, piece,* or *loaf* are required to count objects, in languages such as Chinese, Vietnamese, and Malay/Indonesian, such classifiers are the rule rather than the exception, and it is part of native-speaker competence to know which of these to use with any particular noun.

Some classifiers are quite general in their applicability, while others are highly restricted and used with only a few lexical items. The choice of classifier is based on the semantic properties of nouns. The set of nouns counted with any particular classifier forms a *lexical field*. (See the glossary for an explanation of this term.)

This exercise will introduce you to six common classifiers in Malay/Indonesian. The data are given in standard Malay/Indonesian orthography.

Examine the following data. Extrapolating from these examples, determine the constitution of the lexical field of nouns used with each classifier illustrated. (You may be reminded of the popular TV game show in which contestants have to guess categories of objects and clues consist of members of the category: "Knife, razor blade, ax, broken glass . . ."—"Things that are sharp!")

1. dua orang laki-laki   'two men'
    tiga orang guru   'three teachers'
    enam orang pemain sepakbola   'six soccer players'
    tiga orang perempuan   'three women'
    seorang tukang besi   'one blacksmith'
    empat orang Tionghua   'four Chinese people'

    Classifier: _____

    Used with: _____

2. lima ekor burung   'five birds'
    tujuh ekor gajah   'seven elephants'
    delapan ekor laba-laba   'eight spiders'
    seekor buaya   'one crocodile'
    sepuluh ekor anjing   'ten dogs'
    lima puluh ekor kerbau   'fifty water buffaloes'

    Classifier: _____

    Used with: _____

3. | sebatang rokok | 'a cigarette' |
    | dua batang pensil | 'two pencils' |
    | sepuluh batang jari | 'ten fingers' |
    | lima puluh dua batang pohon | 'fifty-two trees' |
    | empat puluh satu batang buluh | 'forty-one bamboos' |
    | dua batang rokok | 'two cigarettes' |
    | sembilan batang kapor | 'nine sticks of chalk' |

    Classifier: _____

    Used with: _____

4. | enam helai kertas | 'six pieces of paper' |
    | sehelai kain | 'a length of cloth' |
    | dua belas helai daun | 'twelve leaves' |
    | enam belas helai bulu | 'sixteen feathers' |
    | sebelas helai rumput | 'eleven blades of grass' |
    | delapan helai saputangan | 'eight handkerchiefs' |

    Classifier: _____

    Used with: _____

5. | tujuh buah kereta | 'seven cars' |
    | tujuh puluh buah rumah | 'seventy houses' |
    | tujuh belas buah sofa | 'seventeen sofas' |
    | tujuh puluh tujuh buah gunung | 'seventy-seven mountains' |
    | sebuah sekolah | 'one school' |
    | lima buah pulau | 'five islands' |
    | sembilan belas buah kedai | 'nineteen shops' |

    Classifier: _____

    Used with: _____
    (*Hint:* Consider size and shape.)

6. | dua belas biji telur | 'a dozen eggs' |
    | enam biji peluru | 'six bullets' |
    | dua puluh satu biji permata | 'twenty-one jewels' |
    | tiga biji buah anggur | 'three grapes' |
    | tiga puluh lima biji benih | 'thirty-five seeds' |

    Classifier: _____

    Used with: _____

Name _____   Section _____   Date _____

5.10   LEXICAL SEMANTICS: Adjective Classes in Persian

Just as verbs are marked in the lexicon to indicate the kinds of subjects they allow, adjectives can be similarly marked to show the types of noun phrases they can modify.

Compared to many languages, English has rather loose restrictions on adjectives and the nouns they qualify. Thus, we can speak of a worried man or a worried look; a courageous parent, a courageous act, or a courageous newspaper article; and a sarcastic remark or a sarcastic teacher. Other languages can have tighter constraints on adjective-noun co-occurrences.

In the following Persian data, the starred NPs are ungrammatical. By comparing the acceptable and unacceptable phrases, you will be able to divide the adjectives in the data into two classes based on the kinds of nouns they can modify. (*Note:* The bound morpheme *-el-ye* is required between a noun and an attributive adjective modifying it; this is not relevant to the present problem.)

Note: In this data, š =IPA [ʃ], č = IPA [tʃ], ǰ = IPA [dʒ], y = IPA [j], and ' = IPA [ʔ].

1. mærd-e mehræban   'kind man'
    *name-ye mehræban   'kind letter'

2. *bæčče-ye biræhmane   'cruel child'
    hæmle-ye biræhmane   'cruel attack'

3. *hærfha-ye bahuš   'clever remarks'
    šagerd-e bahuš   'clever student'

4. *bæččegan-e mohæbbætamiz   'affectionate children'
    hærfha-ye mohæbbætamiz   'affectionate remarks'

5. *mærd-e mehræbanane   'kind man'
    hærf-e mehræbanane   'kind word'

6. mærd-e bašæræf   'honorable man'
    *ǰæng-e bašæræf   'honorable war'

7. bæččegan-e bamohæbbæt   'affectionate children'
    *hærfha-ye bamohæbbæt   'affectionate remarks'

8. ræftar-e sæfahætamiz   'foolish behavior'
    *pedær-e sæfahætamiz   'foolish father'

9. *mæqale-ye nafæhm   'stupid article'
    ræhbær-e nafæhm   'stupid leader'

10. *valedein-e sorudamiz   'joyful parents'
    mouqe'-e sorudamiz   'joyful occasion'

11. *mo'ællem-e tæ'neamiz   'sarcastic teacher'
    hærf-e tæ'neamiz   'sarcastic remark'

12. pesær-e gostax   'rude boy'
    *goftar-e gostax   'rude speech'

13. zæn-e biræhm   'cruel woman'
    *kar-e biræhm   'cruel deed'

14. karha-ye bišærmane   'shameless acts'
    *zænan-e bišærmane   'shameless women'

15. *soxæn-e doroštxuy   'harsh speech'
    qazi-ye doroštxuy   'harsh judge'

16. *ræhbær-e šærafætmændane   'honorable leader'
    tæsmim-e šærafætmændane   'honorable decision'

17. mærdom-e šadman   'joyful people'
    *mouqe'-e šadman   'joyful occasion'

18. kæleme-ye dorošt   'harsh word'
    *mo'ællem-e dorošt   'harsh teacher'

19. soxæn-e koframiz   'blasphemous speech'
    *ǰævan-e koframiz   'blasphemous young man'

20. ræhbær-e kohnepæræst   'old-fashioned leader'
    *šælvar-e kohnepæræst   'old-fashioned trousers'

21. *særbazan-e tæhævvoramiz   'courageous soldiers'
    karha-ye tæhævvoramiz   'courageous acts'

22. *karha-ye bišærm   'shameless acts'
    zænan-e bišærm   'shameless women'

23. *ǰæng-e ba'edalæt   'just war'
    ræhbær-e ba'edalæt   'just leader'

24. *doxtær-e gostaxane   'rude girl'
    hærfha-ye gostaxane   'rude words'

Name _____   **Section** _____   **Date** _____

A. What is the relevant distinction between the two classes of adjectives in the data?

_____

_____

B. Using the following chart, divide the adjectives into the two classes you have determined. Write the characterization of each class at the head of its column in the spaces provided.

	Class I	**Class II**
Characterization:	_____	_____
	_____	_____
affectionate	_____	_____
blasphemous	_____	_____
clever	_____	_____
courageous	_____	_____
cruel	_____	_____
foolish	_____	_____
harsh	_____	_____
honorable	_____	_____
joyful	_____	_____
just	_____	_____
kind	_____	_____
old-fashioned	_____	_____
rude	_____	_____
sarcastic	_____	_____
shameless	_____	_____
stupid	_____	_____

C. Do any morphological clues allow you to predict which class an adjective will fall into? Explain.

_____

_____

_____

6

Pragmatics

KEY TERMS AND SYMBOLS

See the glossary.

Agent	Implication	Particle
Commissive	Indefinite	Passive
Cooperative principle	Maxim of Manner	Pragmatic function
Declaration	Maxim of Quality	Referential meaning
Definite	Maxim of Quantity	Representative
Directive	Maxim of Relevance	Speech act
Expressive	New information	Verdictive
Function word	Old information	

Name _____   Section _____   Date _____

EXERCISES BASED ON ENGLISH

6.01   CATEGORIES OF INFORMATION STRUCTURE:
Old Information and New Information

Examine the following excerpts from newspaper articles. Write N above any underlined expression that represents *new information* and O above any that represents *old information.* (Excerpts, two slightly adapted, are taken from the *Los Angeles Times,* February 16, 1998.)

                        N   N   N   N

EXAMPLE   Taking <u>a cue</u> from <u>fans</u> around the world, <u>members</u> of <u>Sam's Army</u>

                      N   N

will do just about anything to call <u>attention</u> to <u>the U.S. soccer team</u>.

         N   N   O   O

At <u>the Gold Cup final</u> between <u>Mexico</u> and <u>the U.S.</u>, <u>the Sammers</u> made

                      N

their presence known with <u>chants</u> and songs.

1. For storing <u>large amounts of data</u>, nothing is more efficient or dependable than <u>a</u>

<u>computer</u>—but only for a while. <u>That's</u> <u>the realization</u> <u>computer scientists</u> and <u>archivists</u> are

coming to now that so many <u>documents</u>—ranging from U.S. census data to <u>images</u> of great

works of art—are being stored in the digital code of 1s and 0s. It turns out that <u>magnetic</u>

<u>tapes,</u> CD-ROMs and other storage media have shorter life spans than originally thought,

and the machines and software needed to read them become obsolete even faster. Ironically,

<u>today's high-tech storage methods</u> are far less durable than <u>ancient traditions</u> of carving

<u>words</u> in stone.

2. <u>A culture clash</u> of sorts is under way at <u>the new Getty Center</u> in <u>Brentwood</u>. While the heart of <u>the museum</u>'s ancient Greek and Roman collections consists of <u>sculptures</u>, <u>urns</u>, and <u>other antiquities</u>, the Getty is embracing 21st century <u>computer-networking technology</u> to help cultivate appreciation for <u>that art and culture</u>.

3. It was loud and lively Sunday at <u>the Los Angeles Coliseum</u> as <u>Mexico</u> defeated the United States, 1–0, to claim <u>soccer's prized CONCACAF Gold Cup</u>. More than 91,000 fans were on hand, most pro-<u>Mexico</u>, many blowing <u>horns</u> with such sustained fervor that it sounded like <u>a huge hornet's nest</u> inside <u>the venerable stadium</u>. A sprinkling of <u>U.S. fans</u>—including a group that calls itself <u>Sam's Army</u>—also made noise, hoping <u>the U.S. team</u> could pull off yet another upset. But <u>it</u> was not to be.

Name _____   **Section** _____   **Date** _____

6.02   CATEGORIES OF INFORMATION STRUCTURE:
Definiteness and Indefiniteness; Old and New Information

In the following paragraphs, write D above any underlined noun or noun phrase that is *definite* and I above any that is *indefinite*. Then write N above underlined nouns or noun phrases that represent *new information* and O above those that represent *old information*. (Paragraphs are taken, slightly adapted, from the *Los Angeles Times,* February 16, 1998.)

I-N   I-N   I-N   D-N

EXAMPLE   Taking <u>a cue</u> from <u>fans</u> around the world, <u>members</u> of <u>Sam's Army</u>

I-N   D-N

will do just about anything to call <u>attention</u> to <u>the U.S. soccer team</u>.

D-N   D-N   D-O   D-O

At <u>the Gold Cup final</u> between <u>Mexico</u> and <u>the U.S.</u>, <u>the Sammers</u> made

I-N

their presence known with <u>chants</u> and songs.

1. In <u>Redwood City</u>, California, the new practice of establishing minimum numbers of <u>traffic</u>

   <u>tickets</u> and <u>criminal arrests</u> that <u>officers</u> are expected to log each month aims to motivate

   <u>police</u>, but it has instead pitted <u>them</u> against <u>residents</u>, <u>city leaders</u> and even one another.

2. Ask <u>John Flynn</u>, <u>the state</u>'s chief information officer, what mischief <u>the year 2000 computer</u>

   <u>problem</u> might cause in <u>state computer networks</u> and <u>he</u> begins by taking <u>a deep breath</u>. . . .

   So <u>Flynn</u> and <u>other government officials from throughout the state</u> are planning to convene

   in <u>Sacramento</u> on <u>Thursday</u> for the state's first intergovernmental conference on the year

   2000 problem.

Most city, county and state officials have already spent the last few years working on

solving the problem, which involves some computer programs' inability to recognize dates

beyond Dec. 31, 1999. But even if individual agencies fix their problems internally, many

government computer systems are interconnected. Welfare data, for example, are passed

from the county to the state to the federal government. One thing Flynn hopes to accomplish

Thursday is the establishment of standards so that repairs are compatible across different

systems.

Name _____   **Section** _____   **Date** _____

6.03   PRAGMATIC CATEGORIES AND SYNTAX:
Agentless Passives in English

An agentless passive sentence is one that lacks a 'by + AGENT' constituent:

(a)   *Active sentence:* Melvin stole the baby's candy.

(b)   *Agent passive:* The baby's candy was stolen by Melvin.

(c)   *Agentless passive:* The baby's candy was stolen.

Note that in these examples (a) and (b) have the same referential meaning, but (c) does not, since it conveys less information: It might be Melvin who perpetrated the dastardly deed or it might not—we aren't told.

English speakers use agentless passives in several situations. One is when the agent of the action is either unknown or irrelevant in the discourse. Another—and the focus of this exercise—is when the speaker wishes to avoid assigning responsibility or blame.

The following example illustrates this second use of the agentless passive:

Gary is talking to his boss, who is asking why a client hasn't received some important correspondence. Gary knows the reason: It was Bob's responsibility to take the mail to the post office Tuesday afternoon, and Bob forgot to do it. Gary doesn't want to get Bob in trouble or appear to be a "snitch," yet he doesn't want to lie to his boss. So rather than saying "Bob didn't take out the mail on Tuesday," he sidesteps the issue of responsibility by saying, "I don't think the mail was taken out on Tuesday." That way, the boss might or might not pursue the question of whose job it was to take out the mail, but at least he knows why the letter hasn't arrived—he won't suspect, for example, that the secretary never typed it.

For each of the following examples, give a context or circumstance in which a speaker can use the agentless passive in question to avoid assigning responsibility or blame. Indicate the speaker's motivation and the "protected" agent in each case.

1.   I indicated the corrections in red on the sheet I gave back to you, but it looks as if the changes were never made.

Circumstance: _____

_____

Motivation: _____

_____

Protected agent: _____

2. Our troops achieved all of their military objectives. Unfortunately, forty civilians were killed or injured in the course of the operation.

Circumstance: _____

_____

Motivation: _____

_____

Protected agent: _____

3. Mommy, my bicycle got broken!

Circumstance: _____

_____

Motivation: _____

_____

Protected agent: _____

4. I *know* there aren't any clean socks! The laundry hasn't been done for three weeks!

Circumstance: _____

_____

Motivation: _____

_____

Protected agent: _____

5. I'll do whatever I can to save Fluffy, but I have to tell you that for her own good, she may have to be put to sleep.

Circumstance: _____

_____

Motivation: _____

_____

Protected agent: _____

Name _____   **Section** _____   **Date** _____

6.04   SPEECH ACTS: Categorizing Speech Acts in English

Six important types of speech acts are:

- Representatives
- Commissives
- Directives
- Declarations
- Expressives
- Verdictives

(If you're not sure of the definitions of these terms, see the glossary.)

Examine the following utterances and choose the most appropriate category for each one.

     EXAMPLE   I'll never leave you.   <u>Commissive</u>

	Type of Speech Act
1. I declare the Games officially open.	_____
2. Columbus discovered America in 1492.	_____
3. Are you sure you can't stay just a few more minutes?	_____
4. Way to go!	_____
5. What a mean-spirited, divisive speech he gave.	_____
6. Go ahead—make me!	_____
7. It's 80 degrees outside and you've got the heat turned way up.	_____
8. I pledge $50.	_____
9. Why don't you like to ski?	_____
10. Why don't you spend less time watching TV?	_____
11. I'm so sorry about your mother, Peggy—my heart goes out to you.	_____

Type of Speech Act

12. Neil Armstrong was the first man on the moon.   _____

13. Buzz Aldrin was the first man on the moon.   _____

14. Buzz Aldrin was not the first man on the moon.   _____

15. Was Buzz Aldrin the first man on the moon?   _____

16. I guarantee that you'll double your money in six months.   _____

17. Thank you so much for your generous gift.   _____

18. That's a lie!   _____

19. Can you reach the blue bowl on the top shelf?   _____

20. Roger Jennings, you are the new SuperDad U.S.A. for 2004!   _____

Name _____   **Section** _____   **Date** _____

6.05   SPEECH ACTS: Sentence Implication

The following sentences are taken, sometimes adapted, from the *Los Angeles Times*. For each of the sentences, provide another sentence implied by the first.

> **EXAMPLE**   The proposed rules would make it even more difficult for most foreign performers to get visas.
> *Implies:* The existing rules already make it difficult to get visas.

1. Arts groups said Thursday that controversy over the rules is certain to intensify.

   Implies: _____

   _____

2. Shakespeare Festival/LA has been awarded a $20,000 grant, the largest of 13 awarded in the arts funding program.

   Implies: _____

   _____

3. In lieu of admission, theatergoers are asked to bring canned food, which will be donated to the Salvation Army.

   Implies: _____

   _____

4. It is Singleton's gift to make us empathize with their hopelessness.

   Implies: _____

   _____

5. Unfortunately, the other two entrees were inedible.

   Implies: _____

   _____

6. Perlman has now fulfilled the promise of his early virtuosity.

   Implies: _____

   _____

7. At least four aircraft chose inappropriate fly-by times during the evening.

   Implies: _____

   _____

8. Surprisingly, attendance at this concert reached only 9,124.

   Implies: _____

   _____

9. She responded by suing two of the eight musicians for slander.

   Implies: _____

   _____

10. Like most arts organizations, this one does not earn enough to support itself.

    Implies: _____

    _____

Name _____   **Section** _____   **Date** _____

6.06   THE COOPERATIVE PRINCIPLE:
The Gricean Maxims in American English

Grice identified four important principles or maxims that underlie ordinary conversation:

- Maxim of Manner
- Maxim of Relevance
- Maxim of Quantity
- Maxim of Quality

(If you're not sure of the definitions of these terms, see the glossary.)

For each of the following conversational excerpts, name a maxim that has been violated and explain how.

> **EXAMPLE**   I'm a multimillionaire. (Actually, you're penniless.)   <u>Quality</u>
> *Explanation:*   <u>The speaker has failed to tell the truth.</u>

Violated Maxim

1. A: When am I going to get back the money I lent you?

    B: Boy, it's hot in here!   _____

    Explanation: _____

    _____

2. How to get to 42nd Street? Easy. Go past the movie theater—
    they're showing a film that I highly recommend, *Ma Vie en Rose*—
    it's in French with English subtitles. Then turn right and take Sixth
    Avenue all the way up.   _____

    Explanation: _____

    _____

3. I'll take appropriate action on your complaint and consider it care-
    fully.   _____

    Explanation: _____

    _____

4. Don't be silly. I *love* working 80 hours a week with no vacation. _____

    Explanation: _____

    _____

5. A: How in the world are you going to pay for all of this?

    B: Space aliens have taken over my body, and you are next!   _____

    Explanation: _____

    _____

6. A: Excuse me—how much is this screwdriver?

    B: $9.95. The saw is $39.50, and the power drill there on the table
    is $89.00.   _____

    Explanation: _____

    _____

7. A: What's playing at the Rialto tonight?

    B: A film you haven't seen.   _____

    Explanation: _____

    _____

8. Dr. Kawashima received his Ph.D. in 1986, his B.A. in 1980, and
    his M.A. in 1982.   _____

    Explanation: _____

    _____

9. A: What should I do to get rid of this awful headache, Doctor?

    B: Take some medicine.   _____

    Explanation: _____

    _____

10. A: Hi, John.

    B: Why, hello, Mary. Your last name is Fleming and you were
    born in Santa Barbara in 1979.   _____

    Explanation: _____

    _____

Name _____   **Section** _____   **Date** _____

6.07   VIOLATING THE COOPERATIVE PRINCIPLE: Indirectness

Speakers sometimes deliberately violate the rules of ordinary conversation to achieve certain ends. For the following conversational excerpts, identify a maxim that has been violated, and give a plausible motivation for the violation.

1. A: Would you like to go out with Andrea?

    B: Is the Pope Catholic?

    Violated maxim: _____

    Motivation: _____

    _____

2. A: I'll pay you back in full next week, I promise.

    B: Sure, and pigs will fly and fish will sing.

    Violated maxim: _____

    Motivation: _____

    _____

3. A: So tell me, do you like what I did to my hair?

    B: Er . . . what's on TV tonight?

    Violated maxim: _____

    Motivation: _____

    _____

4. A: What are the three most important things in real estate?

    B: Location, location, and location.

    Violated maxim: _____

    Motivation: _____

    _____

5. A: How are your son and daughter doing?

    B: Cindy is in her second year of med school—she's doing fine. (Silence follows.)

Violated maxim: _____

Motivation: _____

_____

6. A: How can I develop a great body like yours?

    B: Choose your parents carefully.

Violated maxim: _____

Motivation: _____

_____

7. A: You're soaked! It must be raining pretty hard outside.

    B: You're a regular Sherlock Holmes.

Violated maxim: _____

Motivation: _____

_____

8. A: I wonder why Dave didn't answer the phone. I know he's home.

    B: It's Thursday night. *ER* is on.

Violated maxim: _____

Motivation: _____

_____

9. A: Would you like to hear my rendition of "Feelings"?

    B: Yes, of course. I'd love to. (It's actually the last thing you want to hear.)

Violated maxim: _____

Motivation: _____

_____

Name _____   **Section** _____   **Date** _____

EXERCISES BASED ON OTHER LANGUAGES

 6.08   PRAGMATIC CATEGORIES AND SYNTAX:
Sentence-Final *ba* in Mandarin Chinese

Chinese has a set of sentence-final particles that have different semantic and pragmatic functions. In this exercise, you will investigate one of these particles.

Examine the following Mandarin sentences, transcribed in Pinyin (see Appendix A). The second sentence of each pair is identical to the first, with the exception of the sentence-final *ba*. By noting the translations, you can determine the function of *ba*. Your goal is to observe the "common thread" that runs through all the *ba* sentences and then provide a general statement that characterizes sentences with final *ba*. (It is *not* sufficient simply to list the different situations in which *ba* can be used and the various associated translations.)

1. a) Wǒ-men   zǒu.
       I PLURAL leave
       'We leave.'

    b) Wǒmen zǒu ba.
       'Let's leave.'

2. a) Dàjiā   hē   chá.
       Everyone drink tea
       'Everyone drinks tea.'

    b) Dàjiā hē chá ba.
       'Have some tea, everyone.'

3. a) Wǒ gēn nǐ qù bówùguǎn.
       I   with you go museum
       'I'll go to the museum with you.'

    b) Wǒ gēn nǐ qù bówùguǎn ba.
       'I'll go to the museum with you, OK?'

4. a) Nǐ shì Wáng Lǎoshī.
       you be Wang Teacher
       'You are Teacher Wang.'

    b) Nǐ shì Wáng Lǎoshī ba.
       'You must be Teacher Wang.'

5. a) Zhèi-ge   cài hěn hǎo chī.
       this CLASSIFIER dish very good eat
       'This dish is very tasty.'

    b) Zhèige cài hěn hǎo chī ba.
       'This dish is very tasty, don't you think?'

6. a) Nǐ děng yi děng.
       you wait one wait
       'You wait a little while.'

    b) Nǐ děng yi děng ba.
       'Why don't you wait a little while?'

7. a) Tā bú   huì lái.
       s/he NEGATIVE likely come
       'S/He isn't likely to come.'

    b) Tā bú huì lái ba.
       'S/He isn't likely to come, wouldn't you agree?'

A. Judging from the data, what is the function of sentence-final *ba*?

_____

_____

_____

B. Does English have a uniform way of marking the same function? If so, what is it?

_____

_____

_____

C. For examples 3 and 6, show how your analysis of the function of *ba* applies.

3. _____

_____

_____

_____

6. _____

_____

_____

_____

D. Translate into idiomatic English:

1. Nǐmen bù gēn tā zǒu ba.

_____

2. Lǜ chá bù hǎo hē ba. (lǜ = 'green')

_____

6.09 PRAGMATIC CATEGORIES AND SYNTAX:
The *shì . . . de* Construction in Chinese

Consider the following two Mandarin Chinese sentences:

(a) Wǒ péngyou zuótiān dào   le.

     I   friend   yesterday arrive

     'My friend arrived yesterday.'

(b) Wǒ péngyou shì zuótiān dào   de.

     I   friend   be yesterday arrive

     'My friend arrived yesterday.'

Both these sentences refer to a completed action in the past. They are translated identically and have the same referential meaning. However, they are not interchangeable. Depending on the information structure of the discourse, only one of the two generally will be appropriate.

Note that (a) contains the function word *le* and (b) contains the word *shì* 'be' and the function word *de*. (Neither *le* nor *de* have been glossed.) By examining the following minidialogues and answering the questions after them, you can discover when to use the *le* construction and the *shì . . . de* construction for referring to completed action in the past.

1. A: Nǐ   péngyou hái zài Xiānggǎng ma?

       you friend   still at Hong Kong QUESTION

       'Is your friend still in Hong Kong?'

   B: Bù.   Tā zuótiān   zǒu le.

       NEGATIVE s/he yesterday leave

       'No. S/He left yesterday.'

2. A: Nǐ   péngyou shì shénme shíhou dào   de?

       you friend   be what   time   arrive

       'When did your friend arrive?'

   B: Tā shì zuótiān dào   de.

       s/he be yesterday arrive

       'S/He arrived yesterday.'

3. A: Nǐ shì zài nǎr   yùjiàn tā   de?

       you be at where meet   s/he

       'Where did you meet him/her?'

B: Wǒ shì zài Xiǎo Běijīng yùjiàn tā   de.
I   be at little Beijing meet s/he
'I met him/her at Little Beijing.'

4. A: Nǐ chī le ma?
you eat   QUESTION
'Have you eaten?'

B: Wǒ zài Xiǎo Běijīng chī le wǎnfàn.
I   at little Beijing eat   supper
'I had supper at Little Beijing.'

5. A: Wǒ érzi zuótiān   shēng le.
I   son yesterday born
'My son was born yesterday.'

B: Gōngxǐ,   gōngxǐ!
congratulations congratulations
'Congratulations!'

6. A: Nǐ shì něi   nián shēng de?
you be which year born
'What year were you born?'

B: Wǒ shì yī   jiǔ qī   wǔ nián shēng de.
I   be one nine seven five year born
'I was born in 1975.'

7. A: Wǒ mǔqin zuótiān   dào   le.
I   mother yesterday arrive
'My mother arrived yesterday.'

B: Zhēn de ma?   Wǒ bù   zhīdào tā yào lái.
real   QUESTION I   NEGATIVE know she will come
'Really? I didn't know she was going to come.'
Tā shì yí ge   rén   lái   de ma?
she be one CLASSIFIER person come   QUESTION
'Did she come alone?'

Name _____   **Section** _____   **Date** _____

A: Bú   shì. Tā bú   shi yí ge   rén lái de.
NEGATIVE be she NEGATIVE be one CLASSIFIER person come
'No. She didn't come alone.'

8. A: Nǐ zuótiān zuò le xiē   shénme shì?
you yesterday do   PLURAL what   thing
'What did you do yesterday?'

B: Wǒ qù le bówùguǎn.
I   go   museum
'I went to the museum.'

A: Nǐ shì gēn shéi qù de?
you be with who go
'Who did you go with?'

B: Wǒ shì gēn wǒ péngyou qù de.
I   be with I   friend   go
'I went with my friend.'

A. Syntactic analysis.

1. Examine all the examples where *le* appears. What is the rule for the position of *le* in these sentences or questions?

_____

_____

2. Repeat for the *shì* . . . *de* examples. What rule determines the position of *shì* and the position of *de*?

_____

_____

B. Pragmatic analysis.

1. Now examine each of the *shì* . . . *de* examples in the minidialogues in terms of information structure. Alongside each example, indicate what, if any, information is *given, old,* or *presupposed* at the time of utterance and what stated or requested information is *new*.

2. Repeat question 1 for the *le* examples.

3. You should now be ready to state your generalization: In statements or questions about completed action in the past, when do Mandarin speakers use the *le* construction, and when do they use the *shì . . . de* construction?

_____

_____

_____

_____

_____

C. Translate the following dialogue into Chinese:

A: 'My mother's left.'

_____

B: 'When did she leave?'

_____

A: 'She left yesterday.'

_____

B: 'Did she leave with your friend?'

_____

A: 'No, my friend didn't leave.'

_____

7

Register

KEY TERMS AND SYMBOLS

See the glossary.

Adverb
Article
Attributive adjective
Conjoining
Conjunction
Contraction
Mood

Morpheme
Person
Postposition
Predicative adjective
Preposition
Pronoun
Register

Semantic role
Speech act
Subordination
Subordinator
Transitive verb

Name _____   **Section** _____   **Date** _____

EXERCISES BASED ON ENGLISH

7.01   HOW REGISTERS ARE MARKED:
Pronunciation of *-ing* in New York City

Below is a line graph representing the pronunciation of *-ing* as /ɪn/ in words such as *working* and *talking* among white adult New York City residents; the speakers are classed into four socioeconomic status groups, and the graph represents pronunciation in three situations of use. Examine the graph and answer the questions that follow.

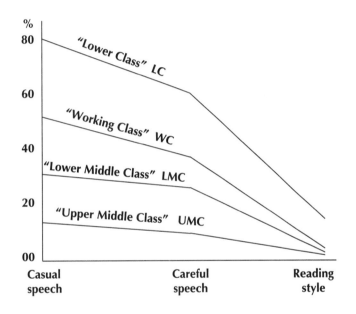

Source: William Labov, *The Study of Nonstandard English*
(Champaign: NCTE, 1970, p. 24)

A. Referring to the Lower Class group as LC, the Working Class group as WC, the Lower Middle Class group as LMC, and the Upper Middle Class group as UMC, list the socioeconomic status groups in order of increasing frequency of pronunciation of /ɪn/

1. in casual speech: _____

2. in careful speech: _____

3. in reading style: _____

B. Which group alters its pronunciation the *most* in moving from one situation/style to another?

_____

Which the *least?* _____

C. In which situation of use is the speech of the four groups most *similar* with respect to this feature?

_____

In which the most *dissimilar?* _____

D. What generalization can be made about the relationship between the pronunciation of /ɪn/ among the social groups and across the situations?

_____

_____

E. If you knew that a particular white adult resident of New York City pronounced *-ing* as /ɪn/ about 30 percent of the time in some situation but you did not know which situation it was, explain why you would or would not have a basis for gauging which of the four socioeconomic status groups that person belonged to.

_____

_____

_____

_____

F. Answer question E for someone using /ɪn/ about 70 percent of the time.

_____

_____

_____

_____

G. For any speech situation, what information does the graph provide about the range of variation across speakers *within* a particular socioeconomic status group?

_____

_____

_____

Name _____   **Section** _____   **Date** _____

7.02   HOW REGISTERS ARE MARKED:
Lexical Domains and Informality

Read through the list of adjectival words and expressions below, all of which can be related to the notion of 'disorder.' Then answer the questions, selecting your answers from the list. You may use the same expression in answer to several questions if appropriate.

bedraggled	indiscriminate	ruffled	squalid
careless	irregular	rumpled	sordid
chaotic	jumbled	scattered	tacky
confused	messy	screwed up	topsy-turvy
deranged	mixed up	seedy	tousled
disheveled	muddled	shabby	unarranged
disorderly	negligent	shoddy	unkempt
frumpy	out of kilter	slipshod	unmethodical
grubby	out of place	sloppy	unorganized
haphazard	out of whack	slouchy	unsystematic
haywire	random	slovenly	untidy

A. Identify four expressions usually associated with 'disorder' in *personal appearance,* and list them from least (1) to most (4) formal:

1. _____   3. _____

2. _____   4. _____

B. Identify four expressions usually associated with 'disorder' in *physical surroundings,* and list them from least to most formal:

1. _____   3. _____

2. _____   4. _____

C. Identify four expressions usually associated with 'disorder' in *workmanship,* and list them from least to most formal:

1. _____   3. _____

2. _____   4. _____

D. Identify four expressions usually associated with 'disorder' in *mental state*, and list them from least to most formal:

1. _____   3. _____

2. _____   4. _____

E. List four expressions usually associated with 'disorder' more generally, and list them from least to most formal:

1. _____   3. _____

2. _____   4. _____

F. Identify and list four expressions you regard as slang, at least as they are used in certain situations:

1. _____   3. _____

2. _____   4. _____

G. Identify and list four expressions you regard as particularly formal:

1. _____   3. _____

2. _____   4. _____

H. Can you make any generalization about the expressions you listed in F and G? That is, can the slang and formal expressions be distinguished on the basis of their form?

_____

_____

_____

Name _____   **Section** _____   **Date** _____

7.03   HOW REGISTERS ARE MARKED: Slang

Slang is a familiar but notoriously tough register to define. Commentators agree that slang occurs in circumstances of extreme informality and serves to "spice up" language. In recent decades, slang has moved unusually quickly into relatively formal channels (such as weekly news-magazines), especially in discussions of such popular topics as computers, sports, criminal behavior, medical and nursing practice, the drug scene, and life in the fast lane. Slang terms are consequently often found in movie and music reviews, lifestyle pieces, and "people" columns.

Although some older slang terms continue in use *(jabber, jackass, malarkey, meal ticket)*, many have lost their edge compared to more current slang terms, such as *dude, sleazoid, oreo, banana, techies, pig out, wimp out, outta here.*

A. Examine a single issue of a current newsweekly or pop culture magazine, and provide six examples of slang terms, with a notation of the lexical category and a gloss for each. Put an asterisk after the terms you believe you can find in your desk dictionary in the sense you have glossed them; then verify your expectation and place a D after glosses that are in fact listed in your dictionary.

| | **EXAMPLE** | "way" | adverb | 'very' |
| | | "stud" | noun | 'sexually attractive male' |

Term	Lexical Category	Gloss
1. _____	_____	_____
2. _____	_____	_____
3. _____	_____	_____
4. _____	_____	_____
5. _____	_____	_____
6. _____	_____	_____

Name and date of magazine: _____

Name of dictionary: _____

B. Provide six slang terms frequently heard on your campus, with their lexical category and a gloss.

	Term	Lexical Category	Gloss
1.	_____	_____	_____
2.	_____	_____	_____
3.	_____	_____	_____
4.	_____	_____	_____
5.	_____	_____	_____
6.	_____	_____	_____

C. Provide a list of six slang terms (plus lexical category and gloss) used by some campus group (for example, band, fraternity, computer science majors) that you are familiar with but that are not widely understood by people outside that group.

	Term	Lexical Category	Gloss
1.	_____	_____	_____
2.	_____	_____	_____
3.	_____	_____	_____
4.	_____	_____	_____
5.	_____	_____	_____
6.	_____	_____	_____

D. Examine the lists you have provided in B and C, and indicate several common arenas in which slang seems to arise on your campus (for example, course names, body parts, personal hygiene).

_____

_____

E. Examine the lists you have provided in B and C, and indicate which lexical categories seem to be most open to slang terms.

_____

Name _____   **Section** _____   **Date** _____

F. Choose a single "subculture" (for example: computers, drugs, music), and list four slang words that originated in that subculture but are commonly understood by outsiders nowadays.

Subculture: _____

1. _____   3. _____

2. _____   4. _____

G. For the italicized words in the following items (taken from *Time* and *Newsweek*), label those you judge to be slang by writing *S* in the column marked "Slang?" Note with Yes (Y) or No (N) in the "Listed?" column whether the items are listed in your desk dictionary, and do the same in the "Label?" column to indicate whether or not they are labeled *slang*. Then check the front matter of your dictionary for its definition of *slang,* and give that definition here. (If no discussion of *slang* appears in the front matter, consult the entry for *slang* in the alphabetical listings.)

_____

_____

_____

_____

Finally, decide whether your dictionary should have marked the word or sense as slang in accordance with *its own* guidelines; write C for consistent (Con) or I for inconsistent (Incon) in the fourth column.

	Slang?	Listed?	Label?	Con/Incon?
1. *wall-to-wall* reruns	_____	_____	_____	_____
2. too *off the wall*	_____	_____	_____	_____
3. *remote-control* medicine	_____	_____	_____	_____
4. just plain *screwy*	_____	_____	_____	_____
5. the *low-impact* story line	_____	_____	_____	_____
6. *laid-back* respect	_____	_____	_____	_____
7. teen *fanzine* favorites	_____	_____	_____	_____

	Slang?	Listed?	Label?	Con/Incon?
8. the *tensomething* crowd	_____	_____	_____	_____
9. to pickle *veggies*	_____	_____	_____	_____
10. popular among *foodies*	_____	_____	_____	_____
11. naked babe *nukes* G-men	_____	_____	_____	_____
12. Ice Cube, the *rapper*	_____	_____	_____	_____
13. diatribes against *whitey*	_____	_____	_____	_____
14. *touchy-feely* comedy	_____	_____	_____	_____
15. a *trek* from the Bronx	_____	_____	_____	_____
16. his emotional *chops*	_____	_____	_____	_____
17. a local *superpig*	_____	_____	_____	_____
18. her fathomless *ditsiness*	_____	_____	_____	_____
19. a kind of *road movie*	_____	_____	_____	_____
20. a fleet of *copmobiles*	_____	_____	_____	_____
21. these *delicious* desperadoes	_____	_____	_____	_____
22. a *blitz* of nutrition advice	_____	_____	_____	_____
23. the latest dietary *bugaboo*	_____	_____	_____	_____
24. there's *life after* croissants	_____	_____	_____	_____
25. *forget* red meat	_____	_____	_____	_____

Name _____   **Section** _____   **Date** _____

7.04   HOW REGISTERS ARE MARKED: Recipe Register

Examine the syntax of recipes as exemplified below. Among other features, note the use of prepositions and articles, the modality (or mood) of verbs, and the use of direct objects with typically transitive verbs. (Recipes adapted slightly from *The New James Beard* [Knopf, 1981].)

1. *Sauteed Brains*

   Parboil the brains as in preceding recipe. Drain and dry. Dip them in flour, then in beaten egg, and then in freshly made bread crumbs. Saute quickly in hot butter until golden brown on both sides. Season with salt and pepper and serve with lemon wedges.

2. *Sauteed Marinated Brains*

   Parboil the brains. Cool and cut in thick slices. Marinate for several hours in a mixture of ½ cup olive oil, 3 tablespoons lemon juice, ¼ teaspoon Tabasco, 1 teaspoon salt, and 1 tablespoon each chopped parsley and chopped chives. Remove from marinade, dip in flour, beaten egg, and fresh bread crumbs, and saute in hot oil until golden brown.

3. *Cioppino*

1 quart clams	2 teaspoons salt
1 cup dry white or red wine	1 teaspoon freshly ground pepper
½ cup olive oil	1 pound crabmeat
1 large onion, chopped	1 pound raw shrimp, shelled
2 cloves garlic, chopped	2 tablespoons finely chopped fresh basil
1 green pepper, chopped	3 tablespoons chopped parsley
4 ripe tomatoes, peeled, seeded, and chopped	[plus other ingredients]

   Steam the clams in the 1 cup white or red wine until they open—discard any that do not open. Strain the broth through two thicknesses of cheesecloth and reserve.

   Heat the olive oil in a deep 8-quart pot and cook the onion, garlic, pepper, and mushrooms for 3 minutes. Add the tomatoes and cook 4 minutes. Add the strained clam broth, tomato paste, and 2 cups red wine. Season with salt and pepper and simmer for about 20 minutes. Taste and correct seasoning. Add the basil and the fish, and just cook the fish through about 3 to 5 minutes. Finally, add the steamed clams, crabmeat, and shrimp. Heat just until shrimp are cooked. Do not overcook. Sprinkle with parsley and serve.

A. Verbs.

1. What mood are most of the verbs expressed in? _____

2. Underline all verbs in other moods.

3. Provide an example of a sentence made up solely of two verbs linked by a conjunction.

_____

B. Prepositions. List three prepositional phrases in the data and three phrases that would usually be introduced by a preposition in conversational English but lack it here.

Prepositional Phrases	Phrases Lacking Prepositions
1. _____	4. _____
2. _____	5. _____
3. _____	6. _____

C. Articles. List four noun phrases that lack an article where conversational English would typically have one.

1. _____   3. _____

2. _____   4. _____

D. List four simple adverbs in the data and characterize their semantic content.

1. _____   3. _____

2. _____   4. _____

Semantic content of recipe adverbs: _____

_____

E. Identify four verbs usually transitive that lack direct objects in the recipes. Why does this register often use transitive verbs intransitively?

_____

_____

F. What other syntactic features strike you as characteristic of this register?

_____

_____

G. Why would it be useful to distinguish two subregisters of recipes?

_____

_____

H. Name two other registers that share some of these characteristics, and specify the shared features.

_____

Name _____   **Section** _____   **Date** _____

7.05   HOW REGISTERS ARE MARKED:
The Syntax and Lexicon of Personal Ads

Examine the personal ads below, adapted from a daily newspaper.

CUDDLER, OUTDOORS LOVER Tall, cute, SWM, 46, N/S, educ. New to Pasadena area seeks youthful, affectionate, playful, nurturing fem to share life with. Do you enjoy getting away from it all & long to build a happy relationship? Attitude more important than age, race, looks. Height & weight proportional plz. P/P nice but not neces.

TRAVEL Woman with sofa, frplc & passprt seeks man to share Sunday paper, capuccino at home, travel and adventure abroad. Attrctv, educ. D/W/F, seeks humorous, n/s, loving, articulate man 48+.

RESPECT & CONSIDERATION Do you know a petite Jewish gal, 30sh, looks like Ms. America, with a heart like my mother's? Please tell her a healthy, unencumbered, comfortable, trilingual, traditional Jewish man wants her for his soulmate.

QUIET EVENINGS AT HOME Attractive, professional, single Filipino lady, 35, never been married, honest, has great sense of humor, one-man woman, no smoking, drinking or drugs, looking for possible serious relationship. Photo pls.

Looking for that special someone to share my life with. Me: 48, SWJM, self employed, successful, stable, honest, sincere, non smoke/drug. You: SWF, age open, sincere, honest.

CLASSIC 1975 GWF Cute, clean, low mileage, good body, no spare tire, rarely overheats, great on curves, cruise control, doesn't smoke. Seeking sexy, in-shape 1975–80 model GWF with skirts.

COULD YOU BE MINE? SBM, 22, N/S, enjoys movies, the beach, dining out, biking. ISO SBF, under 26, N/S.

SEEKS ATHLETIC MALE Good looking GWM, 18, blond, blue eyes 5-11, 155#, college student, fit, healthy, athletic, into swimming, volleyball, new to Southern California. Seeks GM 18–25.

DINING Sensitive SWM 39, tall, successful, out-going, wishes to meet good looking lady, 25–35 for possible relationship.

BEACH WALKS, DINING Physician (Anesthesiologist), Bus. Man (Owner of Co.), 40+, Ambitious, Sweet, Generous, Shy, Oriental Gentleman, No Games, Seeks Vry Honest, Kind, Sweet, Beautiful, Attractive Female, 20–30, for Sharing Good Life &/or Future Committed Relationship. Photo, Telephn # & Description to:

Identify the linguistic features that characterize the personal ads register, including the use or absence of personal pronouns; whether the ads are written in the first person *(I, you)* or third person *(he, she),* and what marks person when pronouns are absent; whether they are consistent in the use of person (or use both first- and third-person pronouns); what information is offered and omitted about the writer and potential respondent; what information is abbreviated; and conventions about the use of nouns, verbs, adverbs, adjectives, and articles that characterize this register.

A. Information offered and abbreviated:

_____

_____

_____

_____

_____

_____

_____

B. Linguistic characteristics:

1. Frequent lexical categories

   _____

   _____

2. Infrequent lexical categories

   _____

   _____

3. Personal pronouns used

   _____

   _____

4. Subjects and verbs

   _____

   _____

Name _____   **Section** _____   **Date** _____

7.06   COMPARING REGISTERS: Natural versus Literary Conversation

Excerpts from three representations of conversation follow: from a novel, a play, and a linguistic transcription of an actual conversation. Notice the common and distinguishing linguistic characteristics of these three conversational registers.

1. **Novel.** (from Tom Wolfe's *The Bonfire of the Vanities* [Farrar, Straus, Giroux, 1987])

   "Craaaaasssssssh!" said Maria, weeping with laughter. "Oh God, I wish I had a videotape a that!" Then she caught the look on Sherman's face. "What's the matter?"

   "What do you think that was all about?"

   "What do you mean, 'all about'?"

   "What do you think he was doing here?"

   "The *land*lord sent him. You remember that letter I showed you."

   "But isn't it kind of odd that—"

   "Germaine pays only $331 a month, and I pay her $750. It's rent-controlled. They'd love to get her out of here."

   "It doesn't strike you as odd that they'd decide to barge in here—right now?"

   "Right now?"

   "Well, maybe I'm crazy, but today—after this thing is in the paper?"

   "In the *paper*?" Then it dawned on her what he was saying, and she broke into a smile. "Sherman, you *are* crazy. You're paranoid. You know that?"

   "Maybe I am. It just seems like a very odd coincidence."

   "Who do you think sent him in here, if the landlord didn't? The police?"

   "Well . . ." Realizing it did sound rather paranoid, he smiled faintly.

2. **Screenplay.** (from Shane Connaughton and Jim Sheridan, *My Left Foot* [Faber and Faber, 1989])

   INT. LIVING ROOM. DAY

   MRS. BROWN *and* MR. BROWN *listen to* CHRISTY *and* DR. COLE.

Mr. Brown:	She's working with him on a Saturday now?
Mrs. Brown:	She has to work with him on her day off. She's doing this voluntarily.
Mr. Brown:	She's a great girl altogether.
Mrs. Brown:	I wish we could afford to pay her.
Mr. Brown:	You were always from the other end of town, Maisie. You're getting it for nothing and you want to pay for it.
Mrs. Brown:	I have me pride as well as you, mister.
Mr. Brown:	I think you're jealous.
Mrs. Brown:	*(Considered)* Do you think that's our Christy up there?
Mr. Brown:	What do you mean?
Mrs. Brown:	Does that sound like our Christy?
Mr. Brown:	It sounds a lot better.
Mrs. Brown:	Not to me it doesn't.

3. **Actual Conversation.** Friends Marguerite (M), Rob (R), and Bobby (B), discussing word processing and computers before dinner. Initial Cap is used for sentence start; CAPS or Í for stress/emphasis; : for lengthened vowel; [   ] for overlapping turns; ⌐⌐ for latched turns; — for incomplete intonation unit; .. for short and . . . for longer pause; ((comments)); and / ?? / for inaudible syllables.

B: Is TA:Ndy—I-B-M comPA:Tible?

M: . . . I: don't KNOW,

B: [. . Well it's —
R: [. . More importantly,   does it ha:ndle WO:RDstar?

M: . . No. And and a LO:T of — She SAID that — Consumer Reports says there's a lo:t of problems with WO:RDstar — that it doesn't DO:,

    . . . a lot of things that you wa:nt it to be A:BLE to do: that it WO:N

    [in the study, and SHE: has the one that] goe:s with . . TA:Ndy —
B: [Tha:t is riDI: culous]

M: that that's much BE:Tter ⌐
R: └ Do you know what the NA:ME [of it is?]
B: [/ ?? /]

M: . . . U:h — . . Í: don't know — something . . . MA:Gnavox, . . Í: don't know . . . ((1 sec.)) u:h . . ((laughs))

B: His MA:Ster's voice

M: . . . Something LI:KE that, . . . but that's not I:T is it.

    That's what it SOU:NDS like.

    . . . ((1.2 sec.)) SO:MEthing VOI:CE, . . something . . . vo:x,

    . . . vo:x PO:Puli ((laughs))

R: ((laughs)) . . . no I don't know what it I:S.

M: . . . Vox DE:I.

Now answer the following questions on a separate sheet.

A. List features of the actual conversation that do not occur in the literary representations.

B. Specify several ways the representation of conversation in the novel differs from that in the screenplay.

C. Explain how the circumstances of literary production influence the representation of conversation in ways that make it different from natural conversation.

Name _____   **Section** _____   **Date** _____

7.07   TEXTUAL DIMENSIONS IN REGISTER VARIATION: Involved versus Informational Registers

Certain linguistic features (including those in Set A below) tend to co-occur frequently in texts belonging to registers that reflect considerable personal *involvement*. Other linguistic features (including those in Set B) tend to co-occur with unusual frequency in texts representing registers whose primary focus is on *information* rather than involvement.

Set A (Involvement Features)

first-person pronouns

contractions *(I'm, doesn't)*

hedges *(kind of, maybe)*

wh-clauses (That's *why he sings*)

clausal coordination *(She went and he stayed)*

second-person pronouns

emphatics *(really, so)*

be as a main verb

private verbs *(think, know)*

zero subordinators *(She said Ø he cried)*

Set B (Information Features)

frequent nouns

longer words

attributive adjectives *(young* people)

frequent prepositions

lexical variety

Below are two passages from an article about Axl Rose and his rock band Guns N' Roses. Passage 1 is Rose's spoken responses to an interviewer in his hotel room (the article doesn't provide the interviewer's questions). Excluding the bracketed words (which were supplied editorially), the passage contains 196 words. Passage 2 is the interviewer's written analysis of Rose and the band. It contains 195 words. (From Robert Hilburn, "Run n' Gun" *Los Angeles Times/Calendar,* July 21, 1991.)

1. Interview with Axl Rose:

I know people are confused by a lot of what I do, but I am too sometimes.   1

That's why I went into therapy.   2

I wanted to understand why Axl had been this volatile, crazy, whatever, for years.   3

I was told that my mental circuitry was all twisted . . . in terms of how I would deal with stress 4

because of what happened to me back in Indiana.   5

Basically I would overload with the stress of a situation . . . by smashing whatever was around   6

me . . .   7

I used to think I was actually dealing with my problems, and now I know that's not dealing with it 8

at all.   9

I'm trying now to [channel] my energy in more positive ways . . . but it doesn't always work.   10

You get a lot of teaching in high school about going after your dreams and being true to yourself,   11

but at the same time [teachers and parents] are trying to beat you down.   12

It was so strict in [our house] that everything you did was wrong.   13

There was so much censorship, you weren't allowed to make any choices.   14

Sex was bad, music was bad.   15

I eventually left, but so many kids stay [in that environment].   16

I wanted to tell them . . . that they can break away too.   17

2. Writer's analysis of Guns N' Roses:

Rose, 29, has been speaking slowly and thoughtfully for more than an hour, outlining the frustrations   1
of his small-town Indiana childhood . . .   2
Just a week before the shows here on the band's first tour in three years, Rose made news by going   3
onstage in his "homecoming" concert in Indianapolis and decrying the forces—including parents and   4
school—that he believes can rob young people of their individuality and aspirations . . .   5
But the Los Angeles–based group's best music is a provocative and affecting exploration of fast-   6
lane temptations and consequences.   7
At the center, Rose is a charismatic performer with an exciting edge of spontaneity—the most   8
compelling and combustible superstar in American hard rock since Jim Morrison . . .   9
You sense in his music and manner a genuine tug of war between healthy and destructive urges—a   10
contest that personalizes for the audience its own struggle over issues as fundamental, and often as   11
paralyzing, as lifestyle, career and relationships. Reflecting in the hotel room on his Indianapolis   12
speech, Rose echoes the classic underdog sentiments that have been a dominant theme in rock ever   13
since James Dean, in "Rebel Without a Cause," articulated youthful anger and pain for the first   14
generation of rockers.   15

A. Underline all attributive adjectives (*mental* circuitry) and double underline all predicative adjectives (*it was strict*) in passage 1.

B. Do the same for passage 2.

C. What function do attributive adjectives serve in texts?

_____

D. What function do predicative adjectives serve in texts?

_____

Name _____   **Section** _____   **Date** _____

E. Why would you expect to find predicative adjectives occurring more frequently in spoken texts than in written texts?

_____

_____

F. Above each of these adverbs in passage 1, mark its adverbial function (T for time, P for place, M for manner, S for speaker's stance): *sometimes* (line 1); *actually* (8); *now* (8, 10); *always* (10); and *eventually* (16). List any other adverbs you find in the passage, and also mark them appropriately.

_____

_____

G. Repeat question F for these adverbs in passage 2: *slowly* (1); *thoughtfully* (1); and *here* (3). List any other adverbs you find in the passage, and mark their function.

_____

_____

H. On the basis of your answers to F and G, how would you characterize the *differences* between common adverbial functions in conversation and in edited writing?

_____

_____

I. The number of occurrences for particular features is provided in the table for one or both passages. Fill out the chart by supplying the missing frequency counts. In cases where space is provided beneath the blank, list as many examples of that feature as the number in parentheses indicates, and give the number of the line where the example occurs.

	Passage 1	Passage 2
Set A (Involvement Features)		
first-person pronouns	_____	____0____
second-person pronouns	_____	____1____
zero subordinator	_____	____0____
(Two)	_____	

	Passage 1	Passage 2
private verbs	_____	3
(Four) _____		
contractions	_____	0
(Three) _____		
emphatics	_____	0
(Three) _____		
be *as a main verb*	_____	2
(Five) _____		

Set B (Information features)

	Passage 1	Passage 2
nouns	25	58
prepositions	24	27
long words (three or more syllables)	15	
(Six; no proper nouns) _____		
lexical variety	126/196	137/195
attributive adjectives	_____	18
(Three) _____		

J. On the basis of these comparisons, determine which passage is more involved and which passage is more informational.

More involved: _____   *More informational:* _____

Name _____   **Section** _____   **Date** _____

EXERCISES BASED ON OTHER LANGUAGES

 7.08   COMPARING REGISTERS:
Formal and Colloquial Registers in Persian

Among the styles of Modern Persian are two that are often termed formal and colloquial. Formal Persian (FP) is the usual language of books, magazines, and newspapers, as well as of radio and television newsbroadcasts, formal speeches, sermons, etc.; Colloquial Persian (CP) is the language of everyday conversation. The two registers are part of the linguistic repertoire of all educated speakers of Persian, who unconsciously switch from one to the other as the situation demands. In this exercise you will discover a few of the phonological, morphological, and syntactic differences between formal and colloquial style.

The following sentences are given in both their FP and CP versions. Compare them carefully, and then answer the questions after them. The data are given in phonetic transcription; parentheses indicate optional elements.

Note: In this data, š =IPA [ʃ], ǰ = IPA [dʒ], and y = IPA [j].

1. FP: mæn æli-ra mibinæm
    CP: mæn æli-ro mibinæm
    'I see Ali'

2. FP: æli šoma-ra mibinæd
    CP: æli šoma-ro mibine
    'Ali sees you'

3. FP: mæryæm an ketab-ra miforušæd
    CP: mæryæm un ketab-(r)o miforuše
    'Maryam is selling that book'

4. FP: an xane bozorg æst
    CP: un xune bozorg-e
    'That house is big'

5. FP: nader midanæd ke iræǰ mæriz æst
    CP: nader midune ke iræǰ mæriz-e
    'Nader knows that Iraj is sick'

6. FP: æbolfæzl miguyæd ke in zæn irani æst
    CP: æbolfæzl mige ke in zæn iruni-e
    'Abolfazl says that this woman is Iranian'

7. FP: mohsen pul-ra be šoma midehæd
    CP: mohsen pul-(r)o be šoma mide
    'Mohsen gives the money to you'

8. FP: kodam ketab asan æst
    CP: kodum ketab asun-e
    'Which book is easy'

9. FP: mæn be xane miayæm
    CP: mæn miam xune
    'I'm coming home'

10. FP: soheyl be ketabxane mirævæd
    CP: soheyl mire ketabxune
    'Soheyl is going to the library'

11. FP: æli mitævanæd be širaz berævæd
    CP: æli mitune bere širaz
    'Ali can go to Shiraz'

12. FP: mæn mitævanæm išan-ra bebinæm
    CP: mæn mitunæm išun-(r)o bebinæm
    'I can see him/her (deferential)'

13. FP: mæn an-ra be xane miaværæm

CP: mæn un-(r)o miaræm xune

   'I'm bringing it home'

14. FP: æbolfæzl ketabha-ra be dæftær
mibæræd

CP: æbolfæzl ketab(h)a-ro mibære
dæftær

   'Abolfazl is carrying the books to
the office'

A. First examine the Formal Persian sentences by themselves, and do a morphemic analysis: Isolate all the morphemes in the FP sentences, and give their meanings or functions. (In this problem you need not account for the function of the postposition -*ra* or for the meaning or function of the verb prefixes—just include these among your listing of morphemes.) Group the morphemes you find according to the following categories.

Nouns

___

Pronouns   **Adjectives**

___

Name _____   **Section** _____   **Date** _____

Verb Stems
_____

Verb Prefixes   **Verb Suffixes**   **Others**
_____

B. Now identify the morphemes in your list that assume a different form in CP. Make another list of these FP/CP pairs.

EXAMPLE   FP   CP
              an   un

C. Examine your list of FP/CP pairs. Some of the variation you have identified can be accounted for by a general phonological rule. State this rule, and indicate which FP/CP pairs it accounts for.

D. Under what circumstances may the *r* in the CP morpheme *-ro* be omitted? State your rule as generally as possible.

E. Circle the numbers of the sentences in the data that exhibit a *syntactic* difference between the FP and CP forms. Determine what these sentences have in common. Then propose a syntactic rule that will account for the difference. Your rule can take the form of a transformation that assumes the FP version represents the underlying word order.

F. Translate into both FP and CP:

'I know that Maryam is bringing the money to the hospital.'

(*Note:* Although you haven't seen the word for 'hospital,' the data provide enough information for you to correctly guess the Persian translation!)

FP: _____

CP: _____

8

Dialect

KEY TERMS AND SYMBOLS

See the glossary.

Auxiliary DO	Inflected verb	Regional dialect/variety
Contraction	Invariant BE	Social dialect/variety
Dialect	Isogloss	Vernacular
Ethnic dialect/variety	Multiple negation	
Gender dialect/variety	Person	

Name _____   **Section** _____   **Date** _____

8.01   REGIONAL AND SOCIAL DIALECTS: English Dialect Identification

In certain phonological, lexical, or syntactic features, each of the expressions below is particularly characteristic of a regional or social dialect. Among the dialects that may be represented are African American English, New York City English, Southern American English, Cockney English, Standard British English, and Chicano English. For each expression, identify in the first column the dialect group whose speech the sample most consistently suggests. In the second column, identify two features from the expression characteristic of that group. In the third column, provide the colloquial Standard American English (SAE) equivalent for the dialect feature identified.

1. [ðə sʌn, i ops tə bi wɪf əm bof, ɪz mʌm n̩ ɪz dæd]
2. [hi pʰæs də tʰitʃər hu wəz sɪtn̩ æt hə dɛs]
3. [hɪm n̩ mi wəz frɛnz ɪn ði ɑrmi]
4. [i bɔʔ ə pʰɑʔ ə flawəz fər ɪz mʌm, uz ɪn ɑspəʔəl]
5. [ɪz ɪt ə nu blu bajk ovə dɛː]
6. [dæt sorər ɑn ðə flɔr ent majn, ɪts hʌz ɔᵊ pʰirəz]
7. [dɛn i wɛn tə baj spɛtʃəl tʃuz fər də wɛrin]
8. [ðə læmps ər ɑn ə fɔθ flɔ, niᵊ ɾi ɛləveɾə]
9. [mɪnɪ ɑːv mɑː frɛnz wɪl se ðɛt ðɛr tʰɑːrd]
10. [ɪz ɪt ə mɪs wɪljəmz hu ɔwez bi wərkən hiᵊ]
11. [hi wetəd ɪn ə kʰju fə ədɪʃənəl pʰɛtrəl fə ðə lɔri]
12. [ʃi juzd ə tʰɔtʃ tə fajnd ðə tʰɪn əv bɪskəts ɪn ðə but]

	Dialect	**Two Features**	**SAE Equivalent**
1.	_____	_____	_____
		_____	_____
2.	_____	_____	_____
		_____	_____
3.	_____	_____	_____
		_____	_____
4.	_____	_____	_____
		_____	_____

Dialect	Two Features	SAE Equivalent
5. _____	_____	_____
	_____	_____
6. _____	_____	_____
	_____	_____
7. _____	_____	_____
	_____	_____
8. _____	_____	_____
	_____	_____
9. _____	_____	_____
	_____	_____
10. _____	_____	_____
	_____	_____
11. _____	_____	_____
	_____	_____
12. _____	_____	_____
	_____	_____

Name _____   **Section** _____   **Date** _____

8.02   REGIONAL DIALECTS OF AMERICAN ENGLISH: Isoglosses

An *isogloss* is a line drawn on a map marking the boundary within which or up to which a particular linguistic feature occurs. On maps representing occurrences of several features, each type of marker represents a particular feature; larger markers represent speakers in several communities.

A. Examine Map A, which identifies the locations where respondents used the expression *I want off* (where speakers of other dialects might say *I want to get off*). On the map, draw the isogloss that represents the northern and eastern limits of that phrase.

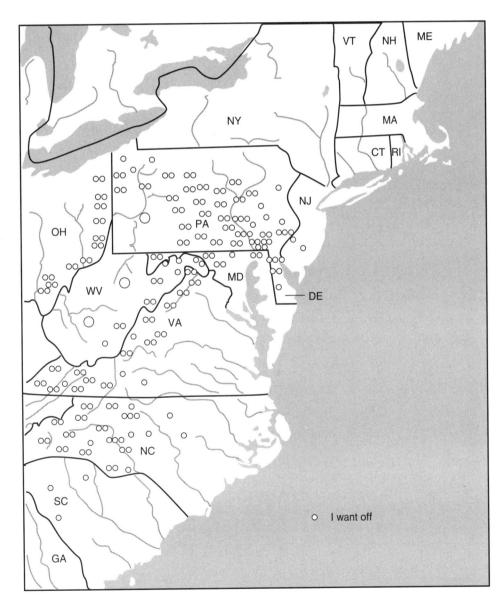

Map A
Distribution of *I want off* in the eastern states
Source: Kurath 1949

B. Map B indicates the locations where respondents used various expressions (other than *saw*) for the past tense of *see*. Using different colors for each feature, draw *(a)* the isogloss that represents the northern limits of *seed*. Then, noting that *see* occurs in three separate areas, draw *(b)* an isogloss representing the southern limits of *see* in the north and, *(c)* and *(d)*, the two isoglosses that completely enclose *see* in the Middle Atlantic states and the south. (*Note:* For drawing certain isoglosses, it may be useful to exclude isolated occurrences of a feature, especially when they occur far away from where the isogloss would otherwise be drawn.)

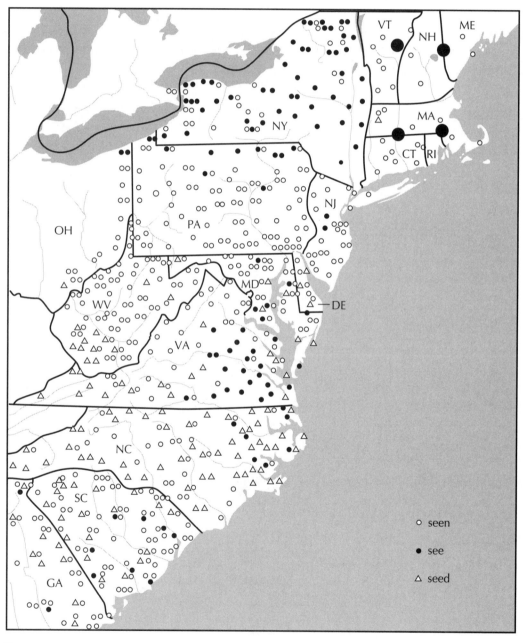

Map B
Words for past tense of *see* in the eastern states
Source: Atwood 1953

Name _____   **Section** _____   **Date** _____

C. Map C indicates the locations in the eastern United States where respondents used various expressions for 'bastard.' Draw the isoglosses that represent *(a)* the southern limits of *ketch-colt;* *(b)* the entire area for *stolen colt; (c)* the southern limits of *come-by-chance;* and *(d)* the northern limits of *woods colt*. (Again, it may be useful to exclude isolated occurrences.)

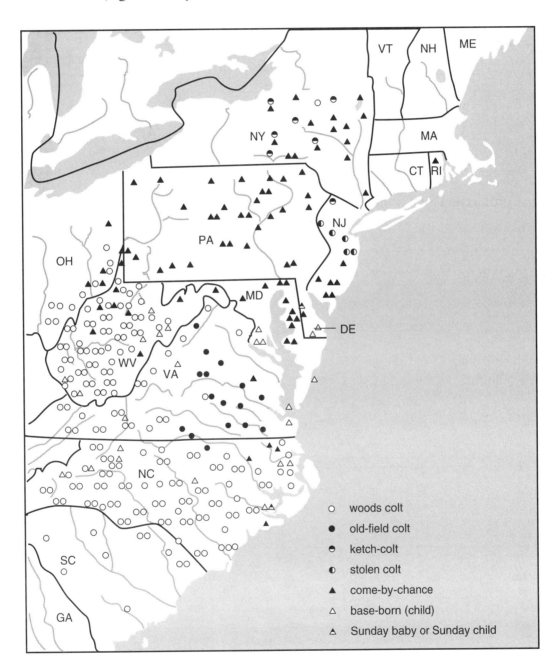

○ woods colt
● old-field colt
◒ ketch-colt
◓ stolen colt
▲ come-by-chance
△ base-born (child)
⧍ Sunday baby or Sunday child

Map C
Words for 'bastard' in the eastern states
Source: Kurath 1949

D. Besides the standard form *saw,* some regions use only a single regional form, while others have several forms for the past tense of *see.* Using Map B and the isoglosses as a guideline, describe in words what usages are found in each of the following locations:

1. Pennsylvania

   _____

2. Maryland

   _____

3. West Virginia

   _____

4. No. Carolina and So. Carolina

   _____

5. New England

   _____

E. Now, using Map C and the isoglosses, describe the geographical distribution of each of the following features:

1. *woods colt*

   _____

2. *come-by-chance*

   _____

3. *bastard*

   _____

F. What do the isoglosses you have drawn suggest about the tidiness of dialect boundaries?

_____

_____

_____

Name _____   **Section** _____   **Date** _____

8.03 REGIONAL DIALECTS OF AMERICAN ENGLISH: *DARE* 1

The *Dictionary of American Regional English* (*DARE*, for short) is a large four-volume dictionary that tracks the distribution of expressions in the fifty states of the United States. The data for *DARE* was gathered by asking residents of 1,002 American communities 1,847 questions such as the ones listed here. (The codes after each question are the identification number of the questions for the *DARE* survey.) Some questions elicited scores of different answers. For example, Frederick Cassidy, *DARE*'s editor, reports that the question seeking other names for the dragonfly elicited 79 different replies.

Answer each of the following *DARE* questionnaire items, using the separate answer sheet on page 271. Then, after your class's responses have been compiled, address the discussion topics that follow the items.

1. Expressions meaning 'confused, mixed up': "So many things were going on at the same time that he got completely _____." (GG2)

2. When someone does something unexpectedly bold or forward, you might say: "Well, she certainly has a lot of _____." (GG5)

3. Names and nicknames for someone who fusses or worries a lot, especially about little things: (GG14)

4. Words for finding fault or complaining: "You just can't please him—he's always _____." (GG16)

5. If you don't care what a person does, you might say: "Go ahead—I don't give a _____." (GG21b)

6. On a day when you don't feel just right, though not actually sick, you might say: "I'll be all right tomorrow—I'm just feeling _____ today." (BB39)

7. When a school child makes a special effort to 'get in good' with the teacher in hopes of getting a better grade: "She's an awful _____." (JJ3b)

8. A child who is always telling on other children: (JJ4)

9. To stay away from school without an excuse: (JJ6)

10. Words or expressions for cheating in school examinations: (JJ7)

11. Somebody who studies too hard or all the time: (JJ9)

12. Joking names for handwriting that's hard to read: "I can't make anything out of his _____." (JJ11)

13. Sayings about a person who seems to you very stupid: "He doesn't know _____." (JJ15b)

14. When you know that somebody has been trying to deceive you, you might say: "He's not fooling me one bit, I'm _____ (him)." (JJ17)

15. To make an error in judgment and get something quite wrong: "He usually handles things well, but this time he certainly _____." (JJ42)

16. Names for somebody who drives carelessly or not well: (NI2)

17. On a trip when you have to change trains and wait a while between them you might say: "I have a two-hour _____ in Chicago." (N38)

18. Vehicles for a baby or small child—the kind it can lie down in: (N42)

19. If you happen to meet someone that you haven't seen for a while: "Guess who I _____ this morning." (II17)

20. Expressions to tell somebody to keep to himself and mind his own business: (II22)

21. What other words do you have for a black eye? (X20)

22. To stare at something with your mouth open: (X22)

23. A mark on the skin where somebody has sucked it hard and brought the blood to the surface: (X39)

24. Words for breaking wind from the bowels: (X55b)

25. Other words for sweat: (X56a)

26. When you are cold, and little points of skin begin to come on your arms and legs, you have _____. (X58)

27. What do you call a man who is fond of being with women and tries to attract their attention—if he's nice about it? (AA6a)

28. What do you call a man who is fond of being with women and tries to attract their attention—if he's rude or not respectful? (AA6b)

29. What words do you have for a woman who is very fond of men and is always trying to know more—if she's nice about it? (AA7a)

30. What words do you have for a woman who is very fond of men and is always trying to know more—if she's not respectable about it? (AA7b)

Topics for Discussion

A. Compare the replies of the members of your class. To the extent they are similar, you might want to compare them to the published results in *DARE* and see how people in other regions of the country answered these same questions.

B. To the extent the replies differ, consider whether the explanation lies in differences among your classmates in regional origins, ages, genders, and ethnicities.

Name _____   **Section** _____   **Date** _____

DARE Questionnaire Answers

1. _____   16. _____

2. _____   17. _____

3. _____   18. _____

4. _____   19. _____

5. _____   20. _____

6. _____   21. _____

7. _____   22. _____

8. _____   23. _____

9. _____   24. _____

10. _____   25. _____

11. _____   26. _____

12. _____   27. _____

13. _____   28. _____

14. _____   29. _____

15. _____   30. _____

Name _____   **Section** _____   **Date** _____

8.04   REGIONAL DIALECTS OF AMERICAN ENGLISH: *DARE* 2

The maps in the *Dictionary of American Regional English* differ from most other maps of regional variation in language in that the states have very different sizes and shapes from those on a conventional map. (Although it is not necessary to do so, you may want to read the front matter to *DARE* or the discussion on pages 376–379 of *Language: Its Structure and Use* to help you complete this exercise.)

The *DARE* maps given here represent the distribution of the verb *to bitch* and the noun *crazy bone*. Examine the maps carefully, and then answer the following questions.

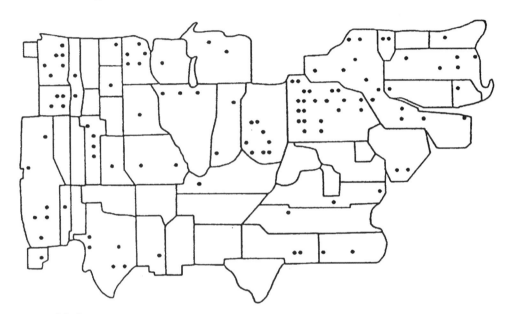

Map A *to bitch*

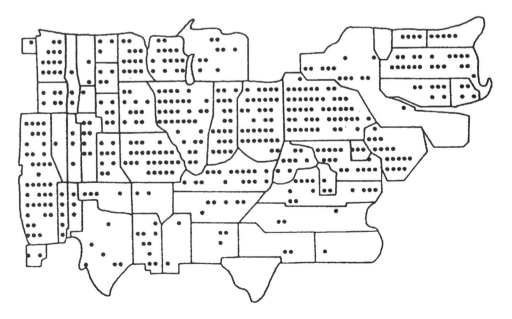

Map B *crazy bone*

A. About *DARE* maps in general.

1. Characterize the difference between a *DARE* map and a conventional map of the United States.

   _____

   _____

2. Are the states on a *DARE* map in approximately the same spatial relation to one another as on a conventional map? Explain.

   _____

   _____

3. On the *DARE* map, Nevada is just a small sliver compared to New York. On a conventional map, Nevada would be about twice as large as New York. What is the basis for the size of the states on a conventional map and on a *DARE* map?

   _____

   _____

4. Hawaii and Alaska are represented on a *DARE* map, but what is unusual about their representation?

   _____

5. In their respective states, write in the two-letter postal abbreviations for Maine (ME), Washington (WA), Florida (FL), Hawaii (HI), and at least fifteen other states on the *DARE* map for *to bitch*. (*Suggestion:* Use pencil in case you change your mind.)

B. About *to bitch*. To elicit *to bitch,* the *DARE* investigators asked this: "Words for finding fault, or complaining: 'You just can't please him—he's always _____.'"

1. In which regions of the country does the use of the verb *to bitch* predominate?

   _____

   _____

2. Name five states where the communities investigated by the *DARE* researchers did not report this usage.

   _____

Name _____   **Section** _____   **Date** _____

3. Name the two states where the largest number of communities reported this usage.

_____

4. Examine the representation for this usage in your home state (or the state you study in). Does your own familiarity with usage in your state square with the usage reported on the *DARE* map? If it does not, offer an explanation for the discrepancy.

_____

_____

C. About *crazy bone*. To elicit *crazy bone,* the *DARE* investigators used this prompt: "The place in the elbow that gives you a strange feeling if you hit it."

1. In which states did the communities investigated by the *DARE* researchers report little use of the expression *crazy bone?*

_____

2. In which state(s) did the investigators find no informants who reported use of *crazy bone?*

_____

3. In which regions of the country does *crazy bone* appear to be in greatest use?

_____

4. In which region(s) of the country does *crazy bone* appear to be in little use?

_____

5. Which states appear to be strikingly different from their immediately surrounding states in terms of their usage of *crazy bone*?

_____

6. Which state's major city appears not to be familiar with *crazy bone,* although some communities in its upstate regions do use the term? What explanation can you offer for this pattern? (*Note:* Although cities are not marked as such on *DARE* maps, this particular city should be obvious from its size and protrusion.)

_____

_____

7. Is *DARE*'s representation of *crazy bone* in your home state (or the state where you attend college) what you would expect, given your own familiarity (or lack of familiarity) with the term? Explain.

_____

_____

Name _____   **Section** _____   **Date** _____

8.05 REGIONAL DIALECTS OF AMERICAN ENGLISH:
Vowel Shifts in North American English

A. The *Northern Cities Shift* (NCS) affects Canadian and major northern U.S. cities, stretching across Syracuse, Rochester, Buffalo, Cleveland, Akron, Detroit, Chicago, Rockford, Milwaukee, and Madison. Some of its characteristic features are listed below:

a) /æ/ is raised and fronted to [iᵊ]: *man, bad* are heard by outsiders as having the underscored vowel of *id**ea***: [miᵊn], [biᵊd]

b) /ɑ/ is fronted to [æ]: *cod* is heard by outsiders as *cad*

c) /ɔ/ is lowered and fronted to [ɑ]: *cawed* is heard as *cod*

d) /ɛ/ is lowered and centered to [ʌ]: *dead* is heard as *dud*

e) /ʌ/ is backed to [ɔ]: *cud* is heard as *cawed*

Assume you speak a dialect *not* affected by the NCS and that you visit a city participating in the Shift and hear speakers say the following. For each one, provide the standard spelling for the underlined word(s) in each sentence that you think the speaker was saying. Also give the letter of the shift as described above.

	Word(s)		Letter(s)	

1. My friend <u>Ian</u> said she loves her new <u>Handa</u> Civic.   _____ _____   __ __

2. Did your friend <u>Tad</u> ever return the <u>lax</u> he borrowed?   _____ _____   __ __

3. Did you ever watch "<u>Mad Skwad</u>" when it was on TV?   _____ _____   __ __

4. It got <u>cot</u> by a <u>hock</u>.   _____ _____   __ __

5. They're now using electric <u>bosses</u> in the central city.   _____ _____   __ __

6. It's too <u>be-ad</u> he didn't take <u>ke-ar</u> of it earlier.   _____ _____   __ __

7. Let's <u>talk</u> in the sheets so the <u>bud</u> looks neat.   _____ _____   __ __

8. I gave my niece <u>Buddy</u> a <u>tuddy</u> bear for her birthday.   _____ _____   __ __

9. She says she can feel <u>gnats</u> in her stomach.   _____ _____   __ __

10. He wants some <u>jully</u> on his <u>brudd</u>.   _____ _____   __ __

11. Are you gonna go to the picnic <u>launch</u> next weekend?   _____ _____   __ __

B. In the southern United States, a shift of vowels called the ***Southern Shift*** is occurring. Among several shifts involved in the Southern Shift are the five listed here:

   a) the diphthong /aj/ is monophthongized to [a]: *hide* sounds like [had] or [haːd]

   b) the vowel /e/ is lowered and centralized to [aj]: *glade* sounds like *glide*

   c) the vowel /o/ is fronted: *code* and *boat* sound like [kɛºd] and [bɛºt]

   d) the vowels /ɪ/, /ɛ/, /æ/ are raised and fronted: *kid* sounds like *keyed, Ted* like *tid, pat* like *pet*

   e) the vowel /u/ is fronted: *cool* sounds like "kewl"

Assume you speak a dialect *not* affected by the Southern Shift and that you visit a city participating in the Shift and overhear speakers say the following. For each one, provide the standard spelling for the underlined words. Also give the letter of the shifts as described above.

		Words		Letters	
1.	Ah hed mah <u>ket</u> <u>spied</u> ez ricomminded bah the SPCA.	_____	_____	__	__
2.	She just <u>petted</u> me on the <u>beck</u> 'n sid, "We'll done."	_____	_____	__	__
3.	How <u>mini</u> skirts hev you <u>prist</u> todye?	_____	_____	__	__
4.	Deon't <u>hodd</u> your <u>prod</u> in your accomplishmints.	_____	_____	__	__
5.	For her birthdye he <u>guyve</u> her a niew sit of <u>tewels</u>.	_____	_____	__	__
6.	Is <u>tiddy kinnidy</u> <u>steel</u> a mimber of the U.S. Senate?	_____	_____	__	__
7.	The <u>eolder</u> she gits the more <u>keolds</u> she ketches.	_____	_____	__	__
8.	Mah brother <u>wide</u> hez niver <u>biked</u> a kike.	_____	_____	__	__
9.	<u>Mah</u> brother night hez niver biked a <u>pah</u>.	_____	_____	__	__
10.	Ah <u>pryed</u> 'n pryed until it kime <u>trew</u>.	_____	_____	__	__
11.	Frad <u>cheekin</u> is mah <u>five-rit</u> dish.	_____	_____	__	__

Name _____   **Section** _____   **Date** _____

8.06   ETHNIC VARIETIES OF AMERICAN ENGLISH:
African American English

The following two passages are transcribed from discussions among African-American teenage girls. Examine them carefully, and then answer the questions about African American English that follow. (Both passages come from Catherine Emihovich, "Bodytalk: Discourses of Sexuality among African-American Girls," in *Kids Talk,* ed. Susan M. Hoyle and Carolyn Temple Adger [New York: Oxford University Press, 1998]. The punctuation has been slightly adapted.)

Passage I

Roslyn: My momma say don't judge Trina. She not like the others say. That's why I talked to

you and got to know you.

Keesha: I feel this way. I was honest with you. I heard things but I like you. I don't believe

what they say.

Katrina: Why they say that? I don't go nowhere. I'm always there *[in the neighborhood].* I

don't bother no one. I sit on the step in the neighborhood by myself. I don't go to

dances, games, I'd rather stay home. I can do things if I ask. How in the world? I'm in

the house always unless I'm at church. So how in the world? I don't hang around

because when I had the chicken pox? What they call that? Oh, that's . . .

Passage II

Katrina: If I had to do it all over again at least a year I would wait. Because it's hard, it's hard

trying to take care of a child while you still in school. Then you want to be doing other

things that your friends be doing. They be like, Well, I'm going out tonight, are you

going to be able to go. I go, Well let me see if my mama can keep the baby first, and

then you be all upset when your mama say like, No not tonight, maybe another time.

A. Invariant *be*.

1. Underline all examples of invariant *be* in the passages.

2. Which of the three speakers use this feature? _____

3. Which use it consistently?

   _____

4. Identify all examples of forms of the verb *be* that are inflected (*am, is, 's,* etc.).

   _____

5. What meaning does invariant *be* seem to carry in the passages?

   _____

B. Negation.

1. Circle all examples of double- or multiple-negative constructions in the passages.
2. Formulate a rule that describes the use of double or multiple negation in this variety.

   _____

   _____

C. Tense marking. For third-person verbs, varieties of English do not typically distinguish singular from plural in the past tense *(she/they walked)*. Many varieties of English, however, make this distinction in the present tense *(she walks/they walk)*.

1. Double underscore all examples of verbs with third-person plural subjects.
2. Draw a box around all examples of third-person singular present-tense verbs whose forms are the same as plural forms.

Name _____   **Section** _____   **Date** _____

D. Auxiliary *do*. Note that Katrina can omit the auxiliary *do* in questions but that she uses it in other constructions.

   1. Identify two instances where Katrina omits *do* and three instances where she uses it.

   _____

   _____

   _____

   _____

   2. Identify any instances of auxiliary *do* in the speech of Roslyn and Keesha, and then state the rule that describes the presence and absence of auxiliary *do* in this speech variety.

   _____

   _____

   _____

E. Contraction versus omission of *be*. Roslyn's speech exhibits an alternation between using contracted forms of the verb *be (That's)* and omitting it altogether *(She not like . . .)*.

   1. Does Katrina's speech show the same alternation? Give examples to prove your point.

   _____

   _____

   _____

   2. Examine the instances where Katrina uses contractions. In your own variety of spoken English, are contractions grammatical in all the same instances?

   _____

   3. Examine the instances where Katrina and Roslyn omit the verb *be* (in any of its forms). In your own variety of spoken English, is such omission grammatical in the same instances?

   _____

4. In your own variety, is it grammatical to contract *be* in those instances where Katrina's and Roslyn's grammar permits them to omit it?

    _____

5. If your spoken variety differs from that of Katrina and Roslyn, what generalization can you make about the relationship between the patterns of *be* omission and contraction in the two varieties?

    _____

    _____

Name _____   Section _____   Date _____

8.07 ETHNIC VARIETIES OF AMERICAN ENGLISH:
A Resolution on Ebonics

In January 1997 in Chicago, Illinois, the Linguistic Society of America (LSA) passed a resolution concerning Ebonics. It is given here in full. The resolution was accompanied by a list of references, which you can find by clicking on "Resolutions/Statements/Guides" in the Members section of the LSA's home page: http://www.lsadc.org. There you will also find the LSA Statement of Language Rights referred to in the resolution.

Examine the Ebonics resolution carefully, and then answer the questions that follow.

Note: The term used here, "African American Vernacular English" (AAVE), refers to the same variety of English as the term used previously, "African American English" (AAE).

LSA Resolution on the Oakland "Ebonics" Issue

Whereas there has been a great deal of discussion in the media and among the American public about the 18 December 1996 decision of the Oakland School Board to recognize the language variety spoken by many African American students and to take it into account in teaching Standard English, the Linguistic Society of America, as a society of scholars engaged in the scientific study of language, hereby resolves to make it known that:

a. The variety known as "Ebonics," "African American Vernacular English" (AAVE), and "Vernacular Black English" and by other names is systematic and rule-governed like all natural speech varieties. In fact, all human linguistic systems—spoken, signed, and written—are fundamentally regular. The systematic and expressive nature of the grammar and pronunciation patterns of the African American vernacular has been established by numerous scientific studies over the past thirty years. Characterizations of Ebonics as slang, "mutant," "lazy," "defective," "ungrammatical," or "broken English" are incorrect and demeaning.

b. The distinction between "languages" and "dialects" is usually made more on social and political grounds than on purely linguistic ones. For example, different varieties of Chinese are popularly regarded as "dialects," though their speakers cannot understand each other, but speakers of Swedish and Norwegian, which are regarded as separate "languages," generally understand each other. What is important from a linguistic and educational point of view is not whether AAVE is called a "language" or a "dialect" but rather that its systematicity be recognized.

c. As affirmed in the LSA Statement of Language Rights (June 1996), there are individual and group benefits to maintaining vernacular speech varieties and there are scientific and human advantages to linguistic diversity. For those living in the United States there are also benefits in acquiring Standard English and resources should be made available to all who aspire to mastery of Standard English. The Oakland School Board's commitment to helping students master Standard English is commendable.

d. There is evidence from Sweden, the US, and other countries that speakers of other varieties can be aided in their learning of the standard variety by pedagogical approaches which recognize the legitimacy of the other varieties of a language. From this perspective, the Oakland School Board's decision to recognize the vernacular of African American students in teaching them Standard English is linguistically and pedagogically sound.

A. Identify several social groups you belong to that contribute to making your own dialect what it is.

_____

_____

_____

B. When they were teaching you, did any or all of your elementary school teachers use the variety of the region where your school was located? Explain.

_____

_____

C. Did any of your elementary or secondary school teachers speak a variety of English that differed from that of the region where you were studying? Explain.

_____

_____

D. Did any of your teachers or ministers, rabbis, or priests have speech characteristics that identified the ethnic group they belonged to? Explain.

_____

_____

E. Name at least two regional varieties of Standard English.

_____

F. Name two other varieties of Standard English and identify the kind of variety they are—e.g., gender, ethnic, regional varieties.

_____

_____

G. Which recent presidents of the United States spoke (or speak) with a distinct regional accent?

_____

H. Why is it so easy for an individual to believe he or she speaks without an accent?

_____

_____

_____

_____

Name _____   **Section** _____   **Date** _____

I. Paragraph a of the LSA resolution implies that AAVE is like Standard English in that both are rule governed. Give two rules of AAVE and two rules of Standard American English.

AAVE: _____

_____

_____

SAE: _____

_____

_____

J. Paragraph a also refers to the fact that Ebonics has sometimes been characterized as "slang," "broken," "ungrammatical," or "lazy."

1. What other varieties of English have been characterized in this way?

_____

_____

2. What explanation can you offer for the fact that the varieties you have just identified are characterized negatively while others that share many of the same characteristics are not?

_____

_____

_____

3. From what you know of Ebonics and your own variety of spoken English, do they contain any slang expressions? Explain.

_____

_____

_____

_____

4. From what you know of Ebonics and your own variety of spoken English, do they contain contractions, abbreviations, and other shortcuts that some might regard as "lazy"? Explain.

_____

_____

_____

_____

K. Paragraph c of the Ebonics resolution refers to "individual and group benefits to maintaining vernacular speech varieties."

1. What is meant by a vernacular speech variety?

_____

_____

_____

2. Identify at least one individual benefit and one group benefit that people derive from speaking a particular regional, gender, or ethnic variety of English. Explain.

_____

_____

_____

_____

3. How do such benefits apply in your particular case?

_____

_____

_____

_____

9

Writing

KEY TERMS AND SYMBOLS

See the glossary.

< > vs. [ ]
allophone
alphabet
ambiguity
diacritic symbol
dialect
digraph

gloss
ideograph
indeterminacy
lexicon
orthography
phoneme
phonetic transcription

pictograph
Roman alphabet
romanization
syllabic symbol
uppercase, lowercase

Name _____   **Section** _____   **Date** _____

EXERCISES BASED ON ENGLISH

9.01   FUNCTIONS OF SPEAKING AND WRITING: English Notices

Notices such as the following are sometimes seen on bulletin boards and other posting places on college campuses:

1. Class canceled today.
2. Applications for Assistant Librarian position now being accepted.
3. Sean. Meet me here at 8 tonight. Erica

A. Explain why each of the three notices above is vague or ambiguous.

1. _____

   _____

   _____

2. _____

   _____

   _____

3. _____

   _____

   _____

B. What is it about how writing differs from speaking that makes these messages vague or ambiguous?

_____

_____

_____

_____

C. What is the difference between using the word *here* and using the word *today* that makes the one but not the other ambiguous on a notice board? Why is it that neither one is typically ambiguous in speech?

_____

_____

_____

_____

_____

D. What have you noticed about the situational similarity of messages on bulletin boards and messages on telephone answering machines? In what ways are the circumstances of composing on such machines more like writing than speaking?

_____

_____

_____

_____

_____

E. Collect several examples from bulletin boards or telephone answering machines in which some very common English expressions (*today, here, now,* etc.) are ambiguous or vague.

_____

_____

_____

_____

_____

Name _____   **Section** _____   **Date** _____

9.02   SYSTEMS OF SPEAKING AND WRITING:
Eighteenth-Century Written versus Spoken English

Daniel Defoe, author of *Robinson Crusoe,* wrote of a visit he made to Somerset, about 150 miles southwest of London, in the first quarter of the eighteenth century.

> . . . when we are come this Length from London, the Dialect of the English Tongue, or the Country-way of expressing themselves, is not easily understood. It is the same in many Parts of England besides, but in none in so gross a Degree as in this Part. As this Way of boorish Speech is in Ireland called, *"The Brogue upon the Tongue,"* so here it is named *Jouring.* It is not possible to explain this fully by Writing, because the Difference is not so much in the Orthography, as in the Tone and Accent; their abridging the Speech, *Cham,* for *I am; Chil,* for *I will; Don,* for *do on,* or *put on;* and *Doff,* for *do off,* or *put off;* and the like.

Continuing, Defoe tells of a pupil reading aloud from the Bible.

> I sat down by the Master, till the Boy had read it out, and observed the Boy read a little oddly in the tone of the Country, which made me the more attentive; because, on Inquiry, I found that the Words were the same, and the Orthography the same, as in all our Bibles. I observed also the Boy read it out with his Eyes still on the Book, and his Head, like a mere Boy, moving from Side to Side, as the Lines reached cross the Columns of the Book: His Lesson was in the *Canticles of Solomon;* the Words these;
>   'I have put off my Coat; how shall I put it on? I have washed my Feet; how shall I defile them?'
>   The Boy read thus, with his Eyes, as I say, full on the Text:
>   'Chav a doffed my Coot; how shall I don't? Chav a washed my Feet; how shall I moil 'em?'
>   How the dexterous Dunce could form his Mouth to express so readily the Words (which stood right printed in the Book) in his Country Jargon, I could not but admire.
>
> (First published 1724–27; cited from Tucker, 61–62.)

Defoe's astonishment that his "dexterous Dunce" read aloud in a "Country Jargon" reveals his view of the relationship between writing and speaking—for example, about which one should be based on which.

A. Describe Defoe's conception of the relationship between spelling and pronunciation as revealed in this anecdote. Did he think spellings should be independent of local pronunciations?

_____

_____

_____

B. If written English is to be relatively uniform across different regional dialects, is it possible to have a standardized spelling system that matches pronunciation in all regions? Explain and give examples to support your answer.

_____

_____

_____

C. If, as Defoe wished, spelling *and* pronunciation were to be uniform, across the English-speaking world, what would have to change—spelling, pronunciation, or both? How practical would this be?

_____

_____

D. Imagine the English spelling system were changed so that spelling varied from region to region to reflect local pronunciation. How feasible would such a change be, and would the consequences be positive or negative? (Consider these questions: Even if a dictionary noted different spellings, which region's spellings would be used in newspapers and for laws, tax records, and information on how to use medicines and assemble bicycles?)

_____

_____

_____

E. Defoe claimed the boy was both "dexterous" and a "Dunce." In what way was he dexterous? Does his dexterity indicate he was a dunce or an accomplished reader? Why?

_____

_____

_____

F. Identify at least four ways the patterns of capitalization and punctuation in the early eighteenth century differ from the familiar patterns of today. What advantages do you see in today's system over the earlier one? What advantages did the earlier system have over today's?

_____   _____

_____   _____

_____

_____

Name _____   **Section** _____   **Date** _____

9.03   WRITING SYSTEMS:
Indeterminacy and Ambiguity in English Spelling

The present-day English spelling system is notoriously difficult to learn. The basic reason for the difficulty is the fact the system does not provide a one-to-one correspondence between sound and written representation. In simple terms, this means you can hear something and not know how to spell it, and you can see something and not know how to say it.

We may call an orthographic system *indeterminate* if the same phonetic form can be written in more than one way. We may call the system *ambiguous* if the same written form can be pronounced in more than one way. With these definitions, the English spelling system is both indeterminate and ambiguous.

A. Indeterminacy. Whenever you have to ask someone "How do you spell that?" you've given evidence English spelling is indeterminate. The question arises most often with proper names. Think of some names you know that have alternate spellings, and list 10 of these below. In some cases, you might discover three or more spellings for the same pronunciation.

     EXAMPLE   [mɑrk]   Marc, Mark

             Transcription   **Alternate Spellings**

1. _____   _____

2. _____   _____

3. _____   _____

4. _____   _____

5. _____   _____

6. _____   _____

7. _____   _____

8. _____   _____

9. _____   _____

10. _____   _____

B. Ambiguity. When you see a new word and have to look up its pronunciation or when you have to ask someone how his or her name is pronounced, you've shown English spelling can be ambiguous.

Suppose you see the English surname Hough in a magazine article but you've never heard it pronounced. Indicate the possible pronunciations English has for this spelling. One answer is provided; you should provide four more.

1. It could be _____[hu]_____ as in _____through_____

2. It could be _____ as in _____

3. It could be _____ as in _____

4. It could be _____ as in _____

5. It could be _____ as in _____

Now provide five of your own examples of words or names whose pronunciations were not clear to you when you first encountered them in written form. In each case, indicate one or more plausible but incorrect pronunciations along with the correct one, and circle the correct one.

EXAMPLES   Sinéad   [sənid], ([ʃəned])

Bette   ([bɛɾi],) [bɛt]   if Bette Davis

[bɛɾi],   ([bɛt])   if Bette Midler

Spelling	Transcription
6. _____	_____
7. _____	_____
8. _____	_____
9. _____	_____
10. _____	_____

Name _____   Section _____   Date _____

EXERCISES BASED ON OTHER LANGUAGES

 9.04   WRITING SYSTEMS: Italian Spelling

A. Examine the following Italian words, given in both Italian spelling and phonetic transcription. Then answer the questions that follow.

Note: In this exercise, č =IPA [tʃ], ǰ = IPA [dʒ], and y = IPA [j].

Italian Spelling	Phonetic Transcription	Gloss
1. circa	[čirka]	'about'
2. chicco	[kikko]	'grain'
3. quota	[kwɔta]	'height'
4. cella	[čɛlla]	'cell'
5. chiosco	[kyɔsko]	'booth'
6. cinque	[čiŋkwe]	'five'
7. accetta	[aččetta]	'ax'
8. quindici	[kwindiči]	'fifteen'
9. chiedere	[kyɛdere]	'to ask'
10. ciocco	[čɔkko]	'log'
11. qui	[kwi]	'here'
12. quercia	[kwɛrča]	'oak tree'
13. socio	[sɔčo]	'member'
14. ciuco	[čuko]	'donkey'
15. cocco	[kɔkko]	'coconut'
16. schivo	[skivo]	'shy'
17. chiusa	[kyuza]	'lock'
18. accetta	[aččetta]	'accepts'
19. qualche	[kwalke]	'some, any'
20. cuocio	[kwɔčo]	'I cook'
21. vecchio	[vɛkkyo]	'old'
22. cucire	[kučire]	'to sew'
23. scalea	[skalea]	'staircase'
24. chiamo	[kyamo]	'I call'
25. chela	[kɛla]	'claw'
26. acquoso	[akkwozo]	'watery'
27. porcellino	[porčellino]	'piggy'
28. questo	[kwesto]	'this'
29. cherubino	[kerubino]	'cherub'
30. chierico	[kyeriko]	'clergyman'

1. Your goal is to determine fully, based on the examples, how the sounds [k] and [č] are spelled before vowels and glides in Italian.

You will need to refer to the Italian vowel system, which follows:

i   u

e   o

ɛ   ɔ

a

Filling in the following chart will help you organize your data and see the patterns more clearly. Indicate the spelling for each phonetic sequence that exists in Italian. (Two of the listed sequences do not exist.) In certain cases, more than one spelling is possible.

[či] _____   [ki] _____   [kyi] _____   [kwi] _____

[če] _____   [ke] _____   [kye] _____   [kwe] _____

[čɛ] _____   [kɛ] _____   [kyɛ] _____   [kwɛ] _____

[ča] _____   [ka] _____   [kya] _____   [kwa] _____

[čo] _____   [ko] _____   [kyo] _____   [kwo] _____

[čɔ] _____   [kɔ] _____   [kyɔ] _____   [kwɔ] _____

[ču] _____   [ku] _____   [kyu] _____   [kwu] _____

2. Now summarize your findings by giving the required spelling rules for [k] and [č]. Be as general as possible.

   EXAMPLE   [k] is spelled _____ before _____ vowels.

_____

_____

_____

_____

_____

_____

_____

Name _____   **Section** _____   **Date** _____

B. Fill in the blanks:

Italian Spelling	Phonetic Transcription	Gloss
1. china	_____	'slope'
2. cima	_____	'summit'
3. _____	[često]	'basket'
4. ciao	_____	'So long!'
5. _____	[kyaro]	'light'
6. taciuto	_____	'withheld'
7. _____	[kwiɛto]	'quiet'
8. _____	[poko]	'little'
9. _____	[pokissimo]	'very little'
10. _____	[skermo]	'screen'

Italian uses the letter *g* to spell the sounds [g] and [ǰ], based on principles similar to those for [k] and [č]. Fill in the blanks as before.

Italian Spelling	Phonetic Transcription	Gloss
11. _____	[garbo]	'grace'
12. _____	[girbo]	'skin'
13. _____	[ǰakka]	'jacket'
14. giammai	_____	'never'
15. _____	[ǰorǰo]	'George'
16. giusto	_____	'right, fair'
17. _____	[gepardo]	'cheetah'

C. We can say a spelling system is *unambiguous* if the phonetic form of a word is always determinable from its orthography. Judging from the data, how unambiguous is the Italian spelling system? Is the pronunciation always clear from the word's written form, or do cases of uncertainty exist? Using the data, explain and illustrate.

_____

_____

_____

_____

_____

Name _____   **Section** _____   **Date** _____

🎧 9.05   WRITING SYSTEMS: Modern Greek

The Modern Greek alphabet consists of twenty-four letters, with the same distinction between upper- and lowercase as the Roman alphabet has. This exercise will familiarize you with the uppercase (capital) letters and with some of the sounds they represent.

A. Compare these Modern Greek words, written in "all caps," with their phonetic transcriptions. (Stress has not been indicated.) By carefully comparing the orthography and the transcriptions, you should be able to determine the most common sound for each written symbol. Write their phonetic values in the following chart. (*Note:* The combinations $\widehat{ps}$ and $\widehat{ks}$ function as single phonemes in Greek.)

ΠΟΛΥΚΑΤΑΣΤΗΜΑ	[polikatastima]	'department store'
ΔΙΟΡΘΩΝΩ	[ðiorθono]	'I correct'
ΓΡΑΦΟΜΗΧΑΝΗ	[ɣrafomixani]	'typewriter'
ΨΕΚΑΖΕΤΕ	[p͡sekazete]	'you sprinkle'
ΞΕΒΓΑΖΩ	[k͡sevɣazo]	'I rinse'

A _____   B _____   Γ_____   Δ _____   E _____   Z _____   H _____   Θ_____

I _____   K_____   Λ_____   M _____   N_____   Ξ_____   O_____   Π _____

P_____   Σ_____   T_____   Y_____   Φ_____   X_____   Ψ_____   Ω _____

B. *Digraphs* are combinations of two letters used to represent a single sound, such as English *sh* for [ʃ]. Determine the digraphs in the following data, and give their phonetic values:

ΜΠΟΡΟΥΜΕ	[borume]	'we can'
ΝΤΡΕΠΟΜΑΙ	[drepome]	'I am ashamed'
ΓΚΡΕΜΙΖΕΙ	[gremizi]	'he pulls down'
ΥΙΟΘΕΤΗΜΕΝΟΙ	[ioθetimeni]	'adopted' (m. pl.)

_____

_____

_____

_____

_____

C. 1.   List the ways the sound [i] can be spelled in Modern Greek.

_____

2.   Speculate on how Modern Greek came to have so many ways to spell the same sound.

_____

_____

_____

Name _____   **Section** _____   **Date** _____

 9.06   WRITING SYSTEMS: Modern Hebrew

The Hebrew alphabet consists of twenty-two letters. Five of these letters change their shape depending on their position in the word. The writing runs from right to left.

All twenty-two letters represent consonants. Two of these, however, are usually "silent" in Modern Hebrew; at the beginning of a word, they indicate the word begins with a vowel. Some letters have more than one pronunciation. Among these ambiguous letters are several that do double duty as vowels.

In the list below, forms in parentheses are "final" letters—variants used exclusively at the end of a word.

1.	א	silent, ʔ		9.	ט	t		17.	(ף)פ p, f
2.	ב	b, v		10.	י	j, i, ɛ		18.	(ץ)צ t͡s
3.	ג	g		11.	(ך)כ	k, x		19.	ק k
4.	ד	d		12.	ל	l		20.	ר r
5.	ה	h, final a		13.	(ם)מ	m		21.	ש ʃ, s
6.	ו	v, u, ɔ		14.	(ן)נ	n		22.	ת t
7.	ז	z		15.	ס	s			
8.	ח	x		16.	ע	silent, ʔ			

With the exception of the three vowel symbols derived from consonants (numbers 5, 6, and 10), vowels are not indicated in ordinary Hebrew texts. Thus the sequence כתב can stand for any of the following:

katav	'he wrote'
kᵊtɔv	'write!' (m. sg. imp.)
kitɛv	'he wrote a lot'
katɛv	'write a lot!' (m. sg. imp.)
kᵊtav	'writing, script'

Even though most vowels are not normally indicated, educated native speakers of Hebrew usually can look at the consonantal outline of a word and determine the correct vowels from context and their knowledge of the language. On occasion, however, ambiguities arise. For this reason—and also to serve the needs of dictionary users and language learners—a system was devised to indicate the normally unwritten vowels. This system of "vowel points," originally invented to fix the pronunciation of Biblical Hebrew texts, can be used in Modern Hebrew not only to differentiate vowels but also to determine the pronunciation of certain ambiguous consonant symbols.

For this exercise, you will need to recognize the following consonant distinctions and vowel symbols:

שׁ	ʃ	כּ	k	בּ	b	פּ	p
שׂ	s	כ	x	ב	v	פ	f

_____ . or _____ ּ֫   i

_____ ..   or _____ ֵ   ɛ

_____ ָ   or _____ ַ   a

_____ ֹ   or _____ וֹ   ɔ

וּ   u

_____ ְ   ə

Thus, בָ ba, בוֹ bɔ, בִי bi, etc.

A. For the letters כ, ב, and פ, formulate a generalization explaining the function of the internal dot.

_____

_____

_____

_____

B. The following Hebrew words are given both in their ordinary and "pointed" forms. Give the phonetic transcription in each case.

שלום	שָׁלוֹם	_____	'hello, goodbye, peace'
כשר	כֹּשֵׁר	_____	'ritually fit or proper'
פורים	פּוּרִים	_____	(a Jewish holiday)
יום כפור	יוֹם כִּפּוּר	_____	(a Jewish holiday)
תל אביב	תֵּל אָבִיב	_____	(place name)
ירושלים	יְרוּשָׁלַיִם	_____	(place name)
עדן	עֵדֶן	_____	(biblical place name)
אדם	אָדָם	_____	(biblical character)
שטן	שָׂטָן	_____	(biblical character)

Name _____   **Section** _____   **Date** _____

9.07   WRITING SYSTEMS: Persian

Persian uses a modified version of the Arabic writing system for its orthography. It has thirty-two letters, twenty-eight of which are borrowed from Arabic; four letters were added to represent the Persian sounds not found in Arabic, namely *p, g, tʃ,* and *ʒ.* The writing runs from right to left.

The six vowels of Persian—*i, u, a, e, o, æ*—are incompletely represented in the orthography. The first three are always written; *e* is written only at the end of a word; *o* and *æ* are indicated very rarely. (Diacritic symbols written above and below the script can indicate all these vowels, but these are used only in special circumstances—dictionaries, children's books, etc.) Most of the vowels that do appear in writing are represented by certain consonants doing double duty as vowels, much the same as the English letter *y.*

This exercise introduces you to twelve Persian letters. Most of these are joined to each other continuously in writing; a few are never joined to the following letter. (Bear in mind that the "following" letter is the one to the *left*!) The chart below shows you the various ways each of these can appear in a word; the most extreme case of variation is with *h,* which has four quite distinct shapes.

Note: Following a nonjoining letter, the next letter is in the initial form unless it is the last letter of the word, in which case it is in the isolated form.

Sound	Shapes				Remarks
	In Isolation	*Initial*	*Medial*	*Final*	
See remarks.	ا	ا	ـا	ـا	Used for [a]. Not joined to the following letter. Initially, indicates the word begins with a vowel.
b	ب	بـ	ـبـ	ـب	
p	پ	پـ	ـپـ	ـپ	
t	ت	تـ	ـتـ	ـت	
r	ر	ر	ـر	ـر	Not joined to the following letter.
s	س	سـ	ـسـ	ـس	
ʃ	ش	شـ	ـشـ	ـش	
f	ف	فـ	ـفـ	ـف	
n	ن	نـ	ـنـ	ـن	
v	و	و	ـو	ـو	Used for [u]. Not joined to the following letter.
h	ه	هـ	ـهـ	ـه	In final position, used to indicate *e*.
j	ی	یـ	ـیـ	ـی	Used for [i]. Notice when the dots disappear!

A. By comparing the following Persian words with the chart, you can match them with their pronunciations and glosses. As you analyze each word, keep in mind that with the exception of ی, *the dots remain intact in all positions* even though the shape of the letter may change.

Write the letter(s) of the transcription that corresponds to each written word in the space provided.

1. رو _____	_____	a. poʃt	'back'
2. راه _____	_____	b. tup	'ball'
3. نان _____	_____	c. behtær	'better'
4. باب _____	_____	d. nan	'bread'
5. سه _____	_____	e. bab	'chapter'
6. سی _____	_____	f. særʃir	'cream'
7. بیش _____	_____	g. orupa	'Europe'
8. توپ _____	_____	h. ru	'face'
9. هوش _____	_____	i. ʃiʃe	'glass'
10. اوف _____	_____	j. ensani	'human'
11. این _____	_____	k. huʃ	'intelligence'
12. است _____	_____	l. æst	'is'
13. پشت _____	_____	m. ræhbær	'leader'
14. ناهار _____	_____	n. navban	'lieutenant'
15. شیشه _____	_____	o. nahar	'lunch'
16. ناوبان _____	_____	p. biʃ	'more'
17. تنور _____	_____	q. uf	'ouch!'
18. فشار _____	_____	r. tænur	'oven'
19. روانی _____	_____	s. beheʃt	'paradise'
20. رهبر _____	_____	t. feʃar	'pressure'
21. بهتر _____	_____	u. piʃræft	'progress'

Name _____   **Section** _____   **Date** _____

22. سرشیر _____ _____   v. rævani   'psychological'

23. اروپا _____ _____   w. rah   'road'

24. اشاره _____ _____   x. eʃare   'sign'

25. تهران _____ _____   y. tabestan   'summer'

26. نیستی _____ _____   z. tehran   'Tehran'

27. بهشت _____ _____   aa. si   'thirty'

28. انسانی _____ _____   bb. in   'this'

29. تابستان _____ _____   cc. se   'three'

30. پیشرفت _____ _____   dd. nisti   'you're not'

B. Fill in the following blanks:

Orthography	Pronunciation	Gloss
1. _____	ba	'with'
2. _____	bi	'without'
3. فارس	_____	'Persian'
4. _____	tab	'warmth'
5. پاریس	_____	_____
6. _____	ʃah	'Shah'
7. _____	sup	'soup'
8. ایران	_____	_____

Name _____   **Section** _____   **Date** _____

 9.08   WRITING SYSTEMS: Korean Hangul

Hangul, the Korean alphabet, appeared in 1446 after King Sejong commissioned it. It is a phonemic writing system, well adapted to the structure of the language it transcribes. This exercise will acquaint you with several vowel and consonant symbols and the way they are put together to write Korean syllables.

A. By carefully analyzing the following Korean words in their Hangul orthography and comparing them with their phonetic transcriptions, you should be able to isolate the five vowel and eight consonant symbols in these data.

1.	공	[koŋ]	'ball'
2.	말	[mal]	'language'
3.	아무	[amu]	'any'
4.	덕분	[təkpun]	'favor'
5.	박	[pak]	'Park' (surname)
6.	누님	[nunim]	'older sister'
7.	로	[ro]	'to'
8.	번	[pən]	'time'
9.	삼	[sam]	'three'
10.	식사	[ʃiksa]	'meal'
11.	눈	[nun]	'snow'
12.	우리	[uri]	'we'
13.	일상	[ilsaŋ]	'daily'
14.	맏	[mat]	'first'
15.	부인	[puin]	'lady'
16.	사람	[saram]	'person'
17.	아니	[ani]	'no'
18.	국	[kuk]	'soup'
19.	비서	[pisə]	'secretary'
20.	사무	[samu]	'office work'
21.	구	[ku]	'nine'

1. List the symbols you have identified, grouping them by consonants and vowels. For each one, give its phonetic value or values according to the data.

	Symbol	**Phonetic Value(s)**
Consonants	_____	_____
	_____	_____
	_____	_____
	_____	_____
	_____	_____
	_____	_____
	_____	_____
	_____	_____
Vowels	_____	_____
	_____	_____
	_____	_____
	_____	_____

2. With the exception of ㅇ, each symbol you have identified stands for a single phoneme in Korean. For those phonemes having more than one allophone in the data, explain carefully how these allophones are distributed. In other words, what determines how the written symbol is pronounced?

_____

_____

_____

_____

_____

Name _____   **Section** _____   **Date** _____

3. Explain the use of ㅇ. Is this symbol ambiguous in context, or is its pronunciation always clearly determined?

_____

_____

_____

_____

B. Fill in the missing Hangul or the missing transcription.

Hangul	Transcription	Gloss
1. 부모	_____	'parents'
2. _____	[tari]	'bridge'
3. _____	[əməni]	'mother'
4. 서울	_____	(place name)
5. 건물	_____	'building'
6. _____	[pusan]	(place name)
7. 기숙사	_____	'dormitory'
8. _____	[paŋsoŋ]	'broadcasting'
9. _____	[kolmok]	'street corner'
10. 사무실	_____	'office'

Name _____   **Section** _____   **Date** _____

🎧 9.09   WRITING SYSTEMS: Japanese Hiragana

Japanese is considered to have one of the most complex writing systems in the world. In addition to *kanji*—characters borrowed from Chinese and used for most roots of nouns, verbs, adjectives, and adverbs—two distinct systems of *kana*, sound-based syllabic symbols, exist. The more important of these, *hiragana*, is used for native Japanese and Chinese-origin words and grammatical morphemes for which the two-thousand-odd *kanji* in common use are not suitable; *hiragana* can also substitute for *kanji* in various situations. The other syllabic system, *katakana*, is used mainly for borrowed words of non-Chinese origin and to transcribe foreign names. Japanese has also two somewhat different forms of romanization, or *roomaji*, used on public signs and for certain abbreviations. Literacy in Japanese entails fluency in all four of these systems, along with the ability to switch back and forth among them instantaneously; all four systems can in fact be used in the same written sentence.

This exercise will introduce you to 20 of the 103 *hiragana* symbols (46 basic and 57 derived or compound symbols).

A. Analyze the following twelve Japanese words, given in *hiragana* and *roomaji*. (Note: <sh> = [ʃ].) Then isolate the twenty different *hiragana* symbols they contain and give the pronunciation of each.

1. さす   sasu   'thrust; indicate'
2. のき   noki   'eaves'
3. あした   ashita   'tomorrow'
4. やがて   yagate   'soon'
5. うら   ura   'back'
6. みこし   mikoshi 'portable shrine'
7. もらう   morau   'receive'
8. かがみ   kagami   'mirror'
9. です   desu   'be'
10. こけし   kokeshi 'wooden doll'
11. だから   dakara   'therefore'
12. げき   geki   'drama'

Hiragana symbols found in these words, with their pronunciations:

1. _____   6. _____   11. _____   16. _____
2. _____   7. _____   12. _____   17. _____
3. _____   8. _____   13. _____   18. _____
4. _____   9. _____   14. _____   19. _____
5. _____   10. _____ 15. _____   20. _____

B. Now answer the following questions:

1. Examine the *hiragana* for the syllables *ko, no,* and *mo.* Is the phonetic similarity among these syllables reflected in their *hiragana* symbols? If so, how?

    _____

2. Now examine the *hiragana* for the syllables *ko, ka,* and *ki.* Is the fact that all three syllables contain the sound [k] reflected in the *hiragana*? If so, how?

    _____

3. Is *hiragana* an alphabet? Why or why not?

    _____

    _____

4. Judging from these data, do any *parts* of individual *hiragana* symbols have identifiable functions? If you find any, be as general as possible in your analysis, and refer to *classes* of sounds. (*Hint:* Consider ˋ.)

    _____

    _____

    _____

5. Here is the Japanese word for 'afternoon' written in *hiragana*. The syllabic symbols it uses are not among the ones you isolated. Nevertheless, you should be able to figure out how it is pronounced:

    ごご   *Pronunciation:* _____

C. The following Japanese words are familiar to many non-Japanese people. Transcribe them into *roomaji*.

すし	_____	さけ	_____
すきやき	_____	さしみ	_____
きもの	_____	からて	_____

Name _____   **Section** _____   **Date** _____

9.10   WRITING SYSTEMS: Chinese Characters

I. Pictographs, Ideographs, and Ideographic Compounds

Many people are under the impression Chinese characters are simply stylized pictures or dia-grams of the objects or ideas they represent. Although in fact the vast majority of Chinese char-acters *cannot* be so analyzed, a relatively small number do conform to this popular notion. In this part of the exercise you will be introduced to a few of these purely "pictorial" characters. (Man-darin pronunciations are given in the Pinyin romanization—see Appendix A.)

A. Pictographs. The Chinese characters that derive from pictures of the objects they represent have mostly evolved to the point where the visual connection between character and object is no longer obvious:

馬		mǎ	'horse'
魚		yú	'fish'
豕		shǐ	'swine'
人	(variant: 亻)	rén	'person'
女		nǚ	'woman'
子		zǐ	'child'

In a few cases, the evolutionary process that derived the modern characters can be inferred and then confirmed historically:

mù 'eye':   ⊂⊃   →   ⊂⊃   →   ⫿   →   目

Here are some examples of the relatively rare group of Chinese characters that still may bear something of a resemblance to what they represent. Try to match each character with its Man-darin pronunciation and meaning. Don't be surprised if the answers aren't entirely obvious! (*Hint:* It may help to look for drops of rain, people under an umbrella, a field divided into sec-tions, and a swinging saloon-type door.)

口	_____	a.	sǎn	'umbrella'
木	_____	b.	tián	'field'
山	_____	c.	mén	'door'
雨	_____	d.	mù	'tree, wood'
川	_____	e.	kǒu	'mouth'
田	_____	f.	yǔ	'rain'
傘	_____	g.	chuān	'river'
門	_____	h.	shān	'mountain'

B. Ideographs. A small group of Chinese characters are simple diagrams that "point to" the idea or relationship in question. Match these characters with their pronunciations and meanings.

中 _____	a. yī	'one'
下 _____	b. èr	'two'
二 _____	c. sān	'three'
一 _____	d. shàng	'above'
上 _____	e. xià	'below'
三 _____	f. zhōng	'middle, center'

C. Ideographic compounds. In this group of Chinese characters, two or more meaningful elements are combined to yield a compound character whose meaning is derived from the meanings of the components.

1. Examine the following compound characters and match them with their pronunciations and meanings. (In a few cases you will have to make an educated guess as to which of several possible alternatives is correct.) You should already know the meanings of most of the components from having worked part A. Here is the additional information you will need:

日 'sun'
月 'moon'
言 'speech'
宀 'roof'

明 _____	a. chuǎng	'force one's way in'
好 _____	b. ān	'safe, tranquil; peace'
信 _____	c. dāi	'slow witted, dull'
林 _____	d. míng	'bright, clear'
家 _____	e. jīng	'brilliant, shiny'
闖 _____	f. hǎo	'good'
安 _____	g. lín	'forest'
晶 _____	h. xìn	'believe'
呆 _____	i. jiā	'household'

Name _____   **Section** _____   **Date** _____

2. For each of these characters, explain briefly how the meaning of the whole is related to the meanings of the component parts.

chuǎng: _____

_____

_____

ān: _____

_____

_____

dāi: _____

_____

_____

míng: _____

_____

_____

jīng: _____

_____

_____

hǎo: _____

_____

_____

lín: _____

_____

_____

xìn: _____

_____

_____

jiā: _____

_____

_____

II. Phonetic Compounds

A common misconception is that Chinese characters are based exclusively on meaning. Actually, about 95 percent of contemporary characters have a partial phonetic basis.

An example will illustrate the basic principle. As you have seen, the word for 'horse' is mǎ, with the following pictographic character: 馬. Now another Chinese word, mā 'mother,' is similar in pronunciation—only the tone is different. Given the phonetic similarity, the character for mǎ 'horse' was *borrowed* to serve as the character for mā 'mother.' However, something had to be done to differentiate the two; otherwise, an unacceptable ambiguity would be created in the written language. To distinguish the two characters, a component was added to the character for 'mother' that would give a clue to its meaning. This component is 女, which as an independent character stands for 'woman.' Thus we now have the following two characters:

馬   mǎ   'horse'

媽   mā   'mother'

The first is a pictograph derived from a stylized picture of the object represented; the second is a *phonetic compound,* with a component (on the left in this case) giving a clue to the meaning and another component (on the right) giving a clue to the pronunciation. (Note that the character for 'mother' is *not* an ideographic compound—if it were, its meaning would probably be 'mare'!)

In phonetic compounds, the element giving a clue to the meaning is called the *signific, determinative,* or *radical**. The element that can hint at the pronunciation is called the *phonetic.*

In each of the following groups of compound characters, one element is common throughout the group. For each group, draw the common element in the space provided. Then determine whether it is the *signific* or the *phonetic.* If the former, make an educated guess as to its general meaning; if the latter, give the range of phonetic values in contemporary Mandarin represented in the data. (The romanization used here is the Pinyin system—see Appendix A.)

1. 請   qǐng   'please'

    清   qīng   'clear'

    睛   jīng   'eyeball'

*The term *radical* is not precisely equivalent to the other two, but the difference does not concern us here.

Name _____ Section _____ Date _____

情 qíng 'emotion'

晴 qíng 'good weather'

Common element:

[   ] Signific *Meaning:* _____

[   ] Phonetic *Values:* _____

2. 淋 lín 'drenched'

漂 piāo 'float'

灣 wān 'bay, gulf'

淚 lèi 'tears'

注 zhù 'pour'

Common element:

[   ] Signific *Meaning:* _____

[   ] Phonetic *Values:* _____

3. 國 guó 'country, nation'

園 yuán 'garden'

圖 tú 'picture, map'

圍 wéi 'surround, enclose'

圈 quān 'encircle'

Common element:

[   ] Signific *Meaning:* _____

[   ] Phonetic *Values:* _____

4. 刨   bào   'plane'

    跑   pǎo   'run'

    雹   báo   'hail'

    飽   bǎo   'full'

    苞   bāo   'bud'

Common element:

[   ] Signific   *Meaning:* _____

[   ] Phonetic   *Values:* _____

5. 肪   fáng   'fat'

    芳   fāng   'fragrant'

    坊   fāng   'lane'

    訪   fǎng   'visit'

    房   fáng   'dwelling'

Common element:

[   ] Signific   *Meaning:* _____

[   ] Phonetic   *Values:* _____

6. 疤   bā   'scar'

    痘   dòu   'smallpox'

    疼   téng   'ache, pain'

    癲   diān   'insane'

    病   bìng   'sick'

Common element:

[   ] Signific   *Meaning:* _____

[   ] Phonetic   *Values:* _____

Name _____   **Section** _____   **Date** _____

 ## 9.11   EVOLUTION OF WRITING SYSTEMS: Malay/Indonesian

Although their names are different, Malay and Indonesian are really two dialects of the same language. Malay speakers in Malaysia and Indonesian speakers in Indonesia usually can understand each other with no more difficulty than speakers of American and British English experience when they communicate with each other.

Nevertheless, the romanized orthography (that is, the method of writing using the Roman alphabet) for the two varieties was significantly different up through the 1960s. The reason for this discrepancy stems from the fact that the Malays and the Indonesians learned the Roman alphabet from different sources: The Malays learned it from the British, the Indonesians from the Dutch. In the early 1970s, the spelling systems in the two countries were unified.

Examine the following data. Columns I and II illustrate some of the earlier spelling conventions—one gives the older Malay spellings, the other the older Indonesian spellings. Column III gives the newer, unified spelling. Columns IV and V give the phonetic transcriptions and glosses.

	I	II	III	IV	V
1.	pulau	pulau	pulau	[pulau]	'island'
2.	tjakap	chakap	cakap	[tʃakap]	'speak'
3.	djalan	jalan	jalan	[dʒalan]	'road, way'
4.	dendang	dendang	dendang	[dəndaŋ]	'raven'
5.	achirnja	akhir-nya	akhirnya	[axirɲa]	'finally'
6.	zalim	dzalim	zalim	[zalim]	'cruel'
7.	sjarikat	sharikat	syarikat	[ʃarikat]	'company'
8.	jang	yang	yang	[yaŋ]	'which'
9.	dendang	dendang	dendang	[dendaŋ]	'song'
10.	masjhur	mashhur	masyhur	[maʃhur]	'famous'
11.	kadi	kadhi	kadi	[kadi]	'Muslim religious officer'
12.	djalan2	jalan2	jalan-jalan	[dʒalandʒalan]	'(various) ways'
13.	berdjalan2	berjalan2	berjalan-jalan	[bərdʒalandʒalan]	'stroll'
14.	leher	leher	leher	[leher]	'neck'
15.	air	ayer	air	[air]	'water'

A. Which column gives the older Malay spellings, and which the older Indonesian ones? How do you know?

_____

_____

_____

B. List the orthographic changes for Malay. (For example, *ch* became *c*.) Then do the same for Indonesian.

Changes for Malay		Changes for Indonesian	

Who do you think had the harder time adapting to the new system, the Malaysians or the Indonesians? Or was the burden equally shared? Give examples to support your position.

C. In what way(s) is the new spelling system superior to each of the old ones? What, if any, are the *disadvantages* of the new system compared to the old ones? Give examples.

D. Is the new system free of ambiguity? That is, does each written symbol in the new system have a unique pronunciation? Explain. Was the situation the same in the two older systems?

10

Historical and Comparative Linguistics

KEY TERMS AND SYMBOLS

See the glossary.

Affricate	Genetic relationship	Reconstruction
Assimilation	Gloss	Referent
Borrowing	Graph	Reflex
Cognates	Inflection	Root
Cognate set	Language family	Stem
Conditioned change	Lexical item	Stop
Consonant cluster	Merger	Subject
Daughter language	Nasalization	Synchronic process
Distinctive	Orthography	Transcription
Environment	Parent language	Unconditioned change
Etymon	Phoneme	
Gemination	Proto-	

Name _____   **Section** _____   **Date** _____

EXERCISES BASED ON ENGLISH

10.01   HISTORICAL DEVELOPMENT IN ENGLISH: A Text across Time

Reproduced here are four versions of the same biblical passage (Genesis 8: 6–11, relating events signaling the end of the forty-day flood) that exemplify the state of the English language at four different periods in its history—Old English, Middle English, Early Modern English, and Modern English. The texts bear striking witness to some of the many changes English has undergone in the past thousand years.

Examine the four versions carefully and compare them to each other. Then answer the questions that follow. Although the different translations are given in chronological order, you may find it easiest to begin with the Modern English version and work backward. (In the Old English version, certain words have been glossed to aid your understanding.) Bear in mind that not all the differences in these passages are reflections of language change; some are simply a result of choices made by different translators. (Texts taken from A.G. Rigg, ed., *The English Language: A Historical Reader* [New York: Appleton-Century-Crofts, 1968].)

Old English (OE)

⁶Ða æfter feowertigum dagum undyde Noe his eahðyrl, ðe he on ðam arce gemacode.
Then   undid   window which   the   made

⁷And asende ut ænne hremn: se hrem fleah ða ut, and nolde   eft   ongean cyrran,
     sent   out a   raven   the   would not again back turn

ær ðan ðe ða wæteru adruwodon ofer eorðan.
before   dried-up

⁸He asende ða eft ut ane culfran, ðæt heo sceawode
                      dove   show

gyf ða wætera ðagyt geswicon ofer ðære eorðan bradnysse.
if   yet   departed   earth's breadth

⁹Heo ða fleah ut and ne mihte findan hwær heo hire fot asette,
                          might   set

for ðan ðe ða wætera wæron ofer ealle eorðan;
because

and heo gecyrde ongean to Noe, and he genam hi in to ðam arce.
        turned   took

¹⁰He abad ða gyt oðre seofan dagas and asende ut eft culfran.
    waited   yet another   a dove

¹¹Heo com ða on æfnunge eft to Noe and brohte an twig of anum elebeame
              evening   an   olive tree

mid grenum leafum on hyre muðe. Ða undergeat Noe ðæt ða wætera wæron adruwode ofer eorðan.
                                    understood

Middle English (ME)

⁶And whanne fourti dais weren passid, Noe openyde the wyndow of the schip which he hadde maad, ⁷and sente out a crowe, which ȝede out and turnede not aȝen til the watris weren dried on erthe. ⁸Also Noe sente out a culuer aftir hym, to se if the watris hadden ceessid thanne on the face of erthe; ⁹and whanne the culuer foond not where hir foot schulde reste, sche turnede aȝen to hym in to the schip, for the watris weren on al erthe; and Noe helde forth his hoond, and brouȝte the culuer takun in to the schip. ¹⁰Sotheli whanne othere seuene daies weren abedun aftirward, eft he leet out a culuer fro the schip; ¹¹and sche cam to hym at euentid, and bare in hir mouth a braunche of olyue tre with greene leeuys. Therfor Noe vndirstood that the watris hadden ceessid on erthe.

Early Modern English (King James) (EModE)

⁶And it came to passe at the end of forty dayes, that Noah opened the window of the Arke which he had made. ⁷And he sent forth a Rauen, which went foorth to and fro, vntill the waters were dried vp from off the earth. ⁸Also hee sent foorth a doue from him, to see if the waters were abated from off the face of the ground. ⁹But the doue found no rest for the sole of her foote, and she returned vnto him into the Arke: for the waters were on the face of the whole earth. Then he put foorth his hand, and tooke her, and pulled her in vnto him, into the Arke. ¹⁰And hee stayed yet other seuen dayes; and againe hee sent foorth the doue out of the Arke. ¹¹And the doue came in to him in the euening, and loe, in her mouth was an Oliue leafe pluckt off: So Noah knew that the waters were abated from off the earth.

Modern English (ModE)

⁶At the end of forty days Noah opened the window that he had made in the ark, ⁷and released a raven, which went flying back and forth until the waters had dried off the earth. ⁸Then he released a dove, to see whether the waters had subsided from the surface of the land; ⁹but the dove could find no resting-place for the sole of her foot, so she came back to him into the ark; for there was water all over the earth. He put out his hand, and catching her, drew her into the ark with him. ¹⁰After waiting another seven days, he again released the dove from the ark; ¹¹in the evening the dove came back to him, and there, in her beak, was a freshly picked olive leaf! So Noah knew that the waters had subsided off the earth.

A. Find three examples in Old English and one example in Middle English of graphs that are no longer used. What sounds did these obsolete letters represent?

OE: _____

ME: _____

B. The letters *u* and *v* were used differently in earlier English than they are used today.

1. What rule accounts for the distribution of *u* and *v* in Middle English?

_____

Name _____   **Section** _____   **Date** _____

2. What is the corresponding rule in Early Modern English?

_____

3. What about Modern English—does such a rule exist today? Explain.

_____

C. The passages illustrate that English has lost lexical items over its history.

1. Find four examples of Old English nouns or verbs that are not found in Modern English, and give the meaning of each. Look for words that have completely disappeared.

_____

_____

2. Find two such examples in Middle English. _____

_____

3. Cite any such examples in the EModE version. If none, explain why.

_____

_____

D. Clauses.

1. Give an "interlinear translation" of the following Old English clauses—that is, write the modern translation of each Old English word directly under it.

   Ða   æfter   feowertigum   dagum   undyde   Noe   his   eahðyrl

   ___   _____   _____   _____   _____   _____   _____   _____

   Ða   undergeat Noe   ðæt   ða   wætera   wæron   adruwode ofer   eorðan

   ___   _____   _____   _____   ___   _____   _____   _____   _____   _____

2. How does the word order of these clauses differ from Modern English syntax? _____

_____

3. Compare the ME versions of these clauses. Is the syntax closer to OE or ModE? Explain.

_____

_____

E. Find 2 different forms of *have* in Middle English. What determines which form is used?

_____

_____

F. Verse 9.

1. Give the corresponding OE and ME versions of this section of verse 9:

   Early Modern English: for the waters were on the face of the whole earth

   Middle English: _____

   Old English: _____

2. How has the word for *were* changed over time? Explain. _____

   _____

3. How do the earlier forms of *were* relate to your answer to part E? _____

   _____

4. Give the subjects of these Old English verbs, and state whether they are singular or plural.

   undyde (6)   _____   geswicon (8)   _____

   gemacode (6)   _____   wæron (9)   _____

   adruwodon (7)   _____   gecyrde (9)   _____

   asende (8)   _____   brohte (11)   _____

   What generalization(s) can you draw about the inflections on these verbs? _____

   _____

   _____

Name _____   **Section** _____   **Date** _____

10.02   HISTORICAL DEVELOPMENT IN ENGLISH:
Lexical Change from Shakespeare to Modern English

Much of the difficulty modern readers have in understanding Early Modern English texts stems from the fact that in these texts, familiar words often have unfamiliar meanings.

Examine the following excerpts from *Hamlet*. Each underlined word is found in present-day English but has an unfamiliar meaning in Shakespeare's play. Write the modern equivalent of each such word in the spaces provided, and then "translate" the entire excerpt into Modern English. To make it easier for you to fill in the blanks, we have provided an alphabetical list of words to choose from; each word in the list is to be used only once. In some instances you may have to make an educated guess as to the correct meaning.

> **EXAMPLE**   . . . it doth much <u>content</u> me   <u>please</u>
> . . . it pleases me very much . . .

bitterest	head	ostentation
catch	hinders	partners
ceremony	inexperienced	pearl
contrary	innocent	pleases
courtesy	intensely	power
frank	knocks	secretly
handkerchief	living	visor
handwriting	at once	

1. If you do meet Horatio and Marcellus,   _____
   The <u>rivals</u> of my watch, bid them make haste. (I, i)

   _____

   _____

2.   For your intent   _____
   In going back to school in Wittenberg,
   It is most <u>retrograde</u> to our desire; (I, ii)

   _____

   _____

3. Would I had met my <u>dearest</u> foe in heaven   _____
   Or ever I had seen that day, Horatio! (I, ii)

   _____

   _____

4. *Ham.* Then saw you not his face?

    Hor. O, yes, my lord! He wore his <u>beaver</u> up. (I, ii)

          _____

5. Affection? Pooh! You speak like a green girl,

    <u>Unsifted</u> in such perilous circumstance. (I, iii)

          _____

6. The air bites <u>shrewdly</u>; it is very cold. (I, iv)

          _____

7. By heaven, I'll make a ghost of him that <u>lets</u> me! (I, iv)

          _____

8. And so without more <u>circumstance</u> at all,

    I hold it fit that we shake hands and part; (I, iv)

          _____

9.   If it will please you

    To show us so much <u>gentry</u> and good will . . . (II, ii)

          _____

10. For we have <u>closely</u> sent for Hamlet hither. (III, i)

          _____

11. . . . ay, there's the <u>rub</u>! (III, i)

          _____

Name _____   **Section** _____   **Date** _____

12. . . . we that have <u>free</u> souls, it touches us not. (III, ii)   _____

_____

13. My lord, the Queen would speak with you, and <u>presently</u>. (III, ii)   _____

_____

14. Pray you be <u>round</u> with him. (III, iv)   _____

_____

15. O heat, dry up my brains! Tears seven times salt   _____
     Burn out the sense and <u>virtue</u> of mine eye! (IV, v)

_____

_____

16. His beard was as white as snow,   _____
     All flaxen was his <u>poll</u>. (IV, v)

_____

17. *Laer.* Know you the hand?   _____
     King. 'Tis Hamlet's <u>character</u>. (IV, vii)

_____

18. How the knave <u>jowls</u> it to the ground, as if 'twere Cain's jawbone,   _____
     that did the first murder! (V, i)

_____

_____

19. 'Tis for the dead, not for the <u>quick</u>. (V, i)   _____

_____

20. But sure the <u>bravery</u> of his grief did put me
    Into a tow'ring passion. (V, ii)   _____

    _____

    _____

21. This <u>likes</u> me well. (V, ii)   _____

    _____

22. And in the cup an <u>union</u> shall he throw   _____
    Richer than that which four successive kings
    In Denmark's crown have worn. (V, ii)

    _____

    _____

    _____

23. Here, Hamlet, take my <u>napkin</u>, rub thy brows. (V, ii)   _____

    _____

Name _____   **Section** _____   **Date** _____

EXERCISES BASED ON OTHER LANGUAGES

10.03   LANGUAGE COMPARISON: Classification of Lexical Similarities

Despite the general arbitrariness of the relationship between a word and its referent, words referring to the same or similar things are sometimes similar in different languages. Four basic explanations for such similarities exist:

1. *Genetic Relationship.* The similar lexical items may be reflexes of an earlier, common source in a common ancestral language.

2. *Borrowing.* One language may borrow a lexical item from another, or both may borrow similar items from an outside source or sources.

3. *Universal Tendency.* In a very limited number of cases, observed similarities are the result of something universal in human physiology, psychology, or perception. An oft-cited example is the observation that many languages, related or not, have an *m* in their word for 'mother,' presumably a consequence of the fact the bilabial nasal is one of the first speech sounds nursing babies learn to produce. Diverse languages often have a high front vowel in words or morphemes denoting smallness or diminution: English *teeny;* Spanish *poco* 'some, a little,' *poquito* 'very little,' *poquitito* 'extremely small amount'—something about the [i] sound seems to convey a "small" feeling. Words that are onomatopoetic—i.e., that attempt to mimic actual sounds—also fall into this category. For example, words for the sounds made by cats, sheep, and cows are often (but not always) similar across languages.

4. *Coincidence.* If no other plausible reason presents itself, we have to conclude that the similarity is due to chance. Clearly, the probability of a chance resemblance is inversely proportional to the length of the word. It is highly unlikely that two seven-syllable words will be similar by coincidence; with short lexical items, chance resemblances can occur more frequently.

For each of the following paired languages and lexical items, determine the most plausible explanation for the similarity. In the space provided, write C for coincidence, UT for universal tendency, B for borrowing, or GR for genetic relationship. In the case of borrowing, also indicate the *source* of the borrowed item: Which language borrowed from which, or was an *outside* source (or sources) involved?

In a few cases you may have to make an educated guess as to the correct explanation. But you usually will be able to arrive at the most plausible answer by a process of deduction, using your knowledge of language families and language change and assessing the likelihood that borrowing occurred. (Some questions to ask yourself: What is the chance speakers of the two languages were in contact? Did any political or cultural influence encourage the borrowing of words? Was it likely the need arose in one or both languages to refer to something "new" for which a convenient word didn't already exist?) One caution to bear in mind: *When two languages are genetically related, it does not necessarily follow that every observed similarity between them is a result of their genetic relationship.*

Note: In these data, words from languages that employ the Roman alphabet appear in their standard orthography (Mandarin Chinese is in Pinyin—see Appendix A), with occasional phonetic transcriptions in brackets. Words from other languages appear in transcription unless otherwise indicated.

1. *Japanese:*   futtobooru   'football'
   English: football
   _____

   _____

2. *Hebrew:*   ʃalɔm   'peace; a greeting'
   Arabic: salaːm   'peace; a greeting'
   _____

   _____

3. *German:*   Haus [haws]   'house'
   English: house
   _____

   _____

4. *Hawaiian:*   aloha   'love; a greeting'
   Maori: aroha   'love; a greeting'
   _____

   _____

5. *Greek:*   ne   'yes'
   Korean: ne   'yes'
   _____

   _____

6. *English:*   Halleluyah
   Hebrew: halᵊluja   'Halleluyah'
   _____

   _____

7. *Portuguese:* libro   'book'
   French: livre   'book'
   _____

   _____

8. *Persian:*   bæradær   'brother'
   English: brother
   _____

   _____

Name _____   **Section** _____   **Date** _____

9. *English:*   tofu

    Chinese: dofu   'tofu'   _____

_____

10. *German:*   fünf   'five'

    Welsh: pump [pɪmp]   'five'   _____

_____

11. *Anc. Greek:*   hüpo   'under'

    English: hypo-   'under' (prefix)   _____

_____

12. *Welsh:*   deg   'ten'

    Latin: decem   'ten'   _____

_____

13. *French:*   weekend [wikɛnd]   'weekend'

    English: weekend   _____

_____

14. *Persian:*   to   'you' (sg. familiar)

    Spanish: tu   'you' (sg. familiar)   _____

_____

15. *Norwegian:*   nei   'no'

    English: nay   _____

_____

16. *English:*   neuron

    Anc. Greek: neuron   'nerve, sinew'   _____

_____

17. *Russian:*   dva   'two'
    Malay: dua   'two'   _____

_____

18. *Hebrew:*   ima   'mommy'
    Malay: emak   'mother'   _____

_____

19. *German:*   Messer   'knife'
    Yiddish: mɛsɛr   'knife'   _____

_____

20. *Polish:*   człowiek   'man'
    Czech: člověk   'man'   _____

_____

21. *Japanese:*   naifu   'knife'
    English: knife   _____

_____

22. *Mod. Greek:* mitera   'mother'
    German: Mutter   'mother'   _____

_____

23. *Hungarian:*   radio   'radio'
    Finnish: radio   'radio'   _____

_____

24. *English:*   snow
    Dutch: sneeuw   'snow'   _____

_____

25. *Arabic:*   ana   'I'
    Hebrew: ani   'I'   _____

_____

Name _____   **Section** _____   **Date** _____

26. *Welsh:*   hi   'she'

    Hebrew: hi   'she'   _____

    _____

27. *Yiddish:*   mɪdbɛr   'desert'

    Hebrew: midbar   'desert'   _____

    _____

28. *French:*   os   'bone'

    Romanian: os   'bone'   _____

    _____

29. *Malay:*   kamus   'dictionary'

    Swahili: kamusi   'dictionary'   _____

    _____

30. *Hungarian:* grépfrút   'grapefruit'

    Turkish: grepfrut   'grapefruit'   _____

    _____

31. *Persian:*   xahær   'sister'

    Welsh: chwaer [xwaer] 'sister'   _____

    _____

32. *English:*   egg

    Norwegian: egg   'egg'   _____

    _____

33. *French:*   grand   'big, great'

    English: grand   _____

    _____

34. *Yiddish:*   ɪz   'is'
    English: is   _____

    _____

35. *English:*   thou
    Icelandic: þu [θu]   'you' (sg. familiar)   _____

    _____

36. *Persian:*   mahi   'fish'
    Hawaiian: mahi-mahi   'kind of fish'   _____

    _____

37. *English:*   taboo
    Tongan: tapu   'forbidden'   _____

    _____

38. *Japanese:*   densha   'streetcar'
    Chinese: diànchē   'streetcar'   _____

    _____

39. *Chinese:*   gōngchang   'factory'
    Korean: koŋtʃaŋ   'factory'   _____

    _____

40. *Malay:*   orang utan   'person of the forest'
    English: orangutan   _____

    _____

41. *Japanese:*   anata   'you'
    Arabic: anta   'you' (m. sg.)   _____

    _____

42. *Malay:*   salam alaikum   'peace be upon you' (a greeting)
    Yiddish: ʃʌləm aleixɛm   'peace be upon you' (a greeting)   _____

    _____

Name _____   **Section** _____   **Date** _____

 10.04   PHONOLOGICAL CHANGE: Greek

This problem concerns a particular phonological development in Greek—the changes in the pronunciation of the Ancient Greek stops. The data below give you the ancient and modern pronunciations of some words common to both stages of the language. You'll notice many changes that took place along the way, but you should concentrate on what became of the original stops. *Note:* The transcription is phonemic—that is, every symbol represents a different phoneme.

	Ancient Greek	Modern Greek	Gloss
1.	agapaoː	aɣapao	'I love'
2.	glüküs	ɣlikos	'sweet'
3.	diapʰtʰeiroː	ðiafθiro	'corrupt'
4.	düstükʰeːs	ðistixis	'unfortunate'
5.	grapʰoː	ɣrafo	'I write'
6.	tʰeatron	θeatro	'theater'
7.	blaptoː	vlapto	'I harm'
8.	karpos	karpos	'fruit'
9.	badizoː	vaðizo	'I walk'
10.	ptosis	ptosi	'fall'
11.	pʰtʰora	fθora	'destruction'
12.	pʰoberos	foveros	'fearful'
13.	kʰtʰes	xθes	'yesterday'
14.	tekʰniteːs	texnitis	'craftsman'

A. On the following chart, indicate the position of each of the Ancient Greek stops.

	Labial	Alveolar	Velar
Voiceless Aspirated			
Voiceless Unaspirated			
Voiced Unaspirated			

B. For each ancient stop, indicate the corresponding sound in Modern Greek. Your answers should consist of statements of the form *A > B, where *A is an ancient stop and B is its modern reflex.

_____

_____

_____

_____

C. Now generalize from the individual sound changes you identified in part B. How did whole *classes* of sounds change in the journey from Ancient to Modern Greek?

_____

_____

_____

_____

Name _____   **Section** _____   **Date** _____

10.05   PHONOLOGICAL CHANGE: Persian

Below you will find transcriptions of some Persian words that contain short vowels. The modern Iranian pronunciation is given alongside the pronunciation at an earlier stage of the language.

Examine the differences between the earlier and modern pronunciations, and then answer the questions that follow.

	Earlier Persian	Modern Persian	Gloss
1.	guft	goft	's/he said'
2.	zærtuʃt	zærtoʃt	'Zoroaster'
3.	ʃæbækæ	ʃæbæke	'network'
4.	sift	seft	'stiff'
5.	sipurdæn	sepordæn	'to deposit'
6.	giriftæ	gerefte	'taken'
7.	gurusnæ	gorosne	'hungry'
8.	nigæh	negæh	'look'
9.	zindæ	zende	'alive'
10.	muslim	moslem	'Muslim'

A. State all the sound changes evident from the data. Determine whether each change is *unconditioned* (occurring across the board, independent of environment) or *conditioned* (occurring only in certain environments). For the conditioned changes, identify the environment in which they took place.

_____

_____

_____

_____

_____

_____

_____

B. Diagram the Persian short vowel system at the two different stages of the language the data represent.

Earlier Short Vowels

Modern Short Vowels

C. Referring to the diagrams you drew in B, what generalizations can you state about the sound changes you've identified?

_____

_____

_____

_____

_____

_____

Name _____   **Section** _____   **Date** _____

    ## 10.06   PHONOLOGICAL CHANGE: Comparative Romance 1

Examine this list of cognates in three Romance languages—Spanish, Italian, and French—and answer the questions that follow.

   Note: The data are given in the standard orthography for each of the languages. In all of these words, <c> = [k].

	Spanish	Italian	French	Gloss
1.	acto	atto	acte	'act'
2.	óptico	ottico	optique	'optic'
3.	obturador	otturatore	obturateur	'shutter'
4.	selectiva	selettiva	sélective	'selective'
5.	flota	flotta	flotte	'fleet'
6.	eléctrico	elettrico	électrique	'electric'
7.	abdomen	addome	abdomen	'abdomen'
8.	apto	atto	apte	'apt'
9.	último	ultimo	ultime	'last'
10.	octubre	ottobre	octobre	'October'
11.	antagonista	antagonista	antagoniste	'antagonist'
12.	septiembre	settembre	septembre	'September'
13.	carta	carta	carte	'card'
14.	correcta	corretta	correcte	'correct'
15.	adoptar	adottare	adopter	'to adopt'
16.	súbdito	suddito	—	'subject'
17.	obtener	ottenere	obtenir	'to obtain'
18.	sospechar	sospettare	suspecter	'to suspect'
19.	letra	lettera	lettre	'letter'
20.	optimista	ottimista	optimiste	'optimist'

A. The data give clear evidence of a phonological change involving adjacent consonants that occurred in the development of one of the languages. Which language was this?

_____

B. Make a "before and after" list of all the sound changes that took place in this language as part of the process you've identified. Your goal is to isolate the *parts* of the words in the data that have changed and thus to "boil down" the data to the essentials.

Before the Change	After the Change

C. Examining the sound changes you've isolated in the previous question, form a *general statement of the process*. Your statement should not include specific cases yet must cover all (and only!) the sound changes in the data that were part of this process. You may want to use the words "assimilate" or "assimilation" in your answer. (See the glossary for a definition of *assimilation*.)

_____

_____

_____

D. Assimilation can be *partial* or *complete* and *progressive* or *regressive*. The former pair of terms refers to whether the sound change results in partial similarity or complete identity; the latter refers to the direction of influence—whether the first sound influenced the second or vice versa. Characterize the process you've identified using these terms:

The process is an example of _____, _____ assimilation.

E. Phonological processes sometimes result in *lexical mergers*—two words or morphemes that have become identical. Does any evidence for lexical mergers exist in the data? Explain.

_____

_____

_____

F. Based on your analysis of the data you've seen and not on any prior knowledge of these languages, can you fill in the missing members of the following two cognate sets with reasonable confidence? Explain how sure you can be of the answer in each case.

Spanish	Italian
contacto	_____
_____	ottava

_____

_____

_____

Name _____   **Section** _____   **Date** _____

  ## 10.07   PHONOLOGICAL CHANGE: Comparative Romance 2

A. Study this list of cognates in Spanish, Italian, and Portuguese, paying particular attention to final vowels. Then answer the questions that follow. *Note:* These data are given in phonetic transcription. The Portuguese transcription reflects Brazilian pronunciation current in Sao Paolo.

	Spanish	Italian	Portuguese	Gloss
1.	libro	libro	livru	'book'
2.	fama	fama	fãmə	'fame'
3.	sentro	tʃɛntro	sẽtru	'center'
4.	grande	grande	grãdʒi	'big'
5.	kwatro	kwattro	kwatru	'four'
6.	alto	alto	awtu	'tall'
7.	kanta	kanta	kãtə	'sings'
8.	diɣo	diko	dʒigu	'I say'
9.	fwerte	fɔrte	fɔrtʃi	'strong'
10.	famosa	famoza	famɔzə	'famous'
11.	nweβe	nɔve	nɔvi	'nine'
12.	alta	alta	awtə	'tall'
13.	seðe	sɛde	sɛdʒi	'seat'
14.	base	baze	bazi	'base'
15.	karo	karo	karu	'dear'
16.	bale	vale	vali	'is worth'
17.	fiesta	fɛsta	fɛstə	'party'
18.	latina	latina	latʃinə	'Latin'
19.	dentista	dentista	dẽtʃistə	'dentist'
20.	tanto	tanto	tãtu	'so much'

1. As evidenced by the data, list the individual sound changes that have occurred in the final vowels of Portuguese. Assume that the Spanish and Italian final vowels, which agree in these data, represent the sounds from which the Portuguese final vowels evolved. You should come up with three statements of the form "*A > B in final position."

_____

_____

_____

_____

2. Fill in the following vowel charts to illustrate this phonological process graphically. On each chart, simply indicate the positions of the three vowels involved in the process.

		Front	Central	Back
Before *the* *Change*	High			
	Mid			
	Low			

		Front	Central	Back
After *the* *Change*	High			
	Mid			
	Low			

3. Now write a single statement that covers all three of the sound changes you've identified. Your statement should not make reference to specific vowels but should be a *linguistically significant generalization* that refers to classes of vowels.

_____

_____

_____

_____

4. The phonological process you've identified is a natural and expected one and has happened in many languages. It would be rare to find a language with the reverse process, i.e., *B > A instead of *A > B in the same environment. Why is the original process natural and the reverse one unusual? (*Hint:* Consider what the process means in terms of your vocal apparatus and why this should be a natural occurrence at the end of a word.)

_____

_____

_____

_____

Name _____   **Section** _____   **Date** _____

_____

_____

B. Now focus your attention on the Portuguese *affricates*. What sound changes have occurred in Portuguese that resulted in these affricates? Again, assume that the corresponding sounds in Spanish and Italian represent the sounds from which these affricates evolved. Find two such sound changes, and then find the single generalization that captures both of them. Were these changes *conditioned* (taking place only in specific environments) or *unconditioned* (independent of environment)?

_____

_____

_____

_____

_____

C. The Portuguese word for 'I could' is spelled *pude*. Assume this spelling represents the earlier pronunciation of the word before the sound changes you have identified occurred. Show by means of phonetic transcription how this word is pronounced today. Then show step-by-step how this pronunciation evolved. (You may be reminded of the type of synchronic phonology problem in which you are required to show how phonological rules apply to an underlying form to yield the correct surface form.)

_____

_____

_____

_____

_____

_____

Name _____   Section _____   Date _____

 10.08   PHONOLOGICAL CHANGE: Borrowed Items

When a language borrows a word, it usually adapts the pronunciation to its own phonological system. Thus, for example, although the Spanish term *burrito* is used by many non-Spanish-speaking Americans to refer to a popular item in Mexican cuisine, its pronunciation is usually anglicized—the first vowel is reduced to a schwa, the strongly-trilled Spanish *rr* becomes an English *r*, the intervocalic *t* becomes a voiced flap, and the final vowel is diphthongized:

Sp. [bur̃ito]   Eng. [bərirоᵂ]

Similarly, many Japanese enjoy playing *gorufu,* wearing *jinzu,* and having *dezato* at the end of their meals.*

Observing what happens to borrowed items can yield information about the phonology of the borrowing language. That is what you will be doing in this exercise, which concerns Arabic borrowings in two unrelated languages, Persian and Malay/Indonesian (MI).

Arabic has had a strong influence on many languages of Asia and Africa. On Persian, the influence has been profound: More than half the lexicon of Modern Persian has been borrowed from Arabic. MI has not absorbed Arabic terms quite so extensively, but the Arabic element in its vocabulary is nevertheless significant.

In the following data, you will find twenty Arabic words, each of which has been borrowed by both Persian and MI. The Persianized and Malayanized loan forms have some interesting differences. Compare these forms with their sources, and then answer the questions that follow.

Notes:

1. The data are transcribed phonemically in modern Standard Arabic, Persian, and MI. If you are not familiar with some of the symbols used in the Arabic, you will find them explained in Appendix B.

2. MI and Persian borrowed from Arabic at different times in their history; however, you can regard the Arabic transcriptions as fairly representative of the language when both the Persians and Malays borrowed these terms, since Standard Arabic has been extremely conservative phonologically.

3. The Persian alterations to the nonlow vowels are the result of a phonological change that occurred in Persian after the time of borrowing. (See problem 10.05.)

4. The glosses given are for identification purposes only and are not necessarily exact for all three languages.

Arabic	Persian	MI	Gloss
1. badan	bædæn	badan	'body'
2. salaːm	sælam	salam	'peace'

*golf, jeans, dessert

	Arabic	Persian	MI	Gloss
3.	ḍarb	zærb	darab	'strike; multiply'
4.	ðˤaːhir	zaher	lahir/zahir	'apparent; visible'
5.	zamaːn	zæman	zaman	'time, period'
6.	hudhud	hodhod	hudhud	'hoopoe' (bird)
7.	ħalaːl	hælal	halal	'religiously permissible'
8.	θaːbit	sabet	sabit	'fixed, constant'
9.	ðikr	zekr	zikir	'remembrance'
10.	ðˤuhr	zohr	zuhur/luhur	'midday; noon prayer'
11.	ħaːḍir	hazer	hadir	'present'
12.	baħθ	bæhs	bahas	'debate'
13.	diːn	din	din	'religion'
14.	ṣubħ	sobh	subuh	'daybreak'
15.	ṣabr	sæbr	sabar	'patient'
16.	ðaːt	zat	zat	'essence; vitamin'
17.	dʒaːhil	dʒahel	dʒahil	'ignorant'
18.	madʒlis	mædʒles	madʒlis	'assembly'
19.	siħr	sehr	sihir	'magic'
20.	laːzim	lazem	lazim	'necessary; usual'

A. For each of the eighteen Arabic consonants in the data, list the correspondences in Persian and MI. Two of these have already been done for you.

	Arabic	Persian	MI
1.	m	m	m
2.	ḍ	z	d
3.	_____	_____	_____
4.	_____	_____	_____
5.	_____	_____	_____
6.	_____	_____	_____
7.	_____	_____	_____
8.	_____	_____	_____
9.	_____	_____	_____
10.	_____	_____	_____
11.	_____	_____	_____

Name _____   **Section** _____   **Date** _____

	Arabic	Persian	MI
12.	_____	_____	_____
13.	_____	_____	_____
14.	_____	_____	_____
15.	_____	_____	_____
16.	_____	_____	_____
17.	_____	_____	_____
18.	_____	_____	_____

B. Based on how the Arabic consonants have been adapted in the borrowing languages, which Arabic phonemes in the data can you conclude are not found in Persian? Which are not found in MI?

Not found in Persian:

_____

_____

Not found in MI:

_____

_____

C. In borrowed items, Persian *s* and *z* each correspond to how many different phonemes in Arabic? List the correspondences.

Persian *s* corresponds to _____ Arabic phoneme(s), namely

_____.

Persian *z* corresponds to _____ Arabic phoneme(s), namely

_____.

D. The Arabic alphabet has a different letter to correspond to each Arabic consonant phoneme. Persian uses a modified version of this alphabet for its orthography. Items borrowed from Arabic are for the most part spelled exactly as they are in Arabic, with no change to accommodate Persian phonology.

Suppose you are a beginning student of Persian and you hear the word *zærbolmæsæl,* which you have reason to suspect is an Arabic loanword. You want to look the word up in a dictionary. As a result of the two fricatives, how many possible spellings do you have to consider? Explain.

_____

_____

_____

_____

E. Arabic makes a phonemic distinction between its two low vowels. Have the borrowing languages kept this distinction? Explain and illustrate.

_____

_____

_____

_____

F. Based on the data, it is clear that Arabic allows final consonant clusters. What can you conclude in this regard about the two borrowing languages? Explain carefully how Persian and MI deal with the original Arabic consonant clusters. (*Note:* If you find that one or the other language does something to break up such clusters, you must state *exactly* what happens. It is not enough, for example, to say, "A vowel is inserted.")

_____

_____

_____

_____

_____

_____

_____

Name _____   **Section** _____   **Date** _____

10.09   RECONSTRUCTION: Proto-Semitic Consonants

The following data consist of a list of cognates in three Semitic languages: Biblical Hebrew, Biblical Aramaic, and Classical Arabic. Examine the consonant correspondences carefully, and determine what consonants the data lead you to reconstruct for the hypothetical parent language, Proto-Semitic. You should be able to reconstruct twenty-five of the twenty-nine consonants usually associated with the protolanguage.

Notes:

1. The data are transcribed phonemically, and the effect of certain phonological rules (e.g., schwa insertion in Hebrew and Aramaic) is not indicated. If you are not familiar with some of the symbols used, see Appendix B.

2. Each cognate set shows items derived from the same *root*, which in Semitic consists entirely of consonants (usually three). However, the forms do not necessarily come from corresponding *stems,* which involve vowels, prefixes and suffixes, and gemination (long or "doubled" consonants). For this reason, you shouldn't try to reconstruct the original vowels based on these data. Stick to the consonants!

3. The glosses given are for identification purposes only and are not necessarily exact for all three languages.

	Hebrew	Aramaic	Arabic	Gloss
1.	diːn	diːn	diːn	'judgment; religion'
2.	zmaːn	zman	zamaːn	'time'
3.	zaːhaːb	dhab	ðahab	'gold'
4.	ṭoːb	ṭaːb	ṭaːb	'good'
5.	ʕaːmoːq	ʕamiːq	ʕamiːq	'deep'
6.	ʃaːloːm	ʃlaːm	salaːm	'peace'
7.	zeruːʕ	zraʕ	zuruːʕ	'seed'
8.	ʃaloːʃ	tlaːt	θalaːθ	'three'
9.	peʃer	pʃar	fassara	'interpret(ation)'
10.	doːr	daːr	daur	'generation; period'
11.	jiktoːb	jiktub	jaktub	'he writes'
12.	ṣdaːqaː	ṣidqaː	ṣadaqa	'charity'
13.	ʔereṣ	ʔarʕaː	ʔarḍ	'earth'
14.	qaːṭalti	qiṭlet	qataltu	'I killed'
15.	ħeleq	ħlaːq	xalaːq	'share'
16.	baːʕaː	bʕaː	baɣaː	'he asked for'

	Hebrew	Aramaic	Arabic	Gloss
17.	zebaħ	dbaħ	ðabħ	'sacrifice; slaughter'
18.	gbuːraː	gbar	dʒabr	'might; man'
19.	ṣaːpar	ṣipar	ṣafara	'he whistled'
20.	ʕereb	_____	ɣarb	'evening; west'
21.	ħemer	ħmar	xamr	'wine'
22.	ṣerur	ʕar	ḍarr	'enmity, foe; harm'
23.	ʃeleg	tlag	θaldʒ	'snow'
24.	ʃaliːṭ	ʃaliːṭ	saliːṭ	'ruler; firm, mighty'

A. First, reconstruct the "easy" protoconsonants—that is, the ones from cognate sets where no variation occurs in the corresponding consonants. Indicate the numbers of the examples in the data that support your reconstruction. One set already has been done for you.

Hebrew	Aramaic	Arabic	Proto-Semitic	Examples
m	m	m	*m	2, 5, 6, 21

Name _____   **Section** _____   **Date** _____

B. Next, do the same for the more interesting cases that show evidence of sound change. You will only need to consider *unconditioned* sound changes—ones in which the given change took place in all environments.

You will find that in several cases you may have to ignore the "majority rules" principle of reconstruction; this is largely a consequence of the fact that the data for this problem have been restricted to three languages.

Hebrew	Aramaic	Arabic	Proto-Semitic	Examples

C. Finally, list the consonant changes that have occurred in each language. Your list should consist of statements of the form *A > B, where *A is a protoconsonant and B is its reflex in the given language. Based on your analysis, which, if any, of these languages has retained more of the original consonants of Proto-Semitic than the others? Explain.

Hebrew	Aramaic	Arabic

Name _____   **Section** _____   **Date** _____

10.10   RECONSTRUCTION: The Spiiktumi Family

Below you will find twenty cognate sets in four languages of the little-known Spiiktumi family. Your task is to reconstruct the etymons (original forms) in proto-Spiiktumi for each of the cognate sets in the data, and to state the sound changes that have taken place in each daughter language.

Examine the data below and answer the questions that follow. (´ indicates stress.)

Note: In this data, š = IPA [ʃ], č =IPA [tʃ], ž = IPA [ʒ], ǰ = IPA [dʒ], and y = IPA [j].

	W	X	Y	Z
1.	pámut	pánti	pámüti	pámut
2.	sít	sído	šíðo	síd
3.	denubó	dembó	denuβó	denubó
4.	lelúk	lerúge	lerúye	lelúg
5.	sudán	sudáno	suðáno	sudã́
6.	únik	úŋga	úniɣa	únig
7.	čomús	čomúsi	čomúši	šomús
8.	láhuk	láhka	láuka	láhuk
9.	banubín	bambíni	banüβíni	banubĩ́
10.	eluǰíl	erǰíla	erüǰíla	elužíl
11.	láhuk	ráhgo	ráuɣo	láhug
12.	héfum	héfmo	héfumo	héfũ
13.	sehúbat	sehúbda	sehúβaða	sehúbad
14.	tehigém	tehgémo	teiɣémo	tehigẽ́
15.	yúnup	yúmbi	yúnüβi	yúnub
16.	ǰút	ǰúda	ǰúða	žúd
17.	famaɣí	faŋgí	famaɣí	famagí
18.	časinokóm	časiŋkómo	čašinokómo	šasinokṍ
19.	sudá	sudá	suðá	sudá
20.	kahihánom	kahhámmo	kaihánomo	kahihánõ

Some helpful hints:

Although no "cookbook" method exists for approaching problems like this, a few general guidelines may help you arrive at a solution.

1. It is often useful to make a list of the sound correspondences in the daughter languages. For example:

A	B	C	D	Examples
b	b	b	b	9
b	b	β	b	3, 9, 13
p	b	β	b	15 etc.

When all the daughters agree, as in the first line, it usually means the etymon is the same as the reflexes and no change has occurred. When disagreement exists, your best bet is to go by the "majority rules" principle unless you find evidence to the contrary; this minimizes the number of independent sound changes you need to posit.

2. The sound changes you propose should account for all the variation in the data. Bear in mind that chronological ordering may play a role here; you should consider the possibility that the output of an earlier sound change served as input to a later one.

3. The sound changes you propose should be plausible and natural. With experience, you will be able to judge whether a proposed sound change is natural or not without much trouble. While you are in the process of gaining that experience, keep in mind that sound changes you have already seen in one language will very likely crop up repeatedly in other languages, related or not. As a general rule, sound changes with an assimilation or other ease-of-articulation basis are usually natural ones.

A. Reconstruct the original forms of each of these words in the parent language, proto-Spiiktumi.

1. _____

2. _____

3. _____

4. _____

5. _____

6. _____

7. _____

8. _____

9. _____

10. _____

11. _____

12. _____

13. _____

14. _____

15. _____

16. _____

17. _____

18. _____

19. _____

20. _____

Name _____   **Section** _____   **Date** _____

B. State the sound changes that occurred in each daughter language, referring whenever possible to classes of sounds. Point out any instances of chronological ordering. Also state whether each change is conditioned or unconditioned; for conditioned sound changes, state precisely under what conditions the change occurred.

Changes in W   **Changes in X**

Changes in Y   **Changes in Z**

C. On the basis of the sound changes you have proposed for the daughter languages, is there any reason to group two or more of them into a subfamily? Give evidence to support your answer.

_____

_____

_____

_____

D. Do [u] and [ü] contrast in language Y, or are they in complementary distribution? Give evidence to support your answer.

_____

_____

_____

_____

E. Is nasalization distinctive in language Z? Again, give evidence to support your answer.

_____

_____

_____

_____

F. Find an example in the data of a _lexical merger_—two words that were originally distinct but later became identical.

_____

_____

_____

_____

Glossary

Note: Boldfaced terms in the definitions are themselves defined in the glossary.

< > vs. [ ]   Angled brackets indicate the written form of an expression; square brackets indicate its pronunciation. Example: In English, <th> is pronounced either [θ] or [ð].

Adjective   A **lexical category** of words that serve semantically to specify the attributes of **nouns** *(tall ships)* and that can be morphologically or syntactically marked to represent degrees of comparison *(taller, most beautiful)*; adjectives can occur in attributive position *(The steep hills)* or predicative position *(The hills are steep)*.

Adverb   A lexical class with wide-ranging functions. Many but by no means all English adverbs carry the **derivational morpheme** -LY *(suddenly, truly)*; the most common adverbs have no distinguishing marks *(soon, very, today)*.

Affective meaning   The information conveyed by an expression about the producer's attitudes and emotions toward the content or the context of expression; together with **social meaning,** affective meaning is sometimes called connotation.

Affix   A **bound morpheme** that occurs attached to a root or stem morpheme (called the **root** or **stem**). **Prefixes** (attached to the beginning of the root or stem) and **suffixes** (attached to the end) are the most common types of affixes. Less common in the world's languages are infixes (inserted within the root or stem) and circumfixes (a part of which is attached at each end of the root or stem).

Affricate   A sound produced when air is built up by a complete closure of the oral tract at some place of articulation and then released and continued like a **fricative.** Examples: English [tʃ] (as in *chin*) and [ʤ] (as in *gin*); German [t͡s] (as in *Zeit* 'time').

Agent   The **semantic role** corresponding to the responsible initiator of an action.

Allomorphs   The alternative phonetic forms of a morpheme in particular linguistic **environments.** Example: The English plural morpheme has three allomorphs: [əz] (as in *buses*), [z] *(twigs),* and [s] *(cats).*

Allophone   A phonetic manifestation of a **phoneme** in a particular phonological **environment.** Example: In English, unaspirated [p] (as in *spin*) and aspirated [pʰ] (as in *pin*) are allophones of the phoneme /p/.

Alphabet   A writing system in which, at least ideally, each graphic symbol represents a **distinctive** sound of the language.

Alveo-palatal consonant   A **consonant** whose place of articulation is between the alveolar ridge and the palate (or velum). Also called *palato-alveolar consonant.*

Ambiguity   A situation in which an expression can be interpreted in more than one way as a consequence of having more than one constituent structure *(elderly men and women)* or more than one **referential meaning** *(river bank* and *savings bank).* Also, ambiguity is sometimes used to refer to an orthographic system in which the same written form can be pronounced in more than one way. Since in English <c> is sometimes pronounced [s] and sometimes [k], the English writing system can be said to be ambiguous.

Antonymy   In semantics, denotes opposite meanings; word pairs with opposite meanings are said to be antonymous, as with *wet* and *dry.*

Approximant   A sound produced when one articulator is close to another but the vocal tract is not sufficiently narrowed to create the audible friction that typically characterizes **consonants.** Examples: [w], [y], [r], [l].

Article   A word like *the* or *a/an* that can indicate **definiteness** or **indefiniteness.**

Aspiration   The puff of air that accompanies the production of certain sounds, as with the *p* in the English word *pot;* represented in **phonetic transcription** by a following raised *h,* as in [pʰ].

Assimilation   The process whereby a sound changes to become more like a neighboring sound. If the second sound changes to become more like the first, the assimilation is called progressive; in the reverse situation, the assimilation is said to be regressive. Example: The pronunciation of the *n* in *income* as [ŋ] is an instance of regressive assimilation, since the **nasal** has changed to become more like the following **stop.**

Attributive adjective   An **adjective** that is syntactically part of the noun phrase whose head it modifies *(a spooky house);* distinguished from a **predicative adjective** *(The house is spooky).*

Auxiliary DO   In English, a form of the verb *do* that functions as an auxiliary, appearing under the AUX node in a tree diagram. In the sentence *Do you know how to do that?* the first occurrence of *do* is Auxiliary DO while the second is Main-Verb DO.

Back vowel   A vowel pronounced with the tongue toward the back of the mouth. Examples: [o] and [u].

Bilabial consonant   A **consonant** whose place of articulation involves both lips.

Blend   A new word created by combining parts of existing words. *Smog* (from *smoke* and *fog*) is a blend.

Borrowing   The process whereby speakers of one language take words or characteristics from another language.

Bound morpheme   A **morpheme** that functions as part of a word but cannot stand alone as a word. Examples: -MENT (as in *establishment*), -ER.

Central vowel   A **vowel** pronounced with the tongue midway between the front and the back of the mouth. Examples: [a] and [ə].

Clause   A constituent unit of syntax consisting of a **verb** with its noun phrases; clauses can function as constituents of a sentence or can stand by themselves as simple sentences.

Cognates   Words or **morphemes** that have developed from a single historically earlier source. Examples: English *father,* German *Vater,* Spanish *padre,* and Gothic *fadar* are cognates because all have developed from the same reconstructed Proto-Indo-European word *(pəter).* The term *cognates* is also used for languages that have a common historical ancestor. Examples: English, Russian, German, Persian, and all the other Indo-European languages.

Cognate set   A set of **cognates,** each in a different language, that developed from a single source in the **parent language.**

Commissive   A **speech act** that commits a speaker to a course of action. Examples: a promise, pledge, threat, or vow.

Complementary distribution   A pattern of distribution of two or more sounds that do not occur in the same position within a word in a given language. Example: In English, [pʰ] does not occur where [p] occurs (and vice versa).

Complex sentence   A sentence that consists of a **matrix clause** and one or more **embedded** (or *subordinate*) **clauses.**

Compound   A word created by putting existing words together. Compounds can be written as one word, as hyphenated words, or as separate words. Examples: *bluebird, cover-up, phone call.*

Conditioned change   A change that occurs only in certain linguistic **environments.** Example: In some languages, the change of [s] to [ʃ] before the vowel [i] but not before other vowels.

Conjoining   The linking of two or more **clauses** or phrases with a **conjunction** to form a new clause or phrase of the same kind. Example: *a gentle dog and a vicious cat.*

Conjunction   A closed class of words that serve to link **clauses** or phrases; **coordinating conjunctions** conjoin clauses *(she went but he stayed)* or phrases *(Alice and I),* while **subordinating conjunctions** embed one clause into another *(Leave when you're ready).*

Consonant   A speech sound produced by partial or complete closure of part of the vocal tract, thus obstructing the airflow and creating audible friction. Consonants are described in terms of **voicing,** place of articulation, and manner of articulation. Abbreviated as C.

Consonant cluster   A sequence of two or more consecutive **consonant** sounds at the beginning or end of a syllable. Examples: *Strikes* contains two consonant clusters—[str] and [ks]; *although* contains none.

Constituent   A syntactic unit that functions as part of a larger unit within a sentence; typical constituent types are the verb phrase, noun phrase, prepositional phrase, and **clause.**

Contraction   A spoken or written expression that represents a fusion of two or more words into a single word; in writing, omitted letters are usually marked by an apostrophe *(can't < cannot; could've < could have),* but some contractions lack an apostrophe *(wanna, gonna).*

Contrast   Characterizes the relationship between two forms when one can be substituted for the other in a given linguistic **environment,** with the substitution resulting in a different expression with a different meaning. In English, [r] and [l] contrast *(lip* vs. *rip)*; [p] and [pʰ] do not.

Converseness   Characterizes a reciprocal relationship between pairs of words, as in *husband* and *wife* or *buy* and *sell.*

Conversion   The functional shift of a word from one **lexical category** to another without an alteration of form. Examples: to *book* a room (N→V), a *run* of bad luck (V→N).

Cooperative principle   The set of four maxims that describe how language users cooperate in producing and understanding utterances in context: Maxim of Quantity (provide the appropriate amount of information), Maxim of Quality (be truthful), Maxim of Relevance (be relevant at the time of utterance), and Maxim of Manner (be orderly and clear).

Coordinate clause   A **clause** of a **coordinate sentence.** (See **Coordinate sentence.**)

Coordinate sentence   A sentence that contains two (or more) **clauses** neither of which functions as a grammatical **constituent** of the other; these clauses are usually joined by a **coordinating conjunction** such as *and* or *but (John went to England, and Mary went to France).*

Coordinating conjunction   A category of **function words** that serve to **conjoin** expressions of the same status or category, such as a **clause** *(He spoke <u>and</u> I wept)* or **adverb** *(slowly <u>but</u> surely).*

Daughter language   A language that has developed directly from another language, known as the parent.

Declaration   A **speech act** that brings about the state of affairs it names. Examples: a blessing, firing, baptism, or arrest.

Deep structure   The abstract form of a sentence before any transformations have applied.

Definite   Refers to a noun phrase marked to indicate that the speaker assumes the addressee can identify its **referent**; opposed to **indefinite.** In English, definiteness is marked by the choice of **determiner** *(the, these,* etc.)

Definite article   A word or morpheme that indicates definiteness. The definite article in English is *the.*

Definite NP   A noun phrase whose **referent** the speaker assumes the listener can identify. Example: *Have you seen the key?* (The speaker assumes the listener can identify which key.)

Deixis   The marking of the orientation or position of entities and situations with respect to certain points of reference, such as the place *(here/there)* and time *(now/then)* of utterance.

Derivation   In morphology, designates a process whereby one word is transformed into another word with a related meaning but belonging to a different lexical class; the **adverb** *slowly* is derived from the **adjective** *slow* by suffixing the **derivational morpheme** -LY.

Derivational morpheme   A **morpheme** that serves to derive a word of one class or meaning from a word of another class or meaning. Examples: -MENT derives the **noun** *establishment* from the **verb** *establish,* and RE- *(repaint)* alters the meaning of the **verb** *paint* from 'paint' to 'paint again'.

Determiner   A word like *a/an, the, this, some,* etc., that occurs with **nouns** as part of a noun phrase. **Articles** and demonstratives are determiners.

Diacritic   A symbol that modifies the meaning of another symbol. Example: The wedge above the *s* in *š* is a diacritic.

Dialect   A language **variety** used by and characteristic of a particular social group—for example, regional, ethnic, socioeconomic, or gender groups.

Digraph   Two consecutive written symbols used to indicate a single sound. Examples: In English, *sh, ch, th,* and *ng.*

Direct object   With **indirect object,** one of two grammatical relations known as *object.* In English, the direct object is the noun phrase in a **clause** that immediately follows the **verb** in **deep structure** and is immediately dominated by the VP. Example: *Peter admires <u>Tracy</u>.*

Directive   A **speech act** intended to get the addressee to carry out an action. Examples: a command, request, invitation, or dare.

Distinctive   Said of a linguistic property in a given language that can be exploited to produce **contrast.** In English, voicing is distinctive, since [z] (voiced) and [s] (unvoiced) contrast.

Embedded clause   A noncoordinate **clause** incorporated into another clause. Example: *Pat thinks Chris should be fired*. Also known as a *subordinate clause*.

Environment   A definable position within a **morpheme,** word, phrase, **clause,** sentence, or discourse. Example: The environment of *g* in *ago* is intervocalic (between two vowels); the environment of *good* in *the good earth* is prenominal (before a noun).

Ethnic dialect/variety   A language **variety** characteristic of an ethnic group. Example: AAE (African American English).

Etymon   The linguistic form from which a word is historically derived.

Expressive   A **speech act** that indicates the speaker's psychological state or attitude. Examples: a greeting, apology, or expression of condolence.

Final position   The **environment** at the end of a word, phrase, **clause,** or sentence. Example: In *hat, t* is in final position.

Free morpheme   A **morpheme** that can stand alone as a word. Examples: ZEBRA, PAINT, PRETTY, VERY. See **Bound morpheme.**

Fricative   A **consonant** sound made by passing a continuous stream of air through a narrowed passage in the vocal tract thereby causing turbulence, such as that created between the lower lip and the upper teeth in the production of [f] and [v].

Front vowel   A **vowel** pronounced with the tongue towards the front of the mouth. Examples: [i] and [æ].

Function words   A class of words such as **determiners** and **conjunctions** whose primary role is to mark grammatical relationships between content words or structures such as phrases and **clauses.**

Gemination   The lengthening or prolongation of a **consonant,** usually indicated in transcription by doubling the consonant symbol. Example: In a language with the words [naso] 'flute' and [nasso] 'nose', gemination exists and is **distinctive.**

Gender   A grammatical property of **nouns, pronouns,** and **adjectives** in certain languages that places such words into categories that can behave differently with respect to grammatical rules. Example: Spanish has two genders; masculine nouns require masculine adjectives, and feminine nouns require feminine adjectives—*cuartos limpios* 'clean rooms', *mesas limpias* 'clean tables'.

Gender dialect/variety   A language **variety** associated with men or women.

Genetic relationship   A relationship based on a common descent from a single ancestral language.

Gloss   A brief translation. Example: 'House' is a gloss for the Spanish word *casa.*

Glottal stop   A voiceless **consonant** produced by complete closure of the glottis.

Grammatical relation   The syntactic role a noun phrase plays in its **clause** (for example, as **subject** or **direct object**).

Graph   A written symbol.

High vowel   A **vowel** pronounced with the tongue in a relatively high position in the mouth. Examples: [i] and [u].

Homonymy   Used in semantics for the state of having identical expression but different meanings (*book a flight* and *buy a book*); *homophonous* is sometimes used with the related meaning of 'sounding alike' but not necessarily having the same written form (*see* and *sea*).

Hyponomy   A semantic relationship in which the **referent** of one term is included in the referent of another. Example: *Blue* is a hyponym of *color;* the relationship between *blue* and *color* is one of hyponomy.

Ideograph   A written symbol for a word in the form of a simple diagram that points to the idea or relationship in question. Example: three lines used to represent the word for 'three'.

Implication   An assertion assumed to be true when another assertion is made. Example: The assertion *Helen has stopped smoking* has the implication *At one time, Helen smoked.*

Indefinite   Refers to a noun phrase marked to indicate that the speaker assumes the addressee cannot identify its **referent;** opposed to **definite.** In English, indefiniteness can be marked by the choice of **determiner** (*a, some,* etc.).

Indefinite article   In certain languages, a word or **morpheme** that indicates indefiniteness. The indefinite article in English is *a*/*an.*

Indefinite NP   A noun phrase whose **referent** is new in the discourse and that the speaker therefore assumes the listener cannot identify. Example: *I was talking to a linguistics professor yesterday.* (The speaker assumes the listener does not know which linguistics professor he is talking about.)

Indeterminacy   Refers to a writing system in which the same phonetic form can be written in more than one way. Since in English [s] is sometimes written as <s> and sometimes as <c>, the English writing system is indeterminate.

Indirect object   One of two grammatical relations known as objects, the other being **direct object.** Indirect objects usually occur in English before the direct object *(He gave the clerk a rose).*

Infinitive   The basic form of a **verb,** often expressed in English with a preceding *to,* as in *to see.*

Inflected verb   A **verb** with at least one **inflectional morpheme** attached to it. Examples: *says, shoved.*

Inflection   The process whereby a language uses **bound morphemes** to mark syntactic or other functions of words in sentences.

Inflectional morpheme   A **bound morpheme** that creates variant forms of a word to mark syntactic or other functions in a sentence. Examples: The suffix -s added to a verb (as in *paints*) marks the verb as agreeing with third-person singular subjects; -ER *(taller)* marks adjectives for comparative degree.

Initial position   The **environment** at the beginning of a word, phrase, **clause,** or sentence. Example: In *hat, h* is in initial position.

Interdental consonant   A **consonant** whose place of articulation is between the upper and lower teeth. Examples: [θ] as in *thin* and [ð] as in *then.*

Intervocalic position   The **environment** between two vowels. Example: The *r* in *Harold* is in intervocalic position.

Invariant BE   In some varieties of English, the word *be* used without markers for **person** and **number.** Example: *She always be on time.*

Invention   A relatively rare process of word formation whereby new words are created from scratch. Example: *zap.*

Isogloss   The geographic boundary marking the limit of the regional distribution of a particular word, pronunciation, or usage.

Labial   A sound whose place of articulation involves the lips.

Labialized consonant   A **consonant** that has been modified by added lip rounding.

Labiodental consonant   A **consonant** whose place of articulation involves the teeth and the lips (usually the upper teeth and lower lip).

Language family   A group of languages that have all developed from a single common ancestral language.

Lax vowel   A **vowel** pronounced with relatively weak muscular tension. In English, [ɪ] and [ɛ] are lax vowels; their tense counterparts are [i] and [e]. See **Tense vowel.**

Lemma   A **lexical item.**

Lexical category   The "part of speech" of a word. Lexical categories include **nouns, verbs, adjectives,** and **prepositions.**

Lexical field   A set of words with an identifiable semantic affinity. Example: *fast, slow, quick, moderate, brisk, swift, leisurely, unhurried, rapid.* Also known as *lexical domain.*

Lexical item   A unit in the **lexicon** of a language, including all its inflected forms. Example: *am, is, are, was, were, be, being,* and *been* constitute the lexical item BE. Also known as *lemma.*

Lexicon   The list of all words and **morphemes** stored in a native speaker's memory. This internalized dictionary includes all the nonpredictable information about words and morphemes.

Liquid   An *r*-like or *l*-like **approximant.**

Low vowel   A **vowel** pronounced with the tongue in a relatively low position in the mouth. Examples: [æ] and [a].

Matrix clause   A **clause** into which another clause, called an **embedded clause,** has been inserted. Example: In *Alan thinks Marvin should be fired,* the matrix clause is *Alan thinks _____.*

Maxim—of Manner, Quality, Quantity, Relevance   See **Cooperative principle.**

Merger   A historical change whereby two originally distinct forms become indistinguishable.

Metaphorical extension   An extension of a word for use beyond its primary meaning to describe **referents** that bear some similarity to the word's primary referent, as with *eye* in *eye of a needle*. Words whose meanings are extended in this way are called *metaphors*. Metaphorical extension is also known as *semantic shift*.

Minimal pair   A pair of words that differ by only a single sound in the same position. Examples: *look/took; take/took; keep/coop*.

Monomorphemic word   A word that contains only one **morpheme.** *Horse* and *water* are monomorphemic; *dogs* and *later* are not.

Monosyllabic word   A word that contains only one syllable. Examples: *dog, dogs, men, strengths, child's.*

Mood   A grammatical category of verbs marking speakers' attitudes toward the status of their assertions as factual (indicative), hypothetical (subjunctive), etc. Although some languages mark mood by inflection on the verb, English has a set of modal verbs (e.g., *must, may,* and *can,* as in *must begin, may arrive, can talk*), which lack typical morphological inflections such as -S and -ING.

Morpheme   The smallest unit of language that bears meaning or serves a grammatical function. A morpheme can be a word, as with *zebra* and *paint,* or part of a word, as in *zebras* and *painted,* which contain two morphemes each (ZEBRA and 'PLURAL'; PAINT and 'PAST TENSE').

Multiple negation   The use of more than one negative marker to indicate negation. For example, *They don't know nothing*.

Nasal   A class of sounds (including the **consonants** [m] and [n]) produced by lowering the velum and allowing air to pass out of the vocal tract through the nasal cavity.

Nasalization   The modification of a sound, most often a **vowel,** by lowering the velum and allowing air to pass through the nose as well as through the mouth.

New information   Content introduced into a discourse for the first time.

Nonreferential NP   A noun phrase that does not refer to a particular entity. See **Referential NP.**

Noun   A lexical category of words that function syntactically as heads of noun phrases and semantically as referring expressions. Nouns can be characterized morphologically by certain inflections—for example, the English possessive case marker *(ship's)* and plural number marker *(ships)*—and syntactically by their distribution in phrases and **clauses.** In traditional grammatical terms, a noun is defined semantically as the name of a person, place, or thing. Abbreviated N.

Number   A grammatical category associated principally with **nouns** and **pronouns** that indicates something about the number of **referents** for the noun or pronoun. Example: *I* and *car* are marked for singular number, while *we* and *cars* are marked for plural number. Number can also be marked on **verbs,** usually in agreement with **subjects,** as in singular *The child sings* and plural *The children sing.*

Oblique   A noun phrase whose grammatical relation in a clause is not that of **subject, direct object,** or **indirect object**; usually marks such semantic categories as location or time. Example: The noun phrase *the game* has an oblique grammatical relation in *He gave Joe the ball after the game.*

Old information   Information currently in the forefront of the hearer's mind, either because it has already been introduced into the discourse or because it is closely associated with something already introduced. Also called *given information*.

Orthography   A system of spelling used to achieve a match between the sound system of a language and the alphabet representing it.

Palatal consonant   A **consonant** whose place of articulation is the palate (or velum).

Parent language   A language that has developed over time into one or more new languages, called **daughter languages.**

Particle   A wide-ranging term used for various types of function words. In English, a particle is usually a directional **adverb** used in conjunction with a **verb** to produce a phrasal verb with an idiomatic meaning. *To* as a marker of the **infinitive** is also a particle. Examples: *out* in *take out, up* in *think up, to* in *to buy.*

Passive   A syntactic construction in which the deep or underlying **direct object** NP functions as the **subject.** Example: *The cookies were eaten by the mouse* is a passive sentence related to the active (nonpassive) sentence *The mouse ate the cookies.*

Person A grammatical category associated principally with **pronouns** marking reference to the speaker (first person), the addressee (second person), a third party (third person), or a combination of these; **verbs** in a **clause** are sometimes marked for person agreement, usually with their **subject.**

Personal pronoun A **pronoun** referring to the speaker (first person), the addressee (second person), or a third party (third person). The personal pronouns in English include *I, me, you, he, him, she, her, it, we, us, they,* and *them.*

Pharyngeal consonant A **consonant** whose place of articulation is the throat.

Phoneme A distinctive and significant structural element in the sound system of a language. An abstract element (defined by a set of phonological features) that can have alternative manifestations (called **allophones**) in particular **environments.** Example: the English phoneme /p/ has several allophones, including **aspirated** [pʰ] and unaspirated [p].

Phonetic symbol A symbol used to represent a sound, based on the principle of one symbol per sound and one sound per symbol.

Phonetic transcription The transcription of an utterance using a particular system of phonetic symbols.

Phonological rule A rule that specifies the **allophones** of a **phoneme** and their distribution in a particular language.

Pictograph A written symbol for a word in the form of a stylized picture of the word's **referent.** Example: a crescent shape used to represent the word for 'moon'.

Polysemy Multiple meanings for the same word or sentence; a word is polysemic when it has more than one meaning.

Postposition A **lexical category** of words that serve syntactically as heads of postpositional phrases and semantically to indicate a relationship between two entities; other than the fact that postpositions follow their complements, they are like **prepositions.** Examples: In Japanese, *no* as in *Taroo no* 'of Taro' and *de* as in *hafi de* 'with chopsticks'.

Pragmatic function The function of a particular linguistic form or process in the marking of information structure—givenness, topic, contrast, definiteness, referentiality, etc.

Predicative adjective An **adjective** that serves syntactically as a complement to the **verb** in a **clause** and predicates something of the **subject** *(The soup is cold);* contrasted with **attributive adjective** *(The cold soup).*

Predictable difference A difference determined by a general rule. Examples: With English **stops,** aspiration is predictable—stops are aspirated at the beginning of a word, unaspirated after *s,* etc. **Voicing,** however, is not predictable: Both voiced and unvoiced stops can occur in the same **environment.**

Prefix An **affix** that attaches to the front of a **stem.**

Preposition A **lexical category** of words that serve syntactically as heads of prepositional phrases and semantically to indicate a relationship between two entities. Examples: *to, with,* and *in,* as in *to school, with liberty, in the spring.* See also **Postposition.**

Productive process A process that is "alive" in a language, in the sense that new forms added to the language are subject to the process. Example: In English, the process that forms plurals by adding -s or -es is productive; plural formation in -en *(ox, oxen; child, children)* is not productive.

Pronoun Several categories of words, all closed classes. Traditionally defined as "taking the place of nouns," **personal pronouns** are the most familiar type. Other types include relative pronouns *(who, whose, which, that),* demonstrative pronouns *(this, that, those),* interrogative pronouns *(who, which, whose),* and indefinite pronouns *(anyone, someone).*

Proto- In historical linguistics, the ancestor of a particular form or language. Example: The ancestor of the Indo-European family of languages is a reconstructed language called Proto-Indo-European.

Reconstruction The process of deducing probable forms in a **parent language** by comparing related forms in **daughter languages.** Also known as *comparative reconstruction.*

Referent The entity (person, object, notion, or situation) in the world referred to by a linguistic expression. Example: The referent of *John's dog* is the four-legged canine belonging to John.

Referential meaning The meaning an expression has by virtue of its ability to refer to an entity; contrasted with **social meaning** and **affective meaning** and sometimes called *denotation.*

Referential NP   A noun phrase that refers to a particular entity. Example: *A good piano teacher* is referential in *Tom knows a good piano teacher* but nonreferential in *Tom wants to find a good piano teacher.*

Reflex   A form in a **daughter language** that developed from a particular form in an ancestral language. Example: Hawaiian /k/ is a reflex of Proto-Polynesian *t (symbolized *t > k).

Regional dialect/variety   A language **variety** characteristic of a particular geographic area.

Register   A language **variety** associated with a particular situation of use.

Representative   A **speech** act that represents a state of affairs. Examples: an assertion, statement, claim, or hypothesis.

Roman alphabet   The familiar alphabet used by the ancient Romans and used today to write English and a great many other languages.

Romanization   A **transcription** using the roman alphabet of a language that uses a non-roman alphabet.

Root   A **morpheme** that can function as the "center" of a word and to which other morphemes may be added. Example: *Faith* is the root of *faiths, faithless, faithlessness,* and *unfaithful.*

Round vowel   A **vowel** produced with rounded lips. Examples: [u] and [o].

Semantic role   The way the **referent** of a noun phrase is involved in the situation described or represented by the **clause;** for example, as agent, patient, or cause.

Semantic shift   See **Metaphorical extension.**

Shortening   A process of word formation by which an existing word or phrase is shortened to create a new word. Examples: *bus* from *omnibus, narc* from *narcotics agent.*

Social dialect/variety   A language **variety** characteristic of a social group, typically socioeconomic groups, gender groups, or ethnic groups, as distinct from regional groups.

Social meaning   Information that words and sentences convey about the social characteristics of their producers and the situation they are produced in; together with **affective meaning,** social meaning is sometimes called *connotation.*

Specific NP   A noun phrase that refers to a particular member of a category rather than to the category itself. Example: In *The unicorn was eating flowers, the unicorn* is specific. In *The unicorn is a mythical beast, the unicorn* is generic (nonspecific).

Speech act   An action carried out through language, such as promising, lying, and greeting.

Stem   A **root** or a root plus one or more **derivational affixes. Inflectional** affixes are added to stems. Example: *Large* is a root and therefore a stem; *enlarge* is a stem consisting of a root and a derivational affix. These stems may take inflectional affixes: *larger, enlarges.*

Stop   A speech sound created when air is built up at a place of articulation in the vocal tract and suddenly released through the mouth; sometimes called *oral stops* when nasals are excluded.

Stress   The relative prominence or emphasis given to a particular syllable of a word or the syllable that receives the most such emphasis. Stressed syllables are usually louder and higher pitched than nonstressed syllables. Example: In *photograph,* the first syllable is stressed; in *photography,* the second syllable is stressed.

Subject   A noun phrase immediately dominated by S in a phrase structure.

Subordinate clause   An **embedded clause.**

Subordinating conjunction   A **subordinator.**

Subordination   The process of embedding a **clause** inside another clause. See **Embedded clause.**

Subordinator   A word that marks the boundary between an **embedded clause** and its **matrix clause.** Example: In *I know that he's lying, that* is a subordinator.

Suffix   An **affix** that attaches to the end of a **stem.**

Surface form   A word's actual pronunciation, generated by the application of a language's phonological rules to the **underlying form;** sometimes also said of sentences. See **Underlying form.**

Surface structure   The constituent structure of a sentence after all applicable syntactic operations have applied.

Syllabic symbol   In certain types of writing systems, a symbol that represents a syllable as a whole. Generally, such symbols cannot be broken down into smaller components that indicate individual consonants and vowels.

Synchronic process   A process that occurs within a language at a particular time in its history without referring to earlier or later stages.

Synonymy   In semantics, the state of having the same meaning (*quick* and *rapid,* for example).

Tense vowel   A **vowel** pronounced with relatively strong muscular tension. In English, [i] and [e] are tense vowels; their lax counterparts are [ɪ] and [ɛ]. See **Lax vowel.**

Transcription   In general, any written form of an utterance. In particular, short for **phonetic transcription.**

Transitive verb   A **verb** that takes a **direct object.** Examples: *Eat* is transitive *(Birds eat worms),* and *sleep* is intransitive *(The mouse is sleeping). Begin* can be both transitive *(He began the project in May)* and intransitive *(The movie began at 3:00).*

Transliteration   The conversion of a piece of writing from one alphabet into another.

Unconditioned change   A change that takes place in all linguistic **environments.** Example: If a language were to replace the sound [θ], regardless of where it occurred, with the sound [t], the change would be unconditioned.

Underlying form   The form of a **morpheme** stored in the internalized **lexicon.**

Uppercase, lowercase   The "capital" and "small" forms of a letter, respectively. *B* is uppercase; *b* is lowercase.

Uvular consonant   A **consonant** pronounced with the aid of the uvula (the piece of flesh that hangs from the soft palate at the back of the mouth). Many languages, including French, German, and Modern Hebrew, have a uvular *r*-sound.

Variety   Any language, **dialect,** or **register.**

Velar consonant   A **consonant** whose place of articulation is the velum, that is, a consonant produced by the tongue approaching or touching the roof of the mouth at the velum.

Verb   A **lexical category** of words that syntactically determine the structure of a **clause** especially with respect to noun phrases; that semantically express the action or state of being represented by a clause; and that morphologically can be marked for certain categories (not all of which are realized in English): tense (present, *walk;* past, *walked*), **mood,** aspect *(walk/walking),* **person** (first, *walk;* third, *walks*), and **number** (singular, *walks;* plural *walk*).

Verdictive   A **speech act** that makes an assessment or judgment. Examples: a ranking or appraisal.

Vernacular   A language or **variety** used for ordinary, everyday conversation.

Voicing   The property of a sound that refers to whether or not the vocal cords vibrate during its production. For example, [z] is voiced (pronounced with the vocal cords vibrating) and [s] is voiceless.

Vowel   One of two major classes of sounds (the other is **consonants**); articulated without complete closure in the oral cavity and without sufficient narrowing to create the friction characteristic of consonants. Abbreviated as V.

Vowel length   The amount of time it takes to pronounce a **vowel.** In some languages, vowel length is **distinctive.** In Latin, for example, *mala* means 'evils' if the first *a* is short and 'apples' if it is long.

The Pinyin Transcription System for Mandarin Chinese

Except for the phonology problems of Chapter 3, the Mandarin examples in this book have been transcribed in *pinyin*.

In the People's Republic of China, *pinyin* is the official system for representing Mandarin in the roman alphabet. It is the standard used for names in Western media, and it is employed extensively in Chinese language education.

Pinyin uses all the letters of the English alphabet except *v*, adding to these only *ü*. Tone marks, although seldom indicated, are the familiar ones: ¯, ´, ˇ, ` for tones 1 through 4 respectively (see problem 3.14).

Listed here with their phonetic equivalents are *symbols that differ significantly from the identical phonetic notation or that require special comment*.

Pinyin	Phonetics	Comments and Examples
p, t, k	[pʰ], [tʰ], [kʰ]	Aspirated voiceless stops (p̲ingp̲āng 'table tennis')
b, d, g	[p], [t], [k]	Unaspirated voiceless stops (B̲ěijīng)
h	[h], [x]	Varies between [h] and [x], tending towards [x] with emphasis (H̲únán)
z	[t͡s]	Unaspirated voiceless affricate (Máo Z̲édōng)
c	[t͡sʰ]	Aspirated voiceless affricate (c̲àidān 'menu')
x	[ç]	Palatal, as in German *ich*, English *hue* (Dèng X̲iǎopíng)
j	[t͡ɕ]	Palatal; closest English sound is the *j* of *jeans* but unvoiced (Běij̲īng)
q	[t͡ɕʰ]	Palatal; closest English sound is the *ch* of *cheese* with aspiration. (tàij̲íquán 'tai chi chuan')
sh	[ʂ]	Retroflex; an *ʃ*-like sound articulated with the tip of the tongue curled up and back toward the palate (S̲hànghǎi)

Pinyin	Phonetics	Comments and Examples
zh	[tʂ]	Retroflex; closest English sound is the *j* of *jerk* but unvoiced (Zhōngguó 'China']
ch	[tʂʰ]	Retroflex; closest English sound is the *ch* of *churn* with aspiration (chǎomiàn 'fried noodles')
r	[r]	Retroflex; in final position very much like an American *r*, in initial position has a hint of a simultaneous [ʒ] sound (èr 'two', rén 'person')
ng	[ŋ]	Appears only in syllable-final position (Shànghǎi)
e	[ɤ]	When syllable-final and not preceded by *i, u,* or *ü;* a mid, back, unrounded vowel, close to [ə] (Máo Zédōng)
en, eng	[ən], [əŋ]	(Zhōu Ēnlái, Dèng Xiǎopíng)
er	[ər] or [ar]	Depending partly on tone (èr 'two')
i	[ɿ]	After the dental sibilants (*s, z, c*); a dental apical vowel (Sìchuān)
i	[ʅ]	After the retroflex consonants (*sh, zh, ch, r*); a retroflex apical vowel; closest English sound is the *ir* of *shirt* (chī 'eat')
ian	[iɛn]	(chǎomiàn 'fried noodles')
ie	[iɛ]	(qiē 'cut')
iu	[io]	(jiǔ 'wine')
o	[ɔ]	This pronunciation does not occur after *a* or before *ng* (wǒ 'I').
ong	[ʊŋ]	(Máo Zédōng)
u	[ü]	}
uan	[üɛn]	} After the palatals *x, j, q,* and *y* (qù 'go', yuán 'garden', xué 'study')
ue	[üɛ]	}
ui	[uei]	(duì 'correct')
un	[uən]	(kùn 'surround')
y	[j]	

Notes:

1. *i* has three pronunciations. For the values of *i* following dental sibilants and retroflex consonants, see the table; the pronunciation of these unfamiliar vowels is best learned from a native speaker. In other environments, *i* is simply [i].

2. Syllable-initial *i* and *u* are respelled *y* and *w,* respectively, before a following vowel; e.g., *uàng → wàng, iǎn → yǎn.* If no vowel follows, *y* is inserted before the *i* (*īng → yīng*) and *w* before the *u* (*ǔ → wǔ*); *y* is also inserted before initial *ü* (see below).

3. *ü* is written as an ordinary *u* after the palatals *x, j, q;* syllable-initial *ü* becomes *yu.* The *ü* appears in *pinyin* only after *n* and *l;* only in these environments do [u] and [ü] contrast, e.g., *lù* 'road', *lǜ* 'green'.

B

Transcription of Semitic Consonants

In the transcriptions of Arabic, Aramaic, and Hebrew in this book, several phonetic symbols may be unfamiliar to you. These are explained below.

q	A voiceless uvular stop
ħ	A voiceless pharyngeal fricative: a strong *h*-like sound, pronounced with pharyngeal (throat) constriction
ʕ	A voiced pharyngeal fricative, usually regarded as the voiced counterpart of ħ
ś	An *s*-like sound found in Biblical Hebrew and Biblical Aramaic, the exact pronunciation of which is uncertain; perhaps palatalized
ç̣	A dot below a consonant, e.g., *ṭ*, indicates that the consonant is pronounced with the back of the tongue raised toward the velum. Such consonants are said to be *velarized* or *emphatic*.
ə, ᵃ	Ultrashort vowels, as in Biblical Hebrew *zᵊmaːn, laʕᵃqoːr*

APPENDIX

Language Index

Exercises

Natural Languages

Akan	3.16
Arabic	3.09, 3.19, 3.20, 3.22; 10.08, 10.09
Aramaic	10.09
Chinese	3.14, 3.18; 4.13; 6.08, 6.09; 9.10
English	1.01, 1.02, 1.03, 1.04, 1.05, 1.06, 1.07; 2.01, 2.02, 2.03, 2.04, 2.05, 2.06, 2.07, 2.08; 3.01, 3.03, 3.04, 3.05, 3.13, 3.17; 4.01, 4.02, 4.03, 4.04, 4.05, 4.06, 4.07, 4.08, 4.09, 4.10, 4.11; 5.01, 5.02, 5.03, 5.04, 5.05, 5.06, 5.07, 5.08; 6.01, 6.02, 6.03, 6.04, 6.05, 6.06, 6.07; 7.01, 7.02, 7.03, 7.04, 7.05, 7.06, 7.07; 8.01, 8.02, 8.03, 8.04, 8.05, 8.06, 8.07; 9.01, 9.02, 9.03; 10.01, 10.02
French	3.20; 4.12; 10.06
German	3.00; 4.14
Greek	3.19, 3.23; 4.11; 9.05; 10.04
Hawaiian	2.12
Hebrew	1.08; 2.14; 3.09; 9.06; 10.09
Hindi	3.08
Hungarian	1.00
Icelandic	3.19

Irish	3.00
Italian	3.11; 4.11; 9.04; 10.06, 10.07
Japanese	3.08, 3.10, 3.15, 3.17; 4.10; 9.09
Korean	9.08
Lakota	1.13; 2.15
Latin	1.12
Malay/Indonesian	1.09; 3.21; 5.09; 9.11; 10.08
Old English	3.02; 10.01
Persian	1.10, 1.11; 5.10; 7.08; 9.07; 10.05, 10.08
Portuguese	10.07
Russian	3.12
Spanish	1.08; 3.06, 3.07, 3.13; 4.10; 10.06, 10.07
Swahili	3.19
Turkish	3.25; 4.15
Welsh	3.24
Wichita	2.13
Yiddish	4.15

Fictitious Languages

Klingon	4.16
Spiiktumi	10.10

Bibliography

Abas, Lutfi, and Awang Sariyan, eds. *Kamus Pelajar* [Student Dictionary]. Petaling Jaya, Malaysia: Delta, 1988.

Adams, Douglas Q. *Essential Modern Greek Grammar*. New York: Dover, 1987.

Atwood, E. Bagby. *A Survey of Verb Forms in the Eastern United States*. Ann Arbor: University of Michigan Press, 1953.

Boas, Franz, and Ella Deloria. *Dakota Grammar*. Washington, DC: U.S. Govt. Printing Office, 1941.

Brown, Francis, S. R. Driver, and C. A. Briggs. *A Hebrew and English Lexicon of the Old Testament*. Oxford: Clarendon Press, 1907.

Burke, David. *Street French: How to Speak and Understand French Slang*. New York: John Wiley, 1988.

Cassidy, Frederic G., ed. *A Dictionary of American Regional English*. Cambridge: Harvard University Press, 1985–.

Ch'en, Ta-tuan, Perry Link, Yih-jian Tai, and Hai-tao Tang. *Chinese Primer*. Princeton: Chinese Linguistics Project, Princeton University, 1987.

Chang, Namgui, and Yong-chol Kim. *Functional Korean*. Elizabeth, NJ: Hollym International, 1989.

Cheng, Chin-Chuan. *A Synchronic Phonology of Mandarin Chinese*. The Hague: Mouton, 1973.

Cohen, A. *The Five Megilloth*. London: Soncino Press, 1946.

Davies, Basil, and Cennard Davies. *Catchphrase: A Course in Spoken Welsh*. Penygroes, Wales: Sain (Recordiau) Cyf., 1980.

Halkin, Abraham S. *201 Hebrew Verbs*. New York: Barron's, 1970.

Harris, Martin, and Nigel Harris, eds. *The Romance Languages*. New York: Oxford University Press, 1988.

Haïm, S. *The One-Volume Persian–English Dictionary*. Tehran: Béroukhim, 1961.

Henshall, Kenneth G., and Tetsuo Takagaki. *A Guide to Learning Katakana and Hiragana*. Rutland, VT: Charles E. Tuttle, 1990.

Hoyle, Susan M., and Carolyn Temple Adger, eds. *Kids Talk*. New York: Oxford University Press, 1998.

Hudoba, Lilla. The First Sentences in Hungarian. <http://www.hungarotips.com/hungarian/b/elso.html>, n.d.

Jones, T. J. Rhys. *Living Welsh*. London: Hodder and Stoughton, 1977.

Jónsson, Snæbjörn. *A Primer of Modern Icelandic*. London: Oxford University Press, 1927.

Jorden, Eleanor Harz. *Beginning Japanese*. New Haven: Yale University Press, 1963.

Kurath, Hans. *A Word Geography of the Eastern United States*. Ann Arbor: University of Michigan Press, 1949.

Lazard, Gilbert. *Grammaire du persan contemporain*. Paris: Klincksieck, 1957.

Li, Charles N., and Sandra A. Thompson. *Mandarin Chinese: A Functional Reference Grammar*. Berkeley: University of California Press, 1981.

Luschning, C. A. E. *An Introduction to Ancient Greek*. New York: Charles Scribner's Sons, 1975.

Melzi, Robert C. *The New College Italian & English Dictionary*. New York, 1976.

Moscati, Sabatino, ed. *An Introduction to the Comparative Grammar of the Semitic Languages*. Wiesbaden, Germany: Otto Harrassowitz, 1980.

Murray, Janette, ed. *Lakota: A Language Course for Beginners*. Guilford, CT: Audio-Forum, 1989.

Nathanail, Paul, ed. *New College Greek and English Dictionary*. Lincolnwood, IL: National Textbook Co., 1990.

Obolensky, Serge, Panagiotis S. Sapountzis, and Aspasia Aliki Sapountzis. *Mastering Greek*. New York: Barron's, 1988.

Ó Dónaill, Niall, ed. *Foclóir Póca: English-Irish, Irish-English Dictionary, 6th ed.* Dublin: An Gúm, 1995.

Okrand, Marc. *The Klingon Dictionary*. New York: Pocket Books, 1985.

Park, B. Nam. *Mastering Korean*. New York: Barron's, 1988.

Peng, Tan Huay. *Fun with Chinese Characters*. 3 vols. Singapore: Federal Publications, 1980–1983.

———. *Chinese Radicals*. 2 vols. Union City, CA: Heian International, 1987.

Perrot, D. V. *Swahili*. London: Hodder and Stoughton, 1951.

Redden, J. E., N. Owusu, and Associates. *Twi Basic Course*. Washington, DC: Foreign Service Institute, 1963.

Rigg, A. G., ed. *The English Language: A Historical Reader*. New York: Appleton-Century-Crofts, 1968.

Rona, Bengisu. *Turkish in Three Months*. Edison, NJ: Hunter, 1989.

Rood, David S. "The Implications of Wichita Phonology." *Language* 51 (1975): 315–37.

Rosenthal, Franz. *A Grammar of Biblical Aramaic*. Wiesbaden: Otto Harrassowitz, 1968.

Shibatani, Masayoshi. *The Languages of Japan*. Cambridge: Cambridge University Press, 1990.

Snell, Robert, and Simon Weightman. *Hindi*. London: Hodder and Stoughton, 1989.

Tiwari, R. C., R. S. Sharma, and Krishna Vikal. *Hindi–English Dictionary*. New York: Hippocrene Books, n. d.

Tucker, Susie I. *English Examined*. Cambridge: Cambridge University Press, 1961.

Underhill, Robert. *Turkish Grammar*. Cambridge, MA: MIT Press, 1976.

Wehr, Hans. *A Dictionary of Modern Written Arabic*. Ed. J. Milton Cowan. Ithaca, NY: Spoken Language Services, 1976.

Weinreich, Uriel. *College Yiddish*. New York: YIVO Institute for Jewish Research, 1967.

Windfuhr, Gernot L., and Shapour Bostanbakhsh. *Modern Persian, Intermediate Level I*. Ann Arbor: Dept. of Near Eastern Studies, University of Michigan, 1980.

Yoshida, Yasuo, ed. *Japanese for Today*. Tokyo: Gakken, 1973.